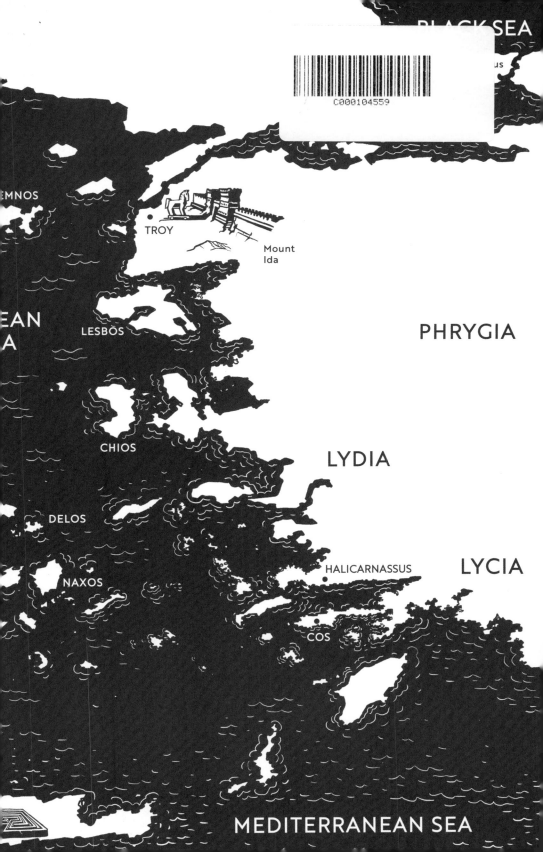

BLACK SEA

...us

...MNOS

TROY

Mount
Ida

PHRYGIA

...EAN
...A

LESBOS

CHIOS

LYDIA

DELOS

HALICARNASSUS

LYCIA

NAXOS

COS

MEDITERRANEAN SEA

"*Gods and Mortals* is a remarkable achievement, a rare combination of great storytelling and deft scholarship. It reads like a novel, with many nested plots, but it is suffused with deep knowledge of the texts. You can read it front to back as a single story, or you can dip in to check what the ancients really wrote about the Titans or that Trojan horse. Johnston has become our best guide to these myths—to what they are and how their characters come to feel alive to people."

—T. M. LUHRMANN, author of *How God Becomes Real: Kindling the Presence of Invisible Others*

"*Gods and Mortals* is a brilliantly executed narration of ancient Greek myth. Johnston outdoes her predecessors, like Bulfinch, Hamilton, and Graves, in the unadorned clarity of her presentation. The book is masterful and promises to help steer a widening interest in this precious body of terrifically good stories."

—PETER STRUCK, author of *Divination and Human Nature: A Cognitive History of Intuition in Classical Antiquity*

GODS AND MORTALS

GODS AND MORTALS

ANCIENT GREEK MYTHS FOR MODERN READERS

SARAH ILES JOHNSTON

WITH ILLUSTRATIONS BY TRISTAN JOHNSTON

PRINCETON UNIVERSITY PRESS
PRINCETON AND OXFORD

Published by Princeton University Press
41 William Street, Princeton, New Jersey 08540
99 Banbury Road, Oxford OX2 6JX

press.princeton.edu

All Rights Reserved
ISBN 9780691199207
ISBN (e-book) 9780691239880

British Library Cataloging-in-Publication Data is available

Editorial: Rob Tempio and Chloe Coy
Production Editorial: Sara Lerner
Text Design: Chris Ferrante
Jacket Design: Tristan Johnston
Production: Erin Suydam
Publicity: Alyssa Sanford and Carmen Jimenez

Jacket, endpaper, and text illustrations by Tristan Johnston

This book has been composed in Goodchild Pro and Brother 1816

Printed on acid-free paper. ∞

Printed and bound in Great Britain by Clays Ltd, Elcograf S.p.A.

1 3 5 7 9 10 8 6 4 2

To the memory of my parents, Phyllis and Robert Iles

CONTENTS

HEROES

THE TROJAN WAR

THE RETURNS

LIST OF ILLUSTRATIONS

GODS AND MORTALS

GODS, MORTALS AND THE MYTHS THEY INHABIT

Imagine for a moment that somehow you've managed to transport yourself back to an ancient Greek city. Look around: you're surrounded by myths. In the marketplace, you see gleaming statues of Athena holding a spear and Poseidon wielding his trident. Nearby, images of Theseus fighting the Amazons look down upon you from a temple. If you're invited to an aristocratic home, you'll be served wine from a bowl painted with a mythic scene and drink it from a cup decorated with another one: Zeus in the form of a bull, surging through the sea with Europa on his back, or the hero Peleus wrestling with the shape-shifting goddess Thetis. If you stay in the city long enough, you'll watch actors performing myths on stage during public festivals—if you're a man, that is. Greek women didn't go to the theater. Women did attend other festivals in honor of the gods, however, where poets recited myths: you might hear about Deianira murdering her husband, Heracles, or Penelope fooling her suitors by means of that most feminine of all contrivances, her loom. If you linger in the city long enough to get married, the song that's sung at your wedding may refer to a great mythic love story, such as that of the doomed warrior Hector and his wife, Andromache. You'll encounter myths in less formal ways, too—as a woman working wool alongside other women who tell myths to pass the time or as a man at a drinking party, where excerpts from the most admired works of the poets are recited.

Nothing in our own culture compares to this—nothing is embraced by all of us with the same fervor and fidelity with which the Greeks embraced their myths. Certainly, there are stories that all of us (or nearly all of us) have at least heard of, but even the most popular of them have not suffused our cultural landscape as thoroughly as myths suffused that of ancient Greece. We wouldn't be surprised to encounter Harry Potter in a book or a movie or miniaturized as a LEGO action figure, but we'd be very surprised to spot his statue gracing a public building or hear a song about his courtship of Ginny Weasley at a wedding. And, leaving aside a few tenacious exceptions, such as the Bible, Shakespeare's plays and the novels of Jane Austen, even our best-loved stories seldom remain popular for more than two or three generations.

In part, this is because diction and manners tend to become stale and remote as time goes by. Samuel Richardson's novel *Pamela; or, Virtue Rewarded* was wildly popular for several decades after it was published in 1740. Now, the smaller group of readers who embark upon *Pamela*'s pages must be willing to decode some of its words (what exactly is a "sauce-box," anyway?) and accept a narrative premise that may seem bizarre (did children and parents really sit down and write lengthy letters to each other, once upon a time, as Pamela and her parents did?). To continue to thrive, even the most wonderful stories need to be updated. But another reason that stories don't remain popular very long anymore is that nowadays, if authors borrow plots or characters from other authors' works, they run the risk of being called derivative, unless they make their own contributions abundantly clear in some way—by completely changing the time, the setting and the names of the characters, for example, as Leonard Bernstein did for *Romeo and Juliet* when he composed *West Side Story*. In contrast, ancient Greek authors didn't hesitate to borrow plots, times, settings, characters and even details from both earlier authors and their own contemporaries. As long as they did this well, adding their own brilliant touches, there was no shame in it—there might even be acclaim. In the process, they continually refreshed the myths, ensuring that they remained exciting and relevant.

Indeed, in ancient Greece, anyone who wanted to narrate a myth had to think about earlier versions because they could be sure that most of the people in their audience knew at least the basics of the story they were about to tell. What we now call Greek myths, most Greeks considered to be part of their history, relayed by poets since the time of Homer. When an author narrated one of them, he was doing something like what Cecil B. DeMille did when he retold the story of Moses in his 1956 film, *The Ten Commandments*. DeMille added intriguing new secondary characters (Queen Nefretiri, for instance) and some thrilling new subplots (Moses's romance with Nefretiri, for example), but no one doubted that he was telling the same story as the Bible had told. In fact, the film won awards from Jewish and Christian organizations for presenting the biblical story to a twentieth-century audience so successfully. Nor was DeMille's film disparaged as derivative: it was a huge box-office hit and is still admired for its accomplishments in filmic narration. Forty-two years later, DeMille's *The Ten Commandments* inspired DreamWorks to create *The Prince of Egypt,* an animated version of the biblical story that introduced its own changes and that also met with commercial and critical success.

Similarly, for example, in 458 BCE, when the tragedian Aeschylus retold the well-known story of Orestes in his trilogy of plays called the *Oresteia*, he innovated upon an old story, too. The final part of Aeschylus's version, which focuses on what happened to Orestes after he avenged his father's murder by killing his mother, alludes to the Areopagus, the place in Athens where the court that tried cases of intentional homicide was located. Aeschylus showed Athena establishing that court so that Orestes could be tried by a jury, which was also presented as a brand-new invention within the world of the play. Earlier versions of Orestes's story had resolved his problem in other ways, which has prompted scholars to suggest that Aeschylus revised the age-old tale in order to celebrate recent Athenian civic reforms—particularly those that cleaned up what had become a corrupt and overly powerful Areopagite court. That's not all that Aeschylus's version of Orestes's story is about, of course. If it's well-narrated, the tale of a young man who is forced to kill his mother in order to avenge his murdered father will always be compelling, and Aeschylus narrated it very well, indeed. He gives us foul-breathed Erinyes who pursue Orestes all the way to Delphi and then onwards to Athens; an Apollo who delivers a clever, protoscientific speech in defense of Orestes; and an Athena who deftly transforms the Erinyes, who are furious at having lost their prey, into kindlier goddesses who promise to nurture Athens. All of these additions that Aeschylus made to the story, as expressed by his glorious language, revitalized a well-known myth. Aeschylus received first prize for his *Oresteia* at the Dionysia, the great Athenian festival that honored Dionysus, the god of drama, and his *Oresteia* continues to be presented on stage today.

It was in this spirit of both tradition and constant innovation that the Greeks told the same myths for more than a millennium, until the coming of Christianity began to mute their voices. Even then, Christianity couldn't silence the myths completely. In the fourteenth century, an anonymous Franciscan monk composed *The Moralized Ovid*, a renarration of Ovid's *Metamorphoses* with allegorizing interpretations that he thought would make it safe reading for Christians. Chaucer redeveloped the myth of Theseus and the Amazons in his *Canterbury Tales*, Shakespeare drew frequently on Greek myths and an army of Renaissance painters and sculptors busily represented them for wealthy men. In the seventeenth century, Monteverdi used the myths of Orpheus and Ariadne as librettos for the first operas and Racine revived tragedy with his own tellings of ancient myths. And the reason you're holding this book now is that we still tell them.

Why do we—and why did the Greeks—love these stories? Certainly, one reason is that they do important cultural and social work. Myths explain and endorse the origins of significant institutions, such as the Athenian jury system. Myths help to instill social codes, such as the expectation that hosts and guests will treat each other honorably. Lycaon didn't abide by that rule, and Zeus turned him into a wolf. They reflect feelings that lie deep within the human heart, such as the difficulty of losing a spouse and the dangers of refusing to come to terms with that loss. Orpheus tried twice to retrieve his wife from the land of the dead but failed and ended up dead himself. They warn against the dangers of character flaws such as arrogance: Odysseus boasted about outwitting the Cyclops Polyphemus, and Polyphemus's father, Poseidon, impeded Odysseus's homeward journey for many years.

Other messages are embedded in the myths, too, not all of which make as much immediate sense to their modern readers as those

I've just mentioned. Most strikingly, in myths the Greek gods are so frequently fickle and cruel in their treatment of mortals that the two groups seem to be eternally pitted against one another. The mortals constantly strive to rise above the limits that confine them and the gods repeatedly smack the mortals down. Why would the Greeks want to imagine that the very gods whom they worshipped would behave that way? Part of the answer lies in the fact that myth and worship expressed two extremes. Myths presented dreadful, worst-case scenarios and what one prayed for during worship presented the best that one could hope for. Together, these articulated the human condition—a persistent aspiration and struggle to become something better, which was often thwarted but could never be extinguished. Of course, the biggest difference between gods and mortals was that the former lived forever and the latter were fated to die. The many myths in which a mortal tries to evade that destiny and fails—not only the story of Orpheus, but also the stories of Sisyphus and Asclepius, for example—repeatedly drive home this point. The gods had infinite time, as well as infinite power, to accomplish almost anything they pleased, and mortals who wished to survive for even the small numbers of years that the Fates allotted them had to live according to the rules that the gods imposed and to tolerate their fickle temperaments. That is why this book is called *Gods and Mortals*; the myths that I tell here often express the crucial differences between the two parties. Yet any purpose that a myth serves is secondary to the telling of the myth itself. Unless an author or artist narrates a myth in a lively, engaging way, no one will bother with it—or at least, they won't bother with the version served up by that particular author or artist. "A man killed his mother because she killed his father" is simply a statement. It was what Aeschylus added to that statement that turned it into a myth. So, too, for the poets who came before and after Aeschylus, each of whom created his Orestes with his own twists: Stesichorus, Pindar, Sophocles, Euripides and so on.

I've tried to make the narratives that I'm offering in this book engaging, too, so that the myths will speak to my readers with at least some of the impact that they had in antiquity. To do this, I've not only chosen my words carefully, but also knit into my stories details about the ancient world in which they're set. I've done this in the hope that if my readers have some sense of the harsher realities of such things as disease and hunger in antiquity, the wilder natural environment that Greek women and men confronted and the tighter social constraints under which they lived, then the myths will resonate more fully. My telling of Pandora's story, therefore, includes details about the household duties of ancient Greek women and the plethora of illnesses that continually lay in wait for human victims. My story of Erigone makes clear how dire a fate it was for a Greek woman to remain unmarried. I've also given some sense of what it was like to worship the gods: my descriptions of Oedipus's and Neoptolemus's visits to the Delphic Oracle express what Apollo's inquirers would have seen and heard at the god's great sanctuary high up in the mountains, and I recount the rituals that the Argonauts performed to appease the anger of the Mother of the Gods. I've woven what we know about the mechanics of ancient looms and the sources of ancient dyes into my story of Arachne and what we know about the ancient way of throwing a discus into my story of Hyacinthus. My stories unfold against the real physical landscapes of ancient Greece and their real fauna and flora.

But as much as I've striven to present my myths within their ancient contexts, I've also been determined not to allow the voices of the ancient authors themselves to dominate my tellings. Although I've drawn my plots and characters from ancient sources and sometimes borrowed their brilliant phrases and imagery, too, I haven't simply translated their narratives into English. Instead, I've created new narratives that have lives of their own. My Odysseus expresses a keener appreciation of his wife's intellect than Homer's did, for instance. And, although the events in my story of Apollo's attempted rape of Daphne closely follow those of Ovid's version, I cast a shadow over Apollo's final action and give Artemis a closing line that is meant to emphasize how little the gods, at least as we meet them in myths, cared about the suffering of their mortal companions.

Indeed, the tone of my stories often parts company with the ancient authors when I narrate rapes or, in the cases of Daphne and Syrinx, attempted rapes. In Greek myths, both gods and mortal men force themselves upon females with alarming frequency, using physical strength, deception or both to satisfy their desires. Ancient narrators often ignored or minimized the damage that these encounters would have wreaked upon their victims. To take but one example, the Homeric *Hymn to Demeter* tells us that Hades snatched Persephone away from her friends and dragged her into the Underworld, but leaves it largely up to us to imagine, if we choose, how this was experienced by the young goddess herself. There were some exceptions to the rule: Aeschylus sympathetically narrates the ghastly ordeals that Io suffered after Zeus decided to rape her, and Ovid evokes our pity for several victims, most notably Philomela. In every case of rape that I narrate, I, too, have tried to convey the shock or horror that the woman or goddess felt—and in the one instance where a goddess sexually violates a man (Salmacis and Hermaphroditus), I've tried to imagine how he felt, too. It's worth clarifying, in connection with this topic, that what we now consider to be two separate situations—rape and seduction—were scarcely distinguished in antiquity. At the root of their conflation lay the fact that women were meant to be controlled by men. A girl was under the guardianship of her father until she married, at which point she came under the guardianship of her husband. If she were widowed, either her father resumed his role or another male relative took it on. The guardian's responsibilities included ensuring that the woman did not have sex without his permission. In real life, this meant that she would have sex only with the husband to whom her guardian gave her in marriage. In myths, some fathers seize other, unusual opportunities to give their daughters to men, as well. For example, Thespius gives his fifty daughters to Heracles because he wants a crop of strong grandsons (chapter 65) and Pittheus gives his daughter Aethra to King Aegeus of Athens because he wants to forge a stronger link with that city (chapter 93). Of course, if your wife or daughter were impregnated by a god, you were expected to count it an honor and duly raise the child, as do several men in these stories. And of course, in both real life and myths there were women and men who, through choice or necessity, became prostitutes and there were slaves of both genders who, as their master's property, owed him their sexual favors.

The notes at the end of this book give information about which ancient narrations and artistic representations of each myth inspired my versions. For those who want to read them, I've recommended translations of those narrations in the essay "Ancient Sources for the Myths." Sometimes, I had to draw not only on what ancient authors tell us but also on my own imagination as well, in order to fill gaps in a plot—gaps where our knowledge of how a story proceeded is fragmentary because our ancient sources themselves are fragmentary. For example, we don't know exactly how it was that Zeus managed to swallow his wife Metis when she was pregnant with their child. After thinking about what little the ancient sources do tell us, I concluded that this myth probably sprang from a folk motif that is shared by many other tales around the world and then developed my version in that direction—you'll find it in chapter 4. Whenever I've filled a gap in that way, I've indicated it in the notes.

From start to finish, this book tells 140 myths. There's no magic in that number, other than the magic of compromise. On the one hand, I quickly realized that telling *every* Greek myth I've ever encountered would make for a book too large to lift. But on the other hand, I wanted to narrate not only all of the myths that one would expect to find in an anthology (the labors of Heracles, the story of how Demeter got her daughter back, and so on) but also some personal favorites that aren't told very often nowadays (the story of Icarius, Erigone and some fatal casks of wine; the tale of how Melampus cured the bovine daughters of Proetus; and a fuller reveal of what happened when Menelaus and Helen sailed home after the Trojan War, for instance). I assembled my choices in an order that makes chronological sense, more or less. That is, my narrative starts with the birth of the cosmos and the gods and it finishes with what happened to the Greek leaders as they returned from the Trojan War. In the eyes of the Greeks, that war was the last great event of the heroic age, before the world settled down into the far less glorious age in which they themselves existed. In between the beginning and the end, I tell stories that characterize the ongoing relationship between gods and mortals, those two tribes between which power was so unevenly divided; stories of the heroes, who challenged the boundary between gods and mortals as they purged the earth of monsters, and of the daring, resourceful women who enabled the heroes to do what they did; and stories of the Trojan War itself, which Zeus brought about in order to quash the burgeoning human population.

Here and there, however, attentive readers will notice that I've had to infringe upon chronology: in chapter 10, for instance, Dionysus advises Hephaestus on how to win a bride, but Dionysus's own birth isn't narrated until chapter 12. It's impossible to arrange Greek myths without a few infelicities of this kind, so tightly entangled are its characters and its events. I say a little more about that entanglement, and the strength that it gave Greek myths, in the essay "The Characters of Greek Myths" at the end of this book. The Greeks themselves certainly knew how to look the other way when chronology threatened to ruin a good story. For instance, although it was events during the wedding of Peleus and Thetis that precipitated the Trojan War, somehow Peleus and Thetis managed to produce a son, Achilles, who was old enough to fight when the war began—and then Achilles himself managed to produce a son, Neoptolemus, who was old enough to join the Greek contingent only nine years later.

Leaving these problems aside, readers who move sequentially from the first chapter, "Earth and Her Children," to the final chapter, "New Lives," will find that the myths I tell earliest sometimes lay the groundwork for those I tell later. However, even if the myths aren't read in the order that I've chosen—even if readers choose to dip into the book here and there, following their own particular interests at any given moment—themes and details will resonate among them. The Greeks, certainly, did not encounter their myths in any fixed sequence. One of the most important ways in which Greek myths were promulgated was through the voices of professional bards who memorized the works of the great poets and then were hired to perform at public festivals and the private parties of the wealthy. In addition, there were poets who could be commissioned to compose new poems to celebrate a glorious athletic victory or a splendid wedding. Those poets often took myths as their subject matter, too. In either case, an audience typically didn't know what myth they would hear until a performance began. You might hear the story of Heracles and the Stymphalian Birds on one occasion and then, some days or months later, hear the story of Heracles's birth, or the story of how Perseus (Heracles's great-grandfather) tricked the Graeae, or the story of how the whole cosmos came to exist in the first place. The art that dotted the landscape continuously evoked a variety of stories that defied chronology, as well. As Greek children grew up, they gradually acquired familiarity with many myths and an understanding of how the characters and events of those myths were knit together into a huge, splendid web.

When I was about halfway done writing this book, I began to experiment with these ideas myself. Every few semesters, I teach a course on Greek myths in an auditorium that holds 740 people. Although it's seldom the case that every seat is filled on any given day, there are always at least 600 students present. The course is an elective; no one is required to enroll and I presume that the students are there because they're interested in the topic. And yet, year after year, here and there in the dim recesses of the auditorium, whispered conversations were always taking place while I delivered my lectures. My colleagues told me that I wasn't alone in this experience; it's hard to retain the attention of so many students, especially when you're standing on a stage, far away from most of them.

One semester, I tried something different. The syllabus that I posted at the beginning of the course included neither a day-by-day list of the myths we'd study nor any list of assigned readings to be done before each session. Instead, when the bell rang each day, my teaching assistant dimmed all the lights except for the spotlight over the stage and I walked in from the wings, wearing a cloak like that an ancient bard would wear. Standing front and center, I read aloud one of the myths that I was writing for this book, with as much drama and feeling as I could muster. I chose to read my own versions of myths, rather than ancient versions, because they were shorter, their diction was more familiar to the students, and in some cases they particularly emphasized certain aspects of the myths that I wanted to discuss.

After eight or nine minutes, when I was done reading, my assistant turned up the lights, I removed my cloak and I delivered a lecture in which I discussed the significance of the myth that the students had just heard—how it expressed ancient social and cultural values, how it articulated the Greeks' view of the relationship between gods and mortals, how it served to explain the existence of a certain animal species, rock formation or a ritual, how it fit together with other myths we'd studied that semester and so on. I showed the students ancient and modern works of art that represented the myth. I also showed them excerpts from ancient authors who had told the same myth. I discussed the differences among those ancient versions and between those versions and my own, explaining how the differences changed what the myth was saying. After each session, the students were assigned to read for themselves the myth they'd heard that day and the ancient versions I'd discussed.

I embarked on these performances in the hope that if the students initially experienced each myth as a *story* that someone was telling to entertain as well as educate them, they might engage more deeply with it. It seems to work; a hush falls over the auditorium as soon as the lights go down. More students visit me during office hours, wanting to talk about the myths.

In one version or another, expurgated or straight, Greek myths have been at the center of my world since I was old enough to choose which stories my mother would read aloud to me. Later, I shared them with my own children and grandchildren; one of my sons, who is now an illustrator, has added his own interpretations of some of them to this book. Over the years, these myths have cheered me, amused me and excited me. They've journeyed alongside me when I traveled and comforted me at times of loss. They've chided me when I did things—or was about to do things—that I knew I shouldn't be doing. The least that I can do in return is to tell them again. I hope that the myths, as I'm offering them now on the pages of this book, will engage, entertain and provoke you, my readers, as well.

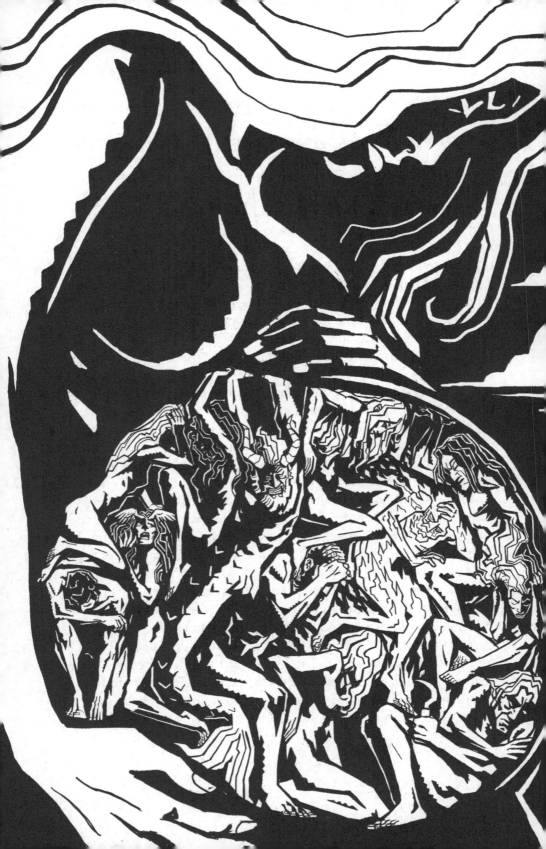

THE GODS

THE COSMOS IS BORN AND GODS BEGIN TO FILL IT

1
EARTH AND HER CHILDREN

In the beginning, there was nothing at all that anyone could have discerned—only a yawning gap that stretched in all directions—featureless, indefinite, without orientation.

Eventually, however, things began to emerge. First came Earth, broad-breasted and standing firm. Next came Tartarus, who lurked beneath Earth, awaiting a time when the greatest of criminals would be handed over to him for punishment. Third came Lust, whose task it would be to loosen the limbs and beguile the senses of gods and mortals alike. Finally, Darkness and Night emerged. Mingling together in love, they created Air and Day.

All by herself, without needing help from any male, Earth gave birth to Sky, Sea and Mountains. Then, entering Sky's bed, Earth conceived more children. Some of these were splendid in appearance and leaders by nature. They wanted to bring order to the new world by setting the sun on its eternal course, channeling the swirling waters and establishing a community. One of them, Mnemosyne, stood by to record her siblings' great deeds so that they'd never be forgotten.

Three other children, the Cyclopes, used their strong arms and skillful hands to forge lightning and thunder. Although they looked like their brothers and sisters in most ways, they had only one eye apiece, bulging forth from the center of their foreheads. Even stranger in appearance, and far too arrogant to take up any work, were the Hundred-Handers, each of whom had fifty heads and a hundred arms.

Sky feared and hated all of his children even before they were born, and came up with a plan to keep them under control. Each time that Earth was about to give birth, Sky shoved the infant back into her womb, imprisoning it before it ever saw the light of day. There, the children languished in crowded confinement while their mother groaned under the weight of her swollen belly. Sky treated the Cyclopes and the Hundred-Handers even more harshly, because he feared and hated them more than the rest. He shoved them not back into Earth's womb, but all the way down into Tartarus, where they lay bound in stout chains.

Things went differently with Cronus, the final child that Sky fathered upon Earth. Devious from the moment he was conceived, Cronus eagerly agreed to a plot that his mother contrived. Reaching deep into her own body, Earth extracted gray adamantine, from which she created a jag-tooth sickle. She handed it to Cronus, telling him to crouch at the mouth of her womb as if he were about to be born and then wait for his chance.

Soon, Sky arrived, lusting to lie with Earth and tugging a blanket of night over their naked bodies. When Sky thrust himself inside of Earth and began to grunt with pleasure, Cronus slithered into his mother's birth canal. Swinging the sickle, he castrated his father. Screaming in pain, Sky limped away to his lair in the lofty air, never to assault Earth again.

Clutching his father's bloody genitals, Cronus triumphantly emerged from between his mother's legs. He flung the bits of flesh into the sea, where they bobbed up and down on the waves, collecting around themselves a foamy froth.

Within this froth, something began to grow and slowly took on the shape of a goddess. After drifting here and there, she stepped with slender feet onto the island of Cyprus, where soft green grass sprang up to greet her. The Graces and the Seasons hastened to anoint her with fragrant oils. Then they gave her an embroidered band to hold up her lovely breasts, translucent silks to veil her beautiful form and sandals to protect her charming toes.

The new goddess was named *Aphro*dite, after the *froth* in which she had been born. Lust and Desire flew to her side the moment they saw her and never departed. She took delight in planting passion in the hearts of gods and mortals—but those who received her gifts would have done well to remember the act of castration that gave her life.

When Cronus threw Sky's genitals towards the sea, drops of blood fell onto Earth and made her pregnant again. In time, she brought forth the fearsome Erinyes, who punished those who betrayed members of their own families; the enormous Gigantes, who were already clad in armor and clutching spears when they were born; and the slender ash-tree nymphs.

2
THE TITANS

Cronus took a long look at the new world that he'd stepped into. When he'd freed Earth from Sky's insistent embrace, a lot of space had been created between his parents. Within it, the children whom Earth had conceived on her own, before she entered Sky's bed, were finally free to grow. Sea and Mountains were spreading outwards and upwards, taking on their destined shapes and appearances. Cronus gasped at the speed with which scrubby pines were already covering the Mountains.

After the cramped conditions that he'd endured inside his mother, Cronus enjoyed all the space, but he soon grew lonely. He helped his brothers and sisters crawl out of their mother and then began to organize them.

He started by announcing that he would be their king—after all, he was the one who had castrated their father. Then he assigned duties to them. He put some of them to work making the cosmos more livable. Helios was told to drive a fiery chariot across the heavens during the day and Selene to drive another one that was less fiery during the night. Other siblings were ordered to establish rules of conduct: Themis was told to articulate the binding power of oaths and establish communications among the different parts of the cosmos. Now that there was so much going on, Mnemosyne was kept busy recording all the new developments for posterity. No god was left idle.

Rhea was given what Cronus considered to be the most important job of all: she became his wife.

From his refuge atop the new cosmos, Sky watched all of this unfold, still nursing his throbbing wound. He fell into the habit of contemptuously referring to his children as "Titans," a word that in his language suggested overweening ambition. He took to darkly predicting that vengeance would soon befall them.

Cronus, in fact, had been fearful from the start that his own children might do to him what he'd done to his father. Well aware that Sky's method of protecting himself had not worked, Cronus thought long and hard about a better solution. Finally, he came up with one that seemed foolproof. As Rhea gave birth to each of his children, Cronus swallowed it down in a single gulp. No one, he chortled, would be able to escape from *his* belly.

Rhea was just as unhappy about this situation as Earth had been about hers, and called on her parents for assistance. They helped her devise a plan that would be executed by Rhea, Earth and Hecate, who had been serving as Rhea's midwife. The three sequestered themselves on the island of Crete, far from Cronus's throne room, and waited for the child's arrival.

Even so, when Rhea finally went into labor, Cronus sensed that something was up. He listened expectantly for Hecate's knock, and when he heard it, he yanked the door open and thrust out his hands, waiting for her to give him the newest bundle.

But in the moments after the child was born, the goddesses had made a quick exchange. Hecate handed Cronus not his newborn son, but a stone wrapped in swaddling clothes. Cronus gulped it down without noticing any difference, burped, and went back to the business of telling his other siblings how to do their jobs.

The real child remained on Crete, safely tucked into a cave. Nymphs cared for him there and Amaltheia, a gentle goat, nursed him. A band of young gods called Couretes stood outside the cave, clashing their spears against their shields every time that he cried, lest the child's squalling reach Cronus's ears.

Meanwhile, Earth had taken a new lover: her son Sea. The two had many children, including a daughter named Ceto and a son named Phorcys. From the waist up, these two looked like their half siblings, the Titans, but from the waist down they resembled the fish of their father's realm.

Mingling in love, Ceto and Phorcys spawned a strange and troublesome brood of children. Among them were the Graeae, who were gray-haired already at the moment of their births and who shared among themselves just a single eye and a single tooth. The Gorgons, who had eagles' wings on their backs and tangles of writhing vipers on their heads where hair should be, were also their daughters. Yet another daughter, Echidna, was a half-breed like her parents: a beautiful goddess from the waist up but a terrible snake, cold and rank, from the waist down. She lurked in a cave at the edge of the world, licking her lips at the thought of raw flesh.

Echidna took to her bed a series of husbands who were just as dreadful as she was and gave birth to monstrous children. One of them was the Chimera, a savage lioness with the head of a fire-breathing goat springing out of her back and a viper for her tail. Another was the three-headed dog Cerberus, who guarded the gates of the Underworld, where his vicious barking resounded like a bronze gong.

The Sphinx, too, was Echidna's child. She had the body of a lion and the head of a woman, behind whose rosy lips lay a maw of needle-sharp teeth that would bring death to mortals in later years. The evil-minded Hydra, a snake with nine heads, and the Nemean Lion, who would be a bane for mortals and their flocks, were Echidna's children as well.

If Cronus's last-born son survived and managed to overthrow his father, he would inherit a cosmos full of challenges. He, his siblings and their children would not only have to conquer the Titans but vanquish these offspring of Ceto and Phorcys, as well.

3
THE YOUNG GODS REBEL

In the cave on Crete the baby grew, nourished by Amaltheia's milk and nestled against her silky belly. Rhea named him Zeus.

Zeus was fascinated by the glinting shafts of light that were cast into the cave by the Couretes' shields, and soon learned to slip away from the nymphs when he wanted to visit the young gods. His development was in all ways prodigious: one day, Cronus spotted unusual activity on the island and rushed over to investigate. Zeus quickly turned the nymphs into bears and himself into a snake, successfully deceiving his father. Although Zeus had responded to that emergency effectively, the incident made it clear that his situation was precarious; the earlier he defeated Cronus, the better. He began to look for a way to do it.

Some of the younger Titans had more in common with Zeus than they did with Cronus. One of them was Zeus's cousin Metis, the daughter of Ocean and Tethys. Metis was the cleverest of all the gods, adept at finding solutions to problems that seemed insurmountable to others. She suggested to Zeus that she slip Cronus an emetic; when the drug did its work, he would vomit up Zeus's brothers and sisters, who were still imprisoned in his belly. These gods would become Zeus's allies.

Zeus and Metis crept to Cronus's stronghold on Mount Othrys. From the shadows, Zeus watched Metis serve Cronus a drink into which she had mixed her drug.

Nothing happened for a few minutes. Then Zeus heard a rumbling sound that reminded him of an earthquake. Cronus turned pale, then began to sweat and gag and retch. Suddenly, up came the stone in its swaddling clothes, followed in quick succession by Hera, Poseidon, Demeter, Hades and Hestia, reversing the order in which Rhea had given birth to them and Cronus had swallowed them. Eventually, Zeus retrieved the swaddled stone and enshrined it at Delphi.

War broke out between the older and the younger gods, with the Titans using Mount Othrys as their base and the younger gods using Mount Olympus, which lay many miles to the north. For ten years, they battled on, their spirits growing weary with the toil of it. So evenly matched were the opponents that victory seemed out of reach for either side.

Then Earth approached Zeus with some further advice. The Cyclopes and the Hundred-Handers, she told him, still languished in Tartarus, where Sky had long ago imprisoned them. If Zeus rescued them, they would be fierce and loyal allies.

So Zeus journeyed down to a part of the cosmos that no god had ever dared to visit before. Once there, he discovered that Tartarus had ordered his ghastly daughter Campe to stand guard over the prisoners. From the waist up, Campe looked like a woman, but below she had a writhing blindworm's body, tipped with a venomous sting that she kept poised above her head, ready to strike. The many arms that sprang from her shoulders ended in talons as sharp as the sickle that had castrated Sky. Deftly thrusting with his spear, Zeus managed to kill Campe—the first great victory of his career. Then he released his uncles, who fell to their knees and swore loyalty to him.

The arrival of the Cyclopes and Hundred-Handers turned the tide of war. The Cyclopes forged thunderbolts for Zeus to hurl and the Hundred-Handers, wrenching great boulders from the soil, barraged the Titans. Soon, many of them lay wounded or bound in chains. The gods' victory seemed certain.

But then Earth took Tartarus as her new lover and in his coiling embrace she conceived Typhon, her most dreadful child yet, a creature so large that his head bumped the stars as he strode across the plains. From his eyes burst spirals of fire and from his mouth came the roaring, barking, squealing, grunting, bellowing and shouting of every creature imaginable, so loud that the hinges on the doors of the younger gods' fortress trembled. Lank, filthy hair grew from his scalp and from his shoulders sprang all manner of writhing vipers, as well as innumerable arms, each hand of which clutched a weapon. Below his waist there were vipers as well, each one thicker than the trunk of an oak tree.

Were it not for the bravery of Zeus, Typhon would have seized power. Most of the gods, upon glimpsing him, had transformed themselves into animals and fled to Egypt, where they lay in hiding. Zeus stood his ground, flinging lightning bolts against Typhon as fast as the Cyclopes could forge them until the monster's body caught fire. Earth, too, caught fire under Zeus's assault; parts of her expanse melted like tin in a blacksmith's ladle and ran in rivulets across her skin. Sea was startled to see flames dancing across his waves. The clamor was terrible; deep within Tartarus the Titans clung to Cronus in fear.

Finally, Typhon was conquered. Zeus wrapped adamantine chains around what remained of him and hurled the bundle deep into Tartarus. Struggling against his bonds, Typhon disrupted Earth's surface far above, forming Mount Etna. Now and then, still roaring with frustration, he sent jets of fire into the air and streams of lava rolling down the new mountain's slopes. From his breath came destructive winds that hurled boats to the bottom of the sea and destroyed what humans had built upon the land.

4
ZEUS BECOMES KING

Zeus was determined to be a different sort of ruler from his father and grandfather; he had observed that tyranny established through force alone was unlikely to endure for very long. One of the first things he did, after the war was over, was to draw lots with his brothers to decide who would rule over the three realms of the cosmos: the heavens, the waters and the Underworld. The surface of the earth would belong to all the gods in common. The Fates gave the heavens, and the kingship that came with it, to Zeus. Poseidon drew the waters and Hades the Underworld.

Zeus's sisters received realms and duties, too. Demeter was put in charge of the growth of grains and Hera became the protector of the marriage bond; together, Demeter and Hera also watched over mothers. Hestia, who swore to remain a virgin, guarded the hearths that lay at the center of every home, which burned brightest when tended by those who had never tasted desire.

Zeus also had to decide what to do with the Titans, who were still imprisoned in Tartarus. Those whom Zeus judged to be irredeemable were either left there to languish or brought above to do jobs that the gods disdained. Atlas was commanded to hold up Sky in order to prevent him from lying on top of Earth again—for although Sky had been castrated by Cronus's sickle, he still had a fondness for Earth's soft, warm body and would have burdened her with his weight once again, if not prevented.

Other Titans, Zeus realized, would have to be restored to the positions that they'd held before the war if the cosmos were to run in an orderly fashion: Helios and Selene went back to crossing the sky each day and night so that the world would have light. Still other Titans were given new roles in Zeus's administration and even higher honors than they'd previously held, in gratitude for their support. Rhea helped Demeter and Hera watch over mothers. Themis and her son Prometheus, who had advised Zeus during the war, continued as his counselors.

The River Styx, which wound her way through the Underworld, had stayed away from the war altogether, but on the advice of her father, Ocean, she now approached Zeus and offered her services.

Zeus decreed that Styx's waters would be the stuff by which the gods would swear their most solemn oaths. Any god who broke such an oath would fall into a dreamless sleep for a year and be banned from the gods' feasts for another nine years.

Hecate received the highest honors of all. Zeus gave her a share of power over the earth, the waters and the heavens. He also decreed that it would be up to Hecate to decide whether mortal prayers reached the ears of the gods. Without her help, no mortal would ever be able to receive the gods' blessings. A fisherman might pray to Poseidon or a mother to Hera, but unless they invoked Hecate as well, their requests would go unheard.

Metis received high honors, too, because she had devised and executed the plot that caused Cronus to vomit up Zeus's sisters and brothers. Zeus admired Metis for more than just her brains, however, and chose to make her his wife. Soon, she was pregnant, and Zeus was looking forward to the birth of what would undoubtedly be a most remarkable child.

Midway through the pregnancy, however, Earth and Sky approached Zeus with a troubling prophecy. Metis's first child, they said, would be as strong as Zeus and as wise as Metis—but would be a daughter, and therefore no threat to Zeus's kingship. Metis's second child, however, would be a son—violent in heart and destined to overthrow his father.

Zeus was deeply worried. He knew himself well enough to realize that he'd be back in Metis's bed as soon as she recovered from their daughter's birth, and he also knew that a god's lovemaking was seldom without issue. His dangerous son would soon be conceived. Reluctantly, he concluded that he must get rid of Metis completely and immediately. He thought carefully about how he might use her strengths to his own advantage and formulated a plan.

All of the gods had the ability to transform themselves into animals, plants and all kinds of other things but Metis had a particularly strong talent for metamorphosis and was proud of it. One day, Zeus began to tease her, claiming that he'd be able to think of something into which even she couldn't change herself. Clever though she was, Metis was foolish enough to accept Zeus's challenge.

First, Zeus told her to become a lion, which she easily did. Then, a giant squid, flopping and gasping on the dusty ground. Then, an oak tree, towering into the skies. Then, a meadow of asphodel, white with flowers. Then, a blazing fire, crackling with sparks.

At that point, Zeus sighed. "Ah, but my darling Metis! I realize now that, so far, I've asked you to become only *large* things. It's much harder, of course, to become something petite, delicate, minute." Provoked by pride, she told him to name his choice. "A butterfly," he replied.

Metis closed her eyes, furrowed her brow, and then poof! She was gone, and a beautiful butterfly, whose wings were graced by purple splashes, sat on the back of Zeus's hand. Zeus raised his hand to his mouth; Metis expected an affectionate kiss. But before she knew what was happening, Zeus's tongue shot out like a frog's and pulled her into his mouth. Down his gorge she tumbled, landing in the nectar that Zeus had drunk that morning.

Metis felt her husband's belly shake with laughter. She twisted and turned but the confining space in which she found herself prevented her from changing into something large enough to break free. She was trapped, just as surely as Zeus's siblings had once been trapped in Cronus's belly, but there was no one on the outside to help her escape, as she had once helped them.

Zeus took Themis as his next wife. Eventually, he set Themis aside and took his sister Hera as his third, and final, wife. This did not mean, however, that Zeus's love affairs were over.

5
PERSEPHONE'S STORY

In between his second and third wives, Zeus wooed his sister Demeter, whose blonde hair rippled like a field of grain bending to the wind. The siblings changed themselves into snakes and twined beneath the ground, making love among the seeds of things waiting to be reborn. Nine months later, Demeter gave birth to their daughter, Persephone.

Persephone was loved by Demeter with an intensity that no one but an only child experiences. Mother and daughter were almost always together and when they weren't, a call from one would bring the other to her side, however great the distance.

But there were some things that Persephone preferred to do with her friends. One of these was flower-gathering, which in any case was properly a task for daughters. Flowers were useful in cooking and healing; every household needed to harvest them when they were in season, dry them and keep them on hand. Wives had duties that might prevent them from going out into the meadows when the blooms were ripe, but daughters' chores were less important and could be postponed. Daughters were also sent to gather flowers so that they could enjoy sunlight and freedom before the yoke of maturity fell upon their shoulders. Every girl was expected to find a husband and bear children, but the responsibilities that came with marriage and motherhood meant that she would spend most of her adult life inside the house, captive to a pregnant belly, hungry infants and a recalcitrant loom. A girl who was allowed some liberty before marriage would be a more dutiful wife and mother—or so ran common wisdom, at least.

Although gods, of course, never needed to be healed and never did any kind of work unless they chose to, they nonetheless saw the advantage of sending their daughters out into the meadows when they were young. The meadow that the young goddesses liked best lay in the shadow of Olympus. The flowers of all seasons grew there together in abundance—crocuses, irises, violets, hyacinths, roses and lilies.

One day, Earth caused a new flower to grow that was taller and more splendid than all the rest: a dazzling narcissus, with a hundred heads springing from a single bulb. Its fragrance was so lovely that the whole meadow laughed with delight.

Persephone wandered away from her friends to find the source of the wonderful aroma. When she reached out to touch the narcissus, however, the ground split open before her eyes. Four horses, black as obsidian, galloped out of the chasm, pulling a golden chariot driven by Hades, the lord of the Underworld.

With a pale but powerful arm, Hades grabbed Persephone around her waist and dragged her into the chariot. His enormous fingers dug into the soft flesh of her thigh and abdomen, leaving bruises that turned blue-black, the color of corpses. For weeks, she would see them every time she undressed. So would he.

In the moments before the chariot plunged back below the earth, Persephone had cried out to her father, pleading for the help that any daughter would expect. Zeus, however, had carefully insulated himself against the appeals that he knew Persephone would be making that day. Early that morning he'd settled down inside one of his temples and focused all of his attention on his worshippers' prayers.

Demeter did hear Persephone's cries, but they echoed off the mountains, seeming to come from all directions at once. A sharp pain seized her heart—where was Persephone? Why was she screaming?

Wrapping herself in a dark cloak and clutching a torch in each hand, Demeter roamed the world for nine days, pausing neither to eat nor to bathe. She asked gods, she asked mortals, she asked birds whether they knew what had happened to Persephone, but no one could answer her.

On the tenth day, Demeter ran into Hecate, who had been lingering in a cave near the meadow on the day that Persephone found the narcissus. Judging from what she'd been able to hear, Hecate feared that Persephone had been abducted but she had no idea who the abductor was. Hecate suggested that they ask Helios, who had probably seen the whole affair as he drove his fiery chariot across the heavens that day. Demeter and Hecate flew to the top of the sky, abruptly alighting in front of Helios's chariot. His horses stumbled to a halt, snorting with surprise at the sudden obstacle in their familiar path.

Helios listened attentively to Demeter's request for help but his reply plunged her into deeper despair. Yes, Persephone had been abducted and the abductor was Demeter's brother Hades. But abduction wasn't what it was being called, Helios continued. Zeus and Hades were presenting the union as a fully legal marriage: they had come to an agreement about bride-price and all the other details some time ago. They had persuaded Earth to serve as their ally and she had cunningly sent forth the narcissus that lured Persephone away from her friends.

According to the strictest interpretation of custom, the fact that the bride and her mother had been neither consulted nor informed about the marriage was irrelevant. Demeter could rage all she wanted, but Persephone was no longer hers. Persephone's father had given her to his brother as a wife.

6
DEMETER'S WANDERINGS

Demeter felt aimless, purposeless, in Persephone's absence. She went about her duties mechanically, blessing the fields as the months turned round so that humans and animals would have food to eat. She shunned the table of the gods—she was angry with some of them and felt humiliated among the others. She took to traveling through the mortal world instead, disguised as an old woman past the age of childbearing, wearing a dusty black cloak.

She wasn't always treated kindly. As Demeter passed through a village on the outskirts of Athens, a woman gave the thirsty traveler a drink. When Demeter downed it in a single gulp, the woman's son snickered and asked whether he should fetch the bucket. Demeter shook the drops that remained in her cup onto his head; he turned into a gecko.

Far worse was what her brother Poseidon did. He spied Demeter walking through Arcadia and was filled with lust when a lock of her beautiful hair fell free of the dark veil she was wearing. Poseidon pursued Demeter; Demeter transformed herself into a mare and hid among other mares who were grazing nearby. Poseidon wasn't fooled, however. Changing himself into a stallion, he raped his sister. Later, she gave birth to the wonder-horse Arion, who would serve as the mount of several heroes. He was a foal that any mother could be proud of, but the brutality of his conception left Demeter even more desolate than she'd been before.

Demeter drifted back towards Athens and sat down at the village well in the town of Eleusis. Four girls approached with pitchers to be filled. Puzzled by the fact that an old woman was sitting there alone, they asked her who she was and whether she needed help.

Demeter spun a tall tale. She said that her name was Giver and that she'd been kidnapped from her home on Crete. Her captors had intended to sell her as a slave, but she'd managed to escape; homeless now, she needed a way to feed herself. She was good at caring for children—did they know of anyone who needed a nanny?

Her question delighted the girls. They were the daughters of King Celeus, they said, and their mother, Metanira, had just given birth to a baby boy named Demophon—an unexpected joy, coming late in her life. Surely she could use the help of a knowledgeable woman! They ran home to tell their mother to prepare for a visitor while dark-robed Demeter followed more slowly behind.

When Demeter crossed the threshold of the room where the women of the household were gathered, her head grazed the lintel and divine radiance filled every corner. Metanira was awestruck; her mouth fell open in amazement and she promptly rose to offer the stranger her chair.

Demeter, however, stood silent and solemn, with her eyes cast down. A servant, Iambe, realized that the stranger was too modest to take a queen's seat and offered her a stool instead, covered with a woolly fleece. Demeter sat, but with a shake of her head she declined the food and drink that Metanira offered.

It was Iambe again who found a way to please her. With bawdy jokes and obscene gestures, she made Demeter smile; only then did Demeter remember her hunger and thirst. She asked Metanira to prepare a soothing drink of water, barley and pennyroyal.

After the stranger had drunk the mixture down, Metanira began to ask about her approach to child-rearing. At what age did she think that babies should be weaned and what should they be fed on afterwards? Goats' milk? Grain mush? What was the best way to get them to sleep soundly? How would she predict when a baby's bowels were about to move so that she could hold him over a pot and prevent his clothes from being soiled?

Demeter told Metanira the answers to all of these questions, and more. She knew how to avert the demons that inflicted dysentery, fever and teething pain, and how to protect babies from the spells of women who envied their mothers' good fortune. Metanira was pleased; she allowed Demeter to take Demophon in her arms and hold the tiny child close to her fragrant bosom. Immediately, he sighed and fell asleep.

As the days and weeks went by, Demophon grew like a wonder. This had nothing to do with milk or mush, however. Secretly, Demeter nurtured him as she'd once nurtured Persephone, anointing his skin with divine ambrosia and infusing her own immortal breath into his body. And each night, while the household slept, Demeter placed Demophon in the hearth fire, as if he were a smoldering log. Slowly, carefully, she was purging the mortal stain from his flesh. Once she'd finished her work, Demophon would never again be ill, never grow old and never, ever die and enter Hades's realm.

But one night, Metanira peered out of her bedroom and glimpsed her son lying among the flickering coals. Misunderstanding what her nanny was doing—and having no idea who the nanny really was—Metanira shrieked and slapped her thighs in anguish. "*O poi-poi*, my little one! What is this strange woman doing to you?!"

Hearing the queen's cries, Demeter angrily snatched Demophon from the fire and dumped him on the floor. "Stupid human!" she screamed. "Your tribe has never been able to tell the difference between good and bad! You've thwarted a glorious future for your son, Metanira; I swear by the Styx that I would have made him ageless and immortal, but now you've brought an end to all that. Learn, at last, who I really am: Demeter, the Giver of gifts to mortals and gods.

"Go tell your people to build me a fine temple on that hill over there, with a splendid altar in front. One day, in the future, I will teach you rituals to perform, so that you might once again earn my favor."

Then Demeter discarded her disguise. Old age melted from her body; she became tall and forbiddingly beautiful. Her hair shone with a blinding brilliance and her robes gave forth the pungent scent of thyme in summer—warm and sharp. Stooping to fit through the doorway, she strode from the house.

Metanira's knees buckled and she collapsed upon the floor, oblivious to the crying child who lay beside her on the cold tiles.

His sisters picked him up, but it took a long time to soothe him, for they were poor substitutes for the nanny that he'd lost.

7
DEMETER AND PERSEPHONE

A grim year followed for mortals. Demeter sat alone in her new temple, longing for her graceful daughter. She ignored the seeds that nestled in the soil and let the fields fall fallow. Without a harvest, mortals were forced to let their animals starve and then, as their stores ran out, the mortals began to starve as well.

Eventually, when the gods noticed that there was no longer any sacrificial smoke rising from their altars, they realized that they had a problem. Zeus sent Iris, his golden-winged messenger, to fetch Demeter back to the company of the gods but Demeter, clutching her black robes more closely around herself, refused the summons. Zeus sent the other gods, one by one, to plead and reason with Demeter, offering many gifts and new honors if she would return to their company and resume her duties, but Demeter remained implacable, insisting that until Persephone returned, she would neither visit Olympus nor allow the earth to send up grain.

Reluctantly, Zeus tried a different solution. He sent Hermes to the Underworld to ask Hades to release Persephone, lest the entire cosmos fall into ruin. After he had listened to Hermes's speech, Hades allowed an enigmatic smile to creep across his face. He conceded that he must obey Zeus, who was, after all, the king of the gods. Then he turned to his wife:

"Go home to your weeping mother, Persephone. But remember what sort of husband you've married: I am the brother of Zeus himself, who rules over all the gods! Mine is a magnificent family! Don't forget, moreover, that as queen of the dead, you receive glory in your own right, and hold immense power over everything that walks or creeps upon the earth. As my wife, you have the authority to punish for eternity anyone who has behaved unjustly or who has failed to honor you properly with sacrifices."

◄ DEMETER AND METANIRA

Persephone rejoiced at Hades's words and then busied herself with preparations for her journey. As she was departing, Hades glanced around to make sure that no one was watching and then gave her a tiny pomegranate seed—blood-red and sweet.

When Demeter saw Persephone arising from the earth, she leapt up and rushed from the temple. Wild with joy, she covered her daughter's face with kisses. Then suddenly, she had a dreadful thought.

"My child, please tell me that you didn't eat anything while you were down below! If you haven't, then you can stay up here in the sunlit world with me forever. But if you *did* eat something, you'll have to return to the moldering realm of the dead for a third of each year as the seasons turn round. And tell me this as well—how did all of this happen, anyway?"

Persephone replied. "Well, Mother, when Hermes came to get me, I was *really* excited. Hades handed me a pomegranate seed and then he forced me to eat it. He did it kind of secretly. I couldn't help it. Really! I swear that's what happened!

"And this is how he snatched me away: we were all playing by ourselves, gathering flowers and having fun. Then I saw this beautiful narcissus. I reached over to pick it and suddenly, there he was! He pulled me into his chariot and took off for the Underworld, even though I kicked and screamed. It really upsets me even to think about all of that, but if you want to know, well, that's exactly what happened, I swear."

Mother and daughter embraced once more, taking pleasure in one another's company. Soon, Hecate arrived to join in their rejoicing and forever after, she accompanied Persephone. Demeter's own mother, Rhea, arrived as well, to escort Demeter back to the gathering of gods. She told Demeter that Zeus had promised to give her whatever she wanted and had guaranteed that Persephone would spend only four months each year below with Hades, if Demeter would relent in her anger and enable the grain to grow again.

And so it was; everything unfolded just as Zeus had planned. But grain was not the only gift that Demeter gave to mortals in her happiness. Summoning the leaders of Eleusis, she taught them the rituals of her mysteries—mysteries that promised their initiates abundance during life and a blissful existence after they descended to Persephone's realm.

8
ATHENA, ARTEMIS AND APOLLO ARE BORN

As the months went by, Metis, who was still trapped in Zeus's belly, fumed with frustration. She had managed to transmute herself from a butterfly back into a goddess, but only a very small goddess, given that she was severely constrained by lack of space. The single part of her that steadily got bigger was her stomach, as the day of her daughter's birth inexorably approached. Zeus, meanwhile, had forgotten all about Metis and their child.

One day, however, Zeus woke up with a raging headache that no remedy could cure. He reluctantly concluded that one of the small demons who wandered the cosmos had somehow managed to crawl inside his skull and that he'd have to resort to extreme measures if he were to stop the throbbing pain.

He summoned his closest advisor, Prometheus, and handed him an enormous double axe. Cast by the Cyclopes out of cold, gray bronze, it had been tempered in the waters of the Styx to ensure that its aim would be true.

"Split open my head," Zeus commanded, bowing his neck to give Prometheus easier access. Prometheus hesitated, but Zeus insisted. The blade whistled down, cleaving the skull of the king of the gods with remarkable ease.

From out of the cleft there jumped a small but perfectly formed female, arrayed in a woman's robes but with a golden cuirass buckled on top. When her skirts stirred, the gods glimpsed golden greaves on her calves. Upon her head was a crested warrior's helmet; on her left arm she wore a golden shield and in her right hand she brandished a javelin.

Before the astonished eyes of the other gods, the figure leapt out of Zeus's head and landed on the floor, rapidly growing larger until her steely gaze, peering through the visor of her helmet, was level with theirs. She let out a battle cry that sent a tremor through all who heard it: Sea heaved, Earth shook and Sky trembled, disarraying his stars. Helios reined in his horses, halting the advance of day as he stared at the new wonder. The gods who had been standing nearby scurried into hiding.

When the cosmos had calmed down again, the young goddess announced that her name was Athena.

Zeus smiled, his headache gone. This marvelous creature was *his* daughter, born from *his* head. In the millennia to come, he would repeat that statement so often that the very existence of Athena's mother would be nearly forgotten. As his daughter's impressive wisdom and talent for strategy became known, Zeus took credit for those, too, although his only real claim to them was that, when motivated by fear, he had been clever enough to trick Metis into his stomach, hijacking her pregnancy.

Zeus also wooed Leto, another of his cousins, during the early days of his kingship, although she never became his wife. She was among the most beautiful of the goddesses, with shining hair that tumbled down to her hips when she released it from its silver combs. She was also an unusually shy and gentle goddess, preferring to sit on the outskirts of the gods' gatherings and work quietly with her spindle and distaff. In that quality, Leto was quite different from Artemis and Apollo, the twins whom she eventually bore to Zeus.

For a time Leto thought that she would never give birth to her twins at all. When Hera discovered that Leto was carrying not just one, but two, of her husband's bastards, she decreed that no land that the sun could see was allowed to offer Leto refuge. The pregnant goddess wandered desperately from city to city and across the countryside, finding no place to rest her weary and increasingly ponderous body. And then one day, her labor commenced. Doubled-over with pain, Leto fled to the tiny island of Delos, a wretched place with only one thing to recommend it: it was a floating island and therefore no land at all, strictly speaking. Delos need not feel bound by Hera's decree.

"Delos," said Leto, "if you'll give me a place to bear my children, great temples will be built upon your soil forever after. Mortals will come from every land, adorning you with wealth. This is your chance to become a respectable place—indeed, a famous place! Moreover, I guarantee that if you give me refuge, you will become fixed to the bottom of the ocean and finally be able to rest. Please help me!"

Delos accepted Leto's offer and Leto gratefully collapsed upon the island's soil. Leto's battle was not yet over, however. When Leto's labor started, Hera wrapped a golden cloud around her daughter Eileithyia, who watched over all childbirths. While in the cloud, Eileithyia could hear neither Leto's cries nor the prayers of all the other goddesses, who had hurried to Delos to help Leto deliver her twins. And without Eileithyia, no child could be born.

After Leto had labored for nine terrible days and nights, the goddesses finally learned what Hera had done. They dispatched Iris to offer Eileithyia a golden necklace long enough to wrap around her neck five times if she would open Leto's womb and allow the twins to be born. Eileithyia accepted.

As soon as Eileithyia set foot on Delos, Leto threw her arms around the sturdy trunk of a palm tree and knelt down with her legs spread wide. Within moments, she bore Artemis, who joined Eileithyia in watching over women in labor. Indeed, as soon as Artemis's feet touched the ground, she turned around to help deliver her brother Apollo.

When the goddesses tried to swaddle Apollo, he thrust the clothing aside and declared, in a perfectly articulate voice, "I am Apollo! Forevermore will the lyre and the curved bow belong to me and forevermore shall I declare the will of Zeus to mortals!" Then he strode forth on a journey across the earth, leaving Delos shimmering with gold—the first return on what Leto had promised the island.

Zeus smiled as he looked down upon his two newest children and wondered who would be the next to arrive. So far, Hera had not been able to produce much of anyone. Their daughter Eileithyia was useful only at times of birth and although their son Ares was helpful in war, he was a crashing bore the rest of the time. Would Hera ever give him a child as impressive as those whom Metis and Leto had borne?

9

APOLLO ESTABLISHES HIS ORACLE

Apollo had claimed the right to transmit the will of Zeus to mortals. This entitled him to reveal things that they wouldn't otherwise know about what would happen in the future, what had happened in the past and what was happening at that very moment, far away.

It was a job that gave Apollo a lot of power, which he relished. Although he couldn't change his father's will to suit himself, he could, when he pleased, speak so cryptically that it was impossible for mortals to be sure what he meant. By that trick alone, Apollo could oppress whomever he wished, either by misleading them or by paralyzing them in a ferment of doubt.

As he settled into the work, Apollo realized that he needed a spectacular place in which to perform it, a place where mortals could congregate as they waited to hear what he had to say and deposit the gifts that they would bring to him—statues made of gold and marble, bronze tripods and cauldrons, animals to sacrifice and more. After looking all over the world, he settled on a spot in Boeotia near a spring. He announced to the nymph of the spring, Telphousa, that he would begin building his oracle.

"Think carefully, Apollo," Telphousa replied. "This is a very noisy place. Poseidon holds his riotous chariot races nearby and mule drivers use my springs to water their animals. If you don't mind a suggestion, I'd say you should try Mount Parnassus, just over the way. It's very quiet up there, and you'd have plenty of room."

So Apollo traveled to Parnassus. The slope of the mountain was exceptionally steep—mortals would find it impossible to climb unless he constructed roads for them—but the view from the terrace where his oracle would stand was magnificent, sweeping vertiginously over the coastal plain in blues and greens. The spot had an ethereal beauty; the boundary between the world of the mortals and the world of the gods was eerily thin there and the very ground exhaled an intoxicating fragrance, as if Earth were murmuring secrets with her own sweet breath.

When he finished building the temple that would contain his oracle, Apollo set out to fetch water with which to dedicate it. As he approached an outcropping behind which he sensed there was a spring, he heard a slithering hiss and caught the fetid smell of reptile on the breeze. Pausing, he fit an arrow to his bowstring.

What he saw when he stepped around the rock was worse than he'd imagined. A massive constrictor lay there, rank and bloated, wallowing in a nest littered with the excreted fur and feathers of her victims. Her cold skin was stretched taut over a distended belly, through which the last, feeble twitches of an unfortunate animal could be seen.

This was Python, a ghastly menace to everyone and everything—mortals, their flocks and even the gods themselves. In her youth, she'd helped to rear Typhon, nurturing him into a monster who nearly managed to defeat Zeus and seize control of the cosmos. Now, sensing Apollo's presence, her nostrils flared with a sticky sound and her head swiveled round. Her yellow eyes stared at the intruder.

"Who dares to transgress Python's domain?" she hissed.

Apollo wasn't foolish enough to waste time answering. He pulled his string and shot Python through the heart. As she writhed in her death throes, slapping her coils against the ground so hard that Parnassus shook, she got her answer.

"I am Apollo! Here you'll die and here you'll putrefy, Python, beneath the merciless rays of the sun."

Stepping over the serpent's carcass, Apollo continued to the spring, filled his pitcher and returned to his temple. Two more things remained to be done before he could open his oracle for business. The first was to punish Telphousa, who, he realized, had intentionally steered him into danger. Striding back to the spring where she dwelt, he shook an avalanche of rocks down upon it, stopping her waters forever.

More challenging was the second task: he needed mortals to staff his oracle. Casting his gaze across the world, he spotted a ship of Cretan sailors who were on their way to Pylos. Transforming himself into an enormous dolphin, Apollo leapt aboard; instantly, the ship veered off course, ignoring the steersman's efforts to control it. It sped across the waves while the great dolphin lay on its deck, glaring at anyone who dared to approach. When the ship reached the bay at the foot of Parnassus, the dolphin changed into a blazing star, which flew off the ship and into Apollo's new temple, terrifying everyone who saw it. Moments later, a handsome young man strolled from the doors and addressed the cowering sailors.

"I am Apollo! You will be the priests of my new oracle. Prepare to serve me."

"But my lord," asked the steersman in a quavering voice, "how shall we feed ourselves in this remote and lofty place?"

Apollo laughed. "Ignorant mortal! Each of you must take a knife in your right hand and wait for the sheep that mortals will bring when they seek my help. As long as my oracle exists, you'll never be short of meat."

Apollo named his new oracle, and the city that grew up around it, Delphi, a word that would remind his priests of the dolphin that had brought them there.

10
HEPHAESTUS'S STORY

While the other gods were gaping at the sight of Athena springing from Zeus's head, Hera sat in the corner, seething with fury. It had been bad enough when Zeus was simply fathering bastards on other goddesses; *this* time, he had borne a child all by himself (or so he claimed, anyway). Hera decided to respond in kind. Mustering her considerable determination, she managed to impregnate herself.

The months hummed along, Hera smugly growing larger and Zeus none the wiser that the child wasn't his. When labor started, however, Hera could stifle her pride no longer. As she lumbered into her bedchamber, supported by Eileithyia and Artemis, she triumphantly announced that the glorious child she was about to bear was hers and hers alone.

But she had boasted too soon. The infant, when he arrived, was misshapen, with one leg shorter than the other. In disgust, Hera seized her baby by the ankle and tossed him over the side of Olympus. He landed in the sea, where the kindly goddess Thetis swam to his rescue. She and her sister Eurynome nurtured the child, whom they named Hephaestus.

When he was older, Hephaestus made his home on Lemnos, an island renowned for its expert craftsmen. The people taught him the art of blacksmithing, at which he excelled. The unreliability of Hephaestus's legs led him to develop muscular arms; this, combined with a wonderful delicacy of touch, enabled him to create works that were both stunningly beautiful and remarkably sturdy. It dawned on Hephaestus that he could use these talents to avenge himself upon his mother.

One day, a splendid golden throne arrived on Olympus, inscribed with Hera's name. The figures engraved on its surface were so lifelike that they seemed to breathe. Its form was so beautifully proportioned that the metal looked as if it had been spun from gossamer. Its curves were clearly meant to embrace Hera's body and no one else's.

Delighted with the tribute, Hera immediately sat down and luxuriated in its comfort, but her weight, when she sat, triggered a hidden mechanism. Slender tendrils of gold stealthily grew from the throne's surface, entwining her thighs and forearms. When she tried to rise, she found that she was trapped. She kicked, she wailed, she cursed, but to no avail.

Zeus, stifling his laughter, tried to free his wife but failed. Her son Ares yanked and pulled but failed as well. Each of the other gods tried in turn to free Hera, without success.

And then it dawned on the youngest of them, Dionysus, that one god had been forgotten: Hephaestus. Although no one had seen him since Hera tossed him into the sea, they'd heard about his fondness for metalwork. They'd treated it as a joke, sneering that Hephaestus was certainly no Olympian; what real god would lift a hand to do such lowly labor—and why would a god want to? Now they began to realize that Hephaestus had discovered a new source of power and claimed it as his own.

Zeus instructed Dionysus to promise Hephaestus whatever he desired in return for freeing Hera. Dionysus descended to Lemnos and tried to persuade his brother to yield. Wouldn't Hephaestus like a golden palace on Olympus, asked Dionysus? No, he could build a better one himself, replied Hephaestus. Wouldn't abundant sacrifices please him? No, he already received them from the people of Lemnos, who loved and admired him.

Finally, Dionysus sighed and ceased negotiating. He conjured two goblets of wine from the air and handed one to Hephaestus, gesturing for him to recline. "Now let us relax and enjoy *my* gift to the world, Brother."

Hephaestus had never tasted wine like this before—indeed, he had scarcely tasted any wine at all. He drank its sweetness and asked for more . . . and more. Dionysus obliged.

When the wine had made Hephaestus more amenable to compromise, Dionysus leaned forward. "Brother," he whispered, "you and I are among the youngest of gods and we're not always respected. Let me advise you. This is your chance to seize a great prize: demand Aphrodite as your wife in return for freeing your mother. You're not a well-built god; this may be your only chance of winning any bride at all, much less the very best of them."

Even when drunk, Hephaestus could see the wisdom of these words. He allowed Dionysus to load him onto the back of a donkey and lead him up to Olympus.

Dionysus announced the terms of the agreement to the assembly of gods. Aphrodite strenuously protested, but her feelings made no difference; Zeus was king and apportioned the goddesses as he chose. He shook Hephaestus's hand (nearly toppling him from the donkey), received the finely wrought cup that Hephaestus had brought along as a bride-price, and formally welcomed Hera's son—or rather, his and Hera's son, as he immediately began to call Hephaestus—into the company of the immortals.

Hephaestus pressed a spring on the throne that was invisible to everyone but him. The golden tendrils disappeared and his mother was free. The ingenuity of the device made the gods gasp; Hephaestus seized the opportunity to expound at length about its construction.

A smile crept across Hera's face; her son was not so defective, after all, even if he was a bit unconventional. Zeus might try to claim him, but the gods, at least, knew the truth about his parentage.

A smile crept across Aphrodite's face, as well. Her new husband seemed to be more besotted by his craft projects than he would ever be by any female. It would be easy enough to deceive him; she saw no reason to terminate her long-standing affair with Ares.

Aphrodite was doubly wrong, however. The time would come when Hephaestus not only learned of her adultery but cunningly trapped her in flagrante delicto. And the time would also come when Hephaestus's eye was caught by another goddess.

That was Athena, who visited Hephaestus's forge one day seeking new armor. Seeing her dressed only in her robes, which more fully revealed the curves of her body, Hephaestus was overcome by lust and wrapped his arms around her.

Athena wrested herself free and ran; Hephaestus pursued her, managing to keep up in spite of his bad leg. He was just overtaking Athena, in fact, when excitement seized him and he ejaculated. His divine sperm hit her divine leg.

Disgusted, Athena wiped it off with a bit of wool and then threw the wool to the ground. Earth, forever fertile, received Hephaestus's seed and became pregnant.

In due course, Earth bore Hephaestus's son. Like many of Earth's children, he was snaky from the waist down, but his upper half resembled his father. Athena, who had a soft spot for children, adopted the creature as her own—as, indeed, he almost had been. She named him Erichthonius.

When Erichthonius was grown, Athena set him on the throne of Athens. He was a good and thoughtful leader, diligently improving the lives of his own subjects. From his father, he learned to smelt silver and make coins, which facilitated trade. He invented the yoke, so that animals could be driven in pairs, and then the plough, to make it easier to grow grain. He designed the first chariot for mortals and established races in honor of Athena.

Erichthonius reigned for fifty years and was followed by his son Pandion. The line of Hephaestus would continue to rule over Athena's city for a long time, although not forever; one day, a son of Poseidon would become Athens's most famous king of all.

11
HERMES THE CATTLE THIEF

Maia was in labor with Hermes, the son of Zeus, for a short but exhausting time: the baby was in such a hurry to be born that he tricked her womb into squeezing what should have been several hours of contractions into just a few, harrowing moments. As soon as Hermes had leapt out from between Maia's legs, a slave helped the weary mother stagger from the birthing stool to the bed, where she fell fast asleep.

Hermes allowed the midwife to wrap him in swaddling bands. He could have seized the moment to announce his grand intentions, as his older brother Apollo had done, but other ideas for which stealth was crucial were swirling around in his tiny head. With his thumb in his mouth, cooing drowsily as babies do, he pretended to sleep. The midwife departed, content that all was well.

As soon as she was gone, Hermes crept out of the cave where Maia made her home. Blinking in the sunlight, he looked around. The heights of Mount Cyllene, deep within the wilderness of Arcadia, were rather lonely, but eventually he saw a tortoise ambling by.

"Well met, my little friend!" Hermes said. "At least for me, that is. Everyone knows you're a marvelous charm against evil when you're alive, but I think I can do something even better with you once you're dead." Hermes flipped the tortoise onto its back and used a chisel to dig the animal out of its shell. Then, adding reeds, oxhide and sheep gut to the empty carapace, he created the first lyre. The song that he improvised as he strummed the new instrument described Zeus and Maia's lovemaking on the night that he was conceived, yet even as he created this masterpiece of imagination, he was plotting his next enterprise: the theft of Apollo's cattle.

After creeping back into the cave and stowing the lyre in his cradle, Hermes darted north to the meadows of Pieria, where the gods kept their cattle, and stole fifty from Apollo's herd, just as the sun was setting. He drove them all the way south to the Alpheus River, forcing them to walk backwards so that they'd leave hoof-prints that he was sure would confound even the keenest detective. He clumped along behind them in sandals he'd made by lashing together branches, twigs and leaves, to disguise his own tracks, as well. The only witness to all of this was an old man tending his grapevines. "Listen, pal," said Hermes, "if you don't want a bad harvest this year, forget that you ever saw me!" And then he hurried onwards.

Once at the Alpheus, Hermes drove the cattle into a stable and set to work inventing fire sticks: whittling a laurel branch to a sharp point, he twirled it against a piece of wood until sparks appeared. Carefully, then, he added tinder until his fire was blazing. Dragging two of the cows from the stable, he threw them to the ground and severed their spinal cords. He butchered them, roasted them and divided their meat into twelve portions as a feast for twelve gods— himself and the eleven Olympians whose circle he was scheming to join. Then he faced the toughest challenge of his young life. The meat's aroma made his mouth water, but gods weren't allowed to eat meat; they were supposed to merely inhale its delicious smell and leave the chewing, savoring and swallowing to humans. Determined to prove himself divine, Hermes ignored his grumbling belly.

Finally, Hermes cleared away the evidence of what he'd done. He threw the leftover bits of the cows into the fire and reluctantly tossed his clever sandals into the Alpheus. Pride wouldn't allow him to conceal everything, however; he carefully spread the cow-hides out on a large rock and petrified them—eternal trophies of his deeds.

Just as the sun was rising on the second day of Hermes's life, he scampered home to Mount Cyllene. Squeezing through the keyhole of Maia's front door, he leapt into his cradle and burrowed under the blankets as if he'd been there all day.

Maia wasn't fooled, however; she'd already realized what sort of child she'd borne when she awoke and found him missing. She warned Hermes to stay out of trouble and particularly advised him to steer clear of Apollo, who was a short-tempered god.

"Oh, stop treating me like a baby, Mother!" Hermes retorted. "I've got plans! You and I deserve the good life, relaxing on Olympus, not squatting here alone. One way or another, I swear I'll get us there."

Apollo, meanwhile, had quickly noticed that fifty cows were missing. Striding forth to find them, he encountered the old man tending his grapevines and asked what he'd seen. Ignoring Hermes's threats, the man described everything, pointing his bony finger at the strange tracks on the ground. Even with this help, however, Apollo failed to find his cattle until he saw an eagle flying overhead—the bird of Zeus. In a flash, he realized that the thief was none other than Zeus's newest son, his own half brother. Apollo burst into Maia's cave and turned it inside out, fruitlessly searching for his cattle. Then he stomped over to Hermes's cradle.

"Where are my cows, you little stinker? Tell me now or I'll hurl you into Hades, where you can play at being king over dead children!"

"How should *I* know where they are?" lisped Hermes in reply. "I'm just a baby! I don't even know what these things . . . cows, I think you called them? . . . are. All I care about are warm blankets and my mother's milk. I swear by Zeus that I never drove any cattle into this cave." Hermes tucked in his chin and fluttered his eyelashes so as to look even more adorable than he already was.

But Apollo, who cared little for cuteness, threw Hermes over his shoulder like a sack of grain and began to carry him away. Thinking quickly, Hermes farted and then sneezed—a mighty stench followed by a puzzling omen. Apollo dropped him to the floor and stood transfixed, his prophet's mind pondering what it all might mean.

It was exactly the reaction that Hermes had hoped for: away he raced to Olympus and his father's throne. Seconds later, Apollo breathlessly arrived as well. The two brothers pled their cases: "Father, listen to me!" "No, Father, listen to ME!" "He's lying!" "*He's* lying!" "He stole my cows!" "But I'm just a *baby!*"

Zeus burst out laughing, delighted by Hermes's clever theft and the boldness of his lies. Calling for silence, he ordered his sons to settle their differences and told Hermes to start by returning Apollo's cattle.

Hermes obediently led Apollo to the stable where the cows were stashed, wondering whether his brother would notice that only forty-eight remained. Apollo did; Apollo obsessively counted everything: the tripods at his temples, the leaves on his favorite laurel trees, the grains of sand on the shore, the pints of water in the sea. Cows were the least of it.

Blustering with indignation, Apollo demanded payment. Hermes, however, calmly settled the lyre in the crook of his arm and, strumming it, sang stories of how the family of gods was born— culminating, of course, with his own birth.

"Good heavens!" exclaimed Apollo. "Did *you* invent this wonderful thing? Why, it would enliven even the dullest party! I underestimated you, Brother; you're clever. If you'll give me this splendid device, we'll forget about those two cows."

So Hermes gave his lyre to Apollo, and Apollo, delighting in its sound, gave Hermes two gifts in return (has Hermes ever failed to come out better in a deal?). The first was a cowherd's goad and with it the honor of watching over cattle. The second was a magic wand, gleaming gold. With it, Hermes grants good fortune to some lucky mortals—but all mortals, at the end of their lives, see him holding it aloft as he leads their souls, gibbering like bats, down to Hades.

12
DIONYSUS IS BORN, AND DIES, AND IS BORN AGAIN

One year when Persephone returned from the Underworld, Demeter saw that her daughter's robes were stretched tight over a ripening belly; Persephone, scarcely more than a child herself, would soon bear a child.

And yet, Persephone spent only four months each year with her husband, Hades. This child, now nearing its birth, must have been conceived the last time that Persephone was above. Who, then, was its father? The gods speculated, but Persephone remained silent, her face downcast, even when questioned by her mother.

Soon, the baby was born—a beautiful boy with startling blue eyes. Persephone fell in love with him at once, holding him close beneath her breasts, rocking him and crooning to him as he stared up at her with an unwavering gaze.

On the following day, Zeus took the child from Persephone's arms and, lifting him high, named him Dionysus. Then Zeus placed Dionysus on a throne next to the one where he himself had sat since conquering the Titans and proudly declared that the child would someday become the ruler of the cosmos.

The identity of the baby's father was now clear. The gods were shocked—not so much, perhaps, by the fact that Zeus had fathered a son upon his own daughter, but by Zeus's anointment of the youngest of them all.

But if the gods were shocked, the Titans were outraged. Defeat at the hands of the Olympians had been a crushing blow; to know that this child would rule over them one day added insult to injury. Some of them who were still free to move about began to plot against Dionysus. Hera, who was furious that Zeus had chosen a bastard as his heir, caught wind of their discontent and offered her help.

It is difficult for anyone to sit upon a throne forever, but for a child it is impossible. One day, Dionysus saw some toys lying nearby on the ground—a spinning top, dice, marionettes, a mirror and golden apples. Quietly sliding down from his seat when no one was watching, he slipped away to play with them.

Instantly, the Titans leapt from their hiding place and seized him. Stifling his cries, they dragged him to their lair at the edge of the world and tore him limb from limb. His beautiful head fell onto Earth below, his startling eyes stared lifelessly at Sky above. Gathering the pieces, the Titans cooked and devoured Dionysus—a grisly feast.

They saved the most coveted morsel for last: his heart, still raw and beating. As they were arguing about how to divide it, Athena caught sight of the smoke rising from their fire and arrived to investigate. In a flash, she took in the gruesome scene; with a shriek, she seized the heart from their hands. Darting to Olympus, she told her father what had happened. Zeus roared with grief and smote the Titans with a thunderbolt.

The Titans' incineration left a greasy smudge upon the ground, which in time began to fester. Like fungus upon a sodden log, the muck eventually spawned new life: a tainted tribe of mortals. As these began to breed with other humans, they infected the whole tribe; Persephone came to regard all people as contaminated by the Titans' murder of her son. As queen of the Underworld, she used her power to blight the afterlife of every mortal who entered her kingdom, condemning their ghosts to linger in eternal gloom and mud.

Zeus carefully preserved Dionysus's heart and used it to resurrect his son in a most curious way. Chopping it up, he mixed the bits into a drink that he served to his lover Semele, the daughter of Cadmus, the king of Thebes. After she drank it, Zeus sired a new Dionysus upon her.

As the months went by and Semele's belly grew larger, Hera learned of her most recent rival and devised a scheme to get rid of both mother and child. Appearing to Semele in the guise of her faithful nurse, Hera asked her about the mysterious lover who appeared in her bedroom each night.

"He claims to be Zeus," Hera said, "but how do you really know? Other men have pretended to be divine to enter women's beds. Ask this 'Zeus' to swear by the Styx that he will give you anything you desire. Once he's sworn, demand that he appear to you in exactly the same form as he appears when making love to Hera. Then we'll see what we shall see . . ."

Poor Semele, her heart filled with doubt, did just as Hera advised. Zeus cheerfully swore the oath she asked him to, but when he heard Semele's unexpected request he was aghast. "You don't know what you're asking, my love—ask for anything else instead!" he pleaded. "Jewels from Egypt! Silks from the East! Perfumes from Arabia! I'll deliver all of this and more to your waiting hands in the blink of an eye!"

But Semele was adamant. Sadly, Zeus cast aside his mortal guise. The bedroom blazed with his splendor and Semele, gazing upon her lover, began to burn.

Quickly, Zeus reached into her womb and rescued his son. Cutting a slit in his own thigh, Zeus slipped Dionysus beneath his skin where, safe from Hera, he could finish gestating. When the time came, Dionysus was born again, this time from the father who had sired him twice.

13
DIONYSUS AND THE PIRATES

Dead once himself, Dionysus harrowed Hades and led Semele up to Olympus.

And dead once himself, Dionysus understood (as much as any god can ever understand) the state of being mortal. Pitying humans,

who lived such a short time and in such a wretched state, he set out to relieve their misery. He invented wine, which provided a respite from suffering while mortals were alive, and invented rituals through which mortals could appease Persephone, so that she would be kinder to them when they entered her gloomy kingdom. He traveled the world, teaching people how to plant grapevines and ferment their fruit. He trained priests to perform the rituals that would protect mortals after death.

But Dionysus's divinity was subtler than that of most gods. He did not declare his grandeur, like Apollo, or arrive with a battle cry, like Athena. He often preferred, like Hermes, to remain unobtrusive, so he might observe the lives of mortals. Because of this, many people refused to believe that Dionysus was a god at all and mocked him as an imposter when he arrived in their villages. His second birth, moreover, had taken place after most of the other Olympians were well established; the pantheon had seemed complete. Eventually, Dionysus realized that to establish himself, he would have to punish those who didn't acknowledge his divinity. He set out to institute his cult in every land.

One day, disguised as a handsome young man with dark hair cascading to his shoulders, he wandered along the seashore. He wore a cloak dyed purple with the ooze of Tyrian shellfish, a mark of wealth and privilege. Tuscan pirates, spotting him from their ship, judged him to be a king's son and steered for the shallows. They dragged Dionysus aboard, meaning to hold him for ransom, and sailed away. When they tried to bind him with withies, however, the bonds fell futilely to the deck and their captive gazed at them with an uncanny smile.

The helmsman saw the truth. "Madmen," he cried, "this is no mortal, but some god! Apollo, or Poseidon, or Zeus—or perhaps a new one! We must set him ashore immediately, before he causes storm winds to blow!"

The captain rebuked him. "*You're* the one who's crazy! Shut up and do your job. Leave this to me; before we reach our next port, he'll tell me who his relatives are and what they're worth." With this, the captain hoisted the sails and the boat moved briskly towards the open sea.

As soon as the shore receded from sight, astonishing things began to happen. Dark wine gushed up between the planks of the deck. Ivy, bright with flowers and berries, spiraled round the mast. Grapevines, heavy with fruit, twined their way across the yard.

The pirates yelled to the helmsman to steer for land, but it was too late. Moments later, Dionysus turned himself into a lion, roaring murderously from the bow, and created a bear to stand amidships, huge, dark and angry. The terrified pirates crouched in the stern, praying for safety, but with a mighty pounce, the lion leapt upon the captain and tore him apart. The other pirates, fearing the same fate, jumped overboard.

As each man fell towards the water, he changed. His face grew broader and his nose grew longer. His back began to arch and his legs fused together, becoming a sturdy tail that ended in a crescent like the new moon. His arms melted into his body but his hands, still free, turned into glistening gray flippers. By the time each pirate hit the water, he was a dolphin.

The helmsman made ready to leap into the sea as well, but Dionysus stopped him.

"Take heart, pious helmsman! I am Dionysus, the god who roars! Zeus is my father and Semele, the daughter of Cadmus, is my mother."

Dionysus blessed the helmsman with abundant good fortune and sent him on his way, commanding him to spread word of a new god's arrival. The helmsman brought the ship to shore and obeyed the god's command.

14
APHRODITE EXPERIENCES DESIRE

The cosmos was still young when Aphrodite began weaving her wiles, for she had arisen from the sea even before the children of Earth and Sky first saw the light of day. Lust had preceded her—it had been Lust who drove Earth and Sky together to begin with—but Lust was coarse, sometimes even brutal. Aphrodite refined sex: she made it into a game and once it was a game there were strategies and tricks, winners and losers, which made everything much more interesting.

She herself had always been a winner, although there had been times when she came close to losing. Once, she and Ares had slipped into bed together, thinking that Hephaestus was far away. Overwhelmed by passion, the lovers failed to notice that thin but sturdy bonds were creeping up through the bedclothes and down from the rafters, weaving a net that immobilized them in midpassion. The harder they fought to free themselves, the more deeply did the fetters bite into their flesh. Hephaestus returned and summoned the other Olympians to witness his wife's shame. The goddesses blushed and stayed away, but the gods gathered around the bed leering, laughing and describing to one another what they'd like to do to Aphrodite themselves.

Hephaestus demanded that Zeus return the goblet he'd paid as bride-price when he married Aphrodite (a demand that Zeus ignored). He also demanded that Ares pay an adulterer's fine. Poseidon agreed to act as Ares's guarantor if Hephaestus would set Ares free, but as soon as Hephaestus released the lovers, Ares ran off to Thrace and Poseidon simply disappeared, leaving Hephaestus behind, empty-handed and humiliated.

As for Aphrodite, she retreated to Cyprus, where the Graces bathed and anointed her. She reappeared on Olympus the following day—sleek, poised and smiling like a cat. She was well aware that the way the fetters bit into her thighs had only heightened the gods' arousal.

Zeus laughed along with everyone else at what happened to Hephaestus. His irritation with Aphrodite, however, was growing. She was constantly infecting him with desire for gods and mortals, females and males—anyone with whom it amused her to pair him. These affairs had cost Zeus no end of quarrels with Hera and no small amount of indignity, given that fear of discovery drove him to disguise himself as all kinds of things.

Nor was Zeus alone in his resentment: almost all of the gods knew what it meant to be Aphrodite's victim. Only Hestia, Athena and Artemis had been spared, because they'd sworn by the Styx to remain virgins as soon as they were born. Even Aphrodite did not tread on such an oath.

Eventually, Zeus had had enough of Aphrodite's tricks. He resolved to humble her with desire for Anchises, a cousin of King

Priam of Troy who made his living herding cattle on the slopes of Mount Ida.

Zeus infected Aphrodite with a yearning so urgent that she trembled. A fever raced beneath her skin, her heart pounded in her ears and her eyes could no longer focus—although divine, she felt close to death. Hurrying home to Cyprus, she ordered the Graces to burnish her already perfect splendor. Perfumes, unguents, silks and jewels were poured, rubbed, draped and dangled upon her luscious flesh. By the time Aphrodite set out for Ida, her allure was so strong that wolves, lions, bears and leopards gathered in her wake, trotting behind her until, overwhelmed by desire themselves, they crept away, two by two, into the woods.

As she approached Anchises's hut, Aphrodite struggled to compose herself. Wasn't this just another game, after all, like so many others that she herself had orchestrated? Couldn't she win it, if she strategized? Adopting the demeanor of a mortal maiden, she approached Anchises. She told him that she was a Phrygian princess, kidnapped by Hermes and whisked away to the mountainside because the gods wished her to become Anchises's bride.

Anchises drew back, suspecting that the maiden was really a goddess in disguise. Although he desired her, he was green with fear of what might happen if he slept with an immortal. Eventually, however, Aphrodite's soft lies and the lure of her body enthralled him. Leading her inside, he removed first her jewelry and then her robes. He gestured towards the pelts of bears and mountain lions that served as his bed. With an artfully shy smile, the goddess lay down and the man lay atop her, mortal merging with divine.

Afterwards, Anchises slept. He awoke to find the maiden standing above him, fully dressed and terrifyingly splendid. The scent of roses, close and pressing, lay heavy in the air. The hut was filled with light, as if a star had burst into the room. The maiden's head, now crowned with a gleaming diadem, grazed the ceiling. Anchises was terrified.

"Arise, Anchises!" she commanded. "See me now as I did not allow you to see me before, in the fullness of my beauty. I am Aphrodite the golden-crowned, the looser of limbs, the mistress of charming deceits.

"For my own pleasure, I lay beneath you. Now, as the months circle round, I shall bear you a son. His name, *Aeneas*, will recall the *an*guish of my desire for you. I will give him to the nymphs to nurture until such time as he may live with you. He will rise in glory and lead the Trojans to a new future. This is what I give you in recompense for the pleasure that I have taken from you.

"Mark this well, though: tell no one what took place here today. It is always dangerous to sleep with an immortal and you would do well to stay silent. Favored though your family is, one of them has already learned this. Tithonus, the son of your grandfather Laomedon, was loved by the goddess Dawn. Dawn asked Zeus to grant him immortality, but she forgot to ask for eternal youth as well. Now, Tithonus cannot die, but his body and strength diminish. He grows smaller and more repulsive with each passing year. In shame, Dawn keeps him hidden, but his tiny voice still chirps away, like the song of a cicada. Take care, lest your fate is even worse."

Anchises swore to remain silent, but eventually he broke his promise and boasted to his friends of bedding a goddess. Zeus struck him with a thunderbolt, crippling his leg.

As for Aphrodite, whatever Zeus had hoped the incident would teach her was quickly forgotten. Nor could it really be said that she had emerged from it the loser. Her son Aeneas survived the Trojan War and led a band of companions to Italy, where he planted the seeds of what would become the mighty Roman Empire. For centuries, the descendants of Aphrodite and Anchises ruled the world.

GODS AND MORTALS

HUMANS LEARN THE WAYS OF THE GODS

15
PROMETHEUS, EPIMETHEUS AND THE FIRST MEN

When it was time to create mortal creatures, the younger gods molded their frames out of materials that they'd found in Earth's body. Then they handed the frames to Prometheus and his brother Epimetheus and told them to finish the job. Zeus gave the brothers a bag of assorted tools and talents from which they could equip each creature. Epimetheus proposed that they divide the labor. He volunteered to distribute the talents and tools if Prometheus would deal with any problems after he was done.

Prometheus should have known better than to accept. Themis had named him Prometheus, which meant "Fore-Thinker," because she discerned in him, already at birth, a mental clarity that enabled him to see the outcome of actions in advance. Her other son seemed to be just the opposite, so Themis had named him Epimetheus, which meant "After-Thinker."

Nonetheless, Prometheus agreed to Epimetheus's proposal, and sure enough, when the job was done, he discovered that his brother had made a terrible mistake. Epimetheus had distributed everything in the bag—claws, talons, hooves, wings, antennae, fur, carapaces, fins, scales, gills, quills, shells, pincers, antlers, horns, beaks, stingers, tentacles, speed, stealth, camouflage and more— without realizing that there would be nothing left when he got to men, who had been last in line.

Poor men! They had nothing with which to clothe their naked flesh, nothing to protect the tender soles of their feet, no way to defend themselves from other animals and no way to flee when they were attacked. Men were surely doomed.

Pitying the feeble creatures, Prometheus slipped into the workshop that Hephaestus and Athena shared and stole the secrets of their crafts. He gave these to men so that they would be able to weave clothing to keep themselves warm and forge weaponry to protect themselves from other animals. He gave them something else that he stole from the workshop, as well: fire. Without it, men's knowledge of crafts would have been useless. As the years went by, Prometheus continued to help men. He taught them seamanship and carpentry, astronomy and meteorology, writing and mathematics, medicine and the divinatory arts.

Men were now on the path to success and were grateful to the gods for all that they had. As soon as they learned how to raise animals, they formed the habit of sacrificing one to the gods every so often, slitting its throat and placing its carcass on a fire so that the aroma of its burning flesh would rise to the gods' noses. The men kept nothing for themselves—not even a scrap of meat, bone, hide or entrails.

Prometheus didn't like this arrangement—why should men do all the work of raising an animal and get no pleasure or use from its remains? He told Zeus that a more equitable deal would have to be made and scheduled a meeting between gods and men in the town of Mecone. He also proposed a way of settling the question.

"The men," he said to Zeus, "will surely want to offer you a sacrifice at this event. After they've killed the animal, let me divide its carcass into two packages. You, Zeus, can choose whichever one you want for the gods and the men will take the other.

"And let's agree," he continued, "that whichever package you choose will set the standard: forevermore, every sacrifice will be divided between gods and men in the same manner."

Zeus raised his eyebrows in surprise but then smiled and nodded.

When the day came, the men killed an ox and Prometheus flayed and butchered its carcass. Before calling Zeus to the altar, he carefully created two parcels. One of them looked disgusting—it was wrapped in the ox's paunch—but inside there was good, rich meat. The other looked delicious—it was wrapped in a sheet of shining fat—but inside there was nothing but bones.

Zeus arrived. "Prometheus, my friend, you've done a very poor job of apportioning the sacrifice."

"Oh my, you're right," sighed Prometheus, feigning surprise while hugging his craftiness close to his heart. "Well—my mistake! Take whichever you want."

And so Zeus, who can never be fooled, chose the fat-covered parcel, knowing full well that doing so would give him an excuse to impose an eternity of grief upon men. Unwrapping it, he thundered, "Prometheus, your cunning has finally undone you! These *men*, these upstart little beasts whom you love so much, will suffer for your deceit. I'm depriving them of fire—they'll no longer be able to cook or smelt metal or warm themselves at their hearths. Let's see how they fare now!"

Thus began a most dreadful time for men—cold, dark and bereft of all comforts.

16
PROMETHEUS STEALS FIRE

Sometime after the disastrous encounter at Mecone, Prometheus slipped into the gods' hall carrying a fennel stalk. Outside, the plant was tough and fibrous, but inside, it was hollow and juicy. Waiting until Hestia was distracted by a household chore, Prometheus stole a smoldering ember from the divine hearth and dropped it inside the stalk.

He ran back to earth as quickly as he could, rolling the stalk between his palms so that the ember wouldn't nestle so deeply into the moist pulp that it extinguished itself. As soon as his feet touched the ground, he slid it onto a pile of dry leaves and gently blew on it until a flame appeared. He nurtured the flame with small twigs until it was blazing.

Gathering men around the fire, he reminded them how to tend and use it. In a few days, small fires were burning all over the land. Zeus looked down and saw the flickering lights. Immediately, he knew what Prometheus had done and summoned him to Olympus. Consumed by fury, he roared, "Titan! You must be very pleased with yourself for stealing fire. But let me tell you: this isn't over yet and the next misery I bring to men will be one that neither your cunning nor your stealth can alleviate. As for you—you'll suffer eternally for your hubris."

Zeus called Force and Power into his presence, and summoned Hephaestus from his forge.

"Take Prometheus to the Caucasus Mountains, in the farthest reaches of the east. Hang him on a cliff; stretch out his arms and legs to either side and pin him down by his wrists and ankles, using adamantine fetters and manacles riveted with bronze. Then drive a shaft through his entrails and deep into the rock beneath so that he can't escape. Leave him there to shiver under winter snows and to be scorched by summer suns until his skin turns to leather."

Power laughed. "We'll teach him he was a fool to try to elude your will, Zeus!"

"I wasn't done speaking!" Zeus thundered. "An eagle will visit you there, Prometheus—a son of Typhon and Echidna, huge and ravenous. He'll tear at your diaphragm until he lays bare your liver, fat and glistening. Then he'll gnaw at it until it's bruised and tattered. He'll gorge himself in the same way every day until the end of time, for as soon as he departs, your liver will begin to grow again, preparing itself for the eagle's next meal."

Hephaestus groaned inwardly, horrified that any god should be treated so barbarically. He groaned, too, at the loss of a companion who, unlike most of the gods, understood the satisfaction of manual labor. He suspected that Zeus's interference with Prometheus and his ideas would prove useless, anyway. Even after they'd been deprived of fire, men had progressed, adapting the skills that Prometheus had taught them to their new circumstances; Hephaestus admired them for their resilience. None of that mattered now, however. Hephaestus sighed and gathered the tools that he'd need to carry out Zeus's will. When they reached the mountains, Force and Power held Prometheus against the cliff while Hephaestus dealt with the fetters and shaft. As they departed, Hephaestus saw the great eagle circling overhead, impatient for his meal.

The bird was not only a greedy eater but also a slovenly one. Each time that he finished a meal, shreds of Prometheus's liver were left dangling from his talons and beak. This led to something extraordinary. Ichor, which ran through the gods' veins instead of blood, dripped from the shreds onto the slopes below. Wherever it fell, new plants sprang up. Their purple flowers were beautiful but their roots were the color of freshly butchered flesh and their juice was dark, oily and viscous. The natives of the area, knowing where the plant had come from, named it the prometheios.

It was Hecate who first discovered the special properties of its juice, which could either heal or harm. She passed the knowledge along to her student Medea, who, sneaking out of her father's palace at night when the moon was waxing, roamed the slopes to harvest it. Eventually, she used the juice to make an unguent that protected the hero Jason from the fiery breath of her father's bulls. Not long after that, prometheios plants stopped growing on the slopes: the hero Heracles had shot the eagle and freed Prometheus from his chains.

By that time, Prometheus had spent one thousand years hanging upon the cliff's face, sorely tormented for the help he had given men.

17
PANDORA'S GIFTS

Zeus had sworn that the next misery he inflicted on men would be impossible for anyone—even Prometheus—to relieve. He planned to create an evil so enticing that men would scramble to embrace it before they realized its dangers.

Chortling at his own cleverness, Zeus mustered his forces. First, he commanded Hephaestus to mix together earth and water and sculpt it into a figure that resembled the goddesses. Once this was done, Aphrodite infused the figure with a beauty that beguiled the minds of all who saw it and made their bodies ache with desire.

It was at this point that the gods noticed the figure was naked. Athena quickly dressed it in shining robes, bound at the waist with a silver belt. The Graces and Persuasion added golden necklaces, bracelets and earrings that gleamed in the light of the hearth fire.

Over its head, Athena draped a finely embroidered veil, on top of which she placed a wreath of spring-blooming flowers, crowned by a golden diadem that Hephaestus had forged. Upon it, he had engraved all of the monsters born from Earth and Sea, so deftly that the creatures seemed to breathe and speak.

Athena gave a few final tugs to the figure's garments and then stepped back to admire her work: the creature was truly a wonder to behold.

Now that its outer form was finished, the gods infused their creation with skills and emotions. Touching its hands, Athena bestowed on them an ability to spin and weave. Touching its breast, Hermes infected it with an audacious mind, a cunning disposition and deceitful ways. Hermes also gave it an alluring voice, without which his other gifts would have lain fallow. And then he gave it a name: Pandora, which meant "All-Gifts." Hermes smiled at his joke; a gift, indeed, would it be to the tribe of men, this creature destined to be the first woman and the mother of all misfortunes.

When Hermes spoke her name, Pandora awoke—no longer clay draped in finery but living flesh, blinking her eyes and shaking her limbs. At Zeus's command, Hermes escorted her down to earth and offered her to Epimetheus as a bride.

Many years earlier, Prometheus had warned his brother never to accept any gifts from the gods. When Epimetheus saw Pandora, however, he forgot that; he could no more decline Pandora than he could cease breathing. And so, Epimetheus hugged Zeus's crafty plan to his silly heart, embracing a life of misery for himself and the tribe of men.

That came later, however. Pandora and Epimetheus settled into marriage happily and Pandora soon bore a daughter whom they named Pyrrha, "Fire," in honor of Prometheus's gift to mortals. Pandora bore other children, too, and in this early age of human existence, she lived long enough to watch them have children, grandchildren and even great-grandchildren of their own.

Pandora used the cunning that Hermes had given her to invent the ways of keeping house. Previously, men had lived from day to day, never troubling to think ahead. As long as each man worked at least one day a year, there had always been plenty to go around. Now, however, there were other people to consider. Pandora, the men thought, wasn't capable of working in the fields or hunting in the forests, especially when she was pregnant. They told her to stay in the house, which was warm in the winter and cool in the summer. The men labored to feed her and her children, which meant that they strove longer and harder than they had before. When some of them married Pandora's descendants and had children of their own, they strove harder still.

Pandora devised ways to store and preserve what the men brought home. She used jars made of clay to stockpile grain, olive oil and other food. By sinking the jars partway into the cool earth of her pantry floor, she was able to keep their contents fresh for a long time. She established the rule that she alone was allowed to open these jars, regulating how much would be consumed and how much would be kept back against the threat of a bad harvest or a lengthy winter.

One day, Pandora discovered that there was an extra jar in her pantry, slightly different from the others. How did this new jar get there, she wondered, and what did it hold? Wheat, oil, dried figs, honey? Something even better—something new and wonderful? A gift from the gods? She knelt on the earth and opened it.

Instantly, a swarm of vermin rushed out, scuttling, slithering and flying in all directions. Some unfurled leathery wings and disappeared into the air; others writhed towards the river and, sprouting scales, flung themselves into the water. Still others, hag-like, darted into the fields or the forests or the dwellings of mortals. These were the evils that would plague humans forevermore, as varied as their number. Some of them worked by night and others by day; some announced themselves boldly to their victims and others, by Zeus's design, worked silently until their wicked jobs were done.

Toil, rank with sweat, lurched towards the fields, his shoulders stooped and his knuckles swollen. Famine shivered along behind him, too gaunt to keep up but determined nonetheless to reach the crops and blight them. Drought, licking her blackened lips, settled atop a fountain and stopped the flow of water.

In house after house, Greed, Jealousy and Betrayal hopped into the men's quarters and squatted there, croaking with glee. Dysentery coiled into kitchens, dribbling brown, malodorous corruption. Diphtheria, wiping drool from her chin with a bony hand, headed for the women's quarters, where she found Childbed Fever already crouching on the coverlets, exuding a putrid ooze. Stillbirth—clammy, flaccid and blue—curled up in the corner where the birthing stool was kept.

Shipwreck propelled himself down the river and into the sea, his tentacles eagerly probing the waters. Only War, reeking of gore, remained squatting by the jar, picking his teeth and waiting for the summons that he knew was soon to come, now that the other evils were at work.

Horrified, Pandora clapped the lid onto the jar again, but it was too late. Everything had escaped except one creature who, by the will of Zeus, had been too slow to get away: Hope. Of all of Zeus's decisions, this may have been the cruelest, for as long as the lid of the jar remained shut, mortals still possessed Hope. Blinded by her to the gravity of their circumstances, they would persevere, whatever challenges they faced.

18
LYCAON TESTS ZEUS

In spite of all the evils that Pandora had released, mortals continued to multiply and spread across the earth. One of the first places they reached was a wild and mountainous land that would later be called Arcadia. Hermes, the god of thieves and liars, was born there, as was Hermes's uncanny son Pan, upon whom human eyes could not gaze with impunity. Civilization arrived slowly; for centuries the inhabitants ignored Demeter's gifts and foraged for acorns on the ground.

One of the earliest kings of this place was Lycaon, a savage, intemperate man who fathered fifty sons upon his numerous wives, the youngest of whom was Nyctimus.

Lycaon worshipped Hermes—indeed, Lycaon had established Hermes's cult—but he doubted that Zeus was a real god and was irked by his constant demand for sacrifices. Finally, Lycaon decided to settle once and for all the question of whether Zeus was really divine. He invited Zeus for a visit, and Zeus, foreseeing an opportunity to put into action a certain plan that he'd long been contemplating, accepted.

After serving Zeus a sumptuous feast, Lycaon escorted him to the best bedroom in the palace. Once Zeus was asleep, Lycaon crept in and bludgeoned him mercilessly. Nonetheless, Zeus slept on, his breaths slow and steady. Puzzled, Lycaon repeatedly stabbed Zeus with a dagger. Zeus merely twitched, as if to shake off flies.

He awoke the next morning looking refreshed and declared he was hungry for breakfast.

Still determined to prove himself right, Lycaon scrambled for a new plan. Glimpsing Nyctimus playing nearby, he grabbed the child with one hand and a knife with the other. Gripping his bewildered son tightly around the waist, Lycaon prepared to slit his throat. When Nyctimus frantically knocked the knife from his father's fingers, Lycaon became enraged and tore the boy's throat open with his teeth.

When the small body stopped moving, Lycaon's rage cooled down. He wiped the blood from his face and thought about how to proceed. Butchering the corpse, he prepared a meal, boiling some of the flesh and roasting the rest. He arranged the food on a platter, summoned a slave and ordered him to carry the meal to Zeus. Lycaon was confident that, lacking a true god's omniscience, Zeus would eat the boy's flesh without realizing what it was, thus giving Lycaon the proof that he longed for.

But Zeus knew immediately what had been placed in front of him—indeed, he had foreseen all of these events long before Lycaon invited him to visit. Rising from his chair, Zeus grabbed the edge of the table with both hands and turned it over, splattering the floor and walls with gobbets of Nyctimus's flesh. Then he strode over to Lycaon, who was cowering in a corner.

"Wicked man—wicked beyond all others! Bad enough that in your smug insolence you denied my divinity; now, by your ghastly actions, you have denied your own humanity, as well.

"Leave this palace that was built for human habitation; leave this kingdom that was foolish enough to look to you as its king; leave the human tribe altogether and run with those to whom you most truly belong."

Zeus glared at Lycaon and instantly the man began to change. The muscles of his back and thighs expanded until his garments split. His sandals tumbled from his feet as his heels disappeared into his ankles. His nose grew longer and his eyes, yellow and bloodshot, moved to either side of it. His ears became pointed. His mouth curled open in a slavering snarl and his tongue lolled out between his teeth. Filthy gray fur covered his skin.

Lycaon had become a wolf. With a howl, he loped out to the forested slopes. The peak where he spent what remained of his life became known as Mount Lycaeon, to mark the awful crimes that he had committed nearby.

In order that the local people might never forget what Lycaon had done, Zeus imposed upon them an enduring burden. Every four years, one of their young men was condemned to become a wolf, just as Lycaon had. If the young man abstained from eating human flesh while living in the wild for nine years, his human form would be restored. That was not, however, Zeus's only response to what Lycaon had done. A far larger group of people was about to suffer a far greater punishment.

19
THE FLOOD

Lycaon's crimes had been only the worst in a long line of dreadful things that humans had done. Theft, murder, rape and adultery had steadily increased. Elderly parents had been neglected, children had been abandoned and starving neighbors had been ignored.

Humans had even begun to forsake the gods. Although none of them went so far as to disbelieve in Zeus, as Lycaon had, many of them were reluctant to share the fruits of their labors with divinities whom they almost never saw and whose contributions to human life had been slowly forgotten. People took the growth of grain and the ripening of grapes for granted, neglecting to thank Demeter and Dionysus. The birth of healthy children no longer brought gifts to Artemis and Eileithyia; sailors no longer thanked Poseidon for safe voyages.

For these reasons, Zeus had been proposing the extermination of mortals for some time. The other gods had objected, arguing that Zeus was being too hasty; they felt that mortals were teachable and wanted to give them another chance. Lycaon's crimes, however, shocked them deeply. Zeus seized the moment, made his proposal again, and the others nodded silently in agreement.

Zeus pondered how to put his plans into effect. At first, he was inclined to scorch the land with his lightning bolts, incinerating everything that walked upon it, but Earth objected, reminding Zeus of a prophecy that fire would bring the entire cosmos to an end one day. So, Zeus proposed instead that Earth should allow Sea to embrace her completely, drowning her inhabitants. To that, she immediately agreed.

Prometheus had foreseen this moment and warned his son Deucalion about it. Deucalion dwelt in Phthia with his wife Pyrrha, the daughter of Pandora and Epimetheus. The couple had led exemplary lives: they were hard-working, law-abiding and pious. For this reason, as well as that of fatherly affection, Prometheus wanted to make sure that Deucalion and Pyrrha survived the Flood that he knew Zeus would one day send and had carefully told his son how to prepare.

When the skies became darker than they'd ever been before and the sea lapped high upon the shore, Deucalion realized that the time had come. He dragged a sturdy wooden chest out into the yard before his house. He had dovetailed its joints and caulked them with pitch to make them watertight. It was just large enough to hold him, Pyrrha and provisions to keep them alive for a while.

They climbed inside it just in time. The waters began to rise and the chest began to float, hitting bushes and tree trunks as it bobbed above what had once been their vegetable garden. Soon, it rose to the windowsills of their house and they watched the water engulf their familiar possessions. They quickly closed the lid of their chest lest it, too, be engulfed.

Other people began to scurry around, scrambling to move themselves and their treasures to safety—a challenge that had to be addressed over and over again as the waters continued to rise. At first, neighbors fought over the best hillside spots, then they fought over access to the highest trees on those hills; eventually, dolphins cavorted among those trees while the people's corpses floated above. Nereids gazed in wonder at their strange new environment: houses, temples and whole cities became their playgrounds. Animals were collateral damage. Neither the stag's speed nor the lion's strength could save it. Birds, finding no place to alight, grew tired and fell into the waters.

After nine days and nights, Earth had been cleansed and Zeus commanded the waters to recede. Deucalion and Pyrrha's chest drifted aground on Mount Parnassus at the very spot where Apollo would one day establish his Delphic Oracle. At the time of the Flood, the spot belonged to Themis, who was the mother of Prometheus and Epimetheus and the grandmother, therefore, of both Deucalion and Pyrrha. As they gazed out over the empty lands, Deucalion and Pyrrha wondered how they, alone, could ever hope to repopulate the earth and called upon Themis in despair.

"Grandmother! We are grieved by the loss of other people, wicked though they were. How we can fill the earth with humans once again?"

"Each of you must throw the bones of your mother over your shoulders," Themis replied.

Deucalion and Pyrrha were perplexed; it would be sacrilegious to do such a thing—if they could even find their mothers' bones in a world that now looked so different. After discussing the matter for some time, they began to reconcile themselves to the fact that they were the last humans.

Then Deucalion realized that Themis's answer was a pun hidden inside a riddle. "*Earth* is the mother of us all, Pyrrha, and her bones are the pebbles—from *pebbles* shall come *people!*"

They gathered up as many pebbles as they could carry and began to walk down the slope of the mountain, throwing them over their shoulders. Men sprang from the soil where Deucalion's pebbles landed and women sprang from the soil where Pyrrha's did. It would have been marvelous to see, had Deucalion and Pyrrha paused to turn around and watch. The heads of the new people emerged from the soil first; as soon as they opened their eyes, they struggled to free their arms and legs, eager to begin their lives.

Having no Deucalion and Pyrrha to foster them, animals returned to the world more slowly. For a long time following the Flood, soft mud lay everywhere, and the embryos of animals developed within it, each one coming to term when its own particular form ripened to maturity. Some of these new creatures survived and reproduced. Others—such as Python, whom Apollo would one day kill—were mercifully exterminated by the gods and their children.

20
IO'S STORY

In the land of Argos there was a river god named Inachus who had a daughter named Io. Inachus was the first to build a temple to Hera. To reward him, Hera appointed his daughter as her priestess.

Soon after assuming her duties, Io began to have alarming dreams. Zeus appeared to her each night in his favorite guise: a majestic man with sensuous lips and dark hair curling over his broad brow.

"Child," he said, "why do you leave the flower of your beauty unplucked, when you could enjoy the most spectacular union of all with the king of the gods? Leave my wife's cold marble temple and come to the meadows of Lerna, where your father pastures his herds and where my desire for you will be fulfilled."

Already in Io's dreams, Zeus's urgent fingers seemed to caress her. Deeply troubled, she went to her father for advice. Inachus sent envoys to Apollo's oracle at Delphi and to Zeus's own oracle at Dodona, asking them what to do. Each told Inachus to relinquish his daughter to Zeus and added that if he didn't, Zeus would strike Argos with lightning, incinerating the city and all its people.

Weeping, Inachus cast Io out of his house. Her feet, as if of their own accord, carried her to Lerna's meadows, where Zeus visited her each night. Io never saw him—he always arrived wrapped in dark clouds, in which he quickly enveloped her as well, in hopes of escaping Hera's notice—but within the clammy mist Io could feel his lips and fingers hungrily exploring her body.

But it is not possible—even for a god—to elude a god forever. One night while Zeus was caressing Io, he saw Hera's hands beginning to part the clouds. Panicking, he did the first thing he could think of: surrounded by Inachus's herds, he transformed Io into a heifer.

"Why Zeus," said Hera, after she had reached the middle of the clouds, "what are you doing here with this beautiful heifer? Absolutely white—not a red hair upon her body! And with horns that curve like the crescent moon. You know how much I love cows—will you give me this one?"

Hera knew full well who the heifer really was, and Zeus knew that Hera knew, but he was trapped, and so Io became Hera's possession. To make sure that Zeus could not rescue her, Hera set an indomitable watchman: Argus, a son of Earth who had one hundred bright blue eyes scattered all over his body. Some eyes slept at some times and others slept at other times, but never were they all asleep at once.

Day after day, Io languished in Lerna's meadows. When the rainy season arrived, the meadows became marshes that rose to her knees. She trembled at the sound of water snakes hissing nearby when she lay down in a patch of mud to rest each night.

Eventually, she wandered back towards her home and Argus followed in her wake. One day, she spotted her father and sisters. Trotting over, she gently nudged them with her nose until she'd drawn their attention. Then, with a clumsy hoof that had once been lovely pink fingers, she traced the letters I and O over and over again in the dirt, until her family understood who she was. They wailed with grief and embraced her, but could offer no help.

The months passed. Finally, as summer's heat arrived, Zeus came up with a plan to relieve Io's distress. He sent Hermes, disguised as a cowherd, down to where Argus lounged in the shade. Hermes befriended Argus and soon enthralled him by the marvelous stories he told. Then, as night began to fall, Hermes took out his pipes and softly played upon them. One by one, Argus's eyes drooped shut; by moonrise, all of them were closed. With a snap of his fingers, Hermes conjured a scimitar from the air and lopped off Argus's head.

Hera immediately sensed that something was wrong. She hurried to the meadow, where she discovered Argus's remains. Thinking quickly, she summoned Argus's ghost, which still lingered nearby, turned it into a gadfly and commanded it to chase Io from the meadow before Zeus could arrive to rescue her. The ghost obeyed, piercing the poor cow's flesh over and over with his razor-sharp mandibles, driving her away from home once more. Meanwhile, Hera, loath to let anything go to waste, knelt by Argus's corpse and carefully pried open each of his many eyelids. Plucking out his beautiful eyes, she attached them to the tail of her pet peacock and decreed that forever after, all peacocks would display the eyes of Argus.

Io ran through the world, never knowing where the fly might chase her next. She traveled west to Dodona and skirted the coast of the Ionian Sea, which took its name from her. She veered north to the land of the gold-hoarding griffins and their enemies, the one-eyed Arimaspians. Eventually, she found herself scrabbling through the Caucasus Mountains, where she found Prometheus, still hanging on his cliff.

Prometheus foretold that Io would make many more arduous journeys before she could rest. She would be driven farther east to the land of the Scythians, a fierce tribe, and then south to the Amazons, who, hating all males, would pity her and guide her across the strait that would become known as the "Cow's Crossing"— Bosphorus. After the gadfly chased her eastwards once more, through the arid lands near the sun's rising, she would reverse her course and travel west to the mouth of the Nile. Following it north until it opened into the sea, she would again encounter Zeus.

Then, Prometheus said, Zeus would touch Io again, but this time with a gentle hand, restoring her human shape. She would bear him a son whom she would name Epaphus, meaning "born from a touch." From his children and grandchildren would descend Europa, Cadmus, Dionysus, Perseus and Heracles—the last of whom would one day kill the eagle that tortured Prometheus, finally freeing him from his agony. Io would be remembered forever after as the ancestor of all these descendants and many others.

And so it all happened, just as Prometheus predicted.

When Zeus restored Io's human shape, she retained her lovely crescent horns. The Egyptians, who witnessed this wonder, recognized by these horns that she who had once been Inachus's daughter was now their own goddess Isis come down to earth, carrying the moon on her head.

21
PHAETHON DRIVES THE CHARIOT OF THE SUN

Princes tend to socialize with other princes. One of Epaphus's friends was Phaethon, the prince of neighboring Ethiopia. Phaethon's mother was Clymene, a daughter of Ocean who had married the king of Ethiopia, but Phaethon's real father (or so Clymene told him) was Helios, whose bright chariot passed through the skies each day.

From time to time, the two princes, each uncertain about his own paternity, taunted one another, each suggesting that the other's father was no god at all. One day, following an afternoon in Epaphus's company, Phaethon made his way to his mother's chambers, disheartened.

"Mother, how do we *know* that Helios was my father? Do you have any proof?"

It was not the first time that he'd asked these questions and Clymene could no longer put him off with soothing reassurances. She admitted that there was nothing she could show him. Having anticipated this answer, Phaethon announced a plan that he'd been thinking about for a long time: he intended to travel to Helios's palace so that he could meet the god and ask whether he was really his father.

Clymene found that she couldn't object. Phaethon would soon enter the world of men; he needed to know who his father was. Someday, he would inherit his stepfather's kingdom; he would never be able to rule it effectively if he weren't sure of his true identity. She had grown peeved, moreover, by his persistent questions, which seemed to cast aspersions on her virtue. Let him discover the truth for himself, she thought.

And so Phaethon began his journey, walking eastwards for many a day. As he drew closer to Helios's palace, he saw many strange sights: gold-mining ants, worms that spun threads finer than spiders' webs, and people who had but one giant foot apiece, which they used as parasols when they lay down on their backs for midday naps. When Phaethon wrapped himself in his cloak and prepared for sleep each night, he wondered what the morning would bring.

One day, he arrived at a field of flowers in colors he'd never seen before. In the middle was a palace built entirely of gold, with adornments of bronze, silver and ivory, all of it so bright that Phaethon's eyes could scarcely look upon it.

Squinting, he ascended the steps and found his way into the audience room, where Helios, wearing a crown made from light, sat upon a golden throne embedded with emeralds and rubies. Trembling in the presence of one so grand, Phaethon asked his question.

Helios looked closely at the young man for a moment, and then, taking off his crown so as to seem less formidable, gestured him forward.

"You are indeed my son, Phaethon," he said. "Your red hair, your blue eyes and your bearing assure me of this. But child, so that no doubt may cloud your heart, I swear by the River Styx to give you anything you might desire as proof."

As bright as Helios might be, he was neither a careful thinker nor a practiced father. His promise had been rash. Unfortunately, it was quickly seized upon by poor, foolish Phaethon.

"I want to drive your chariot, Father—just for a day! Let me experience what it is to do my true father's job before I inherit the throne of the man who has only been standing in for you."

Helios's ruddy face turned ashen at this answer, and he argued eloquently against the idea, but the more he did so, the more his son insisted upon it. And so, Helios reluctantly began to prepare Phaethon for what lay ahead.

He advised Phaethon to keep a tight rein on the horses, who were only too eager to reach the end of their journey and return to their stables. He cautioned him against straying either too far north or too far south, but also against driving straight through the center of the sky: it was best to strive for an elliptical curve through the heavens. He warned Phaethon against drifting too close to the monsters that dwelt in the sky: Cancer, the gigantic crab; Leo, the ravenous lion; and Taurus, the angry bull with dreadful horns.

Helios had many other useful pieces of advice to give, but Phaethon wasn't really listening. He'd already climbed into the splendid chariot—a slave had to fetch a stool to help him do so—and was clutching the gilded reins in his fists. The horses, sensing his inexperienced hands, were exchanging sidelong glances that made Helios nervous.

Then Dawn threw open the stable doors to begin her own journey and Phaethon's horses, knowing they were next, snorted with impatience. A few moments later, they were away and galloping, following so closely upon Dawn's heels that she could feel their fiery breaths.

From the start, Phaethon struggled to keep the horses under control; they yanked at their bits and tossed their heads. His small weight, so much less than Helios's bulk, could not hold the chariot steady. He began to veer off course. For the first time in centuries, the starry snake that winds around the northern pole was enlivened by the sun's warmth and roused itself for attack. In terror, Phaethon neglected to maintain his altitude as he swerved southwards. The chariot skimmed the earth, burnishing the skin of both his own people and those of Epaphus.

Yanking the horses upwards, Phaethon found himself facing Cancer's clicking claws on one side and Leo's yawning jaws on the other. Plunging down again, he scorched the ground so badly that it cracked open. Persephone gazed up, bewildered, as sunlight penetrated the Underworld.

Earth pleaded with Zeus to intervene, fearing that she would soon be incinerated. Zeus responded in the only way that he could, by striking Phaethon with a lightning bolt.

Phaethon fell from the chariot and the horses raced onwards. Eventually, they reached the western edge of the world, where they waited for their real master to reclaim him.

Phaethon's seven sisters searched far and wide for his body, which they found, still burning, in a marsh near the Eridanus River. They stood on the banks and wept until grief broke their hearts.

The gods, pitying such sorrow, changed the sisters into poplar trees. Yet still they wept, their slender branches bowing in the breeze. Then the gods honored the sisters' tears: as each one trickled down its tree trunk, it became a drop of amber, as golden as the sun.

22
EUROPA AND THE BULL

Io's son Epaphus married Memphis and they had a daughter named Libya. Poseidon fell in love with Libya and they had two sons, Belus and Agenor.

Agenor became the king of Phoenicia, a palm-shaded land of seafarers that lay on the eastern shore of the Mediterranean. There, his wife Telephassa bore him many children, including a son named Cadmus and a daughter named Europa, who inherited Io's beauty.

One day, Europa and her friends were picking cornflowers in a meadow that sloped down to the sands along the sea. The day was hot: shimmers of haze hung over the dunes, deceiving the eyes, suggesting shapes that might or might not really be there.

Europa saw, or thought she saw, a bull striding up the beach as if he'd emerged from the sea itself, perfectly white and larger than any in her father's herds. She squeezed her eyes shut for a moment, to clear them, but when she looked again, the creature had reached the meadow and was undeniably real.

He was magnificent. The whiteness of his coat shone even more brightly now when seen against the green grass and the blue cornflowers. Indeed, the contrast was so stark that Europa's senses were overwhelmed; for a moment she lost any notion of where she was. When she shook herself into alertness again, the bull was close enough that she could see the intelligent expression on his face and smell the saffron sweetness of his breath. Now, he nuzzled her shoulder; now, he gently pushed her down onto the grass; now, dropping to his knees, he lay his head in her lap.

The other girls, intrigued by the beast, came running with the flowers they'd gathered. Weaving a garland, they handed it to Europa, who twined it around the bull's horns. When she finished, she gently pushed his head from her lap and climbed astride his shoulders to tie the ends of the garland together behind his head.

With surprising agility, the bull rose to his feet, and Europa, suddenly sliding down his back, clutched at his neck to steady herself. The other girls laughed, cheering on the game and hoping for a turn themselves.

But in the next moment, the bull was running towards the sea with Europa holding on for dear life; a moment more and the water was lapping at her ankles and dampening her crimson robe. Another moment more and the water reached the bull's chest. He began to swim and the beach receded from Europa's sight.

They traveled towards the setting sun with astonishing speed. Soon, they were at least as far west as any of Agenor's ships had ever sailed.

Eventually, she saw an island rising on the horizon. The bull waded ashore and knelt to let his passenger disembark. Europa slid, knees first, onto the sand. Her legs trembled from straddling the bull for so long, but she scurried as best she could towards a grove of scrubby pines, hoping that he wouldn't be able to squeeze his bulk between their trunks.

Just as she reached the grove, she heard a voice behind her. "Be not afraid, Europa," it said, in a tone so commanding that she was compelled to turn around.

The bull was gone and a man stood in his place.

"I am Zeus, who has admired you from afar for many months. I made the cornflowers bloom brightly this morning to bring you to the meadow by the shore, and now I have brought you here to Crete, my birthplace, to fulfill my desire for you.

"I am no bad lover; with a gentle touch I delivered your great-great-grandmother Io of our son, Epaphus, from whom sprang all the glory of your family. Lie down with me here, now, and I shall make your fame even greater than hers."

Seeing no way to refuse, Europa submitted to the god. Afterwards, Zeus gave her a necklace that Hephaestus had forged from gold, with serpentine links so closely joined as to flow like liquid. It nestled between her breasts as if it were seeking her heart.

She bore three sons to Zeus before he finally gave her in marriage to Asterius, the king of Crete. Minos, who was the eldest son, became king when Asterius died. Rhadamanthys, who was the second, sat in judgment over the souls of the dead. Sarpedon, who was the youngest, was killed at Troy, bringing terrible grief upon his parents.

Back in Phoenicia, Agenor tried to learn what had happened to his daughter. Her friends could tell him only that a bull had carried her into the sea. Weeping in distress, Agenor ordered Cadmus to seek her far and wide, forbidding him to return without his sister by his side. Cadmus failed in that quest, although his wanderings gave rise to a family that wove its own bonds with Zeus.

23
CALLISTO'S STORY

A few mortals, here and there, managed to survive the great Flood by retreating to the mountaintops. When Earth was dry again, they descended and continued their lives alongside the people who had sprung from the pebbles thrown by Deucalion and Pyrrha.

One of these was Lycaon's daughter Callisto, who lived in the land that was later called Arcadia. While still a girl, Callisto had joined a group of young women who followed Artemis. Like the others, she had sworn to honor Artemis by remaining a virgin.

The women spent their days hunting with Artemis in the fields and forests, clad in tunics so short that they couldn't get tangled in the underbrush and in boots that protected their feet from brambles. When it was hot, the women paused at midday to bathe in a stream or spring. At night, they slept on the ground, covered by the pelts of animals they'd killed.

Callisto was the most beautiful of Artemis's companions. Zeus, predictably, noticed her running through the woods one day, her brown legs flashing bare in the sunlight, and was overwhelmed by lust.

It took Zeus some time to figure out how to catch her. He realized that it was impossible to approach her disguised as an animal, as he'd approached Europa and some of his other conquests, because Callisto would be likely to hurl a spear at any beast whose form was majestic enough for him to assume. The single creature in whose presence she might relax and drop her guard, he came to realize, was Artemis herself, his own daughter. The corollary to this proposition was perverse, but desire drove Zeus to accept it. Summoning all his metamorphic skill, he assumed the shape of Artemis and, on feet that were now exquisitely lovely, he crept to where Callisto lay sleeping in the shade of a tree. Snuggling up behind her, Zeus ran his finger along the top of her ear.

"Wake up, Callisto!" he whispered. "It is I, Artemis, who desires your embrace," he said.

Surprised but flattered, Callisto opened her eyes and rolled over to greet her mistress. She was met with an ardent kiss and a caressing hand.

But suddenly, Artemis was no longer Artemis. A beard scratched Callisto's chin and large hands fondled her breasts. Then a heavy body lay itself on top of her; it was impossible to flee. By the time she'd made sense of what was happening, it was over. Zeus was standing above her, adjusting his robes.

"Say nothing of this to my daughter, lest her temper prove to be hasty and sharp," he said. "In time, I shall make plans for you and the child you now carry."

And then he was gone.

As the months passed, Callisto's only sign of Zeus was her swelling stomach. For a while, she was able to hide this beneath her tunic: as the days grew colder, Artemis and her friends bathed less often and when they did, Callisto always managed to position herself behind a rock or clump of reeds.

But one day, her secret was revealed. While Artemis and the others were leaping into a spring-fed pool, Callisto dawdled at the edge, hoping to slip into the water after the others were distracted. A friend, teasing Callisto for being slow, threw water at her. Callisto's wet tunic clung to her body, announcing her pregnancy just as loudly as nakedness would have.

"Slut!" shouted Artemis. "How dare you linger among virgins when you have betrayed your own promise of celibacy? If you prefer the pleasures of coupling and motherhood to my company, then become a beast who wallows in them."

Callisto's skin, once lovely and smooth, began to sprout coarse brown hair. Her slender neck grew thicker and merged into sloping shoulders from which hung menacing arms. Her hands and feet became longer; deadly claws protruded from her toes and fingers. The desirable lips that Zeus had once kissed and the nose above them melted together into a snout. Her shining green eyes shrank into beady black points. Although she still stood upright, she did so only clumsily and soon fell forward onto what were now her forepaws.

Callisto had become a bear. Or rather, she had taken on the appearance of a bear: inside, she was still herself. Artemis, piling cruelty upon cruelty, had left Callisto's mind and soul intact so that she would understand the horror of her fate. Indeed, Callisto occasionally forgot what her outer body had become, which brought its own fresh terrors: when she saw other bears in the woods, she ran away in fear, forgetting that they were now her proper companions.

When Callisto delivered her child, she did so easily, as bears always do, and then licked her infant all over to shape its form, as bears always do. It was a human boy, whom she named Arcas. The name evoked the word for bear in the language she'd spoken while still human but it also marked his descent from Arcadia's ruling family. With a clumsy tongue and growling throat, she taught him to say it as best she could.

Three years passed. Callisto realized that Arcas was becoming too quick on his feet for her to keep easily by her side, and she sadly left him near a shepherds' settlement. The shepherds, recognizing a royal bearing in the naked child, took him to the palace, where he was raised to adulthood.

One day, while hunting in the forest, Arcas crossed Callisto's path. She recognized him immediately and in her joy again forgot what she looked like. Rising onto her hind legs, she stretched out her arms to embrace her son. In response, Arcas raised his spear to kill the beast who seemed to threaten him.

Terrified that her son might commit matricide, Callisto lumbered away as quickly as she could, but Arcas pursued her, his hunter's zeal aroused. She kept running. Eventually, she entered a clearing in the woods and found a simple structure that she took to be an abandoned woodsman's hut. She darted inside.

Arcas arrived close behind but paused at the door, recognizing the structure as a temple that Zeus had once ordered the Arcadians to build. No creature, Zeus had declared, should be allowed to enter once it had been finished, upon pain of death. Arcas had his quarry cornered now, and without putting a foot across the forbidden threshold himself, he could easily kill her—indeed, by doing so he would be fulfilling Zeus's orders.

But as Arcas readied his spear, Zeus finally made good on his promise to Callisto. He lifted the terrified mother up into the heavens and made her the starry Bear that turns forever around the north pole. He lifted their son to the heavens, too, making Arcas the Bear Guardian, who follows his mother across the skies as if to protect her.

24
DAPHNE AND APOLLO

Apollo had many talents, as he had proclaimed to an astonished group of goddesses only moments after he was born. He played the lyre beautifully, he was an excellent archer and he conveyed the will of Zeus to mortals in an effectively cryptic manner.

He was, however, a spectacularly unsuccessful lover. Some of the women and boys whom he wooed preferred other suitors, some accepted Apollo but later betrayed him, some simply died after one of the terrible accidents that seemed to blight every mortal he pursued.

It didn't help that Apollo treated Lust with scorn, belittling his talents. Like Apollo, Lust carried a bow and quiver. His equipment was smaller and simpler than Apollo's, which was heavily orna-mented with gold and ivory, but that was good: Lust's aim was not to look glorious but rather to work furtively as he infected hearts with desire. Traveling light was an advantage.

One day, Apollo spotted Lust lounging in a corner of the gods' courtyard.

"Nothing to do, today?" asked Apollo. "Or is it just that you've run out of sufficiently slow targets?"

Lust smiled. "We'll see who's slow."

As soon as Apollo's back was turned, Lust quietly drew two arrows from his quiver. One was tipped with gold, gleaming hot. The other was tipped with lead, as cold as death.

He shot the first one between Apollo's shoulder blades. So sharp was its point that Apollo never felt it entering his heart.

The other one was destined for Daphne, daughter of the river god Peneus. Lust had selected her carefully, in hopes that he could settle his score with two gods at once. Daphne, like Callisto, had chosen to follow Artemis, and like Callisto, therefore, Daphne had sworn to remain a virgin. Lust had long been irritated by Artemis's iron-clad requirement of celibacy; if he could destroy one of her keenest acolytes while making a fool of Apollo, so much the better.

Indeed, the lead-tipped arrow, which was designed to kill desire in those it pierced, was, strictly speaking, unnecessary in Daphne's case, so steadfastly did she follow Artemis's rules. But by pairing it with the golden arrow that he shot at Apollo, Lust guaranteed that Daphne would spurn Apollo not simply because she'd sworn to remain a virgin but also because she found Apollo himself to be repugnant. Given that Apollo considered himself to be the most handsome of all the gods, it would be delicious to watch her reject him.

Daphne, the pawn on whom Lust's strategy depended, drew admiring eyes even without the help of his arrows. She was beguiling in the way that the daughters of river gods often were. Slender and lithe, when she ran with the hunt she seemed to skim over the ground, her hair streaming dark behind her. She didn't tie it back at the nape of her neck as Artemis and her other companions did; binding it made her feel shackled. Instead, she let it undulate down her back or fly behind her in the wind. Watching it move, it was easy to imagine her at home in the water of her father's river.

As soon as Lust's arrow pierced Apollo's heart, he felt an unaccountable urge to visit his sister and descended to where she and her companions were hunting. Scarcely had his foot touched the ground when he spotted Daphne, walking somewhat apart from the others as she tracked a lynx.

Immediately, he desired her. Materializing a few steps in front of her, Apollo presented himself in what he thought to be the truest of all his forms: fair-haired and youthful, with a smile that was meant to be charming. But just as immediately, Daphne was revolted. Stopping short, she turned on her heel and walked back towards her companions. Yet there was Apollo, uncannily standing in front of her once more.

Alarmed, Daphne feinted to the right and then dashed to the left, running out of the underbrush and into a meadow that sloped down to her father's river. She sprinted onwards, grasshoppers leaping up in front of her, stridulating a chorus of distress.

Apollo pursued her, enjoying the chase. His ardor burned even more brightly now that he saw her splendid hair flying out behind her. How beautiful it will be, he thought, once I've taught her to tame it with silken ribbons and ivory combs!

In terror, Daphne kept running, although her vigor was flagging and her heart was hammering. She prayed that she'd reach her father's sheltering banks before her strength was gone. Apollo kept running, too, steadily gaining on Daphne as when a dog, chasing a rabbit, draws closer and closer, until his nose grazes her fur.

Just as they reached the river's banks, Daphne stumbled. Seizing his chance, Apollo reached out and encircled her waist with his arm. She made a desperate plea.

"Save me, Father, however you can, from this loathsome man!"

And Peneus did the best he could.

Apollo, who was now pressing his hips into Daphne's back, felt her stiffen.

"Don't be afraid," he whispered. "I will be gentle with you."

But still Daphne didn't relax. Apollo nuzzled her neck, hoping to arouse her, but his lips scraped against skin that was rough and hard. Puzzled, he tried to stroke her beautiful hair, but found that it was gone; where it should have been, there were leaves instead.

Apollo stepped back and gazed at Daphne in amazement—even he, a god who knew what gods could do, was astonished. Bark had encased her legs, body, arms and neck and was racing towards her mouth, which stood open in a silent scream. A moment later, there was no mouth, no face at all, anymore. Peneus had turned Daphne into a small but exquisite tree.

Sighing in frustration, oblivious to anyone's pain but his own, Apollo fingered its sweetly scented leaves.

"Foolish girl—why did you run from me? You may have won *this* race, but nonetheless, I will possess you forever."

He began to harvest the twigs that bore her foliage. Too fresh and pliant to break easily from their branches, they tore raggedly under his eager hands, bleeding sap upon the ground. From their fragments, Apollo fashioned a wreath and placed it on his head. Ever since, he has used Daphne to crown himself.

Artemis, to the disappointment of Lust, said very little about the loss of the companion he had presumed she valued: only, "What a stupid girl, to leave her hair unbound."

25
ARTEMIS AND ACTAEON

After Cadmus had searched for Europa for many months, the gods told him to stop. At their command, he founded Thebes, the first city in Greece, and became its king. Zeus gave him Harmonia, the graceful daughter of Aphrodite and Ares, as his wife. Their wedding was a grand affair, attended by gods as well as mortals.

Hephaestus had thought carefully about what to give the bride. Harmonia had been born of the ongoing affair between his wife and her lover, which had shamed and distressed him for centuries. Innocent though Harmonia herself might be, her wedding provided an opportunity for him to finally avenge himself upon her parents. As his gift, therefore, Hephaestus forged a necklace like the one that he'd once made for Zeus to give to Europa, gleaming gold and sinuous as a snake. When he alloyed the gold for this second necklace, however, he added some new ingredients: blood from a Gorgon, quills from a Harpy and an adder from Tisiphone's hair—dark elements that would curse the lives of all who wore the necklace and the lives of those they loved.

It was many years later that Harmonia herself felt the curse of the necklace, but before that she watched it smite the lives of her four daughters. Semele, the mother of Dionysus, was consumed by fire when she insisted upon seeing Zeus in his true form. Ino was driven mad by Hera for nursing Semele's motherless infant and in that madness jumped from a cliff with her own son in her arms. Agave and her son Pentheus foolishly called Dionysus a false god. When Dionysus struck her with madness, Agave tore Pentheus limb from limb.

The fourth sister, Autonoë, married Aristaeus, the son of Apollo and Cyrene. For a long time, her life was happy. She bore several children to Aristaeus, including Actaeon, who was sent to the centaur Chiron to be reared alongside other young heroes. Chiron taught his students music, prophecy, healing and hunting skills. It was the last of these that most excited Actaeon. When he returned to Thebes, he spent most of his time hunting beasts of all kinds, accompanied by his friends and his pack of dogs.

One day, after a morning's hunt, Actaeon and his friends sought a cool place to rest while the sun was high. They descended into a valley and made themselves comfortable. Some of them dozed under trees, some waded in a nearby stream and others sprawled along its banks, eating and drinking. Actaeon spotted a cave in the distance. Guessing that the spring that fed the stream lay within it, he and his dogs set out to investigate. If he were right, a short hike would reward him with deeper shade and colder water.

He wasn't the only one looking for relief from the day's heat, however. Just within the cave's mouth, in a pool below the spring, Artemis was bathing after her own morning of tracking animals.

Her companions attended her. Some shook out her tunic, removing the burrs and thorns that had snagged it as Artemis raced through the thickets. Others, kneeling beside her in the pool, poured water over her body, while still others stood behind her to brush out her coppery hair, which they'd released from its combs. The skin of the goddess, burnished by the sun, glowed in the dimness of the cave.

As Actaeon entered that dimness, it took him a moment to understand what he was seeing. When he did, he froze—first in wonderment and then in terror. His heart began to pound and he seemed to hear its peculiar echo bouncing erratically off the cave's walls. He felt as if he could no longer trust his senses and he wasn't sure where, or even who, he was.

Artemis rose to confront the intruder, careless of how much more of herself she revealed by doing so. Her companions rushed to stand in front of her, but the goddess's naked shoulders and face, now pale with fury, loomed above them. She spoke.

"Foolish, impious man, to gaze upon a naked goddess—and you, a hunter who has often honored me with sacrifices! Go—tell others what you have seen, if you still have a mouth to tell it with."

And then she splashed Actaeon. Wherever the water touched his skin, fur began to grow. As she continued to splash him, his body changed shape. His arms grew longer and his hips merged into his back, skewing his balance; he fell forward onto what used to be his hands. His eyes moved around to either side of his head and antlers sprouted from his skull. Actaeon had become a stag, prime quarry for the hunter he once was.

The dogs, who had lingered outside, caught a new scent and bounded into the cave. Vaulting over them, Actaeon sped into the forest, filled with a strange new fear. At first, he thought that he could run to cover, but he had trained the dogs too well: they chased him towards an open field and then ran him hard until his strength gave out. When, finally, they'd surrounded him, he tried to call their names—"Storm! Tigress! Tempest! Ebony!"—but his tongue was no longer able to form the syllables. Grunts emerged from his mouth instead, until finally, he fell silent.

Afterwards, the dogs searched for Actaeon, eager for his praise, but he was nowhere to be found. They howled for their master until Chiron, who divined what had happened, created a statue of Actaeon to soothe them. They lay down around it and slept, resting their muzzles on their paws.

When Autonoë learned of Actaeon's death, she searched until she found his bones, which she buried. He was the first, but not the last, of Cadmus's descendants to fall foul of a god.

26
NIOBE AND LETO

Most of the early kings of Thebes were descended from Cadmus and Harmonia, but for a while the city was ruled by Amphion, the son of Zeus and Antiope. Amphion married Niobe, a daughter of King Tantalus of Lydia and Dione, a daughter of Atlas.

The family of Tantalus was fortunate enough to have close relationships with the gods, who treated them almost as equals. Niobe was particularly friendly with Leto, the mother of Apollo and Artemis.

That should have been enough to satisfy any mortal. Once Niobe became queen of Thebes, however, a new, invidious strain of pride corrupted her heart. Constantly, in her thoughts and in her words, she compared herself to Leto and insinuated—subtly at first, but then with increasing boldness—that she was at least the equal of Leto in appearance and accomplishments.

"I'm a sort of divinity, myself, you know—my mother is Atlas's daughter and my husband is the son of Zeus! Leto is the daughter of two Titans whom no one even talks about anymore . . ."

Or: "One would think that a goddess such as Leto would outshine any mortal woman in beauty, but if you look at *me* now, you'll see that that's not so."

Or worse yet: "Leto is so proud of those twins of hers, but heavens! I have *seven* sons and *seven* daughters, all of them attractive and accomplished."

And: "Why does Apollo still keep his hair so ridiculously long? And Artemis—wearing men's hunting boots and hanging around in the woods with girls? What are we to make of *that*, hmmm? You could take away six of my daughters and six of my sons and I would still be luckier than Leto."

For a long time, Leto, who was more tolerant than most gods, chose to ignore such remarks. But when the Fates have decided that a family must fall, madness festers in a mortal mind until divine anger is provoked. And so it was that one day Niobe finally went too far. Striding through the streets of Thebes, dripping with jewels and wearing a robe spun from gold, she burst into Leto's temple, where incense was being burned in honor of the mother and her twins. Niobe commanded the participants to remove the laurel wreaths that they were wearing and stop the ritual. If they wanted gods to worship, they should look no further than their local palace, she said.

Gentle Leto had finally reached her limit. She called Apollo and Artemis to her side. Before she could even finish describing Niobe's offenses, the two were on their way to Thebes.

Apollo found Niobe's sons out hunting and, pulling the swiftest arrows from his quiver, killed them all, one by one. Their bodies fell to the forest floor, startling the animals they'd been stalking.

Meanwhile, Artemis traveled to the palace. There, she found Niobe's daughters in the women's chambers, choosing their clothes for the day and arranging one another's hair. Her arrows flew as swiftly as her brother's. The girls soon lay dead, their blood staining the tessellated floor.

When Niobe discovered what had happened, her grief was as intense as her arrogance had been. She tore her hair, she clawed her cheeks, she ripped her beautiful robes. She cried *eleleleu! Eleleleu!*

And she wept. She wept until her eyes were swollen and her face was mottled; she wept until the shreds of her robes were wet. Her slaves tried to comfort her, her cooks tempted her with food, but she walked the empty halls of her palace inconsolably, a woman blessed with children but now childless.

The gods, taking pity on her, turned Niobe into stone and sent a whirlwind to carry her back to the land of her birth. There they placed her, still petrified, upon a crag of Mount Sipylus. Even as a stone, however, she cried tears that trickled down the mountain. The crag came to be feared by local shepherds, who heard uncanny wails echoing from it through the night. Uncannier still was the form of a crouching woman that they could see from afar but that vanished each time they climbed the slopes to confront her.

And the corpses of Niobe's children? No one performed their burial rites because when the gods turned Niobe to stone, they turned her entire household to stone as well. For nine days, the children's bodies lay abandoned until finally, the gods buried the children themselves.

27
ARACHNE AND ATHENA

Before Niobe became queen of Thebes, while she was still just a girl in Lydia, she knew another girl, named Arachne. Although they came from different social classes—Niobe was the daughter of King Tantalus whereas Arachne's father, Idmon, was of no particular importance—they were bound by a common love of textiles. Niobe loved to drape herself in beautiful fabrics and Arachne loved to create them.

Arachne was, in fact, renowned throughout Lydia for her skill as a spinner and a weaver. The neighboring nymphs would leave their springs and trees to watch her work, marveling at how fine were the threads that she teased from her spindle, how evenly she beat her weft and how gracefully she strode back and forth before her loom, passing her bobbin through the shed of the warp. Her fingers caressed the threads as she worked and when she lay down at night, her empty fingers continued to move, longing for threads that were no longer there.

But it was for color, and the stories that color helped her to tell, that Arachne was most renowned. Idmon was a dyer by trade, coaxing yellow from buckthorn berries, red from madder, purple from the local shellfish. Arachne had grown up surrounded by hanks of newly dyed thread, drying bright in the sun. She gazed at yellow and saw Callisto's pelt, at red and saw Hephaestus's forge, at purple and saw Europa's robe. The green extracted from delphinium became, in her mind's eye, the Arcadian forests through which Pan wandered and the blue extracted from woad became the sea from which Aphrodite sprang.

All of these colors and more suffused her textiles; all of these stories and more were narrated by her fingers. When she cut a finished piece from her loom and unrolled it, finally making visible the entire tale, her admirers stood enthralled. Justifiable was Arachne's fame; justifiable were the praises she won.

It takes only a moment for a life to change ineluctably, but more than a single footstep to reach the fatal precipice. Arachne fell into the habit of considering her art to be completely her own; her mother had died when she was young and she felt that she had learned little from local women. Her gifts seemed to flow from her fingers of their own accord. Lacking real rivals, she had never learned the grace of humility. Sometimes, admirers would tell her that she had been blessed by Athena, but she understood this only metaphorically.

One day, when a townswoman repeated that phrase, Arachne mumbled, never breaking her pace in front of her loom, "Blessings or not, let Athena descend and compete with me. I bet my life that I'd win."

Though mumbled, the words reached Athena's ears. Disguising herself as an old woman, she squeezed through the crowd around Arachne.

"Be careful, child," Athena said, "it is one thing to claim preeminence among mortals—and you rightly do so—but another to claim supremacy over a god. Athena can be merciful; ask her pardon now and you may yet escape her wrath."

Arachne answered. "Go home and preach to your kinfolk, grandma. Let Athena see to her own affairs."

Suddenly, the old woman vanished and Athena was there. The sun seemed to dim against her steely brilliance; the air grew cooler and the spirit of the crowd turned somber. Everyone but Arachne fell to their knees and bowed their heads.

As for Arachne, she was caught unprepared. Her cheeks turned first red, then ashen white. She stood still as a stone in front of her loom and for once, her fingers stopped moving.

But no one excels without cultivating determination. Arachne—poor, foolish girl—shook herself into action. She ripped from her loom a half-done textile and prepared the header of a new one. Conjuring her own loom from the air, Athena did the same.

How different were their chosen topics! At the center of Athena's web was her own triumph over Poseidon, when the two, bestowing gifts, had contended for the city that became Athens. The olive tree that she'd given and the spring that was his gift were so wondrously lifelike that it seemed as if the first could be watered by the second. Around this centerpiece Athena wove warnings to Arachne. Scene after scene showed mortal hubris and its wages: people turning into mountains, birds and trees for contending with divinities.

Arachne depicted the lustful predations of the gods. Here was Zeus as a bull, cutting through blue waves with a terrified Europa on his back; there he was as a snow-white swan, nestling against Leda; there he was again, as a spotted green snake, raping Persephone. Nor was it only Zeus that Arachne portrayed: Poseidon, in the form of a black stallion, was mounting blonde Demeter; Apollo, cloaked in shepherd's brown, was impregnating the nymph Isse. The scenes that Arachne depicted, censuring the gods, were astoundingly varied but through the subtlety of her skill, she managed to suggest a dreadful unity.

The textiles done, the weavers stepped back to regard them. It was immediately clear whose was technically superior: neither

Athena nor Envy herself could find fault with Arachne's artistry or her skill as a weaver.

Ice-gray fury filled Athena's heart. She kicked at her own loom weights, sending them spinning across the ground like tops, and then, her anger unrelieved, turned her wrath against Arachne's work. Betraying the very craft that she claimed to champion, Athena tore the beautiful fabric to shreds. Then, seizing a bobbin, Athena beat its creator over the head. Arachne, too proud to endure such humiliation, looped a noose around her neck and jumped. Before she could die, however, Athena grabbed her by the waist, slackening the rope.

With a trace of pity in her voice, Athena said, "Live on, blasphemous girl—even if you hang forever."

And then she sprinkled upon Arachne the juice of an herb that Hecate had cultivated. Immediately, Arachne's hair, nose and ears fell off. She rapidly shrank, until she could scarcely be seen. Her arms and legs disappeared into her abdomen, making it bulge like a tiny ball. Arachne was now a spider.

When Athena took away Arachne's arms, she also took away Arachne's thumbs, an artisan's most useful tools, but she permitted Arachne's restless fingers to remain. Now they sprang from her bulbous abdomen, four to a side. With them, Arachne learned to work such colorless threads as she could still spin and to weave a new kind of textile, although each one was as drab as the next.

And whenever a fly or moth dared to disturb her weaving, Arachne paralyzed it with poison and spun her threads around it like a tiny bobbin—a grim trophy of her skills.

28
BAUCIS AND PHILEMON

It was difficult for mortals to recognize the gods when they visited the earth, for the gods were masters of disguise. They could make themselves look shorter and less attractive than they really were, wrinkling the skin on their faces and commanding their heads to sprout gray hair. They could mask the lovely scents that wafted from their bodies behind the human odors of dirt and sweat. They were even willing to turn themselves into animals, if doing so would accomplish their purposes. So skilled were the gods at camouflage that they could be lurking anywhere, at any time.

Zeus disguised himself particularly often, not only because he had a weakness for seducing mortal women, but also because he felt that, as king of the cosmos, he ought to keep track of how humans were behaving. The best way to do this, he'd found, was to live among them for a while, incognito. He often took Hermes along on these trips. Hermes knew the ways of humans better than the other gods did, and that was often a help.

One day, the two were wandering through the low hills of Phrygia. They passed into a prosperous valley that was sheltered from the winds and rich in soil for farming. The people were fat, healthy and satisfied—too satisfied, perhaps: not a single person bothered to welcome the travelers. Indeed, when Zeus and Hermes asked for a shady place to rest at midday, everyone turned them away with excuses: my house is too small, I'm airing the bedding, the baby is sleeping.

Late in the day, as the coolness of evening was falling, Zeus and Hermes moved higher into the hills, where they spotted a humble cottage. In it lived Baucis and Philemon, wife and husband. They had been married in front of the cottage when they were young and had grown old together within its walls. They were poor, but they wore their poverty lightly, using contentment to lessen the load.

As the gods approached the cottage, Baucis hurried out to invite them in. She stirred the ashes of the previous day's fire, nurturing the sparks with her breath until a blaze began to crackle. She hung a pot over the heat and set water to boil while she fetched a cabbage from the garden. Meanwhile, Philemon took a slice of ham down from the rafters, a remnant from last year's butchering. He threw it into the pot and soon the lovely smell of pork filled the room.

Once the cabbage was simmering in the pot alongside the ham, Baucis dragged out a simple willow frame on which she placed a mattress stuffed with sweet grasses. She covered it with a cloth that she usually reserved for festival days. Judged by the best standards, it was tawdry, but in the dimness of the cottage, it gleamed like a treasure. She invited her guests to sit down. In front of them she placed a table and arranged upon it all of the wealth that their labors had produced: olives, both black and green, cherries pickled in vinegar, birds' eggs roasted in ashes, cheeses, nuts, dried figs and dates, grapes, apples and a honeycomb. A rough wine accompanied this, poured into cups carved from beechwood.

After a while, Baucis and Philemon noticed something odd: no matter how much wine their guests drank, the level in the mixing bowl never fell. They exchanged looks of alarm: their guests must be gods—their piety was being tested!

Leaping to their feet, they apologized for the inadequacy of their offerings and prayed to be forgiven. Then, racing outside, they began to chase their goose, a faithful guardian whose honking had kept four-legged marauders away from their garden for many years. Its meat could honorably replace the cabbage stew that they had planned to serve as the main course for the meal. The goose was too quick for them, however, and too clever as well; it ran behind the gods as if to ask for sanctuary.

Hermes spoke then. "Spare your goose, mortals. We are gods, as you have guessed, but we are already satisfied with your hospitality. Your neighbors in town will be punished for their selfishness, but you will be rewarded for sharing what little you had. Come with us now, up the mountain."

When they reached the peak, Zeus and Hermes bid the mortals to turn and look down on the valley. The village where people had once lived was now covered by water; only their own cottage remained, perched on the shore of a new lake. Then, as they watched, the cottage grew into a temple, large and stately. Its rough beams became marble columns. A new roof, covered with gold, gleamed in the setting sun. Tucked below the roof were pediments on which the gods' deeds were celebrated.

Zeus spoke. "Baucis and Philemon, how can we reward your piety?"

The two whispered to one another for a moment and then Philemon said, "Make us the priests of this new temple, so that we may serve you. And when we die, let us die together, so that neither of us will be burdened with the duty of burying the other."

Zeus did as they asked. For years, they faithfully tended the temple until one day, Baucis saw leaves sprouting from Philemon and Philemon saw leaves sprouting from Baucis. As they stood wondering at this, bark was encasing their bodies and then their necks. Just before it reached their mouths, each one smiled and said, "Farewell, my love!"

Baucis had become a linden tree and Philemon an oak. Yet they grew from a single, miraculous trunk, their branches entwining.

29
HYRIEUS AND HIS OX

In the countryside near Thebes there lived an old man named Hyrieus who, with the help of an equally elderly ox, scratched a living out of the rocky soil.

Hyrieus had been widowed while still young and had never been able to find another woman who suited him as well as his wife. He was accustomed, therefore, to a solitary life. Nonetheless, he was hospitable to the bone: no traveler passed his gate without being invited to share in one of the stews that Hyrieus made from the beans that he planted, harvested and dried every year, along with a salad of whatever greens he could find.

One evening, as Hyrieus and the ox were returning from their day's work, Hyrieus spotted three men walking along the road. Inviting the travelers to rest inside the house where it was cool, he followed them in, tied up the ox in its accustomed corner and filled its manger with hay. Then, fetching a skin of wine from his cupboard, he mixed it with water and ladled some out for the man sitting nearest to him. "Ah, thank you," said the visitor, "but you should serve my brother Zeus first, you know."

The speaker regretted his words as soon as they had escaped the fence of his teeth, but even a god cannot erase what he has said. The visitors' disguises were now useless and they discarded them with astonishing swiftness. They grew upwards until their heads grazed the underside of the roof. Their coarsely woven cloaks vanished, revealing skin that filled the house with a brilliance that was painful to Hyrieus's eyes. The air became pungently heavy, as in the moments before a storm breaks; Hyrieus struggled to breathe and his ears rang. He felt small, confused and vulnerable.

After what seemed like a very long time, the youngest visitor spoke in a voice that compelled Hyrieus to meet his gaze. "I am Hermes," he said. "This is Poseidon and this is my father, Zeus. We are traveling the earth to learn whether mortals still honor us."

Hyrieus thought about the tiny room that was his home, and how little its single cupboard contained. How could he possibly honor these gods? Panic-stricken, he seized his kitchen knife in one hand and the nose ring of his ox in the other. The beast obediently turned aside from the manger. Trembling, Hyrieus pulled back its head and slit its throat. His companion of so many years dropped to the floor and gurgled out its life.

When the ox lay still, Hyrieus dragged its body outside, flayed it and butchered it. He lit a fire and laid the thigh pieces upon its flames. As the smoke began to rise, the gods rushed from the house and crowded around the burning meat, inhaling its aroma.

At last they were sated and remembered the man who was cowering nearby. "You have honored us well," said Hermes, "and to mark this, so that other mortals may emulate your piety, we will give you whatever you desire. A river nymph to take to your bed? A kingdom? Shall we topple Polydorus from the throne and give you Thebes? Shall we lend you Hades's cap of invisibility so that you can steal from Midas's treasury undetected?"

Hyrieus wanted none of these things, yet he knew that refusing the gods' offer altogether was sure to offend and anger them. He longed for his wife, but recalled from stories he'd heard how ill-advised it was to ask for the dead to return.

Glimpsing the sad remains of his ox, he realized that he was now both lonely and without help, and remembered something that he had always wanted but had assumed—until now—was beyond all hope.

"I would like a son," he said, "a son with the strength of an ox."

The gods stared down at him. "We have offered you a nymph for your bed," said Hermes, "and minglings with nymphs are never without glorious issue."

Hyrieus cleared his throat and summoned his courage. "Thank you, but I would prefer, please, a son who is like me—a son who is mortal, to share my lot."

The gods conferred among themselves for a moment. Then they laughed—it was not a pleasant laugh—and said to Hyrieus, "Bring us the hide of that gelded beast you sacrificed."

Hyrieus dragged it over, stooping with the effort. When he straightened up again, he saw that the gods had hitched up the skirts of their chitons, exposing themselves. Embarrassed—indeed, terrified—by his glimpse of the gods' genitals, he quickly turned away, wondering what was going to happen.

He heard more laughter and then the sound of piss hitting leather.

"Turn around, Hyrieus," said Hermes, "and receive the gift of your gods. Bury this hide that we have anointed within the Earth, who is the mother of all, and wait nine months. You will have your son, as strong as an ox—and mortal."

And then the gods disappeared.

Hyrieus did as he'd been ordered. He dug a hole, lay the sodden hide within it and covered it with dirt. One morning, he was awoken by the sound of squalling and found a newborn boy lying on the ground. Lifting him up, Hyrieus named his son Orion.

30
ORION

Orion was already larger than normal when Hyrieus found him on the ground, thanks to the nourishment he'd received while cradled in Earth's womb, and he continued to grow prodigiously in both size and strength. He was a great help in the fields as his father grew older and frailer.

He was also extraordinarily handsome. As soon as the bloom of youth had graced his cheek, Orion turned the head of every girl he encountered. Rumor claimed that by the time he was twenty, he'd already fathered fifty sons on as many mothers. Women who didn't consent to his lovemaking soon discovered that he had no scruples about rape. The Pleiades escaped his grasp only by praying to Zeus, who turned the fleeing sisters first into doves and then into stars.

But Orion's greatest passion was the hunt. Already as a child, he stalked any animal that was unlucky enough to wander onto the farm. Hares, squirrels, hedgehogs, badgers, martens, weasels, shrews, lizards, whip snakes, grass snakes, turtles and tortoises fell victim to Orion's sticks and stones.

Later, armed with bow, quiver and club and accompanied by his dog, Sirius, he tracked animals in forests, meadows and swamps, over mountains and across hills, now running, now skulking, now pouncing to capture and kill his prey. The carcasses of boars, bears, mountain lions, panthers, lynxes, jackals, wolves, roe deer, fallow deer, red deer, ibexes and foxes littered his wake. No living creature was able to escape Orion, once he'd decided to pursue it.

One summer morning, the people of Chios, who were famous for their wine, awoke to discover that most of their vines had been destroyed. Some had been pulled from the soil and their roots had been gnawed. Others had been stripped of their ripening grapes. The next morning brought more of the same. The cause was easy to guess: the winter had been mild and the animals of the island had not been winnowed down by cold and disease. An army of creatures, emboldened by hunger, had moved out of the forests and into the vineyards.

Oenopion, the king of Chios, sent for Orion and promised him the hand of his daughter, Merope, if the problem were solved. Orion arrived immediately—Poseidon had given him the ability to run across the waves—and set to work. By the end of the day, a pile of dead animals lay outside of Oenopion's door. The vines were safe and Orion wanted his prize.

Oenopion, however, withdrew his promise. He offered Orion anything else he desired instead, but Orion was implacable. That night, he took what he wanted: he raped Merope within the very walls of her father's palace, covering her mouth with his hand to prevent her desperate cries from being heard.

When Merope told her father what Orion had done, Oenopion's face became as dark as the wine in which he took so much pride. Sneaking up to Orion while he slept, Oenopion blinded him. Orion leapt up, roaring with pain and fury, but his quarry had fled.

Hephaestus took pity on the stumbling giant. He lent Orion a slave, Cedalion, who served as his guide by riding on Orion's shoulders and whispering in his ear. Hephaestus told Orion that the only hope of healing his blindness lay in Helios and that he should seek the god where he rose from his bed each day.

And so Orion and Cedalion walked east towards Helios's palace. At last they reached a land where the rays of the rising sun were so bright that even Orion's ruined eyes could detect a trace of light. As they continued eastwards, Orion's sight became clearer each day until, finally, it was as good as it had been before. Keen to return to the hunt, Orion ran all the way home, shaking the ground beneath his feet, Cedalion hanging on for dear life.

By now, Orion's prowess as a hunter had caught the attention of Artemis, and she invited him to join her on Crete. The two spent many happy days together, tracking and killing the island's animals. One evening, they lay on a hillock, discussing the day's hunt. Orion had come closer than ever before to equaling Artemis in the number of animals he'd killed. Flushed with success, he boasted that he could stalk and kill any animal that Earth could produce.

Arrogant words provoke divine anger. Earth, his mother, heard what he said and was enraged by her son's insolence. In her anger, she created an animal that Orion couldn't stalk because he wouldn't even know it was there. It was small, silent and stealthy like its cousins, the spiders, but armed with a tail that carried venom more lethal than any spider possessed. This creature, the first scorpion, crept through the leaves that littered the ground and stung Orion on the thigh.

Immediately, he felt a searing pain where the scorpion had struck and soon its venom was doing deadly work inside his body. His massive muscles twitched, he drooled and sweated, his heart pounded erratically and he struggled to breathe. He vomited up the meat that he'd gobbled down only an hour before. He leapt here and there, trying to escape the venom's grasp. After death finally brought an end to his agony, Orion awoke to find himself in an infernal meadow, filled with the ghosts of all the animals he'd ever slaughtered. He was condemned to hunt them forevermore, eternally chasing prey that he would never catch.

Artemis had been peeved by the loss of her companion, but not so troubled as to intervene. Earth was a formidable opponent and Orion would have died sooner or later, anyway; mortals were vexingly short-lived. She decided to establish a lasting reminder of her companion's downfall, however. She placed Orion's image in the stars, accompanied by faithful Sirius. Halfway around the circle of the sky she placed the scorpion. Orion and the scorpion eternally pursue, and are pursued by, one another, neither ever catching the other.

31
ERIGONE AND ICARIUS

Early in his journey through the world to bestow his gifts upon mortals, Dionysus stopped on the outskirts of Athens. As twilight was falling, he appeared at the door of a farmer named Icarius and his daughter, Erigone, who gave the stranger a simple meal of vegetables and a place to sleep that night.

In the morning, Dionysus revealed who he really was. He gave Icarius a taste of the wine that he carried. He taught Icarius how to plant and nurture grapevines and how to ferment the fruit when it had ripened. He also gave Icarius advice: however exhilarating the new drink might be, it should be enjoyed in moderation.

It took several years for Icarius's vines to mature and produce fruit, and several more months for the first vintage to be ready. Finally, just as bleak winter was drawing to an end, Icarius judged the moment to be right. He opened one of his casks and tasted the liquid—not as good as what Dionysus had served him, but a lot better than water. That evening, he called together the neighboring men and shared his wine, duly warning them not to drink too much, just as Dionysus had cautioned.

But it is easier to heed advice given by a god than by another human. Once the wine began to warm the men's blood, they lost all sensibility and ignored Icarius's warnings. They rolled more casks out of Icarius's house and caroused in his fields. Finally conquered by the wine, they passed out in the cold plow ruts and lay there till morning.

When they awoke feeling sicker than they ever had before, they concluded that Icarius had tried to poison them. Dragging him into the woods, they murdered him and hid his body under dirt and leaves.

Erigone had been at the village well when her father was taken. As she came around the final curve in the homeward path, she spotted the family dog, Maera, waiting at the gate, whimpering. When Maera saw Erigone, she leapt up and seized the girl's robe with her teeth. She tugged Erigone onwards, swerving through the fields and into the woods. When they reached the mound under which Icarius lay, Maera pawed at it until she uncovered first a hand and then the blood-spattered arm to which it was attached.

With a shriek, Erigone knelt and swept clean her father's face. She tugged his stiffening body into her arms and rocked back and forth, howling *eleleleu! Eleleleu!*

She mourned for her father, but she mourned for herself as well. Her father was dead and she had no brother, no uncle, no grandfather who could assume his responsibilities, seeking a marriage for her, negotiating the dowry, leading her forth from his house and placing her hand in that of her new husband. And if she had the grimmest of lives to look forward to, her afterlife would be even worse: by dying a childless virgin, she would be doomed to wander restlessly between the realm of the living and the realm of the dead. She would be cut off from even the spartan comforts that Hades offered to the ghosts of those who had lived complete lives, and easy prey for any magician who cared to conjure her into his service.

As she lamented, Erigone began to notice things that didn't belong in a forest. Littered here and there in the underbrush were a belt, a sandal, a chiton pin that she recognized as belonging to the men with whom her father had shared Dionysus's gift the night before. She began to understand why her father had met his end—or at least at whose hands he had met it. Maddened now by both grief and fury, she swore vengeance.

With that decision, a cold composure descended upon Erigone's mind and she saw her way clear. The fate of a suicide's ghost was no better than that of a virgin's, but if she killed herself, she could at least choose the circumstances under which she died, and ensure her revenge.

She returned to the house to fetch a rope and pail. Carrying them back into the woods, she made a noose in one end of the rope and threw the other over a sturdy branch of the tree under which Icarius's body lay. She secured it firmly around the tree trunk, tugging to make sure it would hold. She placed the up-turned pail beneath the dangling noose and stepped upon it. She looped the noose around her neck, looked down at her father's motionless body and then, lifting her arms heavenwards, shouted, "Dionysus, hear my curse! As I swing here, so may all Athenian daughters swing!" Then she jumped and then she died: kicking, squirming, gagging, her back arched, her fists clenched, saliva flecking her lips and chin. It was neither a quick death nor a beautiful one.

A few days later, a strange madness seized the city of Athens. Girls began to cry inconsolably, tearing at their clothing and running through the streets. They claimed that they were being driven from their homes by a hideous wraith with red eyes, a swollen tongue and a bent neck. If their parents did not forcibly restrain them, the girls hanged themselves. Sometimes, even when their parents did restrain them, they fought their way free and hanged themselves, so set upon destruction did their madness make them.

The Athenians sent an envoy to the Delphic Oracle, begging Apollo for help. Apollo commanded them to find and punish Icarius's murderers and to establish two rituals to appease Erigone's ghost, to be performed by the girls of the city each year when the new wine casks were opened. In one, called the "Swinging," the girls were to sit on planks suspended from trees and swing back and forth. This would fulfill the letter, if not the spirit, of Erigone's curse. In the other, called the "Wanderer," the girls were to dance in imitation of the zigzagging trip through field and forest that Erigone made when Maera led her to Icarius's corpse.

The murderers were discovered hiding on the island of Ceos and were executed. Each year, as winter died and the new casks were opened, the Athenian men prayed to Dionysus that only good, not evil, might come of the wine that year, and Athenian girls swung and danced to keep Erigone's ghost away from their doors.

32
APOLLO AND HYACINTHUS

Hyacinthus was the son of Amyclas, one of the first kings of Sparta. His mother was Diomede, a daughter of the king of the Lapiths, a tribe from the wild, northern regions of Greece. The combination had produced a beautiful young man. Hyacinthus was slender and well-proportioned. His nose was straight and his steadfast eyes were framed by long lashes. His dark hair curled around a high forehead.

One day, just as the first signs of a beard were beginning to show on Hyacinthus's face, Apollo glimpsed him hunting on a mountain ridge and was immediately seized by desire. Soon, the god and the mortal became inseparable. Apollo tutored Hyacinthus in Apollo's own favorite pursuits: archery, music, prophecy, medicine and athletics. He lent Hyacinthus his chariot and the swans that pulled it through the air so that Hyacinthus might visit the marvelous, faraway lands to the north that Apollo himself loved best.

Apollo wasn't the only god to notice Hyacinthus, however. Zephyr, the west wind, had also been seized by desire and tried to lure Hyacinthus away from Apollo. Hyacinthus ignored Zephyr's persistent murmurings, but this only made Zephyr angry. He swore that he'd find a way to take Hyacinthus away from Apollo, and waited for his chance.

One day, Zephyr spotted Hyacinthus in a clearing, where Apollo was teaching him how to throw a discus. The two of them had removed their tunics and their skin shone with the olive oil that they'd rubbed into it. Zephyr quietly slipped into the branches of a nearby tree to watch.

As Hyacinthus stood to one side, Apollo demonstrated how to plant the right foot firmly on the ground in preparation for a throw. Then he twisted at the waist, stretching his right arm out to the back. He explained how to rotate that arm as the body turned, leveling the discus before it was released. Finally, spinning around, Apollo did just as he'd described and launched his discus into the air.

As the discus sailed past Zephyr, he vigorously blew against it. Instantly, it dove towards the ground. Bouncing hard on its edge, it leapt back up into the air and flew straight at Hyacinthus, hitting him squarely on the forehead. The young man crumpled to the ground.

In the moment that it took Apollo to reach Hyacinthus, the youth's blood had already begun to stain the soil where he lay. When Apollo tried to lift him, his neck drooped listlessly. The god used every healing art he knew—herbs, potions, incantations, infusions of nectar and ambrosia—but none of them helped; Hyacinthus died.

Zephyr emerged from the tree then, laughing. He taunted Apollo, jeering that in spite of all the god's foresight and skill, he'd been robbed of his beloved by nothing more than another god's breath. At that, Apollo drew an arrow from his quiver and shot Zephyr, who flew away, howling, to the western edge of the world.

Apollo did what he could to ensure that Hyacinthus would never be forgotten. He asked Earth to send up a new flower from the blood-soaked soil and Earth complied, creating the first hyacinth. Its purple petals were streaked with white marks that spelled out *ai-ai*, a wailing cry of grief. And Apollo commanded the Spartans to establish a festival called the Hyacinthia, celebrated each year at the time of the first new moon. Even if the Spartans were at war, he ordered, they were to cease fighting until the soldiers could travel home, honor Hyacinthus, and then return to the battlefield.

Apollo knew that he'd done everything he could but still, his heart was melancholy. Hermes gently chided him: "When you fell in love with Hyacinthus, Apollo, you knew that you were giving your heart to a mortal; don't grieve now for his mortality."

33
LEDA AND HER CHILDREN

As the years passed, the descendants of Amyclas continued to rule over Sparta. His grandson Oebalus married Gorgophone, the daughter of Perseus, and had by her a son named Tyndareus.

For a time, Tyndareus was in exile, having been driven out of Sparta by his half brother Hippocoön, a bastard son of Oebalus, but with the help of the hero Heracles and Thestius, the king of Pleuron, Tyndareus recovered the throne. He married Thestius's daughter Leda and settled down to rule Sparta.

One day, Leda looked to the sky and saw a snow-white swan fleeing in terror from an eagle, the bird of Zeus. Just as the eagle was about to catch his prey, the swan dove into Leda's lap, quivering with fear. The eagle returned to the heavens and disappeared.

Leda tried to calm the trembling bird, murmuring soothing words. Comforted, he nestled his head between her breasts and she began to stroke his silky feathers.

Snuggling closer, the swan nudged Leda's robes higher on her legs, laying bare her skin. Soon, his webbed feet caressed her knees. Soon, his downy underbelly tickled her thighs. Suddenly, his wings enveloped her completely and unfamiliar flesh coiled between her legs. The great bird shuddered and gasped—and then, all at once, he disappeared. Leda discovered that a man was gazing down at her; hastily, she sat up and tugged her robes down over her legs.

"Fear not, Leda, for I am Zeus," he said. "I have chosen you, among all mortal women, to receive my embrace. In time, you will bear me two children—both of them immortal. One is fated to be a hero; the other is fated to be the ruin of heroes.

"But hear this, too. Tonight you will be visited by your husband and you will conceive two more children. Though mortal, they will share their siblings' fates—one will be a hero, the other the ruin of heroes."

And then Zeus vanished.

When her time came, Leda groaned in pain as women always do, but into the waiting hands of the midwife there fell not babies, but two eggs. From one of them hatched Clytemnestra and Castor, who were the children of Tyndareus; from the other hatched Helen and Polydeuces, the children of Zeus.

Clytemnestra was a good but unremarkable child. Her looks and her lineage were sufficient to attract Agamemnon, the king of Mycenae, and she bore him four children. Only later did she show how resolute she could be when pushed to her limit.

The natures of Leda's three other children were clear from the start. Already as a child, Helen was wondrously beautiful. While still a girl, she was kidnapped by Theseus, who intended to make her his wife when she came of age. Zeus had other plans for Helen, however, and sent her brothers to rescue her, although they were still young themselves.

Indeed, Castor and Polydeuces were strong, adept and intrepid from an early age. Castor was an excellent horseman and Polydeuces an excellent boxer; both excelled at sailing and could meet almost any other physical challenge. They used their talents not only to retrieve their sister but also to help other heroes. They accompanied Jason on his quest for the Golden Fleece and hunted the Calydonian Boar with Meleager. It was an exploit closer to home that finally brought their careers to an end.

The two were approached by Idas and Lynceus, brothers from Messenia who had been their shipmates aboard the Argo. Idas and Lynceus had taken it into their heads to raid a large herd of cattle and needed Castor and Polydeuces's help.

Together, the four set out; together, they stole the cattle. When it came time to distribute the plunder, however, Idas categorically took charge. Slaughtering one of the cows, he divided it into four parts and declared that whoever ate his portion fastest would receive half of the stolen cattle and whoever came in second would receive the other half.

The four sat down to their meal. Each ate prodigiously, but Idas finished first—and then turned to what was still lying in front of his brother and gobbled that up, too.

Then he burped, rose from the table and drove all of the cattle home to Messenia with Lynceus chortling by his side and Castor and Polydeuces galloping behind in swift pursuit. Storming Messenia, Castor and Polydeuces carried off not only all the cattle but also many other spoils, as well.

Once they were safely away, Castor and Polydeuces stashed the cattle in a stable and crawled into a hollow oak tree, planning to lie low for a while. They forgot, however, that Lynceus had been born with an unusual gift: his eyes were sharp enough to see across enormous distances and keen enough to penetrate solid objects. Searching for the cattle thieves, Lynceus climbed to the top of Mount Taygetus and began to scan the Peloponnesus. Soon, he spotted the twins within the oak and shouted their location to his brother waiting below.

Idas yanked Castor out of the tree and killed him. Polydeuces leapt out then and killed Lynceus, who had just arrived. Zeus, who had been observing all of this, killed Idas with a thunderbolt and snatched Polydeuces up into the heavens, intending that his son should finally enjoy life as the god he really was.

Polydeuces, however, wept inconsolably for Castor. He begged his father to kill him, too, so that he might descend to Hades and join Castor there—or if not that, then to allow them to share one immortal life between them.

Zeus agreed to the latter request. Forevermore, he declared, the brothers would spend one day together in Hades and the next day together in the heavens, inseparable as they had always been. Indeed, although they were not really twins—they had different fathers, after all—to honor them Zeus placed a new constellation in the sky that he called The Twins, depicting them with their arms around each other's shoulders. Soon, he was calling them the Dioscuri, "the sons of Zeus," proudly linking the accomplishments of Tyndareus's son, as well as his own, to his personal glory.

34
MELAMPUS AND THE DAUGHTERS OF PROETUS

Melampus, a seer who came from the city of Pylos, began his career with an unusual act of kindness.

One day, he chanced upon his slaves killing some snakes who had made their home in an oak tree. Feeling sorry for the creatures, Melampus built a funeral pyre and duly cremated their corpses. Then, he reared their orphans.

The young snakes, grateful to Melampus, crept into his chamber while he was asleep and licked his ears, endowing him with the ability to understand the languages of all animals. When he awoke the next morning, Melampus was surprised to hear the birds outside his window talking to one another. As the day wore on, he heard other animals talking to one another as well, discussing all sorts of things that humans didn't know—where lost objects were to be found, what was portended when people twitched and why certain people had certain illnesses.

Melampus used the gift that the snakes had given him to help solve people's problems. It even saved his own life and the lives of others once, when he overheard two woodworms discussing the fact that a roof would collapse as soon as they'd chewed through the last bits of a beam. Just in the nick of time, Melampus persuaded everyone to leave except for one stubborn doubter who stayed behind and was crushed when the roof came crashing down.

As time went on, Melampus acquired other valuable skills, as well—some from animals, some from other seers, some from the gods. These included an array of techniques for curing divine madness. It was by putting those to work that Melampus won wives for himself and his brother, Bias.

At that time, the kingdom of Tiryns was ruled by Proetus. He had three daughters, each more beautiful than the next and each just as skilled at spinning and weaving as she was beautiful. Fortune had smiled generously upon these girls.

But Fortune's generosity had made them complacent. As time went on, their complacency grew into conceit and then conceit became insolence. They treated everything, and everyone, with contempt. One day, they released the golden pins that held their robes together at the shoulders, allowing the soft fabric to fall to their waists. Flaunting their white breasts, they began to dance lewdly in front of Hera's temple. Hera's statue looked down in horror, as did the goddess herself.

Hera's anger had already condemned other girls to spinsterhood for a variety of offenses; as the goddess of marriage she could blight, as well as fulfill, a girl's ambition to marry. What Proetus's daughters had done, however, was so outrageous that mere spinsterhood would be an insufficient penalty. After thinking for some time about how she might punish them, Hera allowed a smile to slip across her face.

"If they choose not to please me as young women, then let them please me as something else that I value," she said, and poured down upon their heads a terrible madness.

Immediately, the girls ran out of the palace and into their father's pastures. They dropped to their hands and knees and, stretching wide their rosy lips, began to crop the grass. When their bewildered father approached, they lifted their heads and, still chewing, gazed at him vacantly. When he waved his hands in front of their faces, trying to awaken them from what he prayed was some passing nightmare, they mooed and resumed their meal. In horror, Proetus realized that his daughters thought they were heifers.

For the first time in centuries, Hera had devised a novel way to punish mortals. Other gods had transformed mortals' bodies into those of animals, which was grim enough: still human in mind and spirit, such victims were forced to live the brutal lives of beasts. But Hera, by transforming the girls' minds while leaving their bodies untouched, made them ongoing spectacles of amusement for Proetus's people. Who could forget the sight of three princesses chewing their cuds? Moreover, Hera reasoned, if she ever chose to restore the girls' sanity, their insolence would be unlikely to return once they'd been told how ridiculous they'd looked as cows.

In spite of Proetus's pleas, no one in Tiryns was able to cure his daughters. Indeed, things got worse. After a few weeks in the pastures, the girls' silken robes had been torn to shreds. They began to twitch their naked buttocks, swishing imaginary tails to ward off the very real gadflies that now tormented their tender flesh. A steady diet of grasses, never meant for the human stomach, left them gaunt and stinking; their shining hair fell out and their radiant skin became mangy. They shivered in the wind as winter approached, macabre shadows of the beautiful girls they'd once been, but they nonetheless wandered far and wide, refusing the shelter of their father's stables.

At his wits' end, Proetus summoned Melampus and offered him one-third of the kingdom and his choice of the girls for a wife if he could cure them. Melampus demurred. Desperate, Proetus promised to give yet another third of the kingdom, and a wife, to Melampus's brother, Bias, too.

Content with that, Melampus set to work. He easily diagnosed the agent behind the problem. Cows were Hera's favorite animals: the madness was stamped with her seal. Melampus therefore began by placating Hera with lavish gifts—gold, peacocks, embroidered robes. Once he discerned that she was amenable to lifting the madness, he used a panoply of substances to purge the girls: black hellebore, a blue squill, sulfur, sea water—and piglets, whose throats he cut while holding them above the girls' heads. Their blood washed away the last of the girls' defilement.

Finally, he led the girls, now docile, to a spring into which he had mixed substances known only to him. They drank its waters and the cure was complete. Proetus's daughters were girls again, in mind and spirit as well as body. In time their beauty—but not their insolence—returned.

Melampus and Bias settled down with their new wives to help rule Proetus's kingdom. From Melampus and his wife sprang a long line of excellent seers and healers, who advised mortals for many generations to come.

35
PAN AND SYRINX

When the great god Pan was born, his mother shrieked in horror at the sight of her child and, breaking free from her attendants' supporting arms, ran from the room as fast as she could.

But the baby's father, Hermes, laughed with delight and tenderly picked up his son. He was an odd child, no question. The buds of tiny horns were just beginning to push through the skin of his scalp and a small but unmistakable beard covered his dimpled chin. His eyes, blinking open for a moment, were yellow. Black pupils slashed sideways across them, like ink dashed upon papyrus.

It was the rest of the child, however, that had most frightened the new mother. Down to the waist, he looked more or less human, but his loins and his legs were like those of the goats tended by her father, Dryops, and a stumpy tail sprang from the base of his spine. Seeing him whole and clear, the mother struggled to comprehend what she had brought forth. A monster? A portent for seers to decipher and then drown?

The man to whom Dryops had given his daughter in marriage seemed normal enough when he arrived at their Arcadian farm—an itinerant goatherd looking for work. Now, however, that goatherd threw off his disguise and stood revealed as a god, shining bright and with feathery wings on the heels of his golden sandals. He named his small son Pan and wrapped him warmly in rabbit pelts. Then, leaving the cottage, he set off for Olympus. Whatever else Dryops's daughter may have wondered about during the years to come, she now knew that her child's peculiar appearance had nothing to do with her.

Hermes proudly introduced Pan to the other gods, who looked with curiosity at the strange creature who slept in his father's arms. They'd transformed plenty of humans into animals and they'd changed themselves into animals, too, when it suited their purposes, but this was something different, this young thing caught forever between god and animal. Had Hermes intended the baby to be some kind of joke? It certainly looked amusing.

But then Pan opened his eyes—quite deliberately, this time— and stared back at the gods. There was a madness in his gaze that discomfited them. After a moment, the baby yawned and then they began to laugh again, but nonetheless they agreed that this child of Hermes belonged (and some of them would have added, "like Hermes himself," were it not for divine politeness) in the pastures and forests of his homeland. Only Dionysus remained untroubled, quietly smiling to himself. He was no longer the youngest god and no longer the strangest, either. He foresaw that he would share many interests with his new nephew.

Like all gods, Pan grew up quickly. Soon, his horns were fully formed and his beard was long. Another goatish attribute had matured as well: Pan found himself in a persistent state of arousal. At first, he released his tension among the flocks that roamed the hills, but as time went on, he yearned for nymphs and shepherd boys.

Pan's looks made it difficult to seduce them—or even to approach them. The moment he came into view, his targets ran away in dizzy terror, hearts hammering, dead afraid of what they'd glimpsed. When Pan did succeed, it was only by taking his quarry by surprise.

One day, he saw Syrinx, an oak-tree nymph, out hunting with Artemis and was captivated by her slender body and her proud face. Indeed, Syrinx looked so much like Artemis that, had she not carried a bow made of horn instead of gold, even Apollo might have mistaken her for his sister.

Her resemblance to the most virginal of goddesses only heightened Pan's arousal. He tracked Syrinx until she fell away from her group, delayed by a broken bowstring. Carefully, he made his way through the trees, remaining in the shadows as long as he could. His familiarity with the forest had taught him how to move noiselessly, like a wolf or a lynx. Trembling with anticipation, he finally stepped into the clearing where Syrinx was fixing her bow.

"Maiden," he said, "come to me and be a maiden no more. Allow your beauty to be enjoyed by one who desires it urgently."

Syrinx looked up and saw him suddenly present where a moment before there had been only empty air. She dropped her bow in surprise and then froze at the sight of his naked and unabashed masculinity. A surge of emotions washed over her: fear, confusion, revulsion, desperation.

And then she fled like a hare. Pan pursued, no longer worrying about stealth: branches splintered, birds scattered, a trail of broken ferns showed the course of their race.

Syrinx ran fast but Pan's goat legs carried him even faster. Eventually, she found herself approaching the river Ladon, a peaceful son of Ocean and Tethys. She realized that his daughters, who were also nymphs, might help her. Stumbling down the muddy bank, Syrinx screamed, "Sisters, save me, however you can!" The nymphs listened and did the best they could.

Pan reached out, expecting his arms to close around Syrinx's body, but found only the lithe reeds into which the nymphs had transformed her. He sighed, familiar with failure but disappointed nonetheless, and the reeds sighed back in reproach. Pan, however, interpreted the sigh as one of longing.

"Fear not, Syrinx," he said, "for I shall kiss your body forever as I teach you to sing my tunes." He yanked the reeds from the mud and snapped them off at different lengths. He fused the dismembered pieces together with beeswax. Each reed produced a different note when he blew across it; together they made a melancholy sound. Pan named his new instrument the syrinx.

36
ECHO AND NARCISSUS

Another nymph whom Pan pursued was Echo. That time, he was successful—she returned his affections and they had a daughter, Iynx.

Iynx enjoyed causing trouble. Once, she used a magic potion to make Zeus fall in love with Io, knowing full well the problems that this would cause for all concerned. When Hera found out what Iynx had done, retribution was swift. She turned Iynx into a bird and then let it be known that the bird was a powerful love charm. Soon, Iynx's broken body was the stuff of sorcery.

Echo didn't learn much from her daughter's horrible end, for not long afterwards she agreed to distract Hera with gossipy chatter while Zeus dallied with the nymphs of the forest. Again, retribution was swift. When Hera discovered what Echo had done, she formulated a curse that would prevent her from ever again being able to distract someone with her idle tongue. Echo would be able to speak only what others had already spoken—indeed, she would be able to speak only the final parts of what they had spoken. An inquiring "Where have I lost my flute?" became the retort "*My flute,*" and the exclamation "I don't want to do that" became the command "*Do that.*"

But although this peculiar impediment stopped Echo from meddling in the love affairs of others, it didn't stop her from falling in love herself. One day, she saw a handsome young man, Narcissus, moving through the forest in search of game. He was the son of the river Cephisus, which flowed down from Mount Parnassus through the Boeotian plain, and the river nymph Liriope.

Although Narcissus was human, the watery nature of his parents shone through. There was an attractive languor about his movements, whether he was brushing a stray hair from his forehead or reclining upon the banks of his father's waters to rest in their coolness. When he chose to move more purposefully, his body was so supple that its discrete motions became one. His face was like something encountered in a dream. The eyes were one degree of green beyond anything else in the world. The lips were so full that they seemed to defy gravity. The skin under his chin, which seldom saw the sun, was translucent in its paleness. Narcissus was like a creature not of this world but of some other place, where it was always afternoon and obligations yielded to desires.

Many came to believe that they loved Narcissus—some would swear that they loved him ardently. But however ardent the suitor, the result was always the same: Narcissus remained cloistered within the private reverie that he inhabited. Eventually, one of Narcissus's admirers, Ameinias, cursed him, lifting up his hands to the goddess Nemesis. "If Narcissus should ever come to love another, let him be spurned as cruelly as he has spurned me!" Nemesis heard Ameinias's plea and made her plans.

When Echo fell in love with Narcissus, she began to follow him through the forests as he hunted. Unable to speak, she was too shy to show herself and was careful to stay behind him, hidden among the grasses that were her natural environment. Eventually, however, Narcissus sensed that someone was near.

"Who's here?" he asked.

"*Here!*" replied Echo.

"Who are you?"

"*You!*"

"Stop that nonsense! And don't pursue me!"

"*Nonsense . . . pursue* me!"

In a fit of exasperation, Narcissus strode away and returned to his hunting. He was used to admirers who fawned upon him, but the silly sort of game that this one seemed to be playing went beyond all toleration. In his irritation, he moved more energetically than usual and grew warm. Lying prone on the banks of a forest pool, he prepared to scoop water onto his face.

But he paused before his hands broke the surface of the water. The most beautiful water god that he had ever seen was looking back at him from the depths: green eyes, sumptuous lips, alabaster skin and an expression of longing that could melt the hardest heart. Nemesis seized the chance to carry out Ameinias's curse: Narcissus finally fell in love.

"Who are you?" Narcissus asked, but heard only the reply of Echo, lingering nearby the bushes, "*You!*"

"Don't tease me!" he cried to his beloved.

"*Tease* me!" came the reply.

"Please caress me!"

"*Caress* me!"

And so it continued: the young man yearning, the nymph yearning and neither of them able to tear themselves away from the unattainable. Autumn came and leaves began to fall upon Narcissus's body, now thin with hunger. He watched in grim fascination as his beloved grew thinner, too, and worried for his health.

"Don't die!" Narcissus pleaded, and Echo, gaunt with hunger herself but still enthralled, replied, "*Die!*"

That command, coming, as he thought it did, from his beloved, broke Narcissus's heart. He lost his will to live and he let his head droop down upon the grass. "Farewell!" he cried to the face in the pool and "*Farewell!*" he heard in return as he breathed his last.

Echo lived only a moment longer and then her withered body crumbled to dust. Her voice, however, lived on, mournfully replying to anyone who came near.

A flower sprang up where Narcissus had died. Its petals, as pale as his throat, surrounded a golden center. The nymphs who searched for him, crying, "Narcissus! Narcissus!" heard their cries resound as they neared the pool where he and Echo had died. There they found the flower instead of the man whom they'd sought and in their grief named it the narcissus. What remained of Echo, lingering near, confirmed their choice, "*Narcissus . . .*"

37
THE GREED OF MIDAS

Midas was born heir to the throne of Phrygia, the land where Baucis and Philemon had once had their humble cottage.

Phrygia had always been a wealthy kingdom with wealthy kings, but when Midas was a child, some ants marched into the cradle where he was sleeping and laid grains of wheat upon his lips. Seers told his father that this meant Midas would be richer than any Phrygian king before him—for what was grain to the ants but their highest form of wealth, the gold of their little realm?

Certainly, Midas grew up to love wealth and particularly to covet gold, the most conspicuous form of it. Once he became king, his slaves were dispatched to forage among the vast ancestral treasuries of the palace, seeking out long-forgotten golden objects with which they could adorn his public rooms and private chambers. Panting with the effort, they dragged forth golden statues, golden lamps, golden plates and goblets, golden footbaths and even golden piss-pots. Golden rings covered Midas's fingers up to the knuckles and heavy golden earrings pulled his earlobes down nearly to his shoulders. His wives were so heavily laden with jewelry that they could scarcely lift themselves from their couches—which were covered with cushions made from cloth of gold.

Midas surrounded himself with other kinds of opulence, as well. His walled gardens were renowned for the abundance and beauty of their roses, which had been gathered from around the world. Each type bloomed at a different time of year and none had fewer than sixty blossoms, ensuring that there was always a splendid play of color. Their fragrance hung so heavy in the air that the effect was like that of the poppy: luscious but somniferous.

It was into these gardens that Silenus, an old satyr who had helped to care for Dionysus when he was young, wandered one afternoon. Drunk when he entered, Silenus inhaled the flowers' intoxicating scent and swooned onto the soft turf. When Midas took his evening walk a few hours later, he stumbled over the sleeper.

When he was younger and not yet so distracted by gold, Midas had sat as a student at the feet of Orpheus, who sang to him about Dionysus and the release from grief that his gifts promised to mortals. Midas had taken up Dionysus's cult and still worshipped the god ardently. He recognized at once who Silenus was, gently awakened him, and hosted him with lavish feasts for ten days.

When the feasts were over, Midas walked out into the garden again with Silenus and lifted his hands to the skies.

"Dionysus! Your foster father Silenus is here with me, having wandered away from your entourage. I will continue to keep him safe until you have need of him again."

Hearing this, Dionysus hastened to the garden, assuming the form of a young man wearing a tunic and short cape, a traveler's hat hanging down his back. His face was handsome, but his deep blue eyes had something of the lynx about them. Almond-shaped and dark-edged as if smudged by kohl, they startled Midas when he saw them gleaming in the twilight.

"Faithful worshipper!" said the god. "Ask me for any boon you please in return for this most welcome favor!"

Midas thought for a moment before answering—but not as long as he should have.

"Gold, my lord! Let everything I touch become gold!"

Dionysus smiled at the promise of entertainment soon to come. He snapped his fingers and said, "All right, then. So be it."

Suddenly, Dionysus and Silenus were gone. Midas's head was spinning, and he reached out for a nearby plinth to steady himself. Expecting to feel cool marble beneath his hand, he was surprised by warmth and looked down at what he had touched. The plinth had become gold: sparkling in the light of nearby torches.

Incredulous, he touched a leaf: it turned to gold. A rose: it became a golden rose. An unfortunate cicada that landed on Midas's arm became a dazzling golden adornment, fit to grace the loveliest hair. A mouse that skittered across his foot became a golden mouse. It was no more beautiful than it had been before, but at least it was golden, and so Midas took delight in it.

Midas ran through the garden cackling with glee, touching this and that, leaving a trail of peculiar ornaments in his wake. As he entered his palace, he continued to touch whatever caught his fancy. The guards' spears became gold—and fell heavily out of their hands onto the floor. The posts on either side of the door to his banquet hall gleamed as he skimmed his fingers over their surfaces. A statue of Aphrodite, carved from pure white Parian marble and delicately colored by the best of artists, became gold. A vase on which the war between the gods and the Gigantes had been painted became gold, too, its story burnished into silence.

Moving into the room, Midas plopped into a chair (now gold) and sighed with happiness. His slaves approached with bowls of grapes and apricots, plums and pomegranates. The king reached out for an apricot and, closing his eyes in blissful anticipation of its juicy flesh, carried it to his mouth. His teeth shuddered against unyielding gold. He quickly raised a goblet to his lips, hoping that wine would blunt the throbbing pain in his gums, but when the wine hit his tongue, it was slick, gummy and golden.

In a panic, Midas tried to eat without touching the food, which proved to be impossible. Horrified, he foresaw a perversity of starvation surrounded by wealth.

"Dionysus! My lord! Take pity on a foolish man and relieve me of your gift!"

Dionysus heard, and smiled once more. At least this mortal had learned his lesson quickly. The god's voice rang throughout the banquet hall, seeming to come from everywhere at once.

"Midas, travel to Lydia and wash yourself in the river Pactolus. You will be cured of your golden touch."

Midas did as he was told; ever since, the sands of the Pactolus have sparkled with gold. He was not cured of foolishness, however. One day, he was rash enough to say that he preferred Pan's piping to Apollo's lyre-playing and Apollo turned his ears into those of an ass. The king wore a turban for the rest of life—but at least it was a turban made of cloth, not gold.

38
TANTALUS TESTS THE GODS AND PELOPS MAKES A BAD DECISION

Tantalus was one of the first sons of Zeus to be born a mortal instead of a god. Although Zeus couldn't change that, he tried to ensure that his son would be happy: he made him king of Lydia and even invited him to the feasts of the gods. Tantalus grew to know his divine aunts, uncles and siblings well.

But Tantalus was unable to digest his good fortune; he became smug and then arrogant. Eventually, he came to believe that he was at least as clever as the gods—perhaps even more so. The gods claimed to be omniscient, but Tantalus suspected that this wasn't true and decided to test his hypothesis in a ghastly way. Having invited the gods to a dinner party, Tantalus seized his son, Pelops, and slaughtered him. Cutting the flesh into chunks, he concocted a grisly stew.

When the dish was set upon the table, it was immediately clear to the gods what lay in front of them. None of them touched the food except Demeter, who was distracted at the time by grief for her kidnapped daughter. Before Demeter realized what she was eating, she'd put a bite of Pelops into her mouth—it happened to be from his right shoulder—chewed it and swallowed it down.

Zeus charged Tantalus with infanticide and cannibalism, two of the vilest acts that any god or mortal could commit. Tantalus didn't even try to deny them; defiantly, he pointed out that one god, at least, had shown herself to be fallible and that such a discovery was worth any number of sons.

Livid with anger, Zeus threw Tantalus into Tartarus, deep below the ground, deep below even the Underworld, where the ghosts of other humans wandered in the comparative blessedness of eternal dimness. Trapped in Tartarus forever, Tantalus suffered a punishment that reminded him of the camaraderie he'd once enjoyed with the gods and the abominable meal that had brought it to an end. Gnawed by hunger and thirst, he stood in a stream of water that ran away each time he stooped to drink; above his head hung branches laden with fruits that flew from his grasp each time he reached up to pluck one. To remind him of the transitory nature of human fortune, a rock hung above his head, poised to fall at any moment.

Clotho, one of the three Fates, was furious that Tantalus had abruptly cut short the lifespan that she and her sisters had given to Pelops when he was born. Putting the remaining gobbets of the boy's body into a cauldron filled with water and herbs, she reconstituted him—except for the part that Demeter had eaten. In recompense, Demeter made Pelops an ivory shoulder, so absolute in its whiteness that it gleamed.

Poseidon was filled with desire when he saw the newly restored Pelops and carried the boy away to be his lover. Under Poseidon's tutelage, Pelops grew to manhood, learning everything that the son of a noble house should know. But eventually, the time came for Pelops to look for a bride. His eye was caught—as were the eyes of many other men—by Hippodamia, the beautiful daughter of King Oenomaus of Elis. Oenomaus himself was inordinately fond of Hippodamia as well and had set a high bar for her suitors: each had to compete in a chariot race with Oenomaus. Those who lost the race would lose their heads as well; the winner (should there ever be one) would marry Hippodamia.

As Pelops approached Oenomaus's palace, he looked with horror at the wall that surrounded it, where the heads of thirteen previous suitors were displayed on spikes. Now, if ever, was the moment to ask his former lover for help. Slipping down to the seashore that night, he stood at the edge of the gray waves and prayed. The waters roiled as Poseidon stepped forward, leading a team of winged horses harnessed to a golden chariot. With this, Pelops could not fail to win the race.

Yet even so, Pelops lacked confidence; perhaps it was in his blood to doubt the gods and their gifts. In his blood, certainly, was a determination to stop at nothing, however despicable, to gain his goals.

Approaching Oenomaus's charioteer, Myrtilus, Pelops offered him a deal. Although Oenomaus would be driving the chariot himself on the following day, Myrtilus would be preparing it. Pelops promised that if Myrtilus replaced the bronze lynchpins with pins made of wax—which would melt once the wheels rubbed against the axles, causing the chariot to crash—then Pelops would allow Myrtilus to enjoy Hippodamia's favors before Pelops himself did. Myrtilus eagerly agreed.

The race was held, with predictable results: Pelops won not only Hippodamia but the kingdom of his now deceased father-in-law. Yet victory only fed the moldering disease that festered in Pelops's blood. Before Myrtilus could claim his prize, Pelops lured him to a cliff and gave him a kick. As he fell, Myrtilus screamed out a curse against Pelops and all his descendants, begging the gods to cause the family that Pelops and Hippodamia were about to establish to rot from within.

For the rest of his life, Pelops congratulated himself that he had somehow managed to escape that curse—he sired six strong sons upon Hippodamia, and two daughters, whom he married off to the sons of Perseus, the powerful king of Mycenae. After he died, he received worship at a shrine near the precinct for the Olympic

Games, which he'd founded at the very spot where Oenomaus had died. Almost as soon as Pelops's body was in the ground, however, two of his sons, Atreus and Thyestes, discovered that Pelops's seemingly fortunate life had been only a respite from Myrtilus's curse, not a reprieve.

39
TITYUS AND LETO

Another mortal son of Zeus was Tityus. His mother, Elara, was the daughter of King Minyas of Orchomenus. Once she became pregnant, Zeus hid her from Hera just as he'd hidden many of his other lovers. In this case, he did a particularly thorough job, tucking Elara away deep beneath the surface of Earth.

Nonetheless, Hera managed to ferret her out and devised a particularly dreadful form of punishment: Elara's fetus grew at an alarming rate until finally, the poor mother's womb burst. Earth could do nothing to save Elara, but she cradled the unborn Tityus in her own belly until the ninth month was finished, releasing him into the upper world near his grandfather's palace.

Earth had already borne many gigantic babies of her own and her capacious womb had given Tityus plenty of room to expand. Even as a newborn infant he was large and he grew into a youth who towered over everyone else. By the time he was an adult, he was as tall as the highest tree. His exceptional size gave Tityus a great deal of power and power made him haughty and cruel; the people of Orchomenus learned to take cover whenever a rumbling of the ground announced that he was approaching.

One day, he went too far. The goddess Leto was on her way to Delphi, where her son, Apollo, was breathing forth prophecies from his laurel-scented oracle. Towards the end of her journey, Leto passed through Panopeus, a town not far from Orchomenus, and paused to watch girls dancing in her honor. The distance between Panopeus and Orchomenus was nothing for someone of Tityus's height and sure enough, he spotted Leto. Seized by lust, he lumbered across the countryside, slung Leto over his shoulder and began to carry her away.

But the distance was nothing for Apollo, either, who heard his mother's cries and rushed to the spot; his sister Artemis arrived right behind him. The two gods loosed their arrows thick and fast. One of the first pierced Tityus's right eye, but even then he didn't relent; tugging out the arrow, he forged ahead, crushing trees, houses and people as he ran. Finally, a shot from Artemis laid him low. Leto disentangled herself from the fallen giant and ran to embrace her children.

Artemis and Apollo had carefully stopped short of killing Tityus, knowing that punishments are better inflicted on living flesh. They cast Tityus into Tartarus and splayed him out supine, as a hunter splays a stag before he guts it. Two enormous vultures with cruel beaks materialized on either side of his abdomen. They tore through his skin, fat and muscles and then gorged upon his liver, the organ from which lust and arrogance seep into the body. Tityus frantically tried to beat the vultures away, but his wrists gyred helplessly in the iron manacles that pinned them to the ground.

The scene played out a thousand upon a thousand times, for each time that the vultures finished their meal, Tityus's liver regenerated itself, relentlessly guaranteeing the birds' next meal and Tityus's eternal punishment.

40
IXION, THE CLOUD AND THE CENTAURS

Ixion was a wicked man, and a stupid one, too. As such, he was a fitting king for the Lapiths—a northern clan that was infamous for its crude and violent behavior. Fortune nonetheless smiled on Ixion: he won the hand of Dia, the radiant daughter of Deioneus.

Tradition decreed that a bridegroom should present gifts to his new father-in-law and Ixion had promised to Deioneus some splendid gold and silver goblets. When none arrived, Deioneus began to ask questions. Ixion hemmed and hawed, unwilling to relinquish either Dia or even the smallest part of his substantial wealth.

When Deioneus persisted and Ixion realized that he could stall no longer, he contrived an abominable plan. He dug a deep pit in front of his palace and built a roaring fire at its bottom. Carefully, he covered the top of the pit with crisscrossed twigs and then a powdery layer of soil, scuffing the edges to blend them into the surrounding dirt. His trap now laid, Ixion invited Deioneus to dinner, promising that he would finally receive what he was owed.

Deioneus arrived, rejoicing in the expectation not only of gold and silver goblets but also of finalizing the bond between two families. Stepping down from his chariot, he strode towards his host, who stood in the doorway with open arms and a treacherous smile. A few steps more and, with a crackle of breaking twigs, the hapless father plunged to a fiery death. At that moment, Ixion became the first person to murder a family member.

When they created humans, the gods had anticipated that such a crime would be committed sooner or later and had laid down rules for dealing with it. To wash away the stain of what he'd done, Ixion would have to find someone to perform rituals of purification on his behalf. Until then, he would be forced to wander aimlessly, outcast and hungry, slowly losing his sanity as the pollution that sprang from the murder seeped ever more deeply into his mind.

So appalled, however, were both Ixion's neighbors and the gods themselves that Ixion could find no one to perform the rituals. Desperate, he pleaded with Zeus (whom some people whispered was Ixion's real father) and Zeus finally relented. Lifting Ixion up to Olympus, Zeus washed away his defilement and then invited the famished man to take dinner with the gods.

The nectar and ambrosia that Zeus gave to Ixion nourished him but also transmogrified him: by eating the food of the gods, he became something of a god himself. When he realized this, Ixion began to make himself at home among those whom he now dared to consider his equals. Casting his eye around the assembled goddesses, each of whom was alluring in her own way, he fantasized about making love to divine flesh. He was particularly captivated by Hera and, to the shock of that goddess, tried to seduce her with sly winks and furtive gestures.

Hera complained to Zeus, but Zeus could scarcely believe that any human he had helped could be so ungrateful as to attempt what Hera described. To settle the matter, Zeus molded a cloud into a perfect replica of Hera and then left it alone with Ixion. Sure enough, Ixion took the cloud-woman to bed, proving that Hera's suspicions had been right.

Zeus was enraged by Ixion's duplicity and resolved to punish him appropriately. This was not an easy task. Because he had shared the food of the gods, Ixion could not be cast into Tartarus as mortal transgressors or Titans might be. Finally, Zeus found a solution: he ordered Hephaestus to make a fiery wheel and then told Hermes to bind Ixion upon it, spread-eagled across its spokes. Once this had been done, Zeus set the wheel—and Ixion—spinning in an eternal orbit around the heavens, from the vantage point of which he could look down upon everything he'd lost through his avarice and treachery.

Ixion's crimes had lasting repercussions not only for himself but also for the world. The false Hera with whom Ixion had lain, whom the gods rather unimaginatively took to calling Nephele, a word that simply meant "cloud," had conceived a child. When her time came, Nephele brought forth Centaurus, a child as brutish as his father. She gave him over to the Lapiths to be raised.

As Centaurus grew, his lust became insatiable. One day, while passing through the meadows near Mount Pelion, he spotted a herd of shapely mares grazing nearby and was seized by desire. Covering each one, he sired creatures unlike anything that either gods or humans had seen before: each of the babies had the shaggy body of a horse from its tail to its forelegs, but where a horse's neck should have been, there rose up instead a human abdomen, chest, arms and head.

Called after their father, these were the first of the centaurs, in whose veins ran the tainted blood of both Centaurus and Ixion. Part Lapith by descent, they envied and resented the people their grandfather had once ruled, who didn't regard the horsey new-comers as real Lapiths. Peace between the two branches of Ixion's family was always precarious.

Dia bore a son named Pirithous—some said his father was Ixion; others said it was Zeus, who had supposedly made love to Dia in the form of a stallion after Ixion attempted to seduce Hera. When Pirithous grew up, he became king of the Lapiths and chose a local woman, Hippodamia, as his bride.

Wishing to bring the two halves of his father's family together, Pirithous invited the centaurs to the wedding. The centaurs, however, accustomed to living wild in the mountains and drinking the milk of goats, had never tasted wine before. They quickly grew drunk. When Hippodamia was formally presented to the wedding guests, the centaur Eurytion grabbed her and ran for the woods. The other centaurs, inspired by Eurytion's example, seized Lapith women as well and a melee broke out. The Lapith men fought with spears to protect the virtue of their women and the centaurs fought with pine trees that they wrenched from the soil.

Pirithous set off after Eurytion, accompanied by his best friend, King Theseus of Athens. Catching up with the centaur, they wrenched Hippodamia out of his arms and then sliced off his nose and ears. Those centaurs who hadn't been killed in the battle were expelled from the territory and eventually retreated further into the rugged lands to the northwest. This was not, however, to be the last that humans saw of them.

41
THE DEATHS OF SISYPHUS

The third great criminal to be punished in Tartarus, alongside Tantalus and Tityus, was Sisyphus, the king of Corinth.

Sisyphus was an accomplished swindler and cheat. His greatest pleasures lay in contriving traps and getting what he wanted by trickery. Not surprisingly, he was a friend of King Autolycus of Parnassus, who was himself the slyest of thieves. Indeed, it was rumored that once when Sisyphus was visiting Autolycus, he had seduced Autolycus's daughter Anticleia and sired Odysseus, who grew up to surpass all other mortals in cunning. When Autolycus learned that Anticleia was pregnant, he quickly married her off to Laertes, who none the wiser raised Odysseus as his own.

Sisyphus was foolish enough, however, to betray Zeus when Zeus was in a similar situation. Zeus kidnapped Aegina, the beautiful daughter of the river god Asopus, and whisked her away to a distant island. When Asopus arrived in Corinth searching for her,

Sisyphus told him the whole story and soon Hera knew, as well. Zeus decided that the day had come for Sisyphus to die.

So Death set out for Corinth with a heart of iron and a soul as pitiless as bronze, skulking through the shadows by the side of the road, as was his habit. He felt his sword, which was as sharp as a Harpy's feather, bumping against his thigh; all was well. He assumed that this job would go according to plan, like the millions of others that he had carried out since the gods had created mortals.

But Death was no match for Sisyphus, who had learned how to spot trouble a long way off. From atop the wall surrounding his palace, Sisyphus saw Death approaching and quickly came up with a scheme.

Creeping down to the gates, Sisyphus signaled to his guards that they should pretend he wasn't there and then hid in the underbrush. When Death arrived, Sisyphus sprang from his ambush with stout chains in his hands. Before Death knew what was happening, he lay bound on the ground, shocked and unable to move.

Sisyphus grinned above him. "Well, I guess I've got the advantage now—and forever, actually. There's no reason I need ever die."

But it wasn't only Sisyphus who didn't die. No one died, once Death was immobilized. At first, this seemed like a wonderful idea. Butchers who carelessly lopped off a hand after a night of carousing didn't bleed to death. Charioteers whose horses ran wild, tossing them onto the ground, survived to tell the tale. Childbed fever didn't carry away new mothers.

But the very old lay suffering in their beds, waiting for Death to release them. Babies born too weak to suckle bleated feebly in their mothers' arms. Warriors whose bodies had been hacked to pieces gasped and shuddered, praying for liberation.

Amid all this mortal rejoicing and pain, Hades sat bewildered on his throne, alarmed by the echoing silence in his entrance hall. There was no longer any crowd of ghosts waiting to be admitted, no longer any gibbering noise that reassured him of his kingdom's strength.

He shared his puzzlement with Zeus, and Zeus asked whether anyone had seen Death recently.

The gods laughed; most of them had never seen Death at all, given that they avoided him like the plague. But then Hermes, whose job it was to escort Death's victims to the Underworld, realized that he'd never been summoned to lead away Sisyphus's soul, as he'd anticipated.

With that clue to help him, Zeus soon discovered where Death was imprisoned. He called Ares to his side.

"This is ridiculous! Go rescue Death, and make sure that Sisyphus is the first person he drags down to the Underworld once he's free."

But Sisyphus had been expecting something like this and prepared his wife, Merope.

"Merope," he'd said, "when I die you must cast my body out into the square and leave it unburied."

And being an obedient wife, she did just that.

When Sisyphus's ghost reached the Underworld, it began to sob and moan so loudly that even Hades and Persephone, sitting far away in their palace, could hear it. Hades summoned it.

"What's your problem?" Hades asked.

"Alas, here I am, stranded, neither fully alive nor fully dead, because my wife—the stupid woman—failed to bury my body. Of course, she's the daughter of Atlas, a Titan; perhaps no one ever told her what to do with a mortal's corpse. If only I could return to life for just a few moments to instruct her! You'd hear no more of my groaning then!"

"Oh, Hades, let him go!" said Persephone. "Poor Merope! How could she have known?"

Hades rolled his eyes and sighed, but nodded. "Go, back then—but be quick about it and return! No tricks, now!"

Sisyphus scurried up to Corinth and ordered his slaves to prepare a feast. He ate, he drank and he had a good laugh at the expense of the gods—for, of course, he had no intention of returning to the Underworld.

Gods, however, always manage to laugh last. Sisyphus was almost too clever too die, but only almost. Death stood waiting for him the next morning at breakfast, sword already drawn, heart even harder than iron and soul even more pitiless than bronze. Before Sisyphus could escape, the sword had done its work and his ghost was scuddering down the slippery path to Hades's kingdom, Hermes grinning at its side.

Once there, Sisyphus was reminded of how futile it is for a mortal to try to outwit a god—even Death, that dimmest of all gods. Persephone pointed to an enormous boulder and ordered Sisyphus to roll it to the top of a hill. Just as Sisyphus approached the peak, infernal gravity took hold and the rock tumbled all the way down again. Sisyphus sighed and sat down, gazing out wearily over the valley of death—but not for long: the Erinyes thrashed him all the way back to the bottom of the hill, where he began his task anew for the first of a billion times.

42
THE DAUGHTERS OF DANAUS AND THE SONS OF EGYPTUS

The descendants of Io's son Epaphus spread out across the earth. His grandson Agenor became the king of Phoenicia. Agenor's daughter Europa was taken by Zeus to Crete, where she became the mother of a royal dynasty, and his son Cadmus, after searching fruitlessly for Europa, founded Thebes.

Agenor's twin brother, Belus, inherited Epaphus's throne in Egypt. Belus had two sons, Egyptus and Danaus, who contended bitterly with one another from their earliest days. They competed with one another even in the begetting of children: Egyptus sired fifty sons upon his numerous wives and Danaus sired fifty daughters upon his.

The day came, however, when Egyptus decided that the two sides of the family should be united. This would happen, he decreed, through marriage: he ordered Danaus to give his fifty daughters to their fifty cousins as wives.

Danaus and his daughters were horrified by the idea and immediately planned their escape. Hiring a ship, Danaus hurried his daughters aboard and sailed away to Argos, the city where once, long ago, Io had lived. Here, Danaus hoped, they would find kinfolk to protect them.

They disembarked safely onto Greek soil and, after washing the grime of travel from their hands in a nearby spring, offered thanks to the gods for their safe arrival. As they were doing this, Pelasgus, the king of Argos, came forth to greet them.

Pelasgus listened to their story sympathetically but found himself in a quandary. He feared that all of Argos would be at risk if the sons of Egypt realized that their intended brides were hiding in the city. His citizens, however, cried out with a single voice in favor of defending their visitors. What protection, they argued, could they ever hope to receive from Zeus themselves if they turned away these women whom Zeus had surely guided to their shores?

The asylum that the Argives offered came none too soon. As the assembled citizens were dispersing to their homes, a dark ship pulled into the harbor, carrying fifty spear-bearing sons of Egypt and a legion of other warriors.

Danaus blanched at the size of the army, which seemed far larger than any that Argos might raise. He feared that his nephews and their men would topple the Argive citadel, seize the city's treasures and rape its women—all as a prelude to dragging his own daughters away into the very marriages that they had fled Egypt to avoid.

Thinking quickly, he contrived a new plan. Handing a knife to each of his daughters, he told them to lie down obediently in their marriage beds and await their new husbands. When the men had sated their appetites and fallen asleep, the women should slit their throats.

Forty-nine daughters obeyed. Forty-nine bridal chambers, flickering bright with lamps, became abattoirs.

But one daughter, Hypermnestra, trembled as she groped for the knife beneath her pillow. Her husband, Lynceus, had declined to consummate their marriage that night. He was content, he said, to wait until she welcomed his embrace. Her hand refused to rob this gentle man of his life. Shaking him awake, she urged him to flee and find sanctuary in some god's temple.

In the morning, Danaus counted the corpses and found one missing. Enraged, he imprisoned Hypermnestra, planning to bring her to trial for defying her father.

Meanwhile, he and his other daughters chopped off the corpses' heads and buried them in nearby Lerna before burying the bodies in Argos. Surely, they hoped, the ghosts of the men wouldn't be able to wreak vengeance on them in such a butchered state. Athena, a virgin herself, sympathized with Danaus and his daughters and purified them of the pollution that clung to them. There was no reason, now, that society need shun them.

But there was sympathy among the gods for Hypermnestra and Lynceus, too. Aphrodite spoke eloquently of the power of love; Artemis spoke persuasively of the honorable way that Lynceus had treated Hypermnestra. The Argives aquitted Hypermnestra and she was released into the arms of her new husband, whom the Argives pledged to protect.

Fortune seemed to smile on all concerned. Hypermnestra and Lynceus had a son, Abas. Danaus found forty-nine other men to marry his daughters, remarkably enough. He lived to see many grandchildren born to his line.

But when Hermes escorted the forty-nine daughters of Danaus to Hades, as he eventually escorted all mortals, he turned onto a seldom used path that sloped steeply downwards. The light, which was never bright in the Underworld under the best of circumstances, grew even dimmer. Each daughter's ghost, when her turn came, shivered in fear as she descended.

That in itself should have alarmed them, for there was only one part of the Underworld in which ghosts retained bodily sensation: Tartarus, where the great sinners were punished. When each daughter reached the end of the path and glimpsed Sisyphus, Tantalus and Tityus, she realized where she was and tried to flee.

The Erinyes swiftly caught them all, however, and dragged them to a spring that gushed with icy water. Handing a jug to each, the Erinyes gestured to a tub that stood some distance away. The message seemed clear: fill the tub. For Greek women, whose girlhood tasks had included fetching water for the household, this seemed easy enough.

The bottom of each jug, however, was riddled with holes. Over and over, the daughters of Danaus plunged their jugs into the water, their arms aching with its coldness. Over and over, the water trickled out onto their shivering bodies. Over and over, they trudged to a tub that remained forever empty.

43

ASCLEPIUS CHALLENGES DEATH

Ares fathered a son upon Chryse, the daughter of a Lapith warrior. When the child, Phlegyas, came of age, Ares set him on the throne of Trikke, a city that lay in the wild northern realm where Chryse's relatives lived. A belligerent man by nature, Phlegyas soon conquered his neighbors' territories, carrying off their cattle and their wealth. He reigned supreme and became accustomed to having his desires fulfilled.

Phlegyas had a daughter, Coronis, whose beautiful black hair was the talk of the kingdom. When neatly bound upon her head, it shone like a raven's wing; when released from its combs and ribbons, it cascaded to her waist like the river of night that Selene unfurled behind her chariot each evening.

One day, the beautiful hair caught Apollo's eye; soon, Coronis was carrying his child. Her father, the son of a god himself, rejoiced in her pregnancy.

"A coup for the family!" he crowed triumphantly. "Be proud, child, that you, like my own mother, were chosen to be the soil that nurtures divine seed!"

But Coronis fell prey to two of the gravest errors that beset mortals—desire for the unfamiliar and scorn for what is already at hand. A handsome young man named Ischys arrived from faraway Arcadia and Coronis yearned to lie with him, in spite of her swollen belly. The lovers crept through the back passages of Phlegyas's palace, mingling in love where they knew that no mortal could find them.

It is not possible to elude Apollo, however. Although he was sitting in his oracle at Delphi when Coronis betrayed him, Apollo's mind perceived what she was doing. In anger, he sent his sister Artemis to punish her. Soon, Coronis's mother was lamenting her daughter's death and Phlegyas was placing her corpse upon a pyre. The fire was lit and the blaze lapped hungrily at the wood.

Apollo watched all of this with satisfaction that turned to horror when he realized that his unborn son would burn as well. Parting the flames, he deftly scooped the baby from his mother's womb and then carried him to the cave of the centaur Chiron, where he could be raised among other young heroes. Apollo named him Asclepius.

Apollo asked Chiron to train Asclepius in the healing arts, a field in which Apollo himself excelled. And so Chiron taught the child the uses of herbs and potions, splints, surgeries, incantations, massages, cold baths and warm baths, the application of healing muds and sucking leeches. The boy showed a natural skill for the work. Even before the first shadow of a beard had appeared upon his cheeks, he went out into the world to heal people. Later, he joined the heroes with whom he'd grown up in Chiron's cave on their expedition to retrieve the Golden Fleece, curing seasickness and soothing the soreness of limbs that rowers suffer. He joined his friends again on their expedition against the Calydonian Boar. Asclepius fell in love with a woman named Epione and they had sons and daughters with whom he shared his skills and knowledge: Machaon, Iaso, Podalirius, Hygeia and Panacea. Little by little, the family began to vanquish the pains and diseases that had swarmed into the world when Pandora opened her jar.

But one day, Asclepius went too far. When Hippolytus, Artemis's favorite disciple, was killed in a chariot crash, she convinced Asclepius to raise him from the dead. Once word of this miracle got around, people begged Asclepius to raise their own loved ones, and he did his best to meet the demand. Ghosts began to disappear from Hades's halls in startling numbers.

Zeus was deeply worried. What if Asclepius taught other doctors how to revive the dead? If mortals stopped fearing death, would they any longer fear the gods? Would they not become something close to gods themselves? Zeus's mind reeled at the possible consequences. Choosing from his armory one of the thunderbolts that the Cyclopes had forged for him, Zeus struck down Asclepius. The healer perished in flames, unable to heal himself.

Apollo was furious at the death of his son, and in his rage sought vengeance. He dared not, and could not, strike down Zeus himself, but he struck down the Cyclopes who had created Zeus's weapon. Apollo paid for this—Zeus declared that if Apollo had no respect for the difference between mortals and immortals, then he should experience what that difference constituted. He sentenced Apollo to serve Admetus, a mortal man, for a year. Admetus treated Apollo kindly, which the god never forgot; later, this bond tempted Apollo to once more blur the boundary between gods and humans.

But Zeus conceded that he, too, had acted hastily when he struck Asclepius down. Reaching into the smoldering ashes of Asclepius's body, he raised the physician up to Olympus and made him a god. Zeus assigned to Asclepius and his children, whom he also made gods, the care of mortals' fragile bodies.

The ill and the disabled gathered at Asclepius's sanctuaries, where his priests bid them to make their beds in sacred chambers. At night, Asclepius and his children visited the sleepers in their dreams, curing them of all sorts of ailments. When they awoke, the blind could see again, the mute could speak and the paralyzed could move their limbs. Even greater miracles occurred, as well: a woman who had been pregnant for five long years finally gave birth, to a child who immediately walked to the sanctuary's fountain and washed the stains of birth from his body.

Great was Asclepius, son of Apollo, twice rescued from the fires of death, a man and then a god!

44
MINOS AND POLYIDUS

Minos, the oldest of the three sons whom Europa bore to Zeus, became the king of Crete and married Pasiphaë, a daughter of Helios whose red hair shone like the sun itself and whose eyes glinted gold like its rays.

One day, when their son Glaucus was still a small boy, he spotted a mouse in a corner of the palace and chased the tiny creature. Glaucus's nanny, distracted by her tasks, didn't notice at first that he was gone; when she did, she found that he had disappeared entirely. An alarm was raised, but to no avail. Glaucus was gone.

Minos consulted his seers and the seers consulted Apollo, who replied that Glaucus would be found by the person who provided the best metaphor for a remarkable calf that had recently been born in Minos's herds. Three times a day, the calf's hide changed color: in the morning, it was white, then it turned red in the afternoon and black in the evening, before becoming white again the next day.

The Cretan seers had little to offer, so Minos ordered his heralds to travel far and wide, announcing a contest with a rich prize for the winner. Poets and seers from many lands gathered on Crete to offer their metaphors.

It was Polyidus, a descendant of the famous seer Melampus, who won.

"Consider the blackberry, my lord," he said. "When it first appears on the bramble, it is white. Then it ripens to red and finally, when it is sweet enough to eat, it is black."

"Perfect!" cried Minos, jumping to his feet. "Now, find my son— then I'll give you your prize."

For several days, Polyidus carefully observed all that happened at the palace. He noticed that an owl patrolled the wine cellar, shooing away bees that were trying to enter. Descending into the cellar, Polyidus found a vat of honey and in the honey, perfectly preserved but dead, he found poor Glaucus.

"I meant that you should find my son *alive!*" roared Minos. "Until you can give me *that*, sit here beside his corpse and ponder your dilemma!" And with that, the king slammed the door and strode away.

Luckily, torches blazed on the walls of the cellar, which enabled Polyidus to witness an instructive drama. A snake crept through a crack into the room and Polyidus, startled, killed him. Moments later, the snake's wife arrived and discovered her husband's corpse. She scurried away and returned with a leaf in her mouth. When she laid the leaf on her husband's body, he was restored to life. The two slithered away then, leaving the leaf behind.

It was but the work of a moment for Polyidus to lay the leaf upon Glaucus's body and the work of less than a moment for the boy to spring to his feet, rosy-cheeked and smiling, licking from his hands the honey that had entombed him.

Polyidus slipped the leaf into his pocket; he intended that the technique for performing this miracle would stay locked in his heart, shared with no one but his own children. He banged on the door. When the guards opened it and saw Glaucus, they shouted for the king and queen.

Minos and Pasiphaë were ecstatic. The Cretan treasuries were opened and Polyidus was told to take whatever he wanted. Like most seers, he was a practical man and stuffed his wallet with gold and a few exceptionally fine gemstones. Everything seemed to have worked out well.

But then Minos—a man who was never satisfied—made another request.

"Polyidus, you're a seer of impressive skills. You solve riddles with ease, you read animal behavior adeptly and now you've shown that you know how to raise the dead. You will stay here and teach Glaucus all you know. I'll reward you even more richly and then allow you to go home."

Crete had become Polyidus's gilded prison; what choice did he have but to train the boy in the techniques of his craft, sharing all his family's secrets?

And so he did. Over the months and years that Polyidus spent with him, Glaucus grew in ability, learning how to read the behavior of birds and the entrails of animals, how to interpret the riddling speech of Apollo's Pythia and the puzzling words of Zeus's dove priestesses. Polyidus taught Glaucus how to heal many illnesses, too.

And under heavy pressure from Minos, Polyidus reluctantly shared with Glaucus his technique for resurrection. Minos made sure Polyidus wasn't cheating him on that; he killed a heifer and left Glaucus alone with it (Polyidus had managed, at least, to convince Minos to leave the chamber, telling him that the miracle wouldn't work in the presence of ordinary people). To Minos's delight, when he returned, the heifer was alive and eating grain from Glaucus's palm.

And so the day finally came when Polyidus was permitted to leave Crete. More gold and jewels were handed over. He and his pupil stood at the palace gates, saying goodbye.

"Glaucus, my child, I have a request that will seem odd to you, but your faithful teacher requests it nonetheless," said Polyidus. "Spit into my mouth."

Puzzled but obedient, Glaucus spat, and in doing so unknowingly returned to Polyidus all the knowledge that he'd acquired. When, later that day, Minos asked Glaucus to perform the resurrection trick for some guests, using Minos's best-loved hunting dog as its star, Polyidus's perfidy became horribly clear.

45
MINOS AND SCYLLA

Once the palace gates had closed behind him, Polyidus fled as fast as he could. Running to the harbor, he jumped aboard a ship that was just casting off and pressed gold into the captain's hand. He disappeared below deck and didn't emerge until the rolling of the ship assured him they were on the open sea.

On the second morning, he awoke to the sight of Aegina and then Salamis passing by; soon, they'd reached the harbor of Megara. The city was ruled by Nisus, the brother of King Aegeus of Athens. Upon hearing the seer's story, Nisus agreed to accept him as a suppliant and give him sanctuary.

And none too quickly. Minos learned from his harbormaster that Polyidus had boarded a Megarian ship. He quickly assembled the navy for which Crete was famous—powerful, sleek and swift—and set out in pursuit. By evening of the day on which Polyidus had arrived, a messenger announced that an ominous ring of Cretan ships was lying to anchor in the Saronic Gulf. At dawn the next morning, the ships disgorged soldiers into rowboats and they beached on the plain before the city. The battle began.

For six months, neither side could seize victory. Polyidus, crouching in the palace, sacrificed animal after animal, searching their entrails for some encouraging message from the gods, but the entrails remained unremarkable; the gods weren't speaking.

Eventually, it was Hera's anger that decided the matter. One day, Nisus's daughter Scylla, while worshipping at Hera's temple, joyfully allowed Boreas to blow her robes here and there, untying her sash to more fully enjoy the north wind's caress. Her silken garments billowed up in the air, revealing her slender legs. Hera was incensed and frightened; it was sights like this that were likely to arouse her husband, Zeus.

And so Hera infected Scylla with the cruelest madness she could think of, turning the girl's heart towards Minos. Once the illness took hold, Scylla climbed each morning to the parapet above the city's gate to gaze down upon her father's enemy. Taller than most men, Minos stood out from the crowd as he strode through the Cretan encampment, exhorting his soldiers. His voice was deep, like an earthquake rumbling in the distance, and so resonant that even her distant ears caught its words.

His menacing persistence fascinated her. Six months encamped through heat and rain: this was not a man to be dissuaded from what he was determined to have. And there, Scylla realized, lay her chance, for she shared a secret known to very few.

Above her father's forehead grew a lock of crimson hair, bright against the muted gray of his middle age. When Nisus was born, the Fates had told his mother, Pylia, that upon this single lock depended the child's own safety and the safety of his city, too. As long as it remained intact, all would be well. If it were cut, all would be lost.

Pylia had kept the lock clipped firmly to the crown of her son's head, fastening it there with a golden clasp shaped like a cicada, the emblem of the royal Athenian line. As he grew, Nisus continued that practice. Decades later, the unshorn lock coiled upon his head like some languid Phrygian cap, the cicada scarcely visible beneath the luxuriant weight of the hair.

What Scylla did, in the silence of the night, was but the work of a moment. Her knife was sharp; her father, fatigued from battle, was deeply asleep. Grasping the lock near its roots—but not so near as to wake the sleeper—she severed it.

Quickly stuffing her trophy into the folds of her bodice, she scurried down to the courtyard and out through a kitchen gate. Soon, she announced herself at the Cretan camp and was led into Minos's tent.

Blushing and stammering, staring at the ground because she found herself unable to look upon the face she had gazed at so often from afar, Scylla explained who she was and what she'd done out of love for him. She was delivering her city into Minos's hands, she said, as surely as she was delivering her father's hair. She handed the lock to him then—limp, damp and tangled from rubbing against her skin as she ran.

"Bitch!" shouted Minos, throwing the hair to the ground. "How could you betray your own father? Never would I allow a creature such as you to touch me or to step onto the sacred island of Crete. Guards—remove her from my sight but keep her close at hand."

And then Minos, who however much he detested his benefactor didn't hesitate to make use of her gift, led a nighttime raid on Megara. The city, lacking its talisman, fell quickly. Nisus became a prisoner, to be taken back to Crete and displayed. Polyidus, the cause of all the trouble, was nowhere to be found.

The next day, Minos's ships were laden with spoils, ready to set sail towards home. One final matter remained to be addressed, however. Minos ordered Scylla to be brought forward.

"Tie her to the stern of my ship. She'll journey to Crete watching her homeland recede before her eyes—until the waves make an end of her, that is. And bring her father up on deck so he can hear her cries."

Up and down plunged the ship, dipping Scylla in and out of the water. The dolphins stared as she passed and the Nereids wondered at this strange new sight. At last Amphitrite, Poseidon's wife, noticed the commotion and swam over to learn its cause. She took pity on the girl—bedraggled and nearly dead—and transformed her into a seabird, the ciris.

But as the new bird flew into the skies, exulting in her freedom, Zeus, who always takes the father's side, saw what was happening and turned Nisus into a sea eagle. Forever after, the father chased his daughter, never catching her but never relenting, over the gray and boundless waters.

46
PASIPHAË AND THE BULL

At the time that Zeus disguised himself as a bull and swam to Crete with Europa on his back, the island was ruled by King Asterius. After Zeus had sired three sons upon Europa, Asterius married her and became stepfather to her children, whom he raised as his own. When Asterius died, his oldest stepson, Minos, inherited his throne.

Some local noblemen, however, complained that Minos's paternity was unproven and his kingship, therefore, was illegitimate. To prove that his sovereignty was divinely sanctioned, Minos announced that the gods would give him anything he wanted. Then he prayed to Poseidon, asking that the god send from the sea a bull that was as large and as absolutely white as the one whose form Zeus had taken on when he kidnapped Europa.

Poseidon responded; a huge bull suddenly charged from the waves onto the beach, snorting and shaking the salt water from his milk-white face. Minos's challengers were silenced and his kingship was secured.

According to the terms of the relationship between gods and mortals, when the gods gave a splendid gift to a mortal, the gift should in turn be shared with the gods themselves. The white bull, therefore, should have been sacrificed and the meat divided in the manner that Prometheus had long ago established at Mecone. Minos's greed was kindled by the thought of the calves that such a magnificent animal would sire, however, and so Poseidon's gift was led not to the altar but to the royal pastures to serve as stud.

Poseidon, furious, was determined to avenge himself. With Aphrodite's help, he contrived a cruel and brutal punishment. The immediate weight of it would fall upon Minos's wife, Pasiphaë, rather than Minos himself, but Poseidon didn't care: Minos would also be humiliated and burdened as the scheme unfolded.

Pasiphaë had already endured a great deal as Minos's wife, long before Poseidon became angry, for Minos was as lustful as his father and bedded any girl he pleased. Eventually, when Pasiphaë could no longer tolerate the situation, she came up with a plan to stop her husband's philandering. Drawing on her knowledge of magic—a knowledge she shared with her sister, Circe, and her brother, Aeëtes—Pasiphaë had concocted a spell that caused Minos to ejaculate scorpions, serpents and centipedes. His partners, stung and bitten in their tenderest parts, died horrible deaths. Word of Minos's condition spread quickly, bringing his love affairs to an end.

Eventually, Procris, an Athenian princess, taught Minos how to neutralize the spell and his eye began to wander again. But in any case, once Poseidon and Aphrodite set their plan in motion, Pasiphaë had bigger problems to worry about than her husband's infidelity, for Aphrodite infected Pasiphaë with a lust greater than any Minos had ever experienced and directed it not towards a human or a god but rather towards the great white bull that now reigned over Minos's pastures.

Pasiphaë yearned for the beast's embrace—if embrace it could be called. She no longer took any pleasure in food and her once voluptuous body withered into gauntness. Each day, she climbed a tower overlooking the pasture and gazed down upon the bull; each night, when she dreamt, her desire played itself out in ways that disgusted her when she awoke. How lucky Europa had been, she thought, to wed a bull who was no longer a bull!

Pasiphaë fell into despair. Then one morning, while making her daily walk to the tower, she glimpsed Daedalus, an ingenious man whom Minos had recently accepted as a suppliant. Daedalus had designed a marvelous circular dancing floor for Pasiphaë's daughter Ariadne and various clever devices for Minos himself. It occurred to Pasiphaë that his talents might somehow solve her own problem. Drawing him aside and swearing him to secrecy, she explained the situation.

Daedalus retreated to his workshop and began to carve a statue of a cow out of limewood. So skillful was his imitation that flies buzzed through the workshop's window and tried to bite its flesh. Verisimilitude stopped at the ends of the statue's legs, however, where Daedalus put wheels instead of hooves, in order to more easily move the creature from place to place.

The statue differed from a real cow in other ways, as well. It was hollow, with a trapdoor in its belly. And, where he'd carved that part of the cow that would most interest a bull, Daedalus had drilled a hole through the wood. When the statue was finished, Daedalus slaughtered a heifer who had just gone into heat. He flayed her, taking care to keep every inch of her skin intact. He stretched it smoothly over his wooden cow, aligning the skin of the heifer's genitals with the hole that he'd drilled.

Pasiphaë crawled, naked, into Daedalus's creation and Daedalus wheeled her out into the pasture and retreated. A moment later, she was screaming—whether in pleasure or in pain, Daedalus couldn't tell. Either way, the bull was quick and the matter swiftly concluded.

Nine months later, Pasiphaë bore a child. Had she not been the daughter of Helios and almost a goddess herself, she would have died in labor. Indeed, even so, Pasiphaë begged for death as the child passed into the light, for although he was human from the neck down, his head and face were entirely those of a bull, with horns as sharp as his father's. Pasiphaë named him Asterius, but as news of the child's true nature seeped out of the palace and spread across the island, the people took to calling him the Minotaur, the "bull of Minos."

As for Minos, he was just as humiliated as Poseidon and Aphrodite had intended him to be. Discovering Daedalus's part in the affair, he demanded that the craftsman make amends by building a prison from which Asterius could never escape. This was what came to be called the Labyrinth—a torturous maze of dark corridors. The poor bull-boy was thrust through a trapdoor in its roof and never saw sunlight again.

47
DAEDALUS AND ICARUS

Daedalus had fled to Crete in the first place because he'd tried to kill his nephew, Perdix.

The two were living in Athens—they were cousins of King Aegeus—and Perdix had been apprenticed to Daedalus to learn how to carve and build. One day, while walking along the seashore, Perdix saw the spine of a fish lying on the sand and was inspired by its serrations to invent the saw. A few weeks later, Perdix invented the potter's wheel. Clearly, the student would soon surpass the teacher.

Envy grew like a weed in Daedalus's heart, crowding out all of his affection for Perdix. Eventually, maddened by jealousy, he pushed the boy off the top of a tower. Athena, seeing Perdix fall, turned him into a partridge before he hit the ground; he flew safely away as Daedalus gaped at the miracle, relieved and ashamed. Grabbing his baby son, Icarus, Daedalus sailed for Crete before Perdix's parents could ask him where Perdix was.

Years later, after constructing the Labyrinth and many other wondrous things for Minos, Daedalus asked for passage back to the mainland. Minos, however, was no more willing to release Daedalus than he'd been to release Polyidus. He commanded the harbormaster to prevent Daedalus from boarding any ship.

Daedalus's fertile mind never stopped working, however. While pacing the beach one day, he noticed feathers lying on the sand, shed by the seagulls that circled the bay. They inspired in Daedalus a plan for escaping through the air—after all, Minos might rule the seas but he didn't rule the skies.

Daedalus spent several days gathering feathers and sorting them according to size. With the help of some beeswax and cedar wood, he constructed wings that looked just like those of gulls except larger, made for a man. He made another, smaller pair for Icarus, who was now eight years old and kept his father company while he worked, chasing stray feathers around the workroom.

Then began a period of learning how to use the marvelous devices. From a hummock on a deserted stretch of beach, the father and son practiced launching, gliding and steering until they were as adept as the birds themselves. Repeatedly, Daedalus cautioned his son about the ephemeral nature of the materials from which their wings were made.

"Don't fly too high, Icarus; if you do, the sun will melt the wax that holds the feathers to the frame and you'll crash, featherless, into the sea. But don't fly too low, either, lest the salt spray cling to your feathers, weighing down the wings and dragging you beneath the waves. Stick to the middle! Be moderate! Follow closely behind me and you'll be fine."

And Icarus, who always tried, at least, to be obedient even if he didn't always succeed, said, "Yes, Papa."

The day came when Daedalus judged the winds to be perfect for their trip, and the two set off from a promontory overlooking the sea. The experience was exhilarating in a way that the practice sessions never had been. For the first time, humans moved through the air as freely as birds!

Initially content with that excitement, Icarus followed his father closely as they headed across the waters towards Sicily. But though obedient, Icarus was also young. Eventually, he forgot his father's warnings and began to chase the gulls, which squawked in alarm. Alerted by the noise, Daedalus looked over his shoulder.

"Child, stop fooling around!"

Icarus, however, was too far away to hear these words. Pursuing a gull, he climbed higher and higher until the inevitable happened. The wax of his wings began to soften and one by one, small feathers dropped off their tips. Some of the larger feathers dropped off too, and Icarus began to lose altitude. Even then, he could have saved himself, had he kept his wits about him, but in his panic he flapped harder, screaming, "Papa, Papa!" and jarring yet more feathers from their softened bed.

At last he had too few feathers left to keep himself aloft. He plummeted into the sea, just off the bow of an elegant ship that was sailing by. Its passengers saw something large and strange fall into the water, but no one could fathom what it was. A few days later, Icarus's body washed up on the shores of a nearby island, where Daedalus buried it, naming the place Icaria. Then Daedalus continued onwards to Sicily, heartbroken but free (or so he thought) of Minos's grasp. He was accepted as a suppliant at the court of King Cocalus.

Minos hunted for Daedalus relentlessly, however, determined to drag him back to Crete. Having failed to find him by ordinary means, Minos resolved to trick him into revealing his whereabouts. He devised a challenge that he was confident only Daedalus could meet, and had heralds announce it in every kingdom, promising an ample reward to whoever solved it.

The challenge was to pass a thread round and round through the spirals of a conch shell and then out a hole drilled in the top. Cocalus, whose treasuries were almost empty, was eager to collect the reward and sought Daedalus's help.

"It's easy," said Daedalus. "Bring me an ant." And then, having tied a thread to the ant's leg, Daedalus gently nudged the tiny creature into a shell's spiral as deeply as his fingers could reach. The ant disappeared into its chambers and then, sure enough, crawled out the top a few minutes later, pulling the thread behind it.

Delighted, Cocalus sent for Minos and Minos arrived. He inspected the shell and immediately said, "Give me Daedalus or the Cretan navy will attack Sicily tomorrow."

But Daedalus had prepared Cocalus for this contingency. "My lord," Cocalus said to Minos, "bathe and rest tonight. Tomorrow, we'll settle this problem."

And so Minos was led away to the palace baths, where Cocalus's daughters awaited him. Grunting with the aches of middle age, he eased himself into a gold-plated tub, closed his eyes and relaxed, anticipating the moment when the girls would pour jugfuls of warm water over his body. But it had been Daedalus who filled the jugs, and he had used boiling water, not warm. Minos screamed and thrashed, and then fell still, as red as a lobster prepared for the table and just as dead.

Surely, thought Daedalus, I'm finally free! Joyously, he boarded a ship for Athens. Stepping from the gangplank at the end of his voyage, he started up a familiar path. Just then a bird burst up from a muddy ditch, flapping his wings and taunting Daedalus with jeering cries. It was a partridge, who had long awaited his uncle's return, and who never left him in peace again.

48
PROCNE AND PHILOMELA

Ares was not a god who mated with mortal women very often, but when he did, he liked to settle the sons born from those unions in the wild lands to the north, where people worshipped him at least as much as they worshipped Zeus.

One of these sons was Tereus, who ruled over a tribe in Thrace. He was an excellent warrior, cut from his father's cloth. When King Pandion of Athens was engaged in a border skirmish with the Thebans, he called upon Tereus for help. When the battle was won, Pandion gave his daughter Procne to Tereus in marriage. Hymen, the god who blessed weddings, refused to accompany the new husband and wife to their bridal chamber, however, sensing trouble ahead; the Erinyes waited for them there instead, unseen.

The day after the wedding, the couple sailed for Thrace. Procne wept as she bid farewell to her younger sister, Philomela, from whom she had never before been parted.

Soon, Procne had a baby to distract her: Itys, a lovely son who had been conceived on the voyage home. Nonetheless, as the years went by, Procne found herself yearning for Philomela. Eventually, she prevailed upon Tereus to sail to Athens and ask Pandion to allow Philomela to return with him for a visit. Philomela, who missed Procne as much as Procne missed her, rejoiced at the idea as soon as Tereus presented it. She wrapped her arms around her father's neck, begging him to agree, and he did.

What Philomela didn't know was that as soon as Tereus had seen her—a woman now, rather than the girl he'd glimpsed at the wedding years before—he was inflamed with lust. He kept himself in check while they were aboard ship, where the eyes of the sailors saw everything, but as soon as they had landed in Thrace, he led Philomela to a hut in the woods, shut the door and prepared to rape her.

She wept, she pleaded, she begged him to respect the bonds of family, but lust deafened him to everything she said. He ripped the combs from her hair and the robes from her body; he pushed her to the floor.

When he was done, Philomela began to scream, imploring the gods to avenge her. Enraged by her audacity, Tereus seized her throat with one enormous hand. Philomela choked and gagged and turned purple; her tongue protruded, so he seized that, too. Releasing her throat but retaining her tongue in his vise-like grip, he yanked his knife from its sheath. He severed the tongue and threw it to the floor, where it wriggled, for a moment, like a mangled snake.

Then he left, locking the door behind him. He went home and, weeping crocodile tears, told Procne that Philomela had died at sea. Over the months that followed, he sent a trusted slave to feed Philomela each day, never revealing who the poor, mute woman really was. He visited her himself sometimes, too, to satisfy his appetites.

Eventually, Philomela prevailed upon him, through gestures and imploring eyes, to bring her a loom, so that she could fill her lonely hours by weaving. His mercy in that matter was his undoing, for Philomela wove a tapestry depicting all that had happened to her. When it was finished, she bundled it up and asked the slave to deliver it to the Thracian queen. Let her enjoy it, Philomela indicated with gestures and smiles, lest it languish in the woods unappreciated forever.

When Procne unfolded the tapestry, she understood its message at once. Emotions flooded her heart: relief that her sister was alive, horror at what had been done to her, hatred of Tereus and a burning desire for revenge.

It happened to be the time of year when Thracian women celebrated Dionysus in nocturnal rituals. Procne dressed herself in the deerskin tunic that Dionysus found pleasing, twined the god's favorite vines into her hair and took up a thyrsus—the god's sacred staff.

Feigning the ecstasy that Dionysus bestows on his worshippers, Procne wandered away from her friends, into the forest. She dashed to the hut and beat her thyrsus against its door until the rotting wood gave way. Quickly draping her sister in deerskin and vines like her own, Procne led her back to the other women, who by now were fully in the god's grasp, dancing and shrieking *euhoe! Euhoe!*, the victory cry of Dionysus. As dawn broke, Philomela slipped into the palace, unnoticed among the exhausted celebrants. Once the sisters were alone, Philomela wept and used her hands to express her shame at having transgressed Procne's marriage bed. But Procne, seething with rage, declared, "*You* have no need for shame and this is no time for tears—it's the sword that we need, or something stronger, if we can find it. Shall I sever Tereus's tongue when next he comes to my bed? Or shall we kill and dismember him then?"

As Procne was speaking, Itys wandered into his mother's chamber. Crawling onto her lap, he tried to kiss away her tears as she had so often kissed away his own. Procne's heart began to soften—what sort of life would Itys have if she killed his father and they were exiled from Thrace? But then she thought of her own father and what had been done to his children. Her resolve grew stronger and a better plan entered her mind. Taking Itys in her arms and warning him not to make any noise, she set out for the palace's wine cellar. She whispered to Philomela, who scurried along behind.

Itys, who was an obedient child, was quiet until they entered the cellar itself, where the light of the torches, leaping here and there on the rough-hewn walls, created monstrous shadows. In terror, he clung to Procne, crying, "Mama, Mama!" but Philomela pried him away and held him fast. Procne drew from her belt the knife that she had used the night before to cut vines in honor of the god. It served equally well for a deed that the god would deplore. Procne stabbed Itys, letting his blood run out upon the floor where it mixed with puddles of wine that had been spilled when the casks were breached the evening before.

The sisters butchered the small body and boiled and roasted its flesh. They arranged the choicest cuts on a tray, which Procne carried to her husband.

"That was delicious, Wife," said Tereus, after finishing his meal. "Now, where is my son? Bring him to me."

"He's already with you," she replied, signaling to Philomela, who emerged from the shadows carrying a smaller tray, on which were arranged the hands, feet and head of the child whom Tereus had consumed. The father bellowed and lunged for the women, invoking the same Erinyes who had watched over his wedding night.

Sometimes, the gods grant what they call pity, even to those who do not merit it. Before Tereus could catch the sisters, Procne became a nightingale, singing mournfully for the child she'd killed, and Philomela a swallow, who scarcely sings at all. Tereus became a hoopoe with a helmet of blood-red feathers. Forevermore he chased the sisters and forevermore they fled, eternally circling in hatred and fear.

49
SALMACIS AND HERMAPHRODITUS

Over the centuries that followed her emergence from the sea, Aphrodite slept with most of the gods, and her lovemaking was never barren. No one was surprised, therefore, that her tryst with Hermes produced a child, but even Aphrodite herself was stunned

by the boy's exceptional beauty. The parents, each of whom took pride in their son's appearance, agreed to name him Hermaphroditus and then delivered him to the nymphs of Mount Ida to be raised.

At the age of fifteen, Hermaphroditus left the mountain and struck out to see the world. Driven by curiosity, he visited many strange peoples and places. Wherever he went, however, he was welcomed: on his face, Hermes's cunning had been softened into a ready smile and Aphrodite's beauty had relaxed into friendly charm.

One day, when passing through a forest on the coast of Caria, Hermaphroditus happened upon a pool whose water was so still and clear that it nearly seemed not to be there. Its banks were free from reeds and rushes; soft green grass ran down to its lips. It was as if the pool were waiting among the trees for someone to arrive and something to happen.

The pool was the home of a nymph named Salmacis, who spent part of each day submerged in its waters and the other part lounging indolently in the shade of the trees, arranging and rearranging her hair with boxwood combs. From time to time, she strolled back to her pool and gazed at the effects in its mirror-like surface. When Hermaphroditus appeared in the clearing, she happened to be among the trees, picking violets to tuck behind her ears. As soon as she saw the beautiful young man, she yearned to possess him. She paused long enough to smooth the creases from the garment she wore—if "garment" were the right term for something that was nearly as translucent as her waters themselves—and then approached Hermaphroditus.

"You look like a god, stranger! And if you're not, then I envy the woman who gave birth to you, the nurse who suckled you and the sister who shared your childhood games. But even more, I envy your wife . . . that is, if you have one? If you don't, then I'll marry you myself, right here! And if you do—well, no matter; she's far away and what she doesn't know won't hurt her. Come, lie down with me now!"

Hermaphroditus blushed and backed away. "Leave me alone! I broke my journey to bathe in this pool, but I can find another!"

That was the last thing Salmacis wanted. She withdrew into the trees and hid, trying to think of what to do next. She watched Hermaphroditus undress and imagined what his skin would feel like next to hers. She saw him walk into her pool and, sighing with pleasure at its coolness, begin to float on his back.

"Oh gods," she murmured as she crept out of the trees, "let there never be another hour that the two of us are kept apart!"

Hermaphroditus's eyes were closed against the sun; he didn't see her discard her clothes and slip into the pond. Nor did he see her body dissolve into the water as easily as smoke dissipates into air. When she resumed her womanly form a moment later, she was next to him. She stroked his slippery body; she kissed his wet lips. Hermaphroditus struggled, but her hands were everywhere at once, like the tentacles of an octopus. He could not escape their entangling embrace.

And then, as when honey is stirred into wine, Hermaphroditus's body began to melt into the water. He tried to wrest himself free, but found that he no longer had a self to command—no arms or legs to carry him to safety, no mouth to pray to his parents for help.

When he once again perceived himself to be embodied, the body was not his. Or rather, it was not *only* his. Soft breasts now cushioned his chest, and behind that part of him that should engender children was another part that should receive the engendering. Hermaphroditus was neither male nor female but both at once, inextricably merged with the nymph who had desired him.

"Why are you so cruel, aunts, uncles, grandparents—*gods*?" he shrieked in a high-pitched voice, stretching newly softened hands towards the heavens. "And you, Father and Mother! Did you stand by and laugh as someone did this to me? Avenge me! If Hermaphroditus is now to be gossiped about, then let this nymph be a matter for gossip, too—or what is left of her. Let her waters be cursed; let no man dare to touch them again lest he, like me, become no man at all."

His parents answered his prayer and carried out his curse. In later years, a great city, Halicarnassus, arose nearby, but no man ever again sought pleasure in Salmacis's waters.

50
PYGMALION AND THE STATUE

After Aphrodite emerged from the sea at the time of her birth, she drifted to the shore of Cyprus, an island that she forever after claimed as her home. It was on Cyprus that the Graces bathed and anointed her and on Cyprus that she adorned herself before setting out to enjoy the embraces of gods and men.

It was particularly distressing for Aphrodite to learn, therefore, that the daughters of Propoetus, a Cypriot man, were denying that she even existed. Shaking with fury, she designed an exquisite revenge. First, she hardened their hearts against the pleasures of love and planted there instead the idea that they might sell their favors. They became the first women to peddle themselves, competing with one another for the grubby gold that men clutched in their hands. Once they had thoroughly degraded themselves, Aphrodite hardened their bodies, as well. Cold and immobile, they became flinty monuments of disgrace.

Pygmalion, a Cypriot sculptor, watched all of this unfold and was appalled that women could act so scandalously. Fearing that all of them were the same, he swore that he would never bring a wife into his home.

But moral superiority is a lonely pedestal, from which occupants are apt to tumble. In spite of his resolve, Pygmalion found himself dreaming of women. And then one day, in a reverie of desire, he took up a block of snow-white marble and began to carve one. Its features and shape were those of a virgin—soft, young and modest. So skillfully did Pygmalion carve that his creation looked as if it were about to move; one leg was slightly bent, as if ready to step forward, a subtle crease behind its knee.

Each day, Pygmalion draped his statue in silks of different colors, adding a band to support its breasts—hardly necessary for breasts carved from marble, but a lovely adornment all the same. He brought it the sort of gifts that would delight a girl: seashells he'd found on the beach, flowers he'd picked in the meadows, drops of amber to dangle from its ears, silver rings set with opals to sweeten its dreams.

When night fell, he lay the statue on his bed, cushioning it with pillows covered by fabrics dipped in costly dyes. He kissed it and pretended that his kisses were returned. He stroked its body, so convinced it was real that he feared his ardor might leave bruises. He fell asleep each night in the comfort of its presence.

The months circled round and the day of Aphrodite's greatest festival arrived. A hundred heifers with gilded horns were sacrificed to the goddess. The aromas of roasting meat and incense rose from her altars. Pygmalion made his own small offering, and as he did so, he prayed, "Lady Aphrodite, Queen of Cyprus, if, as they say, you grant lovers' wishes, then grant that I may have as a bride . . ." He paused in embarrassment at what he'd almost said. He thought again and then continued, ". . . a woman *like* my marble statue."

Aphrodite heard and answered his prayer. When Pygmalion returned to his house, he went to his bed, on which he'd left his statue. Leaning over, he kissed it, as he always did upon returning home.

Her lips felt warm and soft; disbelieving what he perceived, he touched her breast—it was warm and soft as well. Little by little, all the marble yielded to his touch just as beeswax yields to an artisan's fingers, becoming suppler as he handles it.

In his joy, Pygmalion kissed her again and was surprised to have his kiss returned. Then the statue sat up, rubbed the sleep from her eyes and smiled at her creator.

Together they walked to Aphrodite's temple and thanked her for the gifts she had bestowed—a wife for one and life for the other. Nine months later, Pygmalion's creation created, bringing forth a boy, Paphos.

51
MYRRHA AND ADONIS

Paphos had a son named Cinyras, who became the king of Cyprus and married Cenchreis. Cenchreis bore him a daughter, Myrrha, who grew up to be as beautiful as her great-grandmother, Pygmalion's statue. Her hair was a burnished red and her eyes were green—the very colors that Pygmalion had painted on his marble woman.

Many men asked for Myrrha's hand in marriage but to her parents' dismay, she refused them all. The cause—which no one knew—was a curse that Aphrodite had laid upon the girl after Cenchreis had boasted that Myrrha was more beautiful than the goddess herself. In revenge, Aphrodite had infected Myrrha with a virulent lust for her own father.

Poor Myrrha! She had no one to whom she dared confide such a shameful problem, and nowhere to seek a cure for the passion that surged through her body. She lay on her bed with her her arms wrapped tightly around her knees, as if trying to stifle the disease. She fasted, she prayed, she made sacrifices to all the gods. She tried to distract herself with spinning and weaving. Nonetheless, her mind kept wandering to what she had observed while visiting her father's stables and pastures. Animals paid no heed to the strictures that humans had invented. She saw bulls mating with the heifers that they had fathered the previous spring and goats expending their lust upon daughters, sisters and even mothers.

And she knew from the poets who visited her father's court that there were human tribes at the borders of the world for whom the terms "father" and "daughter" blurred easily into "husband" and "wife." What of the gods themselves, moreover? Hadn't Earth taken to bed her sons Sky and Sea? Hadn't Zeus fathered Dionysus upon his own daughter? Why should humans be the only group in which parent and child were so cruelly separated?

With each month that passed, her parents grew more perplexed by Myrrha's refusal to marry. One evening, Cinyras put his arm around his daughter's waist and pulled her close.

"I wish to see you happy, Myrrha. What sort of husband would please you? Tell me and I'll find the man."

Faint in the pleasure of his embrace, Myrrha stammered out an answer. "One just like you, Father."

He kissed her on the forehead. "What a good and loving daughter I have!" At the word "loving," she blushed with desire; at the word "good," she burned with shame at how far from good she really felt herself to be.

One night, her endurance finally failed and concealment came to an end. Unable to bear her predicament any longer, she threw a length of cloth over a beam in her bedroom and tied the end around her neck. Just as she was about to step off the chair upon which she stood, ending her life in the ugliest of ways, her old nurse entered the room.

"Child! What are you doing!" she screamed, lifting the noose from Myrrha's neck.

Myrrha wept, collapsing into her arms. Then, with a little urging, the whole story came out.

". . . So you understand now why I must die," Myrrha concluded.

"Live, child! I will find a way for you to sleep with your . . ." The nurse's tongue refused to shape the word "father"; ". . . with your beloved."

An opportunity soon arose. The festival of Demeter arrived, a time when married women sequestered themselves for several days, leaving their husbands to amuse themselves as best they could. The nurse approached Cinyras one evening after he had drunk enough to be pliant and whispered that a slave girl had fallen in love with him. Too bashful to approach the king herself, she had sent the nurse to ask Cinyras whether she might join him in bed that night.

The king agreed. The nurse went on to explain that the girl's shyness required that the bedroom be absolutely dark and then led the stumbling man to his unlit chamber. After Cinyras lay down, Myrrha slipped into bed beside him. She trembled and he calmed what he took to be the natural fears of a virgin by promising to be gentle. She kept her silence, afraid that her voice would give her away, and awaited what she had dreamt of for so long.

The deed was done—and done again on subsequent nights.

Eventually, Cinyras became curious as to who this ardent yet mysterious girl was. After they had finished making love one night when the moon was full, he slipped out of bed and went over to the window, which the nurse had covered with a heavy curtain. Pulling the fabric aside, he forced the moon to reveal his daughter and his guilt. Horrified, he snatched his sword and tried to kill Myrrha, intending to follow her into death himself.

But Myrrha escaped and ran from the palace. Wandering eastwards for many months, she eventually came to Arabia. By then, her pregnant belly was huge with the shame she carried. At last, tired of life but afraid to die, she prayed to the gods for mercy and they listened.

Myrrha's legs sank into the soil and her toes grew long and sinuous as they explored the dirt. Her waist, although still burdened with her child, grew longer, and her arms reached towards the sky, becoming sturdy branches.

Myrrha was now a small but lovely tree. She wept then, with both remorse and relief, and her tears, trickling through her bark, became a fragrant resin—the myrrh that mortals soon began to burn in honor of the gods. When her son was ready to be born, Myrrha's bark split open to release him into the arms of the nymphs who attended her labor. They named him Adonis.

Sometimes, the actions of the gods travel down paths that even they cannot foresee. Adonis, conceived by Aphrodite's curse, doubly inherited, from both his mother and his father, the beauty of the statue that Aphrodite had once brought to life for Pygmalion. He grew into an astonishingly handsome man, with whom Aphrodite herself fell in love. The two became inseparable. Indeed, Aphrodite swallowed her vanity and learned to wear a tunic and hunting boots so that she could accompany Adonis into the forests.

She did this out of fear, as well as love. Some years earlier, Aphrodite had contrived the death of Hippolytus, a man who was dear to Artemis, and Artemis had sworn to avenge Hippolytus's death by eventually seizing someone dear to Aphrodite. Each time that Adonis hunted, he entered Artemis's territory; Aphrodite was on constant guard for any signs of danger.

But Artemis watched patiently for a day when Aphrodite was away and goaded Adonis's dogs into rousing a boar from its lair. The matter was over before Adonis knew what was happening: white tusks punctured his groin and his blood gushed onto the ground. Aphrodite heard his cries, but even a god cannot breach time: she arrived to find Adonis dead.

Aphrodite gave Adonis what immortality she could. She poured nectar onto the bloody soil and within the hour a bright red flower sprang up—the anemone, as appealing as a lover's glance but as evanescent as a human life.

HEROES

EXTRAORDINARY MORTALS TAKE ON THE WORLD— AND THE GODS

52
DANAË AND THE SHOWER OF GOLD

The children, grandchildren and great-grandchildren of Io and Zeus scattered across the earth and had children of their own. In the seventh generation was born Abas, who was the son of Hypermnestra, the only daughter of Danaus who hadn't killed her husband on their wedding night, and Lynceus, her husband. Abas ruled over the city of Argos peacefully for many years.

But the sibling rivalry that had blighted the lives of Danaus and Egyptus still festered in the family's blood. Abas's twin sons, Proetus and Acrisius, were already quarreling in their mother's womb and they continued to quarrel once they had emerged. After a rancorous childhood and adolescence, they parted ways. Proetus became king of Tiryns and Acrisius stayed behind on their father's throne.

Acrisius's problems were far from over, however. His wife soon bore a daughter, Danaë. Acrisius sent envoys to Apollo's oracle at Delphi to inquire about how he could sire a son, too. Apollo said nothing about that, but he did reveal, to Acrisius's shock, that his future grandson—a son whom Danaë would bear—would one day kill him.

Acrisius quickly contrived a way to trick the oracle—or so he thought. He ordered his men to dig a deep hole in the middle of the palace courtyard and to lower into it a huge vessel made of bronze—high enough inside to stand up in and large enough to include several rooms.

Pushing aside his sobbing wife, Acrisius lowered tiny Danaë and her nurse into the vessel. He slammed shut the hatch in the top and told the workers to shovel dirt back in around it. The hatch, which peeped out of the earth, would be opened only by him—he himself would pass down the food, water and copious amounts of lamp oil that his prisoners' subterranean existence would require. Acrisius felt certain that by taking these precautions, he had confounded the oracle. After all, how could anyone even fall in love with an unseen Danaë, much less impregnate her?

Yet gods forge paths that humans cannot foresee. Danaë grew up a happy girl, never yearning for the upper world because she had no recollection of it. She grew up to be beautiful as well, in spite of her captivity. Her skin was whiter than alabaster—whiter, even, than Aphrodite's skin—because the sun had never touched it. When a stray lock of her black hair fell against her neck, it was as if a raven's feather had drifted onto the snow. Her lips, which the wind had never chapped, were perfectly soft and red. It was inevitable that Zeus would discover such exquisiteness—bronze and soil are no impediment for divine eyes—and once he had, he was determined to have Danaë.

Zeus prided himself on pleasing his partners—whenever possible, at least, and for as long as was convenient for him. He had delighted Europa's eyes as a white bull striding through a field of flowers; he had stroked Leda's knees as a swan; he had embraced a flattered Callisto while disguised as Artemis. But Danaë had seen no animals before and no humans, either, other than her nurse. She would be terrified by the sudden epiphany of any creature, however lovely it might be. Zeus thought carefully about what to do.

One day, a shimmering cloud of golden dust appeared before Danaë's eyes. It glittered in the lamplight, changing shape from this to that, teasing her when she reached out to touch it by darting away and then returning. At last it paused long enough for the girl to draw near. Immersing her hands in its warmth, she let the gold flow through her fingers like water, marveling at its unexpected weight. She sat down and gathered a mass of it into her lap, mounding it into gleaming hills and valleys.

Suddenly, though, the gold billowed and heaved, caressing her abdomen, kissing her neck and trickling down between her breasts. Danaë laughed at the absurdity of the thing, whatever it was. But then it crept beneath her dress and between her legs. Now she felt not warmth but heat, and found herself pressed back against her couch.

And then, all at once, it was gone, departing as mysteriously as it had arrived.

Nine months later, Danaë gave birth to Perseus, a joyous gift whom she and her nurse adored and nurtured in their bronze prison, taking care that the child never had reason to cry and betray his presence. One day, however, he laughed. His grandfather happened to be approaching the hatch with the week's provisions; bewildered, he yanked it open. Peering into the gloom, Acrisius discovered Perseus.

The nurse was summarily executed. Danaë, with Perseus in her arms, was shunted from her bronze chamber to a wooden chest no larger than that which had once held Deucalion and Pyrrha at the time of the Flood. Acrisius's men heaved it into a boat and, ignoring Danaë's desperate pleas, rowed it out into the sea, where they pushed it overboard.

Acrisius congratulated himself. He assumed that he'd guaranteed the death of Danaë and her son without actually killing them. Strictly speaking, his hands were clean. He tried to forget all about his unfortunate daughter and grandson.

The chest bobbed and floated across the waves. Danaë, although terrified by what she, too, assumed was imminent death, focused on keeping Perseus happy. Holding him close, she crooned him to sleep and when he awoke, she made a game of the seabirds that circled and swooped overhead.

Several days went by. Danaë grew ever hungrier and was beginning to hope that death would come soon when, in the distance, she saw an island rise on the horizon. Zeus ordered the winds to guide the chest towards its shore. A fisherman spotted the chest and with a cast of his net brought Danaë and Perseus onto the beach of Seriphus.

53
POLYDECTES AND THE GORGON'S HEAD

Dictys, the fisherman who had rescued Danaë and Perseus, was a kind man. Appalled by what Danaë told him of her adventures, he offered the pair his home and his protection. As the years went by, he helped to raise Perseus and taught him to fish, although Dictys knew that one day Perseus would have to take his place among aristocratic men.

Dictys was not a complete stranger to that crowd. His own brother, Polydectes, had risen to become the king of Seriphus. One day, when the king was paying a visit to his brother's cottage, he glimpsed Danaë kneading bread. By now, the sun had burnished her skin to a healthier hue, making her even more beautiful than when Zeus had first glimpsed her.

"Brother! You've found yourself a most wonderful wife!" exclaimed Polydectes.

"No—not a wife but a helpmeet all the same. She and her son were castaways, brought to my door by the waves."

"Indeed! Well, wherever she comes from, her bearing suggests good blood. Perhaps, then, *I* have found a wife!"

The courtship that ensued pleased no one but Polydectes himself. It didn't please Dictys, who knew that his brother was a short-tempered and imperious man, and it didn't please Danaë, who after a life of dark captivity was quite happy to remain where she was on the seashore.

For many months, Danaë and Dictys did everything they could to forestall the king's wooing. Meanwhile, Perseus grew up. One day, a messenger arrived, inviting him to attend a feast at Polydectes's palace, where all the noble young men of the island would gather together. The message implied that this would mark the beginning of Perseus's ascent into the island's upper class, eventually bringing him property and power. So excited was Perseus that, with the headstrong enthusiasm of a young man, he blurted out, "Why, I'll attend that feast even if I must behead Medusa to do so!" The messenger duly carried Perseus's reply back to Polydectes, who, upon hearing it, laughed softly to himself.

On the evening of the feast, Perseus dressed in his best clothes and walked to the palace. When he arrived, he saw that the courtyard was full of well-bred foals; Polydectes had omitted to tell him that all the other guests had promised to bring a horse as a gift for their host. Perseus blushed and apologized for his ignorance—not that knowing would have made much difference, given that he had no means of buying a horse—and begged the king's pardon.

Polydectes showed his teeth in a simulacrum of a smile.

"But my dear Perseus, no apology is necessary! I didn't expect a horse from you—you promised me something far more interesting! Now: when will you be setting out to fetch me the head of the Gorgon Medusa?"

The other young men had been enjoying the spectacle that Perseus's embarrassment provided, but now their faces paled at what Polydectes had asked. All three of the Gorgons were fearsome monsters. Daughters of Ceto and Phorcys, they were reputed to be women with bronze claws, from whose backs sprang mighty eagles' wings. Where their hair should have been, there were vipers, instead. Two of these sisters were immortal but the third one, Medusa, was not; she could be killed. Something else set Medusa apart, as well: everyone, and everything, that looked at her turned to stone. For this reason alone, obtaining the head of Medusa was surely impossible. Polydectes, like Acrisius, thought he had found a way of killing Perseus without dirtying his own hands.

When the feast was over, Perseus hiked to a hill overlooking the sea and thought about what to do. Suddenly, out of the darkness where the sky met the water, a man appeared, dressed in a traveler's hat and a short cloak, holding in his right hand a staff so sinuous that Perseus gasped, thinking at first that the man held a snake. From the man's mouth came a voice as smooth as water.

"Perseus, set aside your troubles and listen to me. I am Hermes, your brother, bearing gifts from Zeus, the father we share. The first is the cap of Hades, our uncle; wear it and you will be invisible. The second is an adamantine sickle, as sharp as the one that castrated Sky. The third is this sack, made of wool so thickly woven that it will hold even a Gorgon's head. The fourth is this shield of highly polished bronze—keep it clean! You may need it. And finally," said Hermes, stooping to fiddle with the strings around his ankles, "here are my own winged sandals, to carry you through the air."

And then another shape took form out of the darkness—tall and shining, with eyes that made Perseus flinch. When it spoke, each syllable cut the air crisply.

"I am your sister Athena. Listen to me carefully, Perseus; I will tell you how to meet Polydectes's demand and fulfill your destiny as a son of Zeus.

"Only the Graeae, three nymphs who are sisters of the Gorgons, can tell you where they live—a secret they guard closely. Use my brother's sandals to travel west to Lake Tritonis. Alight there and find the cave where the Graeae dwell. Then use your wits—if you are our brother, you surely have some—to win the information you need."

Then Perseus found himself alone again, stunned but heartened. He walked home to Dictys's cottage and prepared for the next day's journey.

54
SOME WEIRD NYMPHS

These Graeae were strange creatures. Born old, they had been gray and wrinkled all their lives, never enjoying the youth and beauty that other nymphs possessed. Worse, they had but one eye and one tooth among them, which they were forced to share. The sister who had the eye at a particular moment might nab a rat as it skittered across the floor, but unless the sister who had the tooth was generous enough to pass it along, the rat nabber could not consume her prey. And vice versa: the one with the tooth might starve in blindness if the sister who had the eye was feeling selfish. The Graeae were compelled by fate to cooperate, but they did so with little grace.

Their parents, Ceto and Phorcys, had spawned many other dreadful creatures as well—Echidna was their daughter; the Hydra, the Chimera, Cerberus and the Sphinx were among their grandchildren—but the Graeae's peculiar handicaps meant that they were of little use in the world of monsters. Therefore, Ceto and Phorcys had parked them in a cave near Lake Tritonis while they were still children and left them there to fend for themselves. They were almost always alone; centuries might pass between visits from gods. Even fewer were the mortals who stumbled into their cave—and so far, those who did had never stumbled out again.

Perseus flew west to Lake Tritonis and then slogged through a swamp that surrounded it, straining to see through the vapors it sent forth. When he finally reached the cave's mouth, he pulled Hades's cap of invisibility over his head and crept in as quietly as he could. He guessed that, having been largely deprived of sight for all of their lives, the Graeae would have developed a keen ability to hear and smell the approach of strangers. The crackling of the fire around which they were huddled helped to mask his footfall, but he could do nothing about his scent, and sure enough, the closest sister, who at that moment happened to possess neither the eye nor the tooth, cried out, "Thithders! Thithders! I thmell the thwead of a mordal! Gib me the eye!" With astonishing rapidity, it was tossed into her upheld hand.

Cramming it into one of her empty sockets, she peered around but saw nothing. After a few minutes, the others began to mock her stupidity, and the one whose turn with the eye had been interrupted demanded it back. This exchange, which unlike the first was not motivated by a possible meal of human flesh, took place slowly and reluctantly.

Watching it, Perseus conceived a plan. He stood stock-still (and downwind) for a while, learning the rhythm by which the eye and the tooth rotated among the three. Then, at the exact moment when the eye was due to pass between the two who were closest to him, Perseus crawled forward on his hands and knees and grabbed it out of one outstretched hand before the other could receive it.

At first, the Graeae suspected nothing, accustomed as they were to each other's reluctance to give up the eye. The one waiting to receive it complained about her sister's selfishness while the giver sanctimoniously insisted that she had already relinquished it; the third sister, who had neither the tooth nor the eye at that moment, cackled at the entertainment that the quarrel provided.

Eventually, however, it became clear that none of them had it. Dropping to the floor, they scuttled around, panicking at the thought that the eye might roll into the fire. When they found nothing, tears trickled from their empty sockets and the cave reverberated with their wails. Shouting over the noise, Perseus announced his presence and laid down his terms: he'd give them back their eye if they told him how to get to the Gorgons' island. The sister with the tooth dashed towards his voice, but Hermes's winged sandals lifted him out of danger. At last the Graeae conceded defeat. The island, they told him, lay farther to the west, near the very edge of the world. They described the shape that it would take when sil-houetted against the sky. Satisfied, Perseus tossed the eye towards the sisters and flew away.

Now he was moving in a gathering dusk, trailing Helios's chariot as it approached the end of its daily journey. From the itinerant bards who occasionally visited Seriphus on their way to more im-portant places, Perseus had heard that there were marvels near the western edge of the world that were even more remarkable than the Graeae: the country of the Cimmerians, for example, who lived in an eternal fog and had learned to tend their sheep, cast their lines and grind their grain in darkness; and Atlas, a Titan whom Zeus had put to work holding up Sky, so that Sky might never again press himself against Earth.

Flying through a dusky sky, Perseus could not see any of these wonders down below. He couldn't see much of anything else, ei-ther; he prayed that Hermes and Athena would guide him towards the island that the Graeae had described before complete darkness fell. If he missed it, he would be left to circle aimlessly over the swirling waters of Ocean until, too exhausted to remain upright, he tumbled into the waves and drowned.

But at last he spotted the shape that the Graeae had described, black against the red sky, and landed on the stony coast with a stumble. He camped there for the night, rolling himself up in his cloak for warmth and clapping Hades's cap of invisibility upon his head for protection.

55
BEHEADING MEDUSA

In the morning, Perseus opened his eyes and was surprised to see meadows stretching up from the shore—poppies, cornflowers and grasses bending to the breeze. This wasn't what he'd expected the Gorgons' island to look like, and he wondered whether he'd made a mistake. After breakfasting on the last of his provisions, he began walking inland, hoping to find the cave in which Medusa and her sisters dwelt. He didn't dare to use the winged sandals for recon-naissance; the speed and height at which they carried him meant that he might glimpse Medusa before he even realized she was nearby and be petrified.

The first part of his walk was discouraging. In the hills that rose from the meadows he saw scrubby junipers and sage bushes; from the corner of his eye he glimpsed small lizards darting for cover and the occasional rabbit or squirrel. There was nothing here that he hadn't seen a million times before on Seriphus.

Gradually, however, he began to notice odd rocks. At first, he thought they were a trick of the eye, prompted by what his brain suggested he would see, but when he stooped to look more closely, he discovered that he'd been right: these rocks were granite versions of the small animals that had been crossing his path since his walk began. They shared a posture: each animal was outstretched in flight but its head was turned backwards, as if to gauge the speed of a pursuer. He realized what this meant: he was now within the zone where Medusa hunted the only flesh that the island usually afforded her. If she was lucky, she caught her victims before they realized that they were being chased; if she was unlucky, they turned to look at her—at which point they ceased to be edible and instead became macabre ornaments for the landscape.

After walking a bit farther, he no longer saw any animals at all, either flesh or stone. Larger granite formations began to dot the area, instead, each one unmistakably the shape of a man who had foolishly tried to approach the Gorgons' home. Many were still crouched in positions of ambush or attack—as if the ordinary tactics used in warfare and the hunt would save them from an enemy who immobilized everything that glimpsed her. Elsewhere, he saw skulls and piles of bones, the remains of mortals Medusa had managed to catch before they could turn their heads.

Walking slowly now, Perseus moved towards a crevice that he'd spotted in the cleft of the mountain. Once there, he stopped and unwrapped his shield from a cloth in which he'd been carrying it to keep it clean, an important part of a plan that he had formulated. He lifted it up before his face like a mirror and carefully began to back into the crevice.

The floor of the narrow passage sloped downwards, making it difficult to negotiate while walking backwards; several times Perseus froze in terror after dislodging small stones that rattled away. He was debating whether he should use his winged sandals to float a few inches above the floor—he'd never tried to make them fly backwards before—when he heard grunting snores and the thump of bodies turning over in sleep.

Cautiously, he moved around the next curve of the path and then he saw them—or rather, he saw their reflections: three torsos with eagles' wings folded over their backs in sleep; three heads crowned by vipers that writhed while they dreamt of their own horrors.

Two of the faces on these heads were repulsive: snaggle-toothed and pop-eyed with flaring nostrils and bearded chins. But the third was that of a lovely girl: her delicately traced brows curved gently over blue-veined eyelids and dark lashes; her nose was straight and well-shaped; her pink lips demurely hid whatever lay inside her mouth. Perseus understood, now, why Poseidon had once yearned to lie with Medusa, journeying far from the warmer parts of the Mediterranean, where he liked to spend his time, in order to do so.

Perseus, too, was transfixed by her beauty, until he remembered that he had a job to do if he wanted to rescue his mother. Slowly he crept backwards, reminding himself that everything he saw in the mirror of his shield was reversed. At last he was in position—at least, he thought he was in position—and he drew from his belt the adamantine sickle that Hermes had given him. He raised it above his head and after a moment's pause to painstakingly recalibrate its position one last time, brought it whistling down onto Medusa's neck.

Still asleep, she died with the smallest of sighs, but her vipers awoke and survived a bit longer; their furious hissing began to rouse Medusa's sisters. Lacking now the luxury for slow, deliberate movements, Perseus lunged backwards and groped for the head. Shoving it into the sack, he ran outside. Leaping into the sky, he headed for home.

Blinking the rheum from their eyes, Medusa's sisters looked around their cave, wondering what had just happened. When they saw their sister's headless corpse, they gnashed their teeth and howled in rage. A moment more and they were outside, snorting like bloodhounds. Leaping into the air, they followed Perseus's scent eastwards, borne aloft on their mighty wings and licking their lips in anticipation of tasty prey. For a moment, it seemed as if they would overtake him, but Hermes's sandals could, when commanded, fly as quickly as thoughts. Eventually, Perseus saw that he was free of his pursuers and paused for breath.

56
ANDROMEDA

The sack, which Perseus had tied around his waist, jostled unpleasantly against his thigh as he flew east towards Seriphus. The thickly woven wool held fast under the weight of Medusa's head, but her blood soaked through it. By the time Perseus was crossing the Libyan desert, it had begun to steadily drip through the fabric. Wherever drops hit the earth, vipers sprang out of the sand. Generations later, when Jason's companions carried the Argo over the desert on their shoulders, one of the vipers bit Mopsus, killing him.

Soon after he'd crossed the desert, Perseus lost his bearings and veered south to Ethiopia, where Cepheus was king. As he flew north along its coast, trying to make his way home, he noticed a young woman chained to a rock overlooking the sea. This was Cepheus's daughter Andromeda, who was paying the price for the vanity of her mother, Cassiopeia.

Cassiopeia had boasted that her hair was lovelier than that of the Nereids, the daughters of the sea god Nereus. The Nereids heard her and were furious that a mortal should dare even to compare herself to them, much less to claim superiority. They prevailed upon Poseidon to send a double curse upon the kingdom: soon, sea water flooded Ethiopia's fields and a sea monster patrolled the shallows of its coastline. Both granaries and fishermen's nets grew empty; the people began to starve. Poseidon refused to relent, however, unless the queen demonstrated her contrition by sacrificing her daughter to the monster. This was why Andromeda stood chained to the rock.

From the moment he saw Andromeda, Perseus was attracted by her beauty and by the defiant way in which she stood upright against the cliff. It was only when he swooped down to speak with her that he saw the hideous monster racing towards her from the open sea, roiling the waves like a ship advancing for battle. There was no time to think; Perseus yanked out his sickle and attacked the beast, thrusting the blade wherever he could here and there between the scales of its carapace. It would have been quicker and surer to pull out Medusa's head and petrify his opponent, but if he did, Andromeda might glimpse it as well and become a stone maiden, standing forever against a stone cliff.

At last the monster's blood trickled out into the water through a hundred cuts—forever after it was called the Red Sea—and the beast sank beneath the waves. Andromeda's parents ran forward to free her as Perseus descended to the beach.

The next day should have seen them married—she was as eager as he was, and her father gratefully approved the match—but years earlier, Andromeda had been betrothed to Cepheus's brother Phineus and Phineus would not relinquish his claim. He and his men arrived at the palace just as the wedding was beginning and a grim battle ensued. Many fell; neither side was able to prevail until at last Perseus cried out, "You deserve this, Phineus, for refusing to respect Andromeda's choice! Friends, look away if you value your lives!"

And then he pulled Medusa's head from his sack, its viperous hair limp and decaying, its eyes glazed by death, but lethal nonetheless. Phineus and his men froze in gray horror at the last sight they saw.

When Perseus and Andromeda arrived on Seriphus a few days later, they found Danaë and Dictys trapped in Athena's temple. As soon as Perseus had departed on his quest for Medusa's head, Polydectes had summoned Danaë, ordering her to prepare to marry him; Dictys and Danaë had fled to the temple for asylum. Polydectes was biding his time until starvation either lured them out or brought death as its own punishment. Perseus, striding into the king's throne room, pulled Medusa's head from its bag and once again turned flesh into stone. His mother and Dictys were free.

As Perseus was resting from his labors, Hermes and Athena arrived to collect the tools that they'd lent to him. He handed the sandals, cap, scimitar and shield back to Hermes and was about to hand over the woolen sack, too, still heavy with its contents, when Athena stopped him.

"Brothers," she said, "I want the head of the Gorgon for myself. Once I fasten it to my breastplate, no enemy will be able to confront me and live." And so it was done, making the most fearsome of goddesses more fearsome still.

Perseus put Dictys on the throne and gave the hand of his mother to the new king—a willing bride this time. Then he departed for the mainland, intending to meet his grandfather and assure him that he had no desire to kill him, in spite of what Apollo's oracle had said so long ago.

Acrisius received his grandson cautiously at first, but as time went on, he learned to trust Perseus and even to be proud of him. One day, however, when Perseus was showing off for Acrisius, a wicked wind seized a discus that he'd thrown and drove it into his grandfather's foot. Acrisius died of the wound.

The king had never fathered the son that he'd longed for; Perseus, therefore, inherited the kingship of Argos. But Perseus was unwilling to sit upon the throne of a man he had killed; he persuaded his cousin Megapenthes, who by now had inherited the throne of Tiryns from Proetus, to trade kingdoms. And so the descendants of two warring brothers came together in accord and the entire family of Io was, at least for a while, at peace.

57
BELLEROPHON AND PEGASUS

When Death finally dragged King Sisyphus of Corinth down to Tartarus, Sisyphus's son Glaucus inherited the throne. He married Eurynome, the daughter of King Nisus of Megara.

Eurynome's face shone like a star and a delicious fragrance wafted from her rosy skin. It was inevitable that she would attract the attention of some god, and one day it finally happened: Poseidon visited her and sired a son, Bellerophon.

Although Glaucus raised Bellerophon as his own, Poseidon watched over the boy from a distance, as well. When Bellerophon reached adolescence, the god appeared and offered him a gift: the horse Pegasus, from whose gleaming white shoulders sprang powerful wings.

"But," said Poseidon, "he is still a wild thing. If you wish to ride him, you must first capture him." And then Poseidon vanished.

Once he had recovered from his astonishment, Bellerophon mused over a particularly odd aspect of his father's gift: if he succeeded in capturing Pegasus, he would soon be riding upon the back of his own brother. Many years earlier, Poseidon, enchanted by the gentle beauty of Medusa's face, had made love to her, fathering twins. One of these was Chrysaor, a mighty giant of a god, and the other was Pegasus.

Medusa's children were still curled in her womb on the day that Perseus crept into the cave that she shared with her sisters, wielding a sickle in his hand. With one fell blow, he decapitated Medusa and then, quickly shoving her head into his sack, he flew away. When Medusa's sleeping sisters opened their eyes a moment later, awoken by the frantic hissing of the snakes on Medusa's head, they beheld a marvelous sight. Two creatures were clambering out of Medusa's severed neck, rapidly growing larger as they escaped their confinement. Chrysaor, whose form was that of a man, was born grasping a golden sword in his hand. Pegasus scrambled out on a foal's shaky legs, unfurled his wings and was gone. It was the last his aunts ever saw of him.

He quickly learned to enjoy himself. The sky was his kingdom and so was the earth below, for with wings that were larger than any eagle's, he could cover great distances. When he was thirsty, he alighted. If there was no source of fresh water nearby, he stamped his hoof upon the soil and a spring of water burst forth, a gift from his father. He was freer than any other creature—freer, even, than the gods themselves, for he carried no responsibilities. How could such a creature be tamed, Bellerophon wondered?

It was rumored that late at night when the land was still, Pegasus sometimes visited the Pirene, a fountain near Corinth's marketplace. For weeks, Bellerophon camped out there. Each time that Pegasus appeared, he waited until the horse bent his neck to drink and then quietly approached him. But time after time, the horse, skittish at even the softest human footfall, sprang into the air before Bellerophon could even draw near.

Finally, Bellerophon asked the seer Polyidus for advice.

"The gods' power easily brings about what mortals consider impossible," Polyidus said. "Make your bed upon the altar in front of Athena's temple. If she favors you, you will receive help."

And so Bellerophon lay down upon the stony altar that evening, wrapping his cloak around himself. He fell asleep and dreamt that Athena stood before him, holding in her hands a golden bridle.

"Awake, Prince of Corinth!" she said. "Awake and receive this enchanted bridle. Tomorrow, sacrifice a white bull to your father. When he appears, show him what I have given you. I think that he will ease your way forward, then."

Bellerophon suddenly found himself wide awake, standing in front of the altar where his cloak still lay in a rumpled heap. In his hands was the bridle that he'd seen in his dream.

The next day, Bellerophon sacrificed a bull just as Athena had instructed him. When Poseidon arrived to receive the gift, he found Bellerophon kneeling before him with the bridle draped over his outstretched palms.

Poseidon lifted an eyebrow and snorted. "Yes, Athena knows horses, too. She's given you a tool to capture Pegasus, so now I'll give you the information you need. Go back to the Pirene tonight and watch. When Pegasus arrives, wait until he's done drinking and then approach him with the bridle in your hands. He'll do the rest."

The night was bright, with the thinnest of clouds cloaking the moon; long before Pegasus landed, Bellerophon spotted him descending over the trees. He alighted neatly at the edge of the fountain and drank.

As Bellerophon drew near, the horse lifted his head. When he saw the golden bridle, he trotted towards Bellerophon. Bowing his head, he pushed his muzzle through the noseband and waited patiently for Bellerophon to pull the crownpiece over his forehead.

When that was done, Bellerophon threw his leg over Pegasus's back and pulled himself up to sit behind the horse's wings. The brothers embarked into the night air.

58
STHENEBOEA

Bellerophon had another brother, Deliades, who was the son of Glaucus and Eurynome. One day when the brothers were wrestling together, as young men do, Bellerophon accidentally killed Deliades. Glaucus had no choice but to exile Bellerophon, ordering him to seek purification at the hands of another king before returning home.

Bellerophon journeyed to Tiryns and knelt before the throne of Proetus, touching the king's knees and chin as was the custom for suppliants. Bidding him to rise, Proetus performed rituals of purification and then, attracted by the young man's thoughtful manner and graceful bearing, invited him to stay on at court as an honored guest.

Proetus's wife, Stheneboea, was attracted by other aspects of Bellerophon, such as his well-built body and handsome face. Soon, she was sending him sidelong glances and secret smiles. When Bellerophon blushed and looked away, she chose to interpret this as the modesty that cloaked virginity, which whet her appetite all the more. She became bolder, brushing up against him when they passed in the hall and lurking in the garden at dusk, when she knew that he liked to walk in the coolness. Bellerophon responded in a manner that he hoped conveyed disinterest, although politeness prevented him from ignoring her altogether.

Finally, a mixture of urgent lust and brazen self-assurance drove Stheneboea to compose a note in which she described, in lewd detail, what she would like Bellerophon to do to her. After reading it, Bellerophon avoided Stheneboea completely.

At last she was forced to acknowledge the truth: Bellerophon wasn't interested in her. Fury and humiliation surged through her body like a fever; her hands trembled so badly that she could work with neither spindle nor loom. She thrashed in her bed and when she finally slept, she saw Bellerophon laughing at her in her dreams.

She composed a second note, drawing again on her talent for erotic detail. Purporting to have been written by Bellerophon to herself, it proposed that the two of them murder Proetus, seize the throne of Tiryns and wallow in a bed of depravity.

"Will you stand still and be assassinated, Husband?" she cried, thrusting the false note into Proetus's hands. "This man—this suppliant to whom you showed mercy and kindness—means to seize your kingdom and debase your wife!"

Proetus was shocked by what he read but paralyzed by doubt; the Bellerophon who his wife claimed had written the note was a completely different man from the guest whom he knew. The king was tugged this way and that, excoriated by Stheneboea as a coward but exhorted by his conscience not to pass hasty judgment on someone whom he'd accepted into his home.

Finally, when he could stand no more, Proetus took the coward's way out. He composed a letter to Stheneboea's father, King Iobates of Lycia, in which he asked Iobates to summarily execute the man who delivered the letter as the would-be seducer of Iobates's own daughter. Proetus melted wax upon the strings that bound it together and sealed it with his ring. Then he called Bellerophon into his presence.

"Please take this letter to King Iobates as quickly as Pegasus can carry you there."

And Bellerophon, happy to serve the man who had treated him kindly, did just as he was asked. Under the gods' watchful eyes he journeyed to Lycia, where he found Iobates's palace on the banks of the Xanthus River. Iobates, who welcomed Bellerophon with the hospitality due to someone who was both a prince in his own right and his son-in-law's envoy, refused to talk business until he had feasted Bellerophon on nine oxen for nine days.

On the tenth day, Iobates sighed with the pleasure of a full belly and asked Bellerophon why Proetus had sent him. Bellerophon handed over the letter and Iobates read it. The king's stomach turned when he realized his situation; he found it just as impossible to kill a guest as Proetus had.

And so, like Proetus, he took a coward's way out.

"Bellerophon," he said, "a terrible monster called the Chimera has been afflicting my people. She slaughters their herds, destroys their crops and sometimes even eats their children. Could you, with your marvelous horse, rid my kingdom of this ghastly pestilence?"

59
THE CHIMERA

Iobates was confident that, even with the help of Pegasus, Bellerophon would not only fail to kill the Chimera but also be killed himself.

The Chimera was the child of Echidna and Typhon and, like most of her siblings, she was an odd conglomeration of animals that humans were used to experiencing separately. Her body was that of a lioness and so was the head that topped its neck, although the head was perversely crowned with the mane that normally belonged to the male of the species. Her tail was a writhing viper—supple, strong and venomous.

Between those two beasts, springing out of the Chimera's spine, were the neck and head of a she-goat. At first glance—particularly given its position between two visibly dangerous appendages—the goat's head looked harmless. The moment she opened her mouth, however, this was disproven: flames and sulfurous smoke belched from her throat. Anything that approached the Chimera from the front would be attacked by the lion, anything that approached from the rear would be bitten by the viper, and anything that approached from the side would find the goat's head swiveling around to sear it. Scorched black patches dotted the pastures of Iobates's kingdom, mute witnesses to bulls that had attacked a strange new beast they found transgressing their territories.

Bellerophon and Pegasus spent a day flying over the broad plain through which the Xanthus flowed, futilely seeking a pattern in these patches that might lead them to the Chimera's den. The next day, they expanded their search into the surrounding foothills, where scruffy cedars competed with broom for the thin soil between outcroppings of stone. Here their luck seemed to be even worse, for there were no burnt patches at all. Perhaps, Bellerophon speculated, nothing that the Chimera stalked in the wild had a defender that would draw the goat's attack. The lion's paws and teeth alone could capture prey to feed the common belly.

And then Bellerophon saw smoke filtering up through the fissures in a rocky peak and steered Pegasus closer. On the hillside he glimpsed what he guessed was the mouth of a cave: the soil in front of it was disturbed and the grasses nearby had been crushed by something large. Surely it served as the home of some animal and what animal, other than the Chimera, produced smoke?

When they returned at dusk, Bellerophon's suspicions were confirmed: from out of the cave slunk the Chimera, embarking on her evening hunt. Bellerophon shuddered as he watched her. Although the lion's body moved with the rippling grace of a cat, the viper and each of the two heads that grew out of the body moved independently of one another. There was no rhythm to the thing, none of the easy elegance with which other animals carried themselves. The viper's undulations, although regular in themselves, periodically brought it thumping against the beast's haunches when the lion's head—which seemed to be piloting the whole thing—ordered the body to leap or change speed abruptly. The goat's head, pivoting here and there, nearly collided with low-hanging branches that the lion's head gracefully slipped beneath.

With a sinking heart, Bellerophon realized that he was dealing with three separate enemies, all of whom would have to be defeated simultaneously. If he managed, somehow, to hack off the viper, the lion and goat would survive and attack him. If he managed to decapitate the goat, he would still have the viper and the lion to contend with. If he speared the lion first, the viper and the goat would remain. Only the body itself was shared by all three; only by efficiently dispatching that body could he really kill the Chimera. But where did that corporate body end and each individual creature begin? Would an arrow to the beast's chest kill the whole thing or only the lion whose head grew from that chest? He went back to the palace and brooded over what to do.

Then some god put it into his head that an enemy might best be defeated by its own talents, and he remembered something he'd seen as a boy in Corinth when he visited the blacksmith's forge. The smith was making lead weights to sell to local merchants. A set of molds stood ready on a bench in the yard. As the smith tipped his brimming ladle into the first of them, his hand trembled with the weight of it and spilled molten lead onto the ground. The grass hissed and shriveled; nothing grew on that spot for the rest of the summer.

Bellerophon leapt up and hurried to the palace forge. He acquired a lump of lead the size of his fist and drilled a hole through the soft metal that was just large enough to accommodate his spear shaft. Removing the spear's bronze point, he slipped the lead onto the shaft and then replaced the point, to hold the lump of lead in place. The next day, he rehearsed Pegasus in the plan he'd made. In late afternoon, the two brothers set out for the cave.

When the Chimera emerged at dusk to hunt, Bellerophon was ready. Hovering overhead on Pegasus's back, he whistled to attract the beast's attention; all three heads looked skywards and the goat, opening her mouth, shot forth flames.

Circling around the Chimera, Pegasus carefully brought Bellerophon as near to her as he dared. When their orbit brought Bellerophon into the right position, he thrust his spear downwards and neatly inserted it, with its lump of lead, into the goat's mouth.

The lead, which instantly melted in the heat of the goat's breath, sizzled down her throat into the beast's shared stomach. Roaring, hissing and bleating in pain, the Chimera dropped to the ground. Bellerophon had killed her, fulfilling the portents of the gods.

60
THE END OF BELLEROPHON

Bellerophon trussed up the Chimera's carcass and tied it across Pegasus's rump. They flew back to the palace, triumphant.

Iobates, however, was less excited by the Chimera's death than Bellerophon had expected. In fact, after a moment of awkward silence, Iobates cleared his throat and asked Bellerophon to do him another favor.

"We have enemies just to the east of us—the Solymoi—who've been causing no end of trouble. Can you stop their raids upon my people?"

And so Bellerophon and Pegasus flew east and conquered the Solymoi. But if anything, Iobates looked even less delighted when they returned this time.

"One more thing. There's this fierce tribe of women to the north, called Amazons, who've also been causing problems. Can you do anything about that?"

And so Bellerophon and Pegasus traveled north through the chilly air and smote the Amazons. When they returned to the banks of the Xanthus this time, it was to discover that Iobates's guards were lying in wait for them. With the help of the gods, however, Bellerophon killed them all.

Bellerophon was shocked and angry now; he had loyally served Iobates three times and now the murderous intent behind each task had been revealed. Striding through the fields to the shore, he stood in the shallows and called upon his father.

"Poseidon, if indeed it was you who sired me, take vengeance upon this wicked king and his people!"

Poseidon listened. As Bellerophon walked away, the waves followed him like obedient dogs, licking the fertile farmland with their salty tongues. The crops wilted and the soil was spoiled.

The Lycian men begged Bellerophon to stop, but he ignored them and continued to stride across the Lycian countryside. Then the Lycian women contrived a plan. Hitching their skirts up to their waists, they walked out to meet the young man. Flustered by what he saw, Bellerophon blushed, turned and hurried back to the sea, drawing the waves along with him.

Iobates slogged through the muddy ruins of his farmers' fields. Kneeling in the sand, he implored Bellerophon to accept his daughter Philonoë in marriage, promising half of his kingdom as well. He revealed the deadly letter that Proetus had sent and begged Bellerophon to forgive a remorseful man.

Bellerophon accepted. He and Philonoë were wed and settled into life at the palace. Soon, the gods blessed them with two sons and a daughter.

Sometimes, however, old injuries come back to rankle. The day arrived when Bellerophon decided to avenge himself upon Proetus and Stheneboea for the plot they'd set in motion. He traveled to Tiryns on Pegasus's back and landed in the palace gardens, startling Stheneboea, who was sitting there alone. Bellerophon launched into a speech that he had carefully prepared.

"Stheneboea! These years I have spent with your sister Philonoë—whose beauty is but the palest shadow of your own— have made me long for the pleasures you once offered, which I was too callow a youth to appreciate. Come away with me now to Lycia! I'll divorce Philonoë and place you next to me on the throne."

Gasping in her eagerness, Stheneboea scrambled onto Pegasus's back and hugged Bellerophon tightly around the waist. Pegasus leapt into the air and soon they were halfway to Lycia, high above the Aegean Sea. Bellerophon glanced down to gauge their altitude and then pried his companion's wandering hands away from his body and pushed her into the waters below. Stheneboea's body, nibbled by fish, washed up on the island of Melos, where it was found by fishermen and conveyed to Proetus for burial.

No one in Lycia reproached Bellerophon for what he'd done. Iobates was dead by then and Bellerophon had long ago told Philonoë about her sister's wickedness. He made ready to enjoy a peaceful old age, surrounded by children and grandchildren.

But repose brought tedium. It occurred to Bellerophon one idle afternoon that he could spur Pegasus to fly higher than they had ever flown before—high enough to surprise the very gods in their palace and be received as their guest.

Up and up the brothers flew until Bellerophon could glimpse the bottom step of Zeus's palace. Zeus, looking out at that very moment, was shocked by the presumptuousness of a man whom the gods had treated kindly. He sent a horsefly to bite Pegasus on the flank. Pegasus reared up and threw Bellerophon from his back. Down and down Bellerophon fell, landing at last upon the plain that lay east of Lycia. He survived the accident but spent the rest of his life wandering through the wilderness.

Pegasus, meanwhile, reached his goal alone. Zeus stabled him on Olympus with the gods' other horses and, to please Poseidon, placed his image among the stars.

61
CADMUS AND THE SERPENT'S TEETH

Cadmus learned that the gods wanted him to stop searching for his sister Europa when he asked for Apollo's help at the oracle of Delphi. Apollo told him nothing at all about Europa; instead, he commanded Cadmus to find a cow with a mark like the crescent moon on her flank—a reminder of the woes suffered by Cadmus's great-great-grandmother Io. He should allow the cow to wander where she wished; wherever she finally lay down to rest, Cadmus should build a city and begin life anew, forgetting about his home and family in Phoenicia.

Cadmus did as the god instructed. After wandering eastwards for three days, the cow sank to her knees in a meadow next to a forest.

In thanks for the portent, Cadmus sent his men to fetch water so that they might offer sacrifice to the gods. The men hiked deep into the woods and found a pool, fed by a spring spilling forth from a cave.

As they knelt to fill their pails, a great serpent slipped from the cave—an ancient, bloated thing that Ares had caused to bubble up from Earth soon after the Flood receded. Lacking sibling or mate, it had brooded alone for hundreds of years, feeding itself on creatures who came to the pool to drink. Its body, armored in scales as black as cinders, moved invisibly among the ferns.

It slithered to the nearest of Cadmus's men and sank its fangs into the poor man's thigh. His heart hammered and his stomach convulsed; groaning, he fell to the ground, his pail clattering beside him. Death came swiftly, but the man lived long enough to watch his comrades fall as well: some bitten, some crushed by the serpent's coils, one poisoned by the serpent's foul breath alone.

When the men failed to return, Cadmus set out to find them. He reached the spring just in time to see the serpent dragging the last of their corpses into the cave for later consumption. Lifting a rock high above his head, Cadmus flung it at the monster, but the rock bounced harmlessly to the ground. The serpent turned, however, and spotted its assailant. It reared up, bringing its eyes level with Cadmus's.

"Who dares transgress the Ismenian Spring of Ares?" it hissed.

Cadmus knew better than to waste time answering. He drove his lance into the serpent's belly where the scales were softer; the tip penetrated deeply before the snake shook itself loose. Blood dribbled from its lipless mouth and its movements grew clumsy but it nonetheless gathered itself together, preparing to spring.

Then some god put it into Cadmus's mind to step slightly to the right. In response, the serpent swiveled, unwittingly positioning itself between Cadmus and an ancient oak tree. Once more, Cadmus drove his lance into the serpent's belly, throwing all his weight behind it. This time, the lance passed through its target and continued into the tree, neatly skewering the snake. With a terrible cry, it died.

After Cadmus had washed himself in the pool, he looked up to see a figure stepping from between the trees—female in form but wearing a golden cuirass. Its gray eyes gazed out from a golden helmet.

"Cadmus," she said, "you are all alone now in an uninhabited land. How will you fulfill the gods' command to build a city? I, Athena, pondered this matter while you were sloughing the grime from your skin in that pool, and prepared the way for you. I yanked the teeth from this nightmare of a creature that my brother engendered—three full rows of them, each as sharp as a thorn— and now I give you half of them, keeping the rest for myself. Plant them where you intended to make your sacrifice and trust in the gods."

Then she was gone.

When he returned to camp, Cadmus did as Athena instructed. When the last of the teeth were nestled in the dirt, Cadmus turned to see a startling sight. Where he had sown the first of them, strange fruits were sprouting from the ground: bronze helmets, crowned with horsehair crests. Soon, entire heads had emerged, followed by shoulders clad in bronze.

Even in the few seconds that he stood gaping at this wonder, new helmets began to grow from the middle of his plot; in the part that he had sown last of all, the dirt was churning as the tips of crests poked out between the clods. In a matter of minutes, the field was filled with warriors, each standing firm with his sword unsheathed.

Terrified, Cadmus began to scrabble in the dirt, grabbing stones and throwing them at this new army. The results were not what he expected, however: as the stones hit their targets, each man turned resentfully against his brothers.

"Did you throw stones at me?"

"Hey, dummy, what's the big idea?"

"I'll teach *you* to attack me!"

A battle broke out—if battle it could be called, so disordered were its maneuvers and so disunified its factions. One by one the warriors fell under each other's swords until only five remained. With Cadmus, they built the city of Thebes; with Cadmus, they became the fathers of Thebes's people.

62
INO AND ATHAMAS

Cadmus married the goddess Harmonia in a splendid wedding that all the gods attended. Hephaestus seized the opportunity to take vengeance for the humiliation he'd suffered when Aphrodite, his wife, had borne Harmonia to her lover, Ares: he presented the bride with a necklace into which he had forged a terrible curse. It blighted Harmonia's life and those of her daughters: Semele, Agave, Autonoë and Ino.

Ino started out well enough: she made an excellent marriage to Athamas, who ruled a neighboring kingdom. Soon, she bore him two sons, Learchus and Melicertes.

But jealousy and ambition, diseases that often travel together, infected Ino's heart. Years earlier, Athamas had married the goddess Nephele; she eventually returned to the sky, entrusting their son, Phrixus, and their daughter, Helle, to his care. At first, Ino was a kind stepmother to Nephele's children, but from the moment she held the newborn Learchus in her arms, she burned with a desire to see her own son, rather than Phrixus, sitting upon Athamas's throne some day.

Finally, Ino contrived a way to rid herself of Phrixus. As queen, she held considerable sway over the rest of the kingdom's women. Calling them together secretly, she instructed them to parch the seed-grain that their husbands had set aside for that year's sowing. The men, knowing nothing of what their wives had done, plowed and planted and waited in vain for crops to emerge from the soil. Soon, famine seized the kingdom.

Athamas prepared to send envoys to Delphi to ask Apollo what to do—but Ino, whispering threats and bribes, persuaded the envoys to return with a false report of her own design: Apollo, they were to say, insisted that the famine would end only when Athamas sacrificed his eldest son to Zeus.

Weeping, Athamas led Phrixus to the grandest altar in the kingdom. Helle clung to her brother's hand, determined to stay at his side to the end. As the priest whet his knife, the crowd of onlookers broke the solemn silence with cries of astonishment. Something, gleaming bright in the sunlight, was descending from the sky. As the thing got closer, the people saw that it was a ram with golden fleece. It landed between Phrixus and the altar that awaited him.

The remarkable ram belonged to Hermes. When Nephele learned that Phrixus was to die, she had asked Hermes for help. Never one to do things simply when they could be done with panache, Hermes had contrived the most arresting mode of deliverance he could imagine. The ram caught Phrixus's eye and Phrixus climbed aboard his back, pulling Helle up behind him. With the children safely aboard, the ram sprang into the sky and disappeared over the eastern horizon.

Phrixus held tightly onto the ram's horns and Helle held tightly onto Phrixus's waist as they sailed across the sea, peering excitedly at all that lay below. As the afternoon wore on, however, they grew tired. Their heads throbbed from the glare of the sun upon the water, their thighs ached from straddling the ram's broad back and their arms began to tremble with the strain of holding on. As they were passing over the strait that divides the Aegean from the Black Sea, Phrixus felt one of Helle's arms slipping from his waist. Before he could help her, she lost her balance and fell into the water below, which has ever since been known as the Hellespont, the "sea of Helle."

Heartbroken, Phrixus traveled on to Colchis, where he was received by King Aeëtes. The ram was sacrificed to Zeus in thanks for Phrixus's deliverance; Aeëtes hung the fleece upon a tree in a grove dedicated to Ares, setting a serpent to guard it.

Soon, Ino presented her husband with another child—not her own, but rather the infant Dionysus, the child that Zeus had fathered upon her late sister Semele. Ino nursed the young god, caring for him as lovingly as she had cared for Learchus and Melicertes. Athamas agreed to help raise him.

It had been Hera who killed Semele, with the intention of killing her unborn child as well. That plan had been foiled when Zeus plucked Dionysus from his dying mother's womb, but Hera knew that sooner or later Dionysus would reappear and had kept careful watch. A smile crept over her face when she finally spotted him in Ino's arms. Stealing down to Hades's realm, she found the corner where Tisiphone, the cruelest of the Erinyes, sat hunched in darkness. Tisiphone listened eagerly to Hera's plan and then hurried off to Athamas's palace.

Yanking out two of the vipers that crowned her head, Tisiphone dispatched them to the throne room, where they invisibly slithered onto the king's and queen's shoulders, exuding pestilential frenzy. Then, Tisiphone decanted gibbering poison into Athamas's and Ino's hearts and swung a sputtering torch three times around their heads. When she had finished, Ino and Athamas were mad.

Athamas, running from the room, stumbled across Learchus and in his delusion mistook the boy for a fawn. Seizing his son by the ankle, Athamas jerked him up into the air and then down onto the floor, staining the tiles with Learchus's brains. Ino howled and ran outside, still clutching Melicertes to her breast. When she reached the cliffs that overlooked the sea, she leapt, still holding him in her arms.

Aphrodite pitied her granddaughter and begged Poseidon for help. He responded by transforming Ino into a sea goddess whose name was Leucothea. He dispatched a dolphin to rescue Melicertes and carry him to the Corinthian isthmus. There, he was worshipped as the god Palaemon, in whose honor athletic games were established.

As for Dionysus, Zeus had dispatched Hermes to whisk him away from the palace before Tisiphone even arrived. Hermes carried the baby to the nymphs of Mount Nysa, who brought him up.

63
THE RETURN OF DIONYSUS

Dionysus grew up wild among the nymphs, unschooled in the conventions of divine society. He was a disquieting child from the start: his blue eyes assessed the world unblinkingly; his smile left its recipients unnerved rather than reassured. He had an affinity with animals that surpassed even that of his caregivers: lions and panthers trotted alongside him and snakes twined round his arms.

As a god raised in exile, he had to work to convert mortals to his worship. When he was old enough to leave the nymphs, he began to travel throughout Lydia and Phrygia, then west through Thrace and south through Thessaly, proselytizing his cult and the gifts that it offered to mortals: wine that brought release from the cares that burdened life and initiations that promised a blessed existence after death. Accompanying him were the bacchantes, women who danced in his honor with ivy crowning their hair and the dappled skins of fawns draped over their shoulders.

Finally, Dionysus arrived in Thebes, where the grave of his mother, Semele, still smoldered with the fire that Zeus had kindled on the night she died. His grandfather Cadmus, now an old man, had abdicated in favor of Pentheus, the son of his daughter Agave and her husband Echion, one of the men who had sprung from the serpent's teeth.

Agave and her sister Autonoë sneered at the idea that Semele's lover had been Zeus: the child she'd spawned was no god, they charged, but only a mortal bastard. Their scorn contaminated Thebes; only Cadmus and his seer, Tiresias, accepted the new god's cult. In fury, Dionysus descended upon the city. Disguised as a priest of his own cult—handsome and young with curls streaming down his back—he deranged the minds of the Theban women. To the mountains they ran, carrying thyrsi, the sacred staffs of the god. They rejoiced in a new title that he'd given them: maenads, "the maddened ones." They banged their thyrsi upon the earth and whatever each one desired gushed forth—water to slake her thirst or wine to heat her blood. When they scratched at the earth with their fingers, milk welled up. Abandoning their infants, they held the young of wolves and gazelles to their swollen breasts to nourish the wilderness. Day by day their madness grew, a madness that brought delight, a madness that was sharp as a thorn pressed into flesh, bright as a bride's necklace and sweet as a mother's kiss—sweet as a stepmother's kiss. The women stayed on the mountain, forgetting their homes. Pentheus seethed with disgust; even his own mother wandered in the mountains now, indulging, he was sure, in orgies that this foreigner was orchestrating. He ordered his guards to capture the charlatan priest.

But far above, in the air of heaven, the gods watched what the humans were doing, marveling at how little they understood. Dionysus allowed himself to be led into Pentheus's presence, smiling, docile, his cheeks flushed with wine.

"Who taught you these enthralling rites, wizard?" spat Pentheus. "For whose pleasures do you prepare the flesh of our women?"

"Dionysus, the son of Zeus. The god himself initiated me and taught me his holy rites."

"What form does this god take, when he addresses his faithful?"

"Many are the forms of the gods. They choose what they please, as the moment demands."

"Enough of your sophistry!" screamed Pentheus, and then turned to his guards. "Bind this man!"

When the guards touched Dionysus, Zeus's thunder suddenly shook the palace and lightning licked at its face. Pentheus's wits were confounded; he skittered here and there, batting at the flames that climbed the walls and thrusting his sword at a phantom of Dionysus that the god himself had created. At last the king dropped exhausted to the floor, resourceless but remorseless, his palace falling around him.

Then a cowherd arrived with a terrifying report. Some man, he said, had goaded the herdsmen into hunting the maenads. In flight, the women had grown more frenzied. Falling upon the grazing cattle, they'd torn the bellowing animals apart with their bare hands. Ribs and horns and hooves were scattered everywhere; scraps of bloody flesh dangled from the trees. Nothing stopped the women: fire didn't burn them and spears fell powerless to the ground.

The god-priest, shaking off his bonds, came forward.

"Pentheus, would you like to see these maenads in action?"

"Oh yes, I'd give a lot to see that!" cried the king in his delusion.

"Then I shall dress you like a bacchant, to pass undetected."

"Must I? A king in women's clothes?"

"If you wish to watch the debauchery, yes."

Dionysus placed a wig on Pentheus's head and draped diaphanous robes upon his body. In the softness of the silk, the king's madness blossomed; he began to preen and primp.

"Do I look like my mother now? Do I look my aunt? Tell me! Am I attractive?"

"You shall attract attention, yes," replied the god.

When they reached the mountain, Dionysus gracefully raised his arm and pulled down the peak of a lofty fir, bending its trunk as easily as an archer bends his bow.

"Sit here, King, to watch the revels."

"Will I be able to see everything?"

"You will see everything."

"What about my mother?"

"She is here. She will go home with you proudly, when all is done."

So Pentheus made himself comfortable among the branches and Dionysus gently released the tree, lifting the king high above the ground, where all could see him.

And then he called to his maenads.

"Faithful ones! Here is the man who mocked our holy rites. Take vengeance!"

Agave cried, "Circle the tree, friends, and grip it tight! Shake loose the blasphemer!" Eager hands yanked the fir from the soil and Pentheus fell to the ground.

Agave inspected him then, a priestess sizing up her victim. He removed his wig and touched her face, crying, "Mother! It's me! Forgive my transgressions against your god!" but she ignored him. Gripping his left arm, she planted her foot on his chest and pulled until his arm ripped free. The other maenads grabbed whatever they could, as prizes of the hunt—fingers, entrails, a foot still warm in its womanish slipper. Finally, Agave impaled Pentheus's head upon her thyrsus and led the way home.

"Father!" she cried as Cadmus stumbled out to meet her. "Look at the head of this beast we've captured! Aren't you proud of your brave daughter? Call Pentheus to see what his mother has caught!"

"Oh child, what have you done?" Cadmus shrieked. "Shake free from the grip of the god and look at what you hold!"

And then, standing atop his mother's tomb, in the cruel finality of vengeance, Dionysus lifted the maenads' madness. Each one gaped at the blood that stained the hands of her companions and then looked down in horror at the redness of her own. Agave recognized her grisly trophy for what it was and then heard the god's command: she was to leave Thebes and live out the rest of her life in exile—polluted, childless, accursed even after death.

The gods accomplish what they wish in ways that mortals can't foresee. Dionysus, hidden and revealed, secured his birthright and established his cult in Thebes.

64
THE BIRTH OF HERACLES

Perseus and Andromeda had a daughter named Gorgophone and three sons named Alcaeus, Electryon and Sthenelus. Alcaeus had a son named Amphitryon, who married his cousin Alcmene, Electryon's daughter. In a fit of anger soon after the wedding, Amphitryon killed his father-in-law and was sent into exile with his wife. The two of them settled in Thebes, the city that Cadmus had built.

The blood of both Danaë and Andromeda ran in Alcmene's veins, making her surpassingly lovely. Once Zeus had seen her, he resolved to have her, and thought carefully about how to accomplish this. It wouldn't be easy; in addition to beauty, Alcmene possessed great virtue and even greater perspicacity. No suspiciously gentle and attractive animal, no mysterious cloud of gold or overly friendly goddess would be likely to lull Alcmene into unguarded intimacy, as Zeus's disguises had lulled other women.

Finally, one day when Amphitryon was away fighting a war on the island of Taphos, Zeus hit upon a plan. Assuming Amphitryon's appearance, dusty from travel, Zeus entered Alcmene's chamber and announced that he had returned, victorious. Surprised but pleased, Alcmene welcomed into her bed someone whom she had no reason to doubt was her husband. Zeus, who felt that he had waited a long time for this moment, asked Helios to hold back his horses for three days, giving him an extraordinarily long night to spend with Alcmene.

Meanwhile, as the Fates would have it, the real Amphitryon arrived in Thebes just as the sun was finally rising, moments after Zeus had departed. Amphitryon entered his wife's chamber, climbed into her bed and began to make love to her.

"Why, Husband! How ardent you are!" gasped Alcmene. "At this rate, you'll surely exhaust me!"

"What do you mean?"

"It was only half an hour ago that you finally left my bed; I didn't expect to see you back again so soon."

Amphitryon, justifiably alarmed, consulted the seer Tiresias and learned of Zeus's deception. He also learned that he and Zeus had each sired a son upon Alcmene that night. According to Tiresias, Amphitryon's son would be an ordinary mortal, but the son of Zeus would become the greatest hero of all time. It would be Amphitryon's job to raise this child as best he could.

Amphitryon dutifully accepted his role as stepfather. Hera, however, was furious about her stepson's very conception. She knew that this child would be different from Zeus's other bastards; she foresaw that he would eventually become a god and sit beside her on Olympus, if she didn't put a stop to the whole thing soon.

And so when Alcmene's labor began, Hera ordered her daughter Eileithyia, whose job it was to help women in labor, to prevent the twins from emerging. Eileithyia sat in a shadowy corner of the hall outside of Alcmene's bedchamber with her legs crossed, her arms crossed and all of her fingers crossed—strong magic that locked shut the mouth of Alcmene's womb. The womb clenched and thrashed, trying to expel its burden, without result. An entire day of labor passed and then another. On the third day, Alcmene began to die of the strain.

Then her friend Galinthias, while passing through the hall with a jug of water, glimpsed Eileithyia sitting crisscrossed in the corner. Instantly, she understood why Alcmene could not give birth and saw a way to rescue her. Galinthias entered Alcmene's chamber long enough to set down the jug and then ran back into the hall, triumphantly shouting to the household, "Rejoice! Alcmene has given birth to healthy twins!"

Eileithyia, bewildered to learn that her magic had failed, leapt to her feet, thoughtlessly uncrossing all of her appendages. Heracles and his brother, Iphicles, immediately slipped out into the light of day. Alcmene, weary but happy, fell into a sound sleep.

It didn't take Eileithyia long to figure out who'd tricked her. She turned Galinthias into a weasel and cursed the females of that tribe forevermore to be impregnated through their ears and to give birth through their mouths. Hecate, however, who watched over women in labor, admired Alcmene's loyal friend. Although she could not undo what Eileithyia had done, she honored Galinthias by making the weasel her own sacred attendant.

Heracles had finally come into the world, but before he was a day old, Hera had contrived another plot to kill him. Summoning two serpents, she dispatched them to the cradle where the twins were sleeping. The serpents slithered into Alcmene's chamber, gliding smoothly past the sleeping mother, the midwife and the slaves. Heracles, however, heard the sound of their scales whispering against the stone floor and awoke. As soon as the serpents peered over the edge of the cradle, he seized them in his tiny fists and squeezed tightly.

The snakes didn't give up easily and their struggle rocked the cradle. Iphicles awoke and began to wail, then the slaves awoke and began to wail as well. Alcmene leapt from her bed, so frantic with fear that she failed to notice she was still undressed. A moment later, Amphitryon burst into the room, brandishing his sword. But the fight was already over and it was abundantly clear which child was his and which belonged to Zeus. One boy was still crying with fear; the other, clutching two dead snakes, was laughing.

Zeus smiled, well pleased with Heracles. And yet, he mused, perhaps another infusion of divinity would truly ensure Heracles's success. He called for Hermes and explained his idea. Then Hermes smiled as well.

Hermes slipped through the keyhole of Amphitryon's house, gathered Heracles up in his arms and flew to Olympus. Ever so stealthily—as stealthily as only Hermes can move—he crept into Hera's chamber, where she lay sleeping on silken sheets. Her robe had fallen open, exposing one breast. Hermes gently placed Heracles there and Heracles began to suckle. At that, Hera awoke and, horrified, thrust the baby away. As she did so, her milk spurted out across the sky, creating the Milky Way.

Laughing at the scene (which he later described in detail to the other gods), Hermes ferried Heracles back home. Alcmene was none the wiser as to her child's adventure, but the divine milk had done its job; Heracles proved to be exceptional not merely among humans but also among heroes.

65
HERACLES MURDERS HIS FAMILY

Amphitryon did his best to raise both Heracles and Iphicles, hiring tutors to train them in the skills that the sons of a noble family should have.

Heracles was a challenging student, however—not because he lacked intelligence but because his temper was exceedingly short. His music teacher, Linus, learned this the hard way. One day, when Linus smacked Heracles for playing the lyre clumsily, Heracles flew into a rage and beat Linus to death with the stool he'd been sitting on. Brought up on charges of murder, Heracles adroitly invoked the law of self-defense that Rhadamanthys had once established, and was acquitted.

At his wits' end over this and similar episodes, Amphitryon finally sent Heracles to a farm that he owned on the outskirts of town. There, Heracles grew into a young man of amazing strength and physical agility. One summer, when Heracles was eighteen years old, a huge lion began to stalk Amphitryon's farm and that of a neighboring king, Thespius. Each night, it slunk down from the heights of Mount Cithaeron and picked off cattle as it pleased. Heracles tracked it and killed it.

Later that day, Heracles visited Thespius to tell him that the problem had been solved. The king, who had fifty daughters, took one look at the muscular young man and contrived a scheme for acquiring a dynasty of heroic grandchildren. After plying Heracles with wine, Thespius helped him stagger into one of the palace's bedchambers. Then, Thespius pushed the first of his daughters through the door. After Heracles made love to her, she crept out. Moments later, one of her sisters entered the room and crawled into bed.

And so it continued, all night long, until each daughter had taken a turn. When Heracles awoke the next morning, hungover but with lingering recollections of a pleasurable night, he laughed to Thespius about the lustiness of the slave girl who had entered his bed. Thespius laughed, too, and then revealed the truth. Nine months later, he welcomed an army of sturdy grandsons into the world.

Soon after this, Heracles fought on behalf of Creon, the king of Thebes, and was offered the hand of the king's daughter, Megara. The marriage was happy; Megara soon bore Heracles eight more sons.

But Hera hadn't forgotten about Heracles; she'd merely been biding her time, knowing that she could hurt him more deeply once he had more to lose. Now, she judged the time to be ripe and ordered Lyssa, the goddess of madness, to infect him. Lyssa balked, reluctant to lay her curse upon an undeserving man, but Hera was adamant and her power was the greater of the two.

Heracles was in the courtyard of his house with Megara, Amphitryon and his sons, preparing to offer a sacrifice to Zeus. A basket of grain—the first, bloodless offering at any sacrifice—had just been passed around the circle when Lyssa descended upon the house with a thunderous crack. Soon, her poison was coursing through Heracles's body. His eyeballs began to bulge and throb like mounds of earth from which some infestation of vermin was preparing to burst. Spittle flecked the corners of his mouth and the veins on his neck were engorged with blood. Initially, he fought back against the madness, heaving and bellowing like a bull, but Lyssa's venom worked ineluctably, hardening his heart and directing his body towards a horrible purpose.

He snatched up each of his sons, one by one. Using the sacrificial knife that he carried, Heracles stabbed them, staining the marble tiles red with their blood. "Father!" screamed one. "What are you doing?" "Papa, don't hurt me!" begged another. But Heracles stared at them pitilessly, failing to recognize his own children.

When he had killed them all, he turned on Megara, behind whose skirts the last and youngest son had tried to hide. When she, too, lay dead, he raised his hand against Amphityron, who trembled in the corner. But by now Athena—who had watched the whole tragedy unfold but had not dared to interfere, knowing what the Fates had decreed for her brother—could tolerate no more. Picking up a rock, she flung it at Heracles, knocking him senseless. The slaves, who had been cowering inside, ran out and bound their master in strong chains.

When Heracles awoke, Lyssa was gone. Sharp grief assaulted his mind, instead. He took what small comfort he could from the fact that his wife and sons had been initiated into Demeter's mysteries at Eleusis. If Demeter's promises held true, his family was now enjoying a sunlit existence of feasts and music in the afterlife.

He, however, faced a life of despair. Eventually, he roused himself to travel to Delphi, where he could ask Apollo for advice.

66
THE NEMEAN LION AND THE LERNAEAN HYDRA

Apollo explained that Heracles would have to atone for the murders of his wife and children. The terms of the atonement would be left to Heracles's cousin Eurystheus, a son of Sthenelus who was now king of Mycenae.

Eurystheus was a thin and sallow man of meager strength. He had been born prematurely, thanks to Hera's machinations. For one day, Zeus had sworn to Hera—knowing that Alcmene was about to give birth to Heracles but not knowing that Hera knew it, as well—that the next descendant of Perseus to see the light of day would rule over all the others.

Hera smiled at Zeus's foolish presumption of her ignorance and, hastening down to Mycenae, caused the womb of Eurystheus's mother to expel its burden two months early. The midwife didn't hold out much hope for the scrawny infant, but Hera devoted herself to his protection, swatting away the illnesses and demons that snatched babies. Eurystheus survived into adulthood, all the while begrudging his cousin's robust health and strength. The prospect of overseeing Heracles's atonement pleased him immensely.

"You shall perform ten labors, Cousin," said Eurystheus contemptuously, "each of which will remind you to take human mortality more *seriously*. For the first, you must kill the lion that has beleaguered our neighbors in Nemea for many years now."

This lion was the son of Echidna and Typhon. Hera had nurtured him when he was a baby, seeing in him the potential to one day kill Heracles if she didn't manage to do it herself. When he was grown, she'd dumped him outside of Nemea, where he quickly became a bane to the people and their flocks, leaving a bloody trail of slaughter wherever he went.

Heracles tracked the lion for several days by following his scat, which was putrid with half-digested flesh. At last he found the cave into which the lion retreated each night, and hid himself in the brush outside the entrance. At evening the lion approached, the fur of his mane clumped with gore from the day's hunt. Heracles leapt from his ambush and cast his spear, but it bounced off the lion's flank and fell uselessly to the ground, its bronze point crumpled. The impact roused the lion, however. He lashed towards Heracles, who quickly drew his sword. That, too, proved useless; the blade bent when it struck the lion's back.

Heracles realized with a shock that the lion's hide was impenetrable. In the next instant, the beast lunged and knocked him to the ground. Absurdly, Heracles found himself embracing the lion like a lover. Almost of their own accord, Heracles's arms began to hug the lion more and more tightly, until the lion's jaws sagged open and gasped for air. Then, his fetid breath stopped altogether.

Heracles rolled out from under the dead body. He was exhausted and in pain; during the fight, the lion had managed to bite off the tip of his smallest finger and the stump throbbed horribly. As he bound up the wound in a strip of linen torn from his tunic, it occurred to him that he ought to flay the lion: an impenetrable pelt could protect him just as it had once protected the lion. But how could he pierce the unpierceable?

And then some god put it into Heracles's head to lift the lion's limp forepaw and use the claws to slit the skin of the beast's belly. Once he'd done this, Heracles slowly peeled the hide from the carcass, taking care to preserve the lion's head and mane. He cured the hide and draped it around himself, tying the forelegs around his neck and letting the tail dangle between his legs. What remained of the lion's head he pulled over his own.

Thus outfitted, he returned to Mycenae. He strode into Eurystheus's palace and declared that his first labor was done. Shrieking with fear at what seemed to be a talking lion, Eurystheus ran behind his throne. Heracles pushed back the head of the pelt and laughed.

"Your next labor," Eurystheus squeaked when he had recovered enough presence to speak, "is to conquer the Hydra of Lerna."

The Hydra—another child of Typhon and Echidna whom Hera had nurtured—was a huge snake that lived in a swamp near the town of Lerna. Size was not her most dreadful aspect, however; the Hydra had nine heads, each of them equipped with a viper's fangs and venom. While her prey skittered to escape one swaying neck, eight others could circle around to attack.

Heracles took Iphicles's son, Iolaus, along on the quest, thinking that the boy might prove useful. When they arrived, they camped in the meadow next to the swamp and fell asleep watching the eerie glow of marsh gas playing over its surface.

As the sun came up and the air grew warm, a stench rolled off the water. Heracles and Iolaus caught the familiar odors of decaying plants and rotting creatures, but behind these lurked another smell: rank, sharp and alive. Soon, its source appeared: the Hydra, seeking her morning meal.

Trusting that his lion skin would protect him from the Hydra's fangs, Heracles waded into the swamp with a sickle in his hand. After watching the way in which the Hydra's necks moved for a moment, he slashed out, severing one of them as neatly as a harvester reaps grain.

He was preparing to sever another when Iolaus shouted out in alarm. Heracles turned to see that the stump of the neck he'd just cut was sending forth two new necks with two new heads. Heracles tentatively hacked off one of them but the results were the same: he gained two new enemies for the one he'd destroyed.

"Grab the torch, Iolaus!" he cried. "Sear the stumps!"

Splashing and ducking, Iolaus flew into action. Soon, the smell of burning snake filled the air—sweetly acrid to their noses.

Hera watched from above, fuming at Heracles's ingenuity. She dispatched a large crab to nip at his feet, hoping to distract him long enough for one of the Hydra's remaining heads to strike. Heracles, however, promptly crushed the thing beneath his heel.

With Iolaus's help, Heracles quickly severed most of the Hydra's heads. The sickle and torch could not defeat the last one, however, which the gods had made immortal. Eventually, Heracles wrenched a great boulder from the meadow's soil and pinned the head beneath it. The Hydra's body continued to writhe and squirm; Heracles slit it open and dipped his arrows in its poisonous gall to ensure that they would bring death to whatever they hit. Even this did not kill the beast; for centuries, travelers continued to see her tail lashing fruitlessly in the swamp.

Dressed in the skin of his first labor and carrying weapons enhanced by his second, Heracles returned to Mycenae to learn where Eurystheus would send him next. Hera, meanwhile, decided to memorialize her efforts to defeat Heracles by placing the lion and the crab next to one another in the stars.

67
THE CERYNEIAN HIND AND THE ERYMANTHIAN BOAR

When Eurystheus heard that Iolaus had cauterized the stumps of the Hydra's necks, he declared that the labor didn't count towards the ten that he'd ordered Heracles to perform because Heracles hadn't done it alone. There were still nine left to do. The next one, Eurystheus continued, was to capture the Ceryneian Hind and bring her back to Mycenae alive.

This hind had once been the nymph Taygete, whom Zeus desired. Taygete begged Artemis to help her escape his embraces; Artemis changed her into a hind that was astonishingly swift and crowned with a strong set of antlers. Later, after Zeus had abandoned his pursuit, Artemis freed the nymph from the hind's body and gave the hind a life of her own. In gratitude, Taygete gilded the hind's antlers and engraved Artemis's name upon them. The hind continued to roam freely in the area around Mount Ceryneia in Arcadia, protected from the wolves that preyed on other deer by her antlers and her speed.

Heracles pursued the hind for an entire year, through forests and meadows, up hills and down valleys, but he could not capture her. Finally, one evening when both Heracles and the hind had paused to eat, Heracles conceded that swiftness alone wouldn't enable him to complete the labor. He drew from his quiver one of the few arrows that he hadn't dipped in the Hydra's gall.

Taking care to move slowly, he approached the tall grass where the hind was resting. He aimed for her foreleg and shot. He lifted the injured animal and carefully wrapped her around his neck, as a shepherd does a sheep, and set out for Mycenae.

When he had nearly reached the city, Artemis and Apollo suddenly appeared in front of him, blocking his path.

"Where are you taking *my* hind, little brother? And what have you done to her leg?" demanded Artemis, while Apollo stared menacingly over her shoulder.

"To Eurystheus of Mycenae, to whom *your* twin has indentured me."

"Ah. Yes. That little matter," said Apollo, clearing his throat. "Sister, let Heracles go on his way; he'll release your hind, whose leg you can easily heal, when he's done."

And so Heracles proceeded to Mycenae and showed Eurystheus the hind.

"Your next labor," said Eurystheus, scarcely pausing to glance at the hind, "is to bring me the boar that has been ravaging the region of Psophis. And again, I want to see this creature *alive*."

Compared with the Nemean Lion and the Hydra, the boar was nothing much: he was merely larger than other boars. But he was also, like the Ceryneian Hind, unusually swift, and this once more proved to be a challenge. Day after day, month after month, Heracles chased the boar over shifting terrains, never getting close enough to grab him. Heracles dared not try to immobilize him as he had immobilized the hind; the boar's legs were so short that they scarcely afforded a target. Heracles might easily hit a more vital part of the boar's body and kill it.

But one day, Heracles realized that the shortness of the boar's legs was his weak point. He renewed his pursuit and steered the boar towards the slopes of Mount Erymanthus, the upper parts of which were blanketed by snow. As the two climbed higher and the snow became deeper, the boar's stumpy legs were unable to move. Heracles walked over to the flailing animal and simply picked him up.

Holding the boar by his back legs, Heracles slung him over his shoulder and began to return to Mycenae. As he approached Eurystheus, the king leapt from his throne in terror and jumped into a huge wine jar that happened to be empty at the moment. Heracles laughed and tried to cram the boar into the jar as well, rump first.

"From now on, my assistant Copreus will be the one to examine anything that you bring home from your labors!" sputtered Eurystheus after he was rescued and sponged off.

During the days and months that Heracles was chasing the boar, he had other adventures as well. One night, he stopped at the cave of Pholus the centaur, who unlike most of his tribe was a quiet, well-mannered creature.

When Heracles introduced himself and asked for a night's shelter, Pholus's eyes opened wide. Years before, Dionysus had left a jar of exceedingly good wine with him, saying, "Don't open this until a time arrives when you serve as host to the hero Heracles." That moment had finally come; the jar was opened and a sweet, inviting aroma filled the cave.

The aroma wafted out of the cave, as well, and over the mountainside where other centaurs made their beds each night among the leaves and pine needles. The thought of wine—which they were seldom able to acquire—drove them wild with excitement; they stormed Pholus's cave and tried to carry it off.

Heracles defended his host by using his arrows to slay the first of the centaurs, but then more arrived, armed with firebrands, axes and small trees that they'd wrenched from the soil. Their grandmother, Nephele, assisted them by sending a heavy rainstorm. In the slick mud, the four-legged creatures had an advantage over two-legged Heracles.

At last, however, Heracles managed to kill most of the centaurs and chase the others away. Pholus thoughtfully regarded the corpses now littering his home. Pulling an arrow from the chest of one, he gazed at it and mused, "To think that such a little thing as this could kill a mighty beast," and then he clumsily dropped it on his foot.

The Hydra's gall still clung to its tip and the poison did its dreadful work. The generous host who had welcomed first Dionysus and then Heracles lay dead.

68
THE STABLES OF AUGEAS AND THE STYMPHALIAN BIRDS

For his fifth labor—or his fourth, as Eurystheus was counting— Heracles was ordered to clean the stables of King Augeas of Elis in a single day. The stables housed Augeas's vast herds of cattle, which were descendants of the beautiful red cows that Augeas's father, Helios, pastured on the island of Thrinacia.

For years, no one had bothered to thoroughly muck the stables out; over time, precipitous heaps of manure had accumulated everywhere, between which the cattle trod narrow paths to their stalls. Clouds of dung-eating flies swarmed up angrily whenever anyone dared to interrupt their meal. Surely, thought Eurystheus, even the strength of Heracles cannot clean out such a mess in one day.

Before Heracles could depart for Elis, word reached him that his friend Jason was assembling a group of heroes to fetch the Golden Fleece, which was guarded by a dragon in Colchis, faraway to the east. It was exactly the sort of quest that Heracles loved: a journey to an exotic land filled with strange new dangers and unexpected trials of strength.

Rushing north to Iolcus, Jason's hometown, Heracles jumped aboard Jason's ship and served the expedition well until the mysterious disappearance of his young lover, Hylas, drew him away from his shipmates. After searching fruitlessly for Hylas for many weeks, the grieving Heracles returned to Greece and remembered his obligation to clean the stables. By the time the Argonauts were nearing home with the fleece, Heracles had finished that labor and done six more, eclipsing Jason's one.

When Heracles arrived in Elis, he kept to himself the fact that he had been ordered by Eurystheus to clean out Augeas's stables. Approaching the king, he made him an offer: if he managed to clean the stables in a single day, Augeas would give him a tenth of the marvelous herd; if he failed, he would receive nothing. Augeas, seeing a way to get rid of at least some of the muck, readily agreed, never expecting that he would have to pay.

The next day, as the sun was rising, Heracles surveyed the stables from a hill nearby. When he noticed that they were located near the spot where the streams of the Alpheus and Peneus Rivers drew close to one another, some god put a clever plan into his head. He ran down the hill, seized a shovel and began to dig furiously, carving channels through the center of each stable nearly to the banks of each river. He then went back and continued each channel in the opposite direction until they joined the rivers downstream.

He paused to wipe the sweat from his brow and then, returning upstream to where just a few feet of soil separated the swiftly flowing rivers from his new channels, he dug the margins away. The rivers swirled into their new causeways and thundered through the stables, carrying all of the muck (to say nothing of the flies) along with them. The mess flowed into the rivers downstream and was swept away.

When this was finished, Heracles restored the waters to their normal courses by closing up the breaches he'd made in their banks. He shoveled the soil back into the channels and then used a broom to clear the last traces of dirt out of the stables. He triumphantly presented himself to Augeas to receive his payment.

In the meantime, however, word reached Augeas that Eurystheus had commanded Heracles to do the job before their own deal had been made; on this basis, Augeas declared that deal null and void. Later, Heracles returned to Elis and made Augeas pay with his life; for the moment, however, he let the matter lie and returned to Mycenae, eager to get on with his work.

Yet news had flown faster than even the swiftest of Zeus's eagles. By the time that Heracles arrived, Eurystheus had heard that he'd been offered a wage by Augeas and declared that *his* deal with Heracles was null and void, as well. Only three labors had been accomplished, by Eurystheus's count. For the fourth labor (or "sixth," said Heracles silently to himself), Heracles had to rid Lake Stymphalia of birds that were snatching up local sheep and sometimes local children, too.

These birds, which had been nurtured by Ares, had rapacious beaks and bronze feathers with points as sharp as arrows. When they chose to, they could shoot those feathers from their wings with great speed and accuracy, skewering prey before swooping down to snatch it.

Heracles camped out near the lake so as to watch the birds when they first arose from the reeds where they nested each night. In spite of the fact that he had heard many reports of them, he was shocked by what he saw when they took flight the next morning: their deadly wings were larger and more muscular than those of even the biggest vultures. That such hulking appendages could lift a bird into the air seemed to defy nature; watching them fly was like seeing a lion or a bear suddenly lift its paws and leap into the clouds.

Shaking himself back into focus, Heracles realized that there were too many birds, and their speed was too great, for him to shoot them all down. He spent the day considering how else he might rid the lake of them. He had nearly given up when out of thin air stepped Athena, giving him quite a start.

"Little brother," she said, "not everything needs to be captured or killed to be defeated. Hephaestus and I have forged for you these tools of bronze from deep in the earth. Use them tomorrow at daybreak—if you have the strength!—and the birds will flee, never to return."

Athena gestured to two enormous castanets lying nearby, each as wide as a discus. And then she dissolved back into the air, leaving Heracles alone once more.

Heracles experimented with ways of holding the unwieldy instruments and clacking them together until the birds returned at dusk. By the time he stopped, his wrists and fingers ached with the strain of the castanets' weight. He sat quietly, then, drowsing but never allowing himself to sleep, lest he miss his opportunity to frighten the birds just before they awoke at dawn.

When the eastern horizon turned gray with early light, Heracles picked up the castanets and clacked them as loudly as he could. The birds shot into the sky, screeching in alarm. They flew away north to the home of Ares, leaving the Stymphalians in peace.

69

THE CRETAN BULL AND THE MARES OF DIOMEDES

Heracles was careful not to tell Eurystheus that Athena and Hephaestus had given him castanets to chase away the birds, lest that labor be disqualified, too. He stood waiting to hear what he had to do next.

"Capture the Cretan Bull," said Eurystheus, "and bring him back for inspection."

This was the bull that Poseidon had once given to Minos: large, white and powerful. This was also the bull that had fathered the Minotaur upon Minos's wife, Pasiphaë, when Aphrodite cursed her with maddened lust. After that disaster, Minos had turned the bull loose into the countryside and allowed him to roam wherever he wished.

Heracles sailed to Crete, tracked down the bull and wrestled him into submission. Dragging him to the seashore, Heracles straddled his back, smacked him on the hindquarters and rode him all the way across the sea to Greece. Once he'd shown the bull to Copreus, Heracles released him again. The bull wandered around the Peloponnese for a few years before crossing the Corinthian isthmus and ambling northwards. Eventually, he ended up in Marathon, where the hero Theseus captured him once more.

Chagrined by how easily Heracles had completed that labor, Eurystheus thought hard about the next. The fastest and most vicious animals of central Greece had proven to be inadequate foes: the Nemean Lion, the Hydra, the Ceryneian Hind, the Erymanthian Boar and the Stymphalian Birds had all been conquered. Sending Heracles south to Crete had not defeated him either.

And then Eurystheus had an idea.

"Go north this time," he ordered Heracles, "until you reach the land of the Bistones, where Diomedes is king. His father, Ares, has given him some mares with tastes that are . . . *unusual*. They dine not on grass or hay or oats, but exclusively on human flesh. Diomedes furnishes their meals from any strangers who are unlucky enough to visit his kingdom. Bring me those mares!"

And so Heracles traveled northwards, taking along his lover Abderus, a handsome young man. They traveled for many days before arriving in Thrace, a land of cold, ferocious people whose bodies were marked with strange, undulating tattoos.

They found the kingdom of the Bistones and made their way to the paddock where Diomedes kept his mares. The animals were just finishing a meal. A mangled arm dangled from the jaws of one, its fingers curling as if making one last plea. Chunks of flesh lay scattered where they'd fallen out of gobbling mouths.

Heracles sidled up to a mare that was drinking from a trough in the shadowy corner of the yard. Throwing a leg over her back, he swung himself up and hung on for dear life, shouting to Abderus to bring him a bridle.

Poor Abderus; he slipped in the muck that lay everywhere and landed on his back. In a trice, the mares were upon him. By the time Heracles reached him, little was left of the beautiful youth.

Diomedes and the grooms had come running at the sound of Abderus's cries and now leaned over the fence, laughing at the sight of Heracles's tears. Enraged, Heracles strode over, yanked the king into the air and threw him to his own mares. In a frenzy of excitement, they made even quicker work of their master than they had of Abderus.

And then a strange change came over them. Tossing their heads and frantically snorting, they scattered to the corners of the paddock and cowered there until Heracles led them away. The flesh of the man who had weaned them on strangers had cured them of their taste for it; from then on, they ate what other horses ate.

Eurystheus had no desire to stable such creatures, even in their penitent state. After Copreus had confirmed the mares' delivery, the king commanded that they be turned loose to wander on their own, like the bull. Years later, while grazing in the hills below Mount Olympus, they were torn apart by wild animals.

Heracles had buried the scant remains of Abderus before he departed for home and founded a city he called Abdera around the grave. It grew into a wealthy place, more civilized than its inland neighbors, where traders who wished to do business with the Thracians would pause on their journeys.

70
ALCESTIS

As Heracles and Abderus were journeying north to capture Diomedes's mares, they paused for the night in Pherae, where Jason's cousin Admetus was king. Admetus had married another of their cousins, Alcestis, after becoming the first of her suitors to meet a challenge set by her father: he drove through the streets in a chariot yoked to a lion and a boar.

Admetus managed this with help from Apollo. The man and the god had become friends after Zeus sentenced Apollo to serve Admetus for a year, to punish him for killing the Cyclopes, whose lightning bolts had incinerated Apollo's son Asclepius. Understanding that it was humiliating for Apollo to serve a mortal, Admetus sent him to the distant meadows to tend cattle—a task that suited the god of herds and that kept him away from people's inquisitive eyes.

Admetus and Alcestis settled happily into marriage and soon had a son and a daughter. One day, however, Admetus fell desperately ill. No doctor could cure him, no wise woman's herbs could help, no offerings to the gods could stop the deadly course of the illness.

Apollo watched from above, unable to ignore this human death as he had ignored so many others. Finally, he invited the Fates to his table and served them nectar laced with wine. The Fates, who had never tasted wine before, were soon drunk. Apollo then persuaded them to extend Admetus's life—with the proviso, added the Fates, that Admetus find someone else to die in his place.

Apollo sighed with relief. Surely, he thought, someone will volunteer to make the exchange! Admetus's parents were plagued by the aches and pains of the elderly. Wouldn't one of them relinquish a few troubled months to save their son? Or one of Admetus's loyal subjects, whom he'd governed with kindness and generosity?

But no one came forward. Admetus's parents wrung their hands and murmured that each hour of life was all the sweeter for being among their last. His subjects coughed and looked away, embarrassed by their selfishness but nonetheless unwilling to make the sacrifice.

And then Alcestis spoke out. "I will die for my husband."

Immediately, Admetus lifted his voice to object, but it was too late: the Fates had heard Alcestis's words. The thread that they were spinning for Admetus became stronger and thicker while that of Alcestis began to fray away, as wool does before it breaks under the spinner's thumb.

Even as Alcestis grew weaker she tried to protect those she would leave behind. After bathing and dressing in her finest clothes, she went to the palace's hearth to offer some grain to Hestia, the goddess who watched over households.

"Take care of my husband for me, goddess," she said, "and watch over my children, who were born within this family that has always honored you. Give them a stepmother who will not be cruel!"

Then she made offerings and prayed at each of the other household altars, as well. At last, when fingers that were once nimble at the loom could no longer carry gifts to the gods, Alcestis retreated to her bed and composed herself to die.

But many surprising things come to pass when the gods so choose. The next day, as Alcestis's body was being prepared for burial, Heracles arrived, asking for a meal and a bed for the night. Admetus, wishing neither to turn away a friend nor to burden one with his grief, welcomed Heracles and then forbade his slaves to mention that Alcestis was dead. Admetus excused himself from dinner that night but ordered his slaves to bring Heracles the finest food and drink.

And so Heracles, being Heracles, ate like a pig and drank like a fish. Only the next morning did he learn from a slave who could not contain her tears that Alcestis was dead.

Heracles strode to the cemetery, found Alcestis's newly covered grave and hid behind a nearby tree. Soon, Death arrived, a grin on his bony face. A filmy shadow arose from Alcestis's grave to meet him, its head bowed.

Suddenly, Heracles sprang from his cover, wrapped his arms around Death and knocked him down. The pair rolled on the ground, each as determined as the other to lead Alcestis away. Now Death clutched Heracles by the throat; now Heracles broke free and pinned Death's arms behind his back. Now Death had his foot on Heracles's chest; now Heracles grabbed Death's shin and flipped him down again.

Finally, Death began to gasp. Admitting defeat, he slouched away. The shadow, which had anxiously watched the wrestling match, began to take on substance. By the time that Heracles had led her back to the palace, she was nearly as much Alcestis again as she had ever been.

She stood by silently as Heracles announced the happy news to Admetus. The gods of the Underworld do not relinquish their citizens easily and the conditions under which they do so must be carefully observed. Not a single word, they had decreed, could Alcestis speak until the sun had set on the third day of her new life. And so with smiles and embraces instead, she made known her joy.

71
HIPPOLYTA'S BELT AND THE CATTLE OF GERYON

"For your next labor go east, into the savage lands that encircle the Black Sea," Eurystheus told Heracles. "My royal geographers tell me that when you reach the place where the river Thermodon flows hot into the sea, you'll find a fierce tribe of women warriors who call themselves Amazons. They're monstrous creatures, covered in strange tattoos that their scanty clothing fails to conceal! It's said that when they're babies, their mothers pinch off their right breasts so they might better draw their bowstrings when they're grown. And they *hate* all men!

"Hippolyta, the queen of these bitches, has a golden war belt that Ares gave her. Bring that belt back to my daughter, who wishes to adorn herself with it."

And so Heracles set out with a band of companions. He sailed across the Aegean Sea and then through the waters of the Hellespont, where Helle had once fallen off the back of the golden ram that was carrying her through the air, and then through the Bosphorus, which his own ancestor, Io, had forded while still in the form of a cow. Sticking close to the southern coast of the Black Sea, he made his way to the mouth of the Thermodon, close to which lay Themiscyra, the city of the Amazons.

He disembarked alone and, carrying a herald's staff, the sign that a parley was desired, approached the guards stationed at the gate. As they drew their swords against him, Heracles spoke quickly.

"I am but one man coming in peace, as my staff shows. You could overpower me at any moment, if you chose to. Take me to your queen, I beg. When she has heard what I have to say, you can do with me as you like."

Hippolyta was fascinated by the strange man dressed in a lion's skin. She listened carefully to his request and his tale of the circumstances that lay behind it.

"Take it, Heracles," she said, unbuckling the heavy belt from her tunic. "The gods are cruel, especially to those who are destined to excel. Good luck."

Hera seethed, watching the scene unfold. However far away Eurystheus might send Heracles (and she had infiltrated Eurystheus's mind in recent months to ensure that he sent Heracles to the most distant lands possible), Heracles triumphed in the most unexpected of ways. Disguising herself as an Amazon, Hera suddenly appeared in front of a group of women who were gathered outside the palace.

"Heracles means to kidnap Hippolyta and enslave her to bear his children!" she screamed.

In moments, the Amazons' well-rehearsed plan for defending their queen was deployed: women marched to the palace like ants, steady and determined. Heracles, hearing them approach, assumed that he'd fallen into a trap. Acting in haste, he strangled Hippolyta—even she, the strongest of women, could not break free of his hands.

When the Amazons discovered what Heracles had done, their cries of grief and fury were so loud that his companions heard them and ran to his defense. Soon, the streets of Themiscyra were littered with bodies, male and female. Heracles fought his way out of the palace, gathered what companions remained and swiftly departed. In a few weeks, he was back in Mycenae. The gods, meanwhile, had told him of Hippolyta's innocence; he mourned her needless death and wept bitterly for his own part in it.

"Go west, now," said Eurystheus, while his skinny daughter tried to strut in a belt too large for her hips to carry. "Fetch me the cattle of Geryon from where he pastures them on the misty island of Erythia."

Geryon was the mortal son of Callirhoë, a nymph, and Chrysaor, who was the son of Medusa and Poseidon. Geryon had emerged from his mother's womb curious in form: three torsos sprang up from his waist, each topped by two arms and a head, and six legs stood underneath.

The hides of Geryon's cattle had been stained red by the waning rays of Helios's chariot, which flew low over the island each evening as it approached the western stream of Ocean. A formidable herdsman, Eurytion, watched over them with the help of Orthrus, a two-headed dog that was brother to Cerberus.

Heracles's journey west was long and wearisome. More than once, he battled strange monsters; more than once, he lost his way among strange peoples. Wandering through northern Libya, he reached the place where it nearly touched the southern expanse of Spain. Realizing that he'd traveled as far west as any mortal before him, Heracles built two pillars, one on either side of the strait, to mark his presence. Onwards he journeyed until at last—frustrated, exhausted and maddened by the unrelenting heat that seared Libya—he took an arrow from his quiver and shot it at Helios, who was passing overhead just then. Helios, none the worse for the arrow, took pity on Heracles and lent him the golden cup in which he and his horses sailed home on the stream of Ocean each night. Heracles bobbed up and down on the waves, riding the currents westwards alongside peculiar creatures who peered up at him through the water. Overhead, the constellations staggered wearily in their tracks as they neared their beds. Finally, he reached the island of Erythia, where it was always twilight and always cool.

When Geryon learned that Heracles had arrived, he buckled three cuirasses upon his three bodies and prepared to defend his cattle. His friend Menoetes urged him to stay back.

"Consider what you're about to confront! This man killed the lion of Nemea, the Hydra of Lerna and many another fearsome beast—as well as countless mortals. The gods can give you new cattle; let Heracles take what he wants!"

"If I'd been born a god," Geryon replied, "this would be a trifling matter. But if I must pass into death, then the honor I leave behind means everything. For my own good name and that of my children, who are dearer to me than my life, I must fight him."

He stopped to visit his mother in her chambers. Callirhoë wept and reminded him of how she, a queen, had nursed him herself, never trusting him to a nanny. Yet he turned aside his faces, now wet with tears, and left the palace.

The battle was brief. When Geryon arrived, Eurytion was already breathing his last, and the great dog sprawled dead with his feet in the air. The smell of blood, as sharp as iron, hung in the air.

Heracles threw an enormous boulder at one of Geryon's heads, knocking off its helmet. An arrow, dipped in the Hydra's gall, quickly followed. The head drooped heavily upon its neck, like the barren bud of a poppy. Poseidon tried to save his grandson then, but Athena held him to the oath that all gods swear not to spurn the Fates' decrees. Heracles made quick work of Geryon's two other heads and then herded the wonderful cattle into Helios's cup, eager to start his voyage home.

Weeping, the people of Erythia gave their king a magnificent funeral and praised his noble death.

72
CACUS AND THE APPLES OF THE HESPERIDES

The journey home from Erythia was just as long and demanding as the journey there had been. After returning Helios's cup and setting out again on foot, Heracles lost his way and ended up driving the cattle through Spain, France and finally Italy. Many people coveted the herd; he was constantly fighting off marauders.

The people of Liguria proved to be especially troublesome. The men and women joined forces to steal the cattle, fighting Heracles with whatever implements came to hand—sticks, shovels, pitchforks, pestles. Heracles used his bow to defend himself until his quiver was empty. Wounded then, he fell to his knees and Zeus realized that the time had finally come to help his son. He caused thousands of stones to rain down upon the ground next to Heracles, supplying ample ammunition. Heracles dragged himself to his feet, flung the stones at his attackers and routed the Ligurians. Centuries later, the stones still littered the field, a testament to Heracles's resilience.

He hadn't traveled much farther before he encountered a grimmer challenge. In a cave on a forested hill lived Cacus, a son of Hephaestus who was brutal in body and depraved in soul. Corpulent and filthy, he lumbered through the countryside doing whatever he pleased, sampling crimes and perversions with the relish of a gourmand. The ground outside his cave reeked with blood that dripped from the flayed faces of travelers whom he'd tortured and killed.

Cacus happened to be squatting on a precipice that overlooked the valley of the river Tiber when Heracles arrived and decided to settle the cattle there for the night; immediately, Cacus resolved to steal some for himself. Waiting until Heracles was asleep, Cacus drove four bulls and four heifers backwards to his cave, cackling at the way that their reversed footprints would confuse Heracles. Once inside, he released a chain that lowered a boulder before the cave's entrance; no passerby would ever guess what lay behind it.

But clever though Cacus was, Heracles was cleverer still. The next morning, when he noticed that eight cows were missing, Heracles drove the rest of the herd all over the area until the sound of their lowing was answered from inside the hill. He circled it three times then, seeking a way into what appeared to be solid rock. Finally, losing his patience, he threw all of his weight against the flinty pinnacle at its top until it snapped.

From the edge of the hole that he'd made in the roof of Cacus's home, Heracles began to pummel Cacus with rocks but Cacus responded with a talent he'd inherited from his father: opening wide his mouth, he belched forth smoke in such abundance that it filled the cave, completely hiding him from sight. Heracles leapt down and blindly groped for Cacus until at last he caught and strangled him. He found the chain that raised the boulder, drove forth his cattle and then dragged out Cacus's corpse, raising a gasp from the crowd of people who had been drawn to the place by the noise and the smoke. Evander, the king of that region, built an altar to Heracles (ignoring Heracles's insistence that he was merely mortal) and the people worshipped him forevermore at the foot of what later became known as the Aventine Hill.

Finally arriving in Mycenae, Heracles gave what remained of Geryon's cattle—lean and lank from their long trek—to Eurystheus.

"Since you know the west so well now, Heracles, go back," said the king. "Indeed, go farther west than before—even farther than our ancestor Perseus went when he killed Medusa! Fetch me three golden apples from the garden of the Hesperides, beyond the stream of Ocean."

When the universe was young, Earth had given the tree that bore these golden apples to Hera as a wedding present; Hera entrusted it to nymphs called Hesperides to prevent the apples from being stolen. Later, however, Hera discovered that the Hesperides themselves were eating the apples and ordered Ladon, a fearsome dragon whose breath was so vile that it scorched the grass, to twine himself around the tree's trunk.

So Heracles trudged off once more—but not towards the setting sun. In hopes of staying on course this time, he decided to seek directions from Nereus, the Old Man of the Sea. Nereus hated to talk with mortals; Heracles had to wrestle him into submission, clinging tightly as Nereus changed himself first into a fish, then into a lion, then into fire and finally into water itself. Exhausted at last,

Nereus told Heracles to seek advice from Prometheus, who was still hanging on a cliff in the Caucasus Mountains.

So Heracles traveled eastwards, following in Io's footsteps for many months until he found the poor Titan. Just as Heracles was about to ask his questions, Zeus's eagle arrived to make his daily meal from Prometheus's liver. Horrified by what the bird was about to do, Heracles shot him dead and freed Prometheus from his chains. Stretching his limbs for the first time in centuries, Prometheus gratefully told Heracles about the landmarks he would pass on the journey westwards. Heracles set out once more. Yet even with all of Prometheus's advice, he again became lost in Libya. Stopping for the night, he asked for a bed in the house of Antaeus.

This Antaeus, an enormous son of Earth and Poseidon, challenged every visitor to a wrestling match. He killed those who lost (so far, that had been everyone) and from their skulls he had been steadily building a temple to his father. His eye gleamed avariciously at the fine shape of Heracles's head as he explained what he demanded of guests.

The match commenced. Although smaller than Antaeus, Heracles seemed to be winning at first, easily toppling his opponent several times. Yet every time he pinned Antaeus to the ground, Antaeus sprang free. The reason (which no one but Antaeus knew) was that whenever Antaeus touched his mother, Earth, his strength was renewed. Finally realizing that something of the sort must be going on, Heracles lifted his opponent off the ground and held him there until Antaeus grew so feeble that Heracles could crush his chest, forcing the ends of his ribs into his liver. Heracles slept soundly that night in Antaeus's bed and then marched onwards.

He became lost again and wandered into Egypt, where Busiris, a wicked king who sacrificed all strangers to the gods, tried to make an offering of him; Heracles slit Busiris's throat at his own altar. Then he marched west to the mountain where Atlas stood, forever holding Sky away from Earth as Zeus had long ago commanded. Prometheus had told Heracles to seek Atlas's advice about how to obtain the apples.

"It's no use my trying to explain such a complicated matter to a mere mortal," said Atlas when Heracles inquired. "You look like a strong man—from what I hear, you beat Antaeus—so why don't *you* hold up Sky for a bit while I sprint westwards and get the apples for you?"

Heracles had little choice but to agree. He bowed his head and lifted his hands; Atlas shifted all the weight of Sky onto Heracles's shoulders.

Atlas soon returned, cradling three golden apples in one enormous hand.

"Mortal," he said, "it's foolish for you to trudge all the way back to Eurystheus when I can deliver these almost instantaneously. Stay here. I'll complete your mission and return—eventually."

Heracles realized that if he didn't think quickly, the job of holding up Sky would be his forever.

"Well, all right," he said, "but first let me fold my lion skin and place it on my shoulders as a cushion. Take over for a moment while I do that."

Atlas obligingly placed the apples on the ground and let Heracles shift Sky onto his shoulders.

"Stupid Titan!" cried Heracles, scooping up the apples and running away.

73
A JOURNEY TO THE UNDERWORLD

Heracles had performed eleven labors for Eurystheus, nine of which the king counted towards the ten he was owed. Now Heracles stood in Eurystheus's throne room, awaiting his last orders.

"Go down this time—go to the Underworld. Fetch me the three-headed dog with razor-sharp teeth who guards the realm of Hades and Persephone—the one they call Cerberus."

Heracles knew little about the Underworld—no mortal knew much, until death brought its own grim revelations—but he did know that its dangers were far greater for those who had not won the gods' protection by being initiated into their mystery cults.

And so he traveled to Eleusis and asked the hierophant of Demeter's cult to initiate him. The hierophant recoiled in horror; Heracles, he said, had been befouled by the murders of many mortals—not only his wife and children but also those whom he had killed while carrying out his labors: Diomedes, Hippolyta, Geryon, the centaurs and others. Heracles was so profoundly stained that he couldn't even set foot in Demeter's sacred precinct.

But Demeter took pity on Heracles. She invented new rituals of purification and ordered her priests and priestesses to perform them on the banks of the Ilissus River, not far from Eleusis. Sitting on a stool that was as humble as the one on which Demeter herself had sat in the royal household so many years before, with his head bowed and veiled, Heracles was cleansed by water, air and fire. He returned to Eleusis, was initiated into Demeter's mysteries and then traveled south to Taenarum, where there was an entrance to the Underworld.

The way down was easy. Although Hades's kingdom was far away from the sunlit world by any ordinary measure of distance, the passage from life to death was always brief. For two obols, the boatman Charon ferried Heracles across the waters of the Acheron and left him on its farther bank, where white poplars susurrated in a breeze that Heracles could not feel. He disembarked and trod through a muddy marsh and then a dusty field. Milling all around him were the wretched ghosts of those who had killed their guests or dishonored their parents and many other ghosts as well—of good people, bad people, the noble and the lowly. By the terrible laws of that place, all were gathered together.

Most of them looked fragile, like leaves blown about in the wind, but one ghost stood out, so vivid and alarming that Heracles fit an arrow to his string.

"Put away your bow, Heracles, for you can't kill the dead and the dead can't kill you. And even if I could kill you, I wouldn't; don't you recognize Meleager, the son of Oeneus?"

"Meleager! How did you come to the land of the dead?" exclaimed Heracles.

"My mother, Althaea, murdered me in the white-hot anger of grief after I'd slain her brothers for behaving dishonorably when we killed the great boar."

Heracles wept at Meleager's fate, but then asked, "My friend, did you leave behind an unwed sister who was dear to your heart, whom I might lead home as my wife, to remember you by when I've returned to the land of the living?"

Meleager answered that his sister Deianira was still unwed and Heracles pledged to marry her when his labors were done.

And then he walked on. In the distance, he saw a palace that flickered dimly in the gloom, like the light of a lamp whose oil is reaching its end. On either side of the road that led to it were gray silhouettes of houses and shops, faint simulacra of human buildings. Through their black windows he could see shadows flitting here and there on some business of their own. Between these buildings he glimpsed tunnels that led into darkness.

The palace, when he finally reached it, was no less dim than it had been at a distance. The dog he had come to fetch lay near the entrance, eyes shut, heads resting on his paws. Stepping over him, Heracles passed inside and wandered through hallways that zigzagged back upon themselves. His footsteps reverberated in the silence.

In the throne room sat Hades. Persephone stood next to him, holding a fourfold torch to break the darkness in which she lived for part of each year. Its light danced against the ebony walls, casting monstrous shadows.

"Welcome, Nephew," said Hades, and, as Heracles's eyes widened in astonishment, he continued, "Don't be surprised that we have anticipated your arrival; very little remains secret among the gods. My brother Zeus boasts of you; my sister Hera spits at your name. Most of my divine nieces and nephews have made it their business to help you along your path and I know that my sister Demeter prepared you to come here so that you might finally expunge the debt you owe Eurystheus.

"I have no objection to your borrowing Cerberus, provided that you set him free when you're done; he'll find his own way back to us. But beware: docile though he is when someone enters my kingdom, he savagely attacks those who try to leave. That's your problem to solve." Hades chuckled, the sound echoing disagreeably against the polished walls.

"I've made it *my* problem to solve, Uncle," said Hermes as he materialized out of the gloom, carrying the luminous golden wand that Apollo had given him long ago. "It's my right to lead mortals down to your kingdom and my right, too, to lead them up again."

"As ghosts!" Hades exclaimed. "This man is no ghost."

"My dispensation from Zeus carries no restrictions. I'll lead him back, and the dog, too."

Hades thought for a moment, then nodded his head and whistled for Cerberus. Heracles bound a leash around Cerberus's necks and the man and the dog slipped effortlessly up the road, pulled along in Hermes's wake. They emerged through a cave near the town of Hermione and then sped over the earth to Mycenae, where Hermes vanished. Heracles tugged the dog along to the palace.

This time, when Eurystheus heard that Heracles had arrived, he decided to inspect the proof of the labor's completion himself, doubtful that any mortal could return from the land of the dead. When he walked into his audience room and saw the great dog straining at the leash, he doubted no longer and leapt, for the last time, into his wine jar. Screaming at Heracles to go away, he released him from his servitude.

74
SLAVE TO OMPHALE

Heracles continued to wander, unable to settle down after so many years of traveling. He visited other lands and grew to know their peoples. Some welcomed him with open arms: he slew the monsters that were a threat to their herds and killed the brigands that were haunting their roads. He fathered upon their women sons who grew up to lead their peoples as warriors and kings.

On one occasion, the gods themselves called upon Heracles's help when the Gigantes—massive, snake-legged creatures who had sprung from Earth when the world was young—tried to topple Zeus from his throne. The battle had already been raging in the fields of Phlegra for a long time when Zeus remembered an old prophecy: the gods would win if a mortal with divine blood in his veins came to their aid. Zeus called upon Heracles, who defended his father's rule over the cosmos.

On another occasion, Heracles heard that Eurytus, the king of Oechalia, had set an archery challenge, with his daughter, Iole, as the prize. Hastening there, Heracles easily won and stepped forward to claim his bride. But Eurytus, red-faced and stammering, refused to hold the wedding. He'd heard (indeed, everyone had heard) that Heracles had gone mad and killed his first wife and their children.

Heracles controlled his temper and returned home, although anger simmered in his heart. Months later, when Eurytus's son Iphitus, searching for some lost cows, appeared on Heracles's doorstep, Heracles accepted the young man hospitably but then lured him to a bastion and cast him to the ground below. And with that, Heracles once again became polluted. As he had so many years before, he traveled to Delphi to seek advice from his brother Apollo. This time, however, the Pythia refused to let Heracles enter the temple. Pushing her aside, Heracles began to plunder the temple's wealth.

He had just seized the most sacred object of all—the tripod upon which the Pythia sat whenever Apollo spoke through her mouth—when Apollo himself showed up. Apollo grabbed at the tripod just as Heracles was carrying it out the door. The brothers tugged it back and forth across the threshold until Zeus hurled a thunderbolt between their feet.

"Heracles will atone for the murder of Iphitus by being sold as a slave to Queen Omphale of Lydia," boomed Zeus from the heavens. "He will serve her for a year. The money that Omphale pays for him shall be given to Eurytus as blood gold."

Thus began a most interesting year in Heracles's life. Lydia was a wealthy kingdom, thanks in part to the gold that washed into its soil from the Pactolus River. Trade routes crisscrossed the land, bringing wares from foreign kingdoms and customers for what the Lydians themselves produced. Even the common folk lived well, filling their bellies with good food and draping their forms in soft wools of vibrant colors.

Omphale, the queen of this wealthy place, stood out even among all the other beautifully dressed women. Only the sheerest silks from India and the finest perfumes from Arabia touched her alabaster skin. Sandals of velvety leather, patterned with colorful designs, protected her feet from the cold mosaic floors of her palace. Amethysts dangled from her earlobes in clusters like gleaming grapes, sparkling in the light as she moved.

But all this luxury had sated Omphale's palate; what she yearned for most was novelty. As soon as Heracles arrived, she pulled him into her boudoir and told him to strip. After she'd bathed him in warm, fragrant water and blotted him dry, she stripped, too. Then she pointed to the silken heap of garments that she had just stepped out of and ordered him to get dressed. Meanwhile, she pulled on his tunic, girded it up around her waist with a stout belt and wrapped his lion skin around herself, rough though it was against her tender flesh. She picked up his club (or at least, she lifted one end of it from the floor and dragged it behind her), led him into her sitting room and pointed to a gilded basket of sheared wool, in which there lay a carding comb.

"Card!" she commanded. And he tried to card. After a few weeks of practice, he was able to produce acceptable wads of wool.

"Spin!" she commanded. And Heracles tried to spin, his callouses snagging the wispy wool each time he rubbed a blob of it between finger and thumb. But after a few weeks of practice, he was able to spin acceptable threads.

Each day, Omphale summoned Heracles to her chambers; each day, the two disrobed and exchanged clothing; each day, he worked wool while she lounged nearby, stroking the fur on the lion skin as she watched.

The practice led to a strange adventure. Late one day, the two set out into the woods so as to be able to greet the dawn in a place sacred to Dionysus, whose festival was due to begin on the morrow. They were spotted by Pan, who was filled with desire for Omphale. He began to track the pair, always staying far enough behind to remain hidden.

Evening was falling when they reached their goal; Omphale and Heracles slipped into a sheltering cave and, certain that they were far from prying eyes, traded clothes before lying down to sleep.

Pan waited until the cave was silent and then crept into its dimness, intending to rape Omphale and then dart away before Heracles could catch him. Fumbling in the dark, he encountered a body covered by a lion's pelt. Not that one! he thought, and turned to the other sleeper, whose form was wrapped in silken robes. Having gently moved them aside, he reached down to part the sleeper's thighs.

His hand encountered a thick matte of coarse hair. Suddenly, there was a roar of fury and Pan was carried outside into the moonlight by the scruff of his neck. When he saw his captive, however, Heracles's anger turned to laughter; smacking Pan on his goatish rear end, Heracles sent him on his way.

And ever since, Pan has preferred that mortals disrobe before they worship him, so that he knows exactly what he's getting.

75
A NEW WIFE AND NEW PROBLEMS

Before his year of slavery was up, Heracles had sired a son, Lamos, upon Omphale. What had begun as punishment ended pleasurably enough. But at last he longed for a home and a wife. Remembering what the ghost of Meleager had told him, he visited Oeneus and asked for Deianira's hand. Oeneus agreed—provided that Heracles defeat her other suitor, the river god Achelous.

And so began the slipperiest wrestling match of Heracles's long career. The river churned and twisted, changing form like quicksilver—now a snake, now a man, now a bull, now something in between them all—but Heracles never slackened his grip. Victorious, he carried away both Deianira and one of the horns that had crowned the river's fleetingly bullish brow.

The two were wed and began the journey back to Heracles's home in Trachis. When they reached the river Evenus, they discovered that recent rains had swollen it so greatly that Deianira could not wade across and Heracles could not carry her. As they were trying to puzzle out a solution, a centaur named Nessus appeared. He offered to ferry Deianira upon his back while Heracles swam alongside. It seemed a perfect solution, and they gratefully accepted.

Once they were in the river, however, Nessus bolted downstream, clamored ashore and prepared to rape his passenger.

Hastening to the bank, Heracles fit an arrow to his string, which seconds later pierced the centaur's flank. The Hydra's gall began its deadly work.

In the moments before Nessus died, he gasped out advice to Deianira: she should collect the blood that gushed from his wound and carefully preserve it, away from heat and light, against a day when she might lose Heracles's love. Nessus assured her that the blood, when rubbed onto a garment for Heracles to wear, would serve as a powerful love charm.

And poor, foolish Deianira, believing what Nessus told her, did as he advised. Emptying a copper bottle, she filled it with the centaur's blood and carried it to her new home. She tucked it into a chest where it languished for years.

Deianira bore many children to Heracles—a miracle in itself, given that his wanderlust returned and kept him away from home for months at a time. One day, when he'd been absent for nearly a year, word came to Deianira that he would join her again on the following day, after he had sacrificed to Zeus on Mount Oeta, but that in advance of his own arrival, he was sending home a captive whom he wanted Deianira to take particularly good care of.

The captive was Iole, whom Eurytus had long ago refused to allow Heracles to marry. Heracles had sacked her city, killed her father and now intended to make her his concubine. The truth, thought Deianira, is that we will be two wives under one blanket, and she is the fresher of the two. Soon, this "concubine" will be mistress of my house.

So Deianira retrieved the blood that she had guarded for so long and smeared it onto a newly woven robe. Wrapping the garment tightly to keep it cool and dark, she called a messenger and said, "Take this to Heracles at Mount Oeta. Bid him wear it as a token of my love when he lights the sacrificial fire."

The messenger departed. Her fear relieved, Deianira relaxed.

When she returned to her chamber later that day, however, a ghastly sight met her eyes. The tuft of wool that she had used to daub the blood onto the robe still lay where she had tossed it on the floor, but the sun, now beating through the window, had worked a change upon it. The soft wisp had melted into a festering liquid, darker than wine.

In a flash, Deianira comprehended Nessus's trick in all its clever cruelty, but it was too late. Even the swiftest rider could not reach Heracles in time to stop him from putting on the robe. Quietly, she chose a sword from the weapons her husband had left behind, sat down upon her marriage bed and pushed the grim blade between her ribs.

Meanwhile, the Hydra's poison, enlivened by the heat of the fire that Heracles kindled for his sacrifice, was doing even grislier work on human flesh than it had done on the wool. As the flames blazed high, the robe clung to Heracles so tightly as to make body and fabric seem a sculpted whole. His flesh began to suppurate; soon, his shoulder blades came into sharp relief as the muscles around them liquified. Then the poison dug deeper still, into his lungs and heart and liver. His breath came fast, his pulse throbbed and his thoughts flew here and there like angry wasps.

He cried out to his son Hyllus, who stood nearby, paralyzed with horror. "Burn me now, child, while I am still sane, lest I destroy you all when greater madness falls upon me!"

Hyllus wept and trembled and refused, until the bonds of his father's hideous necessity grew tighter, compelling obedience. He helped his father climb onto a hastily built pyre and then Heracles's friend Philoctetes touched a torch to its base.

Many and strange were the agonies that Heracles suffered during his life; many and strange were his sorrows, but there was nothing in them that was not part of Zeus's plan. In the moment before Heracles died, Athena descended and took her brother by the hand. Carrying him to Olympus, she tugged him eagerly towards their father. The adamantine rule was broken; Heracles, born mortal, became a god. Hera, reconciled to the inevitable, offered her daughter Hebe to Heracles as his third, and final, wife.

Below, the flames consumed his weary body. Hyllus buried his mother and married Iole. And then, fulfilling his father's dying wish, he bestowed Heracles's great bow upon Philoctetes; its career was not yet over.

76
ATALANTA

The Theban nobleman Schoeneus was desperate for a son. When his wife delivered a girl, he commanded a slave to carry the baby into the woods and kill her. The slave pitied the child, however, and left her lying near a spring, where he reasoned that she might at least find water. The gods, protecting her, inspired a mother bear to lumber over to where the child lay. The bear's cubs had been killed by hunters and her breasts were bursting with milk; she lay down and suckled the child. For some days, this arrangement continued, both parties content, until the hunters who had killed the cubs spotted the odd pair and killed the poor bear. They took the child home to be raised by their wives, who named her Atalanta.

The bear's milk had had its effect, however: Atalanta found it hard to accommodate the ways of humans and spent most of her time alone, roaming the mountains. She grew up strong, beautiful and determined, daring to vie for the same prizes as men did. She accompanied the Argonauts on their journey and beat her shipmate Peleus in a wrestling match. She drew first blood from the Calydonian Boar. Many men were attracted by her lovely face and form, but when she returned their gazes with a boldness uncommon to women, they found themselves flustered and at a loss for words.

Eventually, Schoeneus learned that his daughter had survived and insisted that she return to the family. Rebuking her virginity, he ordered her to marry. She reluctantly agreed, with the stipulation that she be allowed to choose her own husband in her own way. She announced that she would race against any man who wooed her. The suitor would be given a head start; if he won, she would be his wife, but if she overtook him before he reached the finish line, he would pay with his life. The spikes atop the wall surrounding her father's palace soon sported the heads of men who had foolishly tested her speed.

Hippomenes, a young man from the nearby city of Onchestus, laughed at the folly of Atalanta's suitors until he happened to join the crowd of spectators at a race one day. Atalanta's blonde hair flew freely over her shoulders and the bright ribbons that she'd tied around her knees rippled in the breeze. As she pressed forward, a pink flush spread over her skin, highlighting the sleekness of her body. By the time she'd reached the finish line, Hippomenes was so determined to win her that he scarcely noticed the executioner leading away that day's unlucky loser.

The gods help those who dare—and those who pray. Hippomenes made a fervent appeal to Aphrodite and Aphrodite listened. It happened that she was in Cyprus at the time, lingering in a meadow that the local people had consecrated to her private use. In it grew a glimmering tree that was laden with golden apples. Plucking three of these, Aphrodite cloaked herself in mist and carried them to Hippomenes. She laid them in his lap and whispered a scheme in his ear.

The next day, when the trumpet gave the signal that began the race, Hippomenes took off so quickly that his feet scarcely touched the ground. The crowd—which had grown tired of watching men go to their deaths—cheered him on. Moments later, however, Atalanta sped after him on feet that were quicker still. When Hippomenes could hear her pounding the earth just behind him, he took the first of Aphrodite's golden apples from a pouch around his waist and threw it to the side of the course. It gleamed in the sun as it bounced along the ground, attracting Atalanta's eye. She paused to pick it up and then kept running.

Once more she gained on Hippomenes, and once more he threw an apple to slow her down. Just as the finish line came into view, he heard her draw close again and flung the third apple as far as he could. Luck was with him: it bounced down a grassy slope, delaying Atalanta just long enough to give him victory.

The wedding was celebrated that very day. Atalanta, to her surprise, found that she savored the physical side of marriage, which provided opportunities to gratify the wilder side of her nature. Hippomenes, in his excitement at winning such an interesting bride, forgot to thank Aphrodite for her help. Not a single prayer of gratitude did he utter; not a single grain of incense did he burn on her altar.

Aphrodite bided her time, waiting for the perfect opportunity to punish the pair. One day, she saw them walking in the forest near a cave dedicated to Cybele, a goddess who prized chastity, and infected them with an irresistible desire to lie together. Stumbling into Cybele's cave, they satisfied their lust in that forbidden place, as images of the ancient gods looked down upon them.

Cybele's vengeance was swift. As the lovers awoke from a nap, each saw tawny hair sprouting from the other's neck. Their fingers, so recently used in delightful ways, curled into deadly claws. Their arms became legs and tails burst from their spines. When they tried to speak, growls issued from their jaws, which were filled with deadly teeth.

Cybele yoked two new lions to her chariot. The beam of the yoke conquered and divided them, enforcing a continence that they themselves had failed to maintain.

77
A MARVELOUS MUSICIAN

Soon after Zeus became king of the gods, he happened to gaze down upon the Pierian Mountains, which rose nearly as high out of the stony northern soil as Mount Olympus itself. He saw a young woman sitting with her back against an outcropping of rock, the wind teasing strands from her neatly coiled hair. Her posture, upright yet relaxed, conveyed tranquility. The expression on her face, however, suggested resolve; her brows were furrowed and her lips were pressed together as she surveyed the countryside below. Intrigued by this creature, Zeus disguised himself as a shepherd and appeared by her side. They lay together in love for nine nights.

When Zeus arose to depart on the tenth day, he got ready to give a speech that he'd already given several times in his young life, which began with a dramatic announcement of his true identity and ended with chivalrous reassurances that he would watch over the offspring that were sure to arrive soon. This time, however, as he began to speak, the woman's lips curled into a smile. She asked him whether he didn't remember his aunt Mnemosyne, the daughter of Earth and Sky.

Mnemosyne was one of the Titans whom Zeus had allowed to remain free after their war against the gods because they could help him bring order to the cosmos. Mnemosyne did this through her gift of memory, through which knowledge could be preserved. Now, she promised Zeus that the nine daughters whom she had conceived—one on each of the nights they had spent together—would be born with similar gifts. They would be able to inspire humans not only with knowledge itself but also with the ability to share it, through story, song and dance. They would become the Muses. The eldest of these sisters was Calliope, whose heart held some of her mother's solemnity. With a voice that murmured like wind in the pine boughs, she inspired poets to sing about the great deeds of gods and mortals and about the birth of the cosmos itself.

Calliope fell in love with Oeagrus, the king of Thrace, a land that lay even farther to the north than Pieria and Olympus did. Oeagrus had inherited the kingship from his father Charops, a pious and perceptive man. While Charops was still a simple farmer, he had warned young Dionysus that Lycurgus, who was king at the time, was about to attack Dionysus's maenads as they marched from Asia into Greece spreading word of his cult. After blinding and then crucifying Lycurgus, Dionysus rewarded Charops by putting him on the throne and teaching him rituals through which humans could win a better existence after death. He ordered Charops to initiate others into his cult.

Calliope and Oeagrus had but one child, Orpheus. Not surprisingly, he was born with exceptional musical gifts: no sooner did his mother tell him a story than he was fashioning it into a poem and setting it to a melody with his voice and lyre. Orpheus sang about the first gods and the coming together of the cosmos. He sang about Demeter's grief-stricken search for Persephone, who was trapped below the earth, and the aid that torch-bearing Hecate gave to the mother and daughter. He sang of how humans could acquire the help of each god by burning the essence of the plant the god loved best—myrrh and frankincense, dried thyme, storax, rosemary and saffron.

And Orpheus sang a story that his father and grandfather had taught him about how Zeus, being exceedingly proud of Dionysus, had set the child upon a throne and announced to the gods that he would one day be their king. He sang of how Hera, furious that her husband favored this bastard son, told the Titans where a tender morsel of divine flesh could be found. He sang of how the Titans enticed Dionysus away from his guardians, tore him limb from limb and then gobbled him down. He sang of how Athena arrived in time to rescue Dionysus's heart from the abominable feast, and how Zeus used that heart to resurrect his son within a new mother's womb. He sang of how Zeus incinerated the Titans and how the first humans spontaneously arose from their sludgy soot. And he sang of the resulting taint that each human had carried ever since and of the rituals through which it could be washed away, rituals that Dionysus himself had invented. Through these songs, Orpheus dispersed all the knowledge that Dionysus had entrusted to Charops and Charops had entrusted to Oeagrus, spreading Dionysus's mysteries among mortals.

Whatever he sang, Orpheus's voice was so entrancing that when people heard it, they abandoned both labors and pleasures, mesmerized by the sound. Girls at the village well stopped filling their pitchers. Noblewomen stopped treading before their looms. Hands lifting cups of wine stopped short of waiting lips. Millers stopped threshing and shepherds forgot their flocks. And it wasn't only people whom Orpheus's songs enthralled. The miller's donkey and the shepherd's sheep listened, too, as did all the other animals. When Orpheus walked through the forests singing, wolves and foxes slunk from the underbrush to trot alongside him. When he passed through the meadows, birds fluttered above his head, trying to memorize his songs. When he sang along the shingle of the sea, fish leapt in and out of the waves. Stones mustered themselves from crevices and rolled behind him. Trees pulled their gnarled roots from the soil to lumber along in his wake. An entire grove of wild oak trees that once grew in the Thracian hills now stood on the seashore in close-set ranks, where they had gathered to bid farewell to Orpheus as he sailed away to carry his songs to the rest of the world.

78
ORPHEUS THE ARGONAUT

Such were the gifts that Orpheus had inherited from his parents and his grandparents. With them, he made a living that suited him well, traveling the world as a singer and a priest of Dionysus, initiating people into the mystery rites that the god had taught to his grandfather Charops.

The two professions converged; as part of their initiations, people listened to Orpheus sing about what they would need to say and do after they died to ensure that Hades and Persephone would send them to the meadows of the blessed. Scribes who traveled with Orpheus engraved the most important lines from his songs onto tiny gold tablets, which family members tucked into the hands or lay across the lips of dead initiates. If their souls were too dazed to remember what they'd learned from Orpheus when they awoke in the Underworld, the tablets would remind them.

Although Orpheus was not a traditional hero who relied on strength and agility as Heracles did, for example, Chiron the centaur had advised Jason to invite Orpheus to join the Argonauts on their quest for the Golden Fleece. Chiron, who had the gift of foresight, knew that the Argonauts would face challenges that only a spellbinding voice could conquer.

On the voyage out to Colchis, Orpheus proved to be as useful as anyone else on board. He strummed his lyre to set a rhythm to which the men could row, and when quarrels erupted, his singing reestablished harmony. He advised the Argonauts to be initiated into the Samothracian mysteries, which protected those who sailed the seas, and taught them the rituals through which they could propitiate the Mother of the Gods after they'd angered her. It was only later, however, when the Argonauts were on their way home, that the value of Chiron's advice became fully clear.

One day, currents began to carry the Argo towards a small island that pleased the eye with promises of soft green meadows and fresh water. Eager for a rest, the Argonauts furled their sails and the steersman set the tiller to bring them to shore. The Argonauts sat down to row.

As they got nearer to the island, a sweet, resonant sound came drifting over the water. It carried no words that anyone could discern, but its quivering tremolo alone was enough to excite the soul. The sound evoked great deeds, wondrous sights and unknown lands. The Argonauts rowed faster, keen to reach its source.

Only Orpheus was hesitant; to his ears, the sound was cloying. His nose sensed something disagreeable, too, as the breeze shifted back and forth; the air carried the odor of putrescence. There was something naggingly suggestive about it all, which Orpheus struggled to identify. A memory sat at the back of his mind but refused to come forward.

And then suddenly, he had it. He remembered a day late in spring, many years ago, when he was a boy. He had been working alongside his grandmother in her garden, harvesting stalks of rosemary and binding them together to dry inside, before the brutal heat of summer sent the plants into dormancy. As they worked, Mnemosyne told him a tale that he hadn't heard before—a family tragedy.

Once upon a time, she said, his mother's sister Melpomene had lain with the river Achelous and borne him three daughters, who grew into girls with alluring voices and feet that danced like rippling water. The three became close friends of Persephone and often wandered with her through the meadows, picking flowers. On the fateful day that Hades had burst through the crust of the earth and dragged Persephone down to the Underworld, Melpomene's daughters had been near enough to hear their friend scream but too far away to save her—not that anyone could have saved her, really, considering that Zeus had already agreed to give his daughter to Hades. Nonetheless, in her maddened grief Demeter cursed the sisters, transforming their lovely feet into raptors' claws and blighting their soft bodies with thick feathers. Only their beautiful faces and voices remained as they were before—bitter reminders of lost happiness.

Ashamed of their appearance, Orpheus's cousins (for the three girls *were* his cousins, after all) retreated to a distant island. As the years went by, with only one another for company, they honed their voices into mesmerizing harmonies and became known as the Sirens—a name that signified the overwhelming power of their voices. Resentful of their fate, they learned to use those voices in the only way that they could still affect the outside world: by luring ships onto the rocks that lay below the waters of their island's coast. Any sailors who managed to crawl ashore after their ships had been wrecked were clawed to death by the sisters. Their bodies were left to rot in the tall grass that looked so green and pleasant from the deck of a ship.

By the time Orpheus realized that the island towards which his shipmates were rowing was the island of the Sirens, the Argo had drawn near enough for each of them to hear in the Sirens' song a celebration of their own deeds: Zetes and Calais heard the story of how they'd rid Phineus of the accursed Harpies; Polydeuces heard how he'd defeated King Amycus in a boxing match; Erginus heard how he'd surprised everyone by winning a footrace on Lemnos. Hypnotized by the pleasure of their individual glories, the Argonauts yearned to hear more and rowed frantically towards their doom.

Orpheus seized his lyre and began to sing with all the skill and power that he could muster. He sang a song that reminded the Argonauts of their homes and what awaited them there. Zetes and Calais began to think of Mount Pangaion and their father Boreas; Polydeuces of Sparta and his mother Leda; Erginus of glorious Miletus, rich in sheep. As Orpheus continued to sing, his friends awoke from their stupor. They shook their heads and blinked their eyes, uncertain of where they were and what was happening. They stopped rowing, but the current still pulled the boat inexorably towards the Sirens' island.

"Row us away!" cried Orpheus, interrupting his song, and then Jason took up the cry as well. And so the Argonauts rowed until their arms ached and their chests were bursting with the strain.

At last they reached the safe waters of the open sea. Orpheus fell silent then, and thought of his own home, in faraway Thrace, of his own parents, and most particularly of his grandmother and her gift of memory.

79
EURYDICE

The Argo dropped anchor in Iolcus and the Argonauts said goodbye to each other, eager to return to their families. Orpheus began to walk north. He planned to stop first in Pieria, to visit his mother and her sisters, and then go on to Thrace, where his father was still king.

He didn't get far, however. Just a few miles into his journey, as he was cutting through a forest near the Peneus River, he saw a group of oak-tree nymphs dancing in a glade. They were a striking sight: slender and supple, taller than human women, with auburn hair that swayed freely around their shoulders as they moved. Orpheus stopped short, half-hidden by the trees.

One of the nymphs, sensing Orpheus's presence when the dance brought her close to where he stood, turned to look at him. When he met her green eyes, he realized that, in spite of all the songs that he'd sung about beauty, he'd never before understood what it was. By the time the dancing stopped, Orpheus had fallen in love with her. He learned that her name was Eurydice.

Their wooing went quickly, for she was as eager as he. Their wedding promised to be splendid; Eurydice's sisters wove roses into her hair and the Muses prepared to sing the bridal song. The local people brought wine and food for a feast. Only Hymen, the god who presided over weddings, was somber; the torch with which he intended to lead the couple to their bridal chamber had been sputtering ominously all day.

Among the guests was Aristaeus, the son of Apollo and Cyrene, the daughter of Hypseus, king of the nearby Lapiths. Aristaeus was a beekeeper by trade and a good one, having inherited from Apollo a passion for order that helped him maintain healthy hives. From Cyrene, however, Aristaeus had inherited the barbarity of his Lapith ancestors. And so, when Aristaeus saw Eurydice and was filled with desire for her, he didn't hesitate to pursue her.

Eurydice ran, as swiftly as only a nymph can run, through the meadows and down towards the river. Neither Aristaeus nor Orpheus, who rushed after Aristaeus, was able to catch her. She was confident that her nimbleness would keep her safe. She planned to scoff at Aristaeus from the shallows of the river, daring him to follow her into deeper water, where she would have an even greater advantage. But doom awaited her. As she sprinted through the grass along the riverbank, she trod upon a viper and was bitten. By the time that Orpheus reached her, she was dead.

Grief-stricken, Orpheus resolved to journey to the Underworld and convince Hades and Persephone to release Eurydice. He traveled to Taenarum in southern Greece, where there was an entrance to the Underworld at the back of a cave.

The descent was surprisingly smooth and easy—suspiciously so, in fact—and Orpheus soon found himself facing his first challenge: convincing Charon to take him across Lake Acheron in spite of the fact that he was still alive. Orpheus picked up his lyre and sang of things that the aged ferryman had not thought about for centuries: his childhood in the home of his mother, Night, and the games he had played with the more pleasant of his siblings—Sleep, Friendship and the Hesperides. With tears in his steely eyes, Charon gestured Orpheus aboard.

Orpheus found his way to the palace and, after wandering through its shadowy halls for a while, entered the audience room. Hades was seated on his throne and Persephone stood next to him, holding a torch that terminated in a horizontal cross, each arm of which held a flaming wick. Even the fourfold light did little to relieve the surrounding gloom.

When Orpheus asked for the return of his wife, Hades laughed dismissively. "If I were to grant this to you, singer, soon everyone would be down here on behalf of their husbands and wives. Do you think you're the only person who ever loved?"

"I'm not the only one who ever loved, my lord," replied Orpheus, "but those who dare great things for love deserve great rewards. For love, I've dared to leave the upper world, where I belong, and enter your realm. For love, you once dared to leave the lower world, where you belong, and enter the sunlit world above."

And then Orpheus began to sing of how, long ago, Hades had burst through the crust of the earth to sweep Persephone away and of how deeply Hades loved his wife. So eloquently did he sing that even Persephone began to cry. Indeed, the entire Underworld ground to a halt in order to listen to the song. Tantalus stood still, caring for neither food nor water. Tityus's vultures forgot their meal. The daughters of Danaus sat down, their chins in their hands, and

listened. Halfway down the hill, Sisyphus's stone stopped rolling. The Erinyes wept so copiously that the foul muck caking their eyes was, for a moment, washed away.

At last Persephone sighed and said, "Take back your wife, Orpheus—on one condition: you must not look at her until you've reached the upper world."

And so the two set out, the silent ghost of Eurydice walking behind her husband. The path that had been easy for Orpheus when he descended was harder going up; the very smoothness that had made the downward trip effortless made the upward journey perilous; one misstep would mean tumbling all the way back to the banks of the Acheron. Several times, Orpheus nearly fell. His heart was in his mouth lest Eurydice do so.

Finally, the path became more like the floor of a cave, with dry soil and small stones underfoot. Orpheus saw daylight in the distance, and at last began to relax. Then suddenly, he heard the sound of pebbles bouncing downhill and sandals skidding on dirt. "Eurydice!" he screamed, turning his head before he realized what he was doing.

For just a moment, Orpheus glimpsed Eurydice's face before she vanished like smoke; he clutched at her but his arms embraced emptiness. Frantic, he searched the shadows of the cave, thinking that she might still be there somewhere, but eventually he had to abandon all hope. Once again, Eurydice was gone.

80
THE DEATH OF ORPHEUS

Orpheus descended into the Underworld again, but was unsuccessful this time. Sing though he might, he was unable to sway Hades and Persephone. He returned to the upper world a broken man.

He also returned a wiser man. On his first trip, he'd been so focused on retrieving Eurydice that he hadn't noticed much else. There was some irony in this, given that much of his career had been spent evangelizing the mystery cults of gods who promised a better afterlife to their initiates. Orpheus had inherited a duty to do this for Dionysus from his father and grandfather, but he'd also been called upon to compose poetry for Demeter and Persephone's cult in Eleusis, which also promised a better existence after death. Had Orpheus not been distracted by grief when he visited Hades for the first time, he would have taken a keen interest in observing how a system that he had proselytized for so long really worked.

On the second trip, he found out. As he made his way through the throngs of the dead on his way to Hades and Persephone's palace, he scanned their faces, hoping to find Eurydice among them. He didn't, but his eye was caught by something else that unsettled him. He recognized the faces of several people whom he'd personally initiated into the mysteries of Dionysus while they were still alive. One was even clutching a small gold tablet in her hand—a tablet promising that, after death, she would enjoy eternal happiness in the sunlit meadows of the blessed. Why was she here, milling around with thousands of ordinary ghosts in a dim, moldering cavern? Had he made some terrible mistake when he performed the rituals to initiate all these people? Had he told them to take the right-hand road in the Underworld when he should have told them to take the left-hand? He kept his eyes open for the road to the meadows of the blessed, hoping to spot at least some of his initiates there, but there didn't seem to be any such road—to either the right or the left.

With horror, he began to suspect that it had all been just a scam—that Dionysus, and for that matter Demeter and Persephone, too, had used him to promote new cults merely in order to extract more sacrifices from mortals. And if that were true, then what about the mysteries that Hecate had commanded him to establish on Aegina, which claimed to ward off insanity? And those on Samothrace, which claimed to prevent disasters at sea? Had his whole life's work been a fraud?

Orpheus became cynical, distrusting all the gods except his mother, Calliope, and his grandmother Mnemosyne, who were keeping Eurydice alive in his memory. Certainly, he no longer believed that any god would help mortals after death. Life was all there really was; the warmth and brilliance of the sun was worth much more than any hope for something after death. Orpheus cast Dionysus aside and began to honor Helios instead, as he rose in the east each morning.

Dionysus was enraged by Orpheus's desertion and contrived a terrible revenge, anchoring it in the love that Orpheus bore for his lost wife. Because he grieved so deeply, Orpheus had shunned other women, although his good looks would have made it easy for him to find welcoming beds. Instead, he'd sought what comfort he could find in the arms of men.

Dionysus whispered into the ears of his maenads that Orpheus had rebuffed their advances because he found them repulsive and that he'd mocked them to his boyfriends. He told the maenads that they'd been disparaged, devalued and denigrated and urged them to punish the man who had done this to them. Dionysus finished his work by infecting the women's minds with madness and then handed them bulging skins of wine.

After a night of drinking, the maenads scrabbled to the top of the hill above the Hebrus River where Orpheus was accustomed to greet the rising sun. There he sat, cross-legged, his lyre in his lap, gazing at Helios, who was halfway above the eastern horizon.

The women fell upon him like ravening dogs. Two seized his legs, two others his arms, and another threw his lyre down the hill. They tugged, they pulled, they battered him with their thyrsi and shrieked *euhoe! euhoe Dionysus!* Finally, with strength born of madness they dismembered him, tossing his arms and legs into the tall grass. Last of all, they ripped off his head and sent it rolling down the hill. It bounced at the bottom and landed on top of the lyre, which was already floating in the Hebrus.

Orpheus's limbs and torso were gathered up by the Muses and buried in Leibethra, below Mount Olympus. His head and his lyre, however, drifted southwards on the river and out into the sea. The waves carried them to Lesbos, where the people who found them were stunned to discover that Orpheus's mouth was still crying out for Eurydice.

Not knowing what else to do, they built a shrine for the head in a cave. For many years, it gave forth oracles, until Apollo, noticing that his own oracles were being ignored, silenced it forever.

81
CHIRON AND JASON

Most centaurs could trace their origin to a single lustful moment. Centaurus, the savage son of Nephele and Ixion, spotted a herd of mares who were grazing nearby, switching their tails, and was consumed by lust. Violating them as they whinnied in distress, he sired a strange tribe of creatures. From its rump to its forelegs, each of them had the body of a horse, but where there should have been a horse's neck, instead there sprang forth a human abdomen, chest, arms and head.

These were the centaurs—a loutish, feral group, constantly fighting with one another and with any humans they encountered. They thought nothing of rape or theft and they scorned the pursuits by which humans sought to make their lives more bearable: art, music, medicine, divination. They made their homes in caves, living hand to mouth.

Chiron, although identical to these centaurs in shape, was peaceful in disposition and studious in inclination. This was because his origin was altogether different from theirs. In the early days of the cosmos, Cronus had mingled in love with Philyra, the gentle, fair-cheeked daughter of Ocean. At the very moment that the couple reached the climax of their pleasure, Cronus's wife, Rhea, abruptly appeared from nowhere. Hoping to evade her, Cronus instantly transformed himself into a stallion. Philyra, who wasn't as nimble at the art of transformation, retained her form. Nine months later, she gave birth to Chiron.

As the years went by, Chiron allowed his curiosity to lead him where it would. He discovered the principles by which herbs, roots, incantations and surgery could heal human flesh, and the way in which music could soothe the soul. He deciphered the hidden codes of divination. He honed his skills as a hunter—not the brutal snatching of animals in which other centaurs engaged, but the reasoned study of a quarry's habitats and behavior and the application of that knowledge in the field. He made himself a home on top of Mount Pelion, where he could pursue his interests uninterrupted.

Soon, the best families in Greece were sending their sons to Chiron to be raised. Actaeon, Castor, Polydeuces, Asclepius and even Dionysus became his students. He taught them everything that he'd learned and also trained them as athletes, preparing them for a day when they would become warriors. He inculcated moderation and restraint, shaping them to become leaders.

One day, a slave whose dress suggested that he came from a noble household arrived at Chiron's cave with a squalling infant wrapped in purple blankets. The baby was Jason, he explained, the son of King Aeson of Iolcus and his wife, Alcimede. Aeson's brother, Pelias, had just seized the throne; Aeson and Alcimede had fled for their lives and were now in hiding. They feared for Jason's survival: although they'd spread the rumor that the baby had died, they knew that Pelias's men would search for him. They asked Chiron to raise him until the moment came when he could reclaim the throne.

Chiron agreed. His wife, the nymph Chariclo, took charge of the baby and saw to his needs. As he grew, he began to sit beside the other boys as Chiron taught them and competed with them in the contests that Chiron set.

Chiron kept a close watch over Jason's development. The boy met all the challenges that he set but excelled at none of them: he was neither the best archer nor the best wrestler nor the best huntsman, physician, musician or diviner.

And yet, Chiron reflected, Jason could be said to have a talent: he was good at managing others. If the group became lost in the woods, it was Jason who assigned the tasks necessary for their survival and return. Jason instinctively knew, just as Chiron knew, which of the youths could be relied upon to bring back game to stave off hunger and which could climb a tree and get the lay of the land that would enable them to plot a course home. Relatively talentless himself, Jason excelled at organizing the talents of others.

One thing made Chiron uneasy, however. Jason's peculiar skill was not always valued, or even recognized, by the other students. This fed a persistent insecurity within the boy. Lacking the easy confidence that the others had, Jason constantly yearned for power and admiration and pushed at the limits of ethical behavior to obtain them. Although he could recite moral precepts back to Chiron with an ease born of memorization, he didn't seem to have digested them completely. And, he didn't hesitate to manipulate the emotions of others if it would profit him.

When Chiron knew that there was nothing more that he could teach Jason, he announced that it was time for him to confront Pelias and demand the return of the kingdom. Foreseeing certain developments, Chiron gave Jason plenty of parting advice, as well. In particular, he made sure that Jason knew who the most talented youths in Greece were—not only those with whom he had grown up, but also those who were scattered elsewhere throughout the land.

82
LOSING A SANDAL AND
RECLAIMING THE KINGDOM

Jason gathered provisions for the journey to Iolcus. He wrapped himself in a cloak, slung a leopard's skin over his shoulder and took up a spear in each hand. Bidding his foster parents goodbye, he set forth down the mountain.

When he reached the Anaurus River, flowing swiftly in its flood season, he saw an old woman dithering on the bank, wringing her hands and looking upwards as if to plead with the gods.

"Are you in trouble, mother?" he asked.

"I must reach my home on the other side of this river, and can't imagine how I'm to do so!" she replied.

Jason lifted her onto his shoulders and then strode into the waters, which soon swirled around his waist. In midstream, his left sandal became hopelessly mired in the mud; unable to free it, he slipped his foot from its straps and continued on without it.

When he reached the other side, he set the woman down upon soft moss and bent over to wring the water from the bottom of his tunic. When he looked up again, she had vanished. He realized then that it was no mortal he'd carried, but some immortal, and prayed that he'd pleased her.

He was dry by the time he reached the marketplace in Iolcus, where a crowd quickly gathered around him. Some whispered that his face bore a familiar look, but no one knew who he was and he himself remained silent. Pelias, who spotted the commotion from a window in the palace, called for his mule cart and drove out to meet the stranger. His crafty heart ran cold when he realized that the man was half-shod, for an oracle had warned him, long ago, that his doom would arrive in just such a form.

"Who are you, boy, and who are your parents?" he asked. "Answer me now, and don't try to lie."

"My name is Jason. I was raised by Chiron and Chariclo alongside other heroes—let my bearing speak for how they did their job. But you know my parents well enough, I think: Aeson and Alcimede, whom you drove from the palace. Many years ago, you thought you watched my funeral procession and heard the women wailing for me, a tiny prince drifting down to Hades, but you were deceived. I'm alive. Now: are there kinfolk of mine among those gathered here? Let us make ourselves known to one another."

His other uncles came forward then, and his cousins. They took him home and celebrated his return with six days of feasting. His father was there, too, and cried at the sight of his son, the fairest thing that he'd seen in twenty years.

After the sixth day of feasting, Jason went to the palace and was received by Pelias. Jason spoke calmly.

"Let us both be reasonable, Uncle. I have no need of cattle or sheep or good grazing land, which most people count as the best of all possessions. All of those things, which you stole from my father, you may keep. Use them to fatten up the wealth that you cherish so dearly. All I want is that scepter in your hand and with it the right to rule my people."

Pelias was silent. He allowed his shoulders to slump forward and his chin to droop so low that his beard touched his chest. He looked up at Jason from the corner of one eye, and put a quaver into his voice.

"Well, I'm old and you're young, Nephew. Perhaps you're right to ask me to hand over this city whose care has been my burden for so many years."

He sighed. "And as it happens, there is a matter of state that requires a young man's touch. The ghost of our ancestor Phrixus—have you heard of him? Did Chiron teach you our family's history?—wants to be brought home from Colchis, that barbaric land to which he flew on the back of a golden ram so many years ago. His ghost told me this himself, in a dream, but he also said that he can't come home unless the fleece of that ram, which now hangs on a tree in Colchis, guarded by a fearsome dragon, is brought home, too."

Pelias sat upright once more and stuck out his chin. "Now, I know that dreams are unreliable messengers, so I went to Delphi to ask for confirmation. Apollo spoke to me there—*Apollo*! The god! Spoke to *me*! He confirmed everything that Phrixus said. So, Jason: if you want the kingdom, then sail to Colchis and fetch back that golden fleece."

Jason agreed to Pelias's terms and hired the carpenter Argus to build a ship. Athena guided Argus's hands; the vessel, which Jason named the Argo after its creator, was a marvelous thing. As a final touch, Athena gave it an oaken figurehead carved in her own likeness. Then Jason sent messengers throughout the land to gather a crew. Among them were Heracles and Heracles's young lover, Hylas; Peleus, who brought with him his brother Telamon and his father-in-law, Eurytion; Castor and Polydeuces, sons of Leda; Zetes and Calais, twin sons of Boreas who had wings that rippled purple in the wind; Echion and Eurytus, twin sons of Hermes; Idas and Lynceus of Messenia; the seers Idmon and Mopsus; Euphemus, a son of Poseidon who could run over the waves; Polyphemus of Thessaly; Meleager of Calydon; Oeleus of Locris; Amphidamas of Arcadia; Jason's cousin Admetus from Pherae; Ancaeus of Tegea, who after Heracles was the strongest of all the Argonauts; Nestor of Pylos; Asclepius the healer; and Orpheus the poet, who knew all the gods' mysteries. After careful thought, Jason also invited the huntress Atalanta to join the expedition, risking the possibility that she would be a distraction for the others. Hera—for it was she whom Jason had carried across the Anaurus, and she was well pleased with him—cast into the hearts of all who sailed on the Argo a yearning for adventure and the fame that would accompany it, even if these should come at the price of death.

Chiron and Chariclo came down from Mount Pelion to bid farewell to the Argonauts. In her arms, Chariclo carried the infant Achilles, whom Thetis had recently entrusted to their care. She held him up for his father, Peleus, to see as he departed.

Mopsus obtained auspicious signs from the gods and sent the crew aboard. When the anchors had been stowed above the prow, Jason took a golden bowl in his hands and offered a libation, calling on Zeus to give them a favorable homecoming. As they sailed from the harbor, Athena's figurehead cried out in eagerness.

83
THE LEMNIAN WOMEN

The gods looked down from the sky, watching their children and grandchildren sail off into the open sea. The next day, the ship approached Lemnos, an island long sacred to Hephaestus, which had fallen under a curse. The women of Lemnos had neglected Aphrodite, allowing her altars to grow cold and her temples to remain unscented by myrrh. At last, spurned and angry, Aphrodite had infused the women's bodies with an odor so vile that their husbands turned away from them and kidnapped new, untainted women from Thrace. Enraged, the Lemnian women killed not only their rivals but also all the men of the island, from youngest to oldest.

By the time that the Argo neared Lemnos, the women had been living on their own for almost a year. Hypsipyle, their queen, had brought order to their new existence: the women had learned how to plow the fields and reap the harvest, how to arm themselves and defend their island. When the Argonauts sent an envoy ashore, asking permission for the ship to come into harbor and take on provisions, the women were inclined to deny the request. They could uphold the obligations that Zeus laid upon all hosts, they reasoned, by rowing provisions out to the ship and sending it on its way again. But then Hypsipyle's old nurse, Polyxo, spoke up.

"What do you think will happen when you die, ladies, and your daughters die? Who will repopulate our island? Let the

Argonauts disembark—and then put the men to good use siring new Lemnians."

Accepting Polyxo's advice, Hypsipyle invited Jason and his shipmates to disembark. Aphrodite, setting aside her anger in order to please Hephaestus, expunged the women's odor and poured desire into the Argonauts, who eagerly scrambled down the gangplank. Hypsipyle claimed Jason for herself; the other men went wherever chance and an enthusiastic hand led them.

A few men stayed aboard the Argo: Heracles, who saw no good in delaying the expedition for such a frivolous reason, and Heracles's closest companions. Day after day, as other men dallied in the women's beds and enjoyed themselves at feasts and games, Heracles simmered with impatience. Finally, he went ashore and bellowed for the Argonauts to gather around him.

"Did we agree to join this expedition because there were no women at home, friends? Will we win glory by plowing Lemnian fields? If Jason has decided to spend his time in a woman's bed, then let him give up on the fleece and release us from our promises, so that we can return to our own countries."

Heracles's speech had its intended effect; the men were suddenly ashamed of their behavior. Soon, each was back on the Argo, preparing the ship for departure. Hypsipyle realized that it was futile to try to restrain Jason but she promised him that, if he returned to Lemnos when his quest was over, the kingship would be his. He declined, reminding her of his obligations in Iolcus, but asked her to send their son, should she be carrying one, to Iolcus when he was grown. Nine months later, Euneus was born. Although he never traveled to his father's land, he served the Greeks well during the Trojan War by sending excellent Lemnian wine across the strait to them.

As evening fell on the day that the Argonauts departed from Lemnos, they drew near to the island of Samothrace. Orpheus urged them to stop so that they might learn, by being initiated into the mysteries there, the secrets regarding how the gods chose which mortals to protect when they sailed the seas. They departed the next morning and at sunset passed through the Hellespont, where Phrixus's sister, Helle, had long ago fallen from the back of the golden ram. Onwards they traveled along the coast of the Propontis until they reached the country of the Doliones, whom King Cyzicus ruled. An oracle had once told Cyzicus that the gods would send a band of heroes to his shores and that he should receive them hospitably, so he ordered his slaves to replenish the Argo's stores and invited the Argonauts to dine with him that night.

Cyzicus was a young king. He had recently brought home a wife, Clite, from whom he reluctantly parted that evening to fulfill his duties as host. After pleasantly trading stories and information with Jason for some hours, he excused himself and rejoined her.

At dawn the next morning, the Argonauts untied the mooring ropes and sailed eastwards. They made good time for most of the day, but as a moonless night was falling, heavy gusts began to blow from every direction. They were tossed violently here and there until eventually they felt the ship scraping against the sandy shallows of an unknown shore. They disembarked under the dim light of a few stars.

Suddenly, they were attacked by the local inhabitants. A pitched battle followed on the darkened shore, neither side sure who their opponents were, but each determined to win, just the same. As the sun rose, a ghastly scene was revealed: the gusts had blown the Argonauts back to the land of the Doliones and each group had taken the other for enemies. Jason discovered that the man he had killed shortly before dawn was none other than King Cyzicus himself.

Cyzicus was buried and grandly mourned for three days by both the Doliones and the Argonauts, after which they held funeral games in his honor. Clite, overwhelmed by grief, hanged herself. The nymphs of the forest cried for her so profusely that their tears formed a spring, which took her name.

84
HERACLES AND HYLAS

Following the funerals of Cyzicus and Clite, the winds blustered continuously for twelve days, preventing the Argonauts from leaving the land of the Doliones. On the twelfth night, the seer Mopsus was keeping watch and saw a halcyon circle over Jason's head as he slept and then fly to the Argo's sternpost. It cried shrilly before it flew away again.

Mopsus roused Jason. "The gods have sent a messenger to tell us how we can escape our troubles. If we climb to the top of Mount Dindymon and appease the one they call the Mother of the Gods, who is angered by the deaths of Cyzicus and Clite, she'll call off the opposing winds. She is powerful and her anger is dreadful—even Zeus makes way when she enters the hall of the gods! But if we appease her, we'll be free to sail."

When dawn broke, the Argonauts climbed the mountain, driving cattle to sacrifice to the Mother. When they arrived in her sacred precinct, they found an old vine stump, withered and tough, which Argus skillfully carved into her image. They gathered stones and made a rough altar, upon which they offered gifts to the Mother and her companions the Dactyls, wise gods who understand the Mother's mysteries. Years before, Orpheus had sat at their feet as a student; now, he told the Argonauts to put on their armor and dance in the Mother's honor, banging their swords against their shields so that she could no longer hear the Doliones grieving for their king and queen.

The Mother, well pleased, made the trees on her mountain burgeon with fruit and the soil bloom with flowers. Wild animals lay down companionably at the Argonauts' feet. A new source of water gushed out from the mountain's face, which the Doliones came to call Jason's Spring. By these signs, the Argonauts knew that the Mother was appeased. Descending, they found that the winds were in their favor and they departed, eager to make up for lost time.

Heracles rowed so strenuously that his oar broke. The Argo put into a cove on the coast of Mysia so that he could fell a tree and carve a new one. The Mysians welcomed them and began to prepare a feast for them on the beach. Heracles dispatched Hylas, his young lover, to find a spring of fresh water.

Hylas stumbled upon one at exactly the hour when the nymphs were gathering for their dance—tree nymphs, mountain nymphs and the nymph of the spring herself. When she saw Hylas kneeling on the banks of her pool, she was transfixed by his beauty. Gliding closer, she softly encircled his neck and tugged until he lost his balance and tumbled into the water. As he fell, Hylas cried out, but the only Argonaut near enough to hear him was Polyphemus. Polyphemus ran towards the spring but saw nothing there at all, because Hylas now dwelt with the nymph, deep below the surface of the water. Polyphemus hastened to where Heracles was carving his oar and told him that Hylas had disappeared. The two scoured the forests and meadows, frantically seeking their friend.

On the beach, meanwhile, the feast was drawing to an end. The Mysians departed and the Argonauts rolled themselves up in their cloaks to sleep in the sand. At dawn a favorable breeze arose and Jason quickly ordered everyone aboard. They rowed out of the cove and raised the sail. Scudding along, they were passing the Cape of Poseidon before anyone realized that Heracles, Hylas and Polyphemus were missing.

Telamon turned on Jason furiously. "This was no accident! You've been looking for a chance to get rid of Heracles ever since the moment, back in Iolcus, when some of us suggested making *him* the leader of this expedition. He declined, as a courtesy to you, but the shadow of his accomplishments continually darkens your own!"

Jason sat bewildered, his heart despairing at the loss of his friends and his mind stunned by Telamon's accusation. Telamon snatched the opportunity afforded by Jason's silence to rush at Tiphys, the steersman.

"I'll not leave the best of us behind—we're turning back!" he yelled. Telamon would have seized command of the tiller if Zetes and Calais had not restrained him. And then suddenly, the waves roiled and an enormous, shaggy head appeared from beneath them, followed by gigantic shoulders and a chest to match. The creature was shaped like a man, but his skin was as gray as a dolphin's and his beard was as green as the tinge that grows on bronze. He grabbed the stern and spoke in a rumbling voice that shook the ship.

"Why do you waste time squabbling about your companions? Heracles is destined to complete twelve labors for Eurystheus and must return to Mycenae to fulfill that fate. Polyphemus will stay behind among the Mysians, founding a new city. As for Hylas: a nymph has made him her husband."

The creature released the ship and returned to the sea; Idmon announced that he was the god Glaucus, who, although wise himself, had been speaking on behalf of Nereus, who was wiser still. Telamon took Jason's hand and begged forgiveness for his stupidity, born of grief. After a moment of silence, Jason replied. "Your accusations wounded me, Telamon; I only hope that you'd fight so hard for me, too, should I need you to." The two sat down on their benches to row.

85
THE HARPIES AND THE CLASHING ROCKS

Soon they came to the land of the Bebrycians, a bloodthirsty people ruled by Amycus, a violent, arrogant man. He exacted a terrible toll on visitors to his shores: someone from each ship had to box with him to the death before the ship could go on its way. Polydeuces stepped forward on behalf of the Argonauts—a slender, youthful contender against a man who loomed like a mountain.

For some minutes, there was an awful thud of hardened leather gloves against flesh and neither contender seemed able to win—but then Polydeuces darted up and struck Amycus above the ear, breaking his skull and spilling his brains out onto the ground. At that, the Bebrycians roared with anger and attacked the Argonauts. Heads were split, bones snapped and teeth shattered before the Argonauts beat off the Bebrycians and departed.

Two days later, they reached Bithynia, a country ruled by Phineus, a man to whom Apollo had granted the gift of prophecy. Reveling in his skill, Phineus soon boasted that he could foresee everything that Zeus would do. To punish Phineus's hubris, Zeus blinded him and then sent against him two of the Harpies—rapacious birds with maidens' faces, from whose wombs dripped the foulest of ooze. Whenever Phineus's attendants set a meal upon the table, the baneful creatures swooped down from the clouds and snatched it away before Phineus could ease his hunger. Now and then, after they had glutted themselves, they allowed Phineus a few morsels, so as to keep his soul imprisoned in his emaciated body, but on other occasions, they squatted over whatever remained of the meal and dribbled their slime upon it.

Phineus had foreseen the Argonauts' visit. When he heard that they had arrived, he hobbled forth to meet them, as gaunt as a skeleton sprung from its grave.

"Jason, fate has decreed that two of your shipmates will rescue me, at last, from the repulsive Harpies. Indeed, it will be two with whom I claim a bond of kinship: Zetes and Calais, sons of Boreas and brothers of my wife, Cleopatra. If they do this for me, I will reveal what lies ahead on your voyage and how you may win the Golden Fleece."

Zetes and Calais came forward, the feathers of their purple wings fluttering in the breeze. They accompanied Phineus to the palace and stood in the shadows while attendants placed a meal before him. Immediately, the Harpies darted down like stormwinds, gobbled up the food and sped away. Zetes and Calais quickly caught up with them, but just as the twins were about to grab the creatures, Iris descended and blocked their way.

"Sons of Boreas!" she declared. "Zeus forbids you to harm the Harpies, who have their roles to play in the cosmos. But he has promised, by the River Styx, that they will never again torment Phineus."

When the brothers returned to the palace, they found Phineus feasting alongside the Argonauts. At last, sighing with pleasure, the king laid aside the lamb shank that he'd been gnawing on and told the Argonauts what he knew.

"Soon after you depart, you will face the Clashing Rocks, through which no ship has ever passed. These are huge crags that rush through the water when they perceive an interloper, crashing together to crush it and then parting again. They've splintered many a vessel! But if you wait nearby and first send a dove between them, the rocks will race towards the dove and then part. That is the moment when you can speed between them. Soon after that, you will encounter deadly birds on an island belonging to Ares—use your wits against them! In that same place, look for help from the grim sea. Once you are in Colchis, trust to Aphrodite—and when your tasks are over, brace yourselves for a tortuous route home."

Thanking Phineus, the Argonauts went aboard and sat down on their benches, preparing to row. Euphemus, before he did so, caught a dove and stowed it safely away.

As the Argo approached the Clashing Rocks, Athena moved to a vantage point atop a cloud, from which she could monitor the ship's progress. It was just then approaching the narrow opening of the strait, where the water roared with such force that the Argonauts could scarcely hear Tiphys shouting out instructions. Euphemus stood on the prow and released the dove; it darted through, losing only a few of its tail feathers as the rocks crashed together. Immediately, Tiphys ordered the Argonauts to row harder and they advanced towards the widening gap between the rocks. The waves, however, tossed them back and forth; for every two measures they gained, they fell back one. At last Athena intervened: with one invisible hand she held back an advancing rock and with the other she pushed the Argo through the gap. The rocks stood still, never to move again.

As the Argonauts rested, Tiphys laughed for joy and thanked Athena, whose presence he had sensed.

"Must you always be so cheerful?" shouted Jason. "That was far too close a call—I'm a wretched captain not to have done a better job! The strain under which I work, overseeing the rest of you, has become unendurable! Why am I even here? I loathe the sea and I loathe the strange people we meet! I dread the dawn of every day!"

Jason said these things to test the loyalty of the Argonauts. After they'd gathered around him, praising him and speaking words of encouragement, he smiled to himself and resumed his duties.

Some days later, they stopped at the land of the Mariandynoi and were welcomed by King Lycus, who told them that Heracles had recently stayed with them on his way to fetch Hippolyta's belt, the ninth of his labors. In the weeks since he had left the Argo, he had completed four others, as well.

86
COLCHIS

The birds that nested on Ares's island were of the same stock as those that Heracles had chased away from Stymphalia: huge and muscular, with feathers as sharp as darts, which they could shoot at their prey. The Argonauts knew that they were close to the island when Oeleus abruptly dropped his oar and crumpled over in pain, a feather sticking out of his shoulder. Amphidamas, thinking quickly, shouted that half the Argonauts must keep rowing and the other half gather their weapons—not to kill the birds, he explained, but to frighten them away by noisily clashing spears against shields. Once this was done, the Argonauts rowed towards the island, curious about why Phineus would send them to such a blighted spot. When they landed, four bedraggled men approached them.

"Help us, we beg you, whoever you are! A storm wrecked our ship and marooned us here!"

Jason asked who they were and where they were going.

"We are the sons of Phrixus, who once traveled to Colchis on the back of a golden ram. We were journeying to our ancestral home in Orchomenus when the storm struck. My own name is Argus and my brothers are Cytissorus, Phrontis and Melas."

"If you're the sons of Phrixus, then I'm your cousin, Jason of Iolcus. Your grandfather Athamas and my grandfather Cretheus were brothers. We're heading *to* Colchis, to fetch home your father's ghost by retrieving the fleece of that ram he rode. If you counsel us, we'll take you to Greece when we return."

The brothers grimaced at one another. "We'll help you," Argus replied, "but our first advice is this: be careful. Our other grandfather, Aeëtes, who rules Colchis, is a ruthless, dangerous man."

They sailed on, past the cliff on which Prometheus still waited to be released by Heracles. They saw the eagle flying overhead and then heard Prometheus's cries echoing down the valley as the bird tore at his liver. Later that afternoon, Argus guided them to the mouth of the Phasis River, which flowed through Colchis. They lowered their sail and dropped anchor in a marsh, where they could hide among the reeds while they strategized.

Some of the gods were strategizing as well. Aphrodite knew that Jason's diplomacy would be wasted on Aeëtes; her gimlet eye fell upon Aeëtes's daughter Medea as the surest means through which Jason could obtain the fleece. Medea had spent her childhood studying the arcane properties of plants and how to put them to use; if she were persuaded to do so, she could use her knowledge to ensure Jason's success.

So Aphrodite descended to where Jason sat alone on the banks of the marsh, dangling a strange device from her hand. A leather cord had been threaded through two holes drilled in the hub of a small, four-spoked wheel. The ends of the cord were tied together to make a loop. When the loop was held taut between two hands and then twisted and pulled, the wheel spun rapidly, emitting an eerie hum that, if accompanied by the proper incantation, would infect whomever one wished with desire. It was an old charm; many had used it. But before Aphrodite had threaded the cord through her wheel, she'd nailed a splayed bird to its spokes, gouging holes in the bird's body that aligned with those in the wheel. The bird was an iynx—in itself a powerful love charm—and iynx was what Aphrodite had decided to call this hybrid device that she'd invented, too. The mangled bird didn't live long, but as it died, its maddening pain passed into the wheel, amplifying its merciless power. Appearing before Jason's astonished eyes, Aphrodite taught him how to use the iynx, and against whom. He carefully hid it away beneath a gnarled tree root.

Hera, for her part, inspired Medea to neglect her usual duties at the temple of Hecate on the following day and linger inside the palace. Thus it was that when Jason and the sons of Phrixus arrived, seeking an audience with Aeëtes, Medea saw them at once. She cried out in surprise at the sight of a stranger and with relief at the sight of her nephews, who had mysteriously vanished from Colchis some days earlier. Her sister Chalciope ran to her side, overjoyed by her sons' return. Soon, a feast was prepared to receive the travelers. After everyone had eaten their fill, Aeëtes asked Jason who he was and why he had come. When Jason explained what he wanted, Aeëtes flew into a rage.

"Be happy that you ate at my table before announcing your mission," he thundered. "If you weren't protected by the strictures that Zeus lays upon me as a host, I'd kill you here and now! Go back to your ship—go back to your country!"

Jason tried to soothe the king, promising gifts and military alliances in exchange for the fleece, but Aeëtes brusquely interrupted him.

"Let's make a deal," he said. "Perform two tasks for me—tasks that I myself have performed many times. If you complete them, I'll give you the fleece; if not, you leave my kingdom. The first is this: I have some bulls that Hephaestus made by hammering bronze into fire-breathing animals. Yoke them together. The second is this: use those bulls to plow the Field of Ares and sow a crop—not the grain of Demeter but teeth from a gigantic serpent, which Athena once gave to me. The teeth will promptly bear fruit: armed warriors, full of fury—reap them, if you can! Do all of this within a single day and the fleece will be yours."

Jason and his friends returned to the ship, debating the best way to meet Aeëtes's challenges. Jason told them of Aphrodite's visit and they agreed that securing Medea's help, through whatever means were necessary, offered the greatest hope of success. So as dusk was falling, Jason walked to the tree among the roots of which he had hidden the iynx and retrieved it. The bird now hung limply from the wheel and ants had begun to eat away its eyes; to Jason, it looked nothing like a love charm. Nonetheless, he twisted the cord as Aphrodite had taught him. When the wheel began to spin and wail, he mumbled the incantation.

At the palace, Medea suddenly awoke. Her mind, which years of studiousness had disciplined to do her will, burned with a longing that she could neither assuage nor understand: she yearned to see the far-off land from which the stranger had come and to sleep in his arms. She shuddered at the thought of what her parents would say to such ideas, but desire kept lashing her mind back to Jason. In despair, she contemplated the poisonous plants that she kept in her collection and wondered whether suicide was the best solution to her dilemma.

As Medea paced in her chamber, Chalciope slipped in. Argus had visited her earlier that evening and explained why he and his brothers had suddenly fled Colchis: they had discovered that their grandfather was plotting to kill them, fearing a prophecy that his doom would come at the hands of one of his descendants. Argus had asked his mother to persuade Medea to help them win the fleece and safely escape to Greece. The two sisters sat down to devise a plan that satisfied them both.

87
THE TASKS

Hera kept watch over Medea for the rest of the night, stoking the fire that burned in her heart. At daybreak, Medea rubbed fragrant oils into her skin, dressed in a crimson robe and wrapped a silvery veil around her head. She ordered a mule cart so that she could drive to Hecate's temple, which lay in the plains outside the city; Argus had arranged for Jason to meet her there.

Then she unlocked the chest in which she kept the rarest and most powerful botanical materials that she had collected over the years. She selected a vial of sap extracted from the root of the prometheios, a flower that sprang from the earth wherever ichor from Prometheus's tattered liver dripped onto the ground. She had harvested it carefully one night after bathing seven times in running water and calling seven times upon Hecate, just as Hecate had taught her to. Those who pleased Hecate with nocturnal sacrifices and then rubbed this sap onto their skin would be invulnerable to bronze and fire for the span of a day. Medea tucked the vial into her breastband and drove to the temple to wait.

When Jason arrived, such ardor raced through Medea's veins that she couldn't lift her eyes to meet his gaze.

"Medea," he said, taking her hand, "don't be shy with me; your sister has told me you'll give me an unguent to protect me from the bulls. Accept my thanks, and know that in gratitude, I'll carry your name home to Greece along with the fleece: our poets will sing of you forever."

Medea took out the vial, but then paused, trembling at the thought of her father.

"Listen to what you must do," she said at last, lifting her eyes to meet his. "At midnight, bathe in the river and dress in a dark robe. Dig a circular pit and slit the throat of a black ewe over it, so that the blood reaches the lower gods. Then burn the ewe's body, pour out a libation of honey for Hecate and pray for her help. Walk away from the spot—don't look back, whatever you may hear, lest you glimpse Hecate arriving for her meal. The next morning, rub the sap over your body, your sword and your shield: for the rest of the day, your strength and endurance will be equal to a god's. As for the earthborn warriors: after most of them have emerged, throw a stone into their midst. I've seen my father do this many times as a cruel amusement for his people: they'll viciously turn on one another. That will give you your chance to kill them."

When Jason saw Medea's face and heard her voice, he, too, was filled with desire. Hera was responsible for this; she hated Pelias and knew that if Jason took Medea back to Iolcus, Medea would be sure to bring about the king's death.

"After I've completed these tasks and won the fleece," Jason said, "perhaps I'll win your hand, as well, by coming to an agreement with your father?"

"People may honor agreements in Greece, but the same does not hold true in Colchis," Medea replied. "You'll discover, I think, that you'll have to fight for the fleece even after you've yoked the bulls and killed the warriors. My father won't keep his word and he certainly won't give you my hand, especially after he learns that I've helped you. Death is likely to be my reward."

"Be patient," Jason said. "I'll find some way to take you with me." And then he departed for the Argo.

At midnight, Jason bathed in the river and dressed himself in a dark purple robe that Hypsipyle had given him when he left the island of Lemnos. He dug a pit on the bank and slit the throat of a ewe. He burned her body, poured out honey and prayed to Hecate. As soon as he turned to walk away he heard dogs barking; already, the goddess was rising from Hades accompanied by her pack. In terror, Jason sprinted back to his comrades and slept close to the fire that night.

In the morning, he rubbed the sap onto his skin, sword and shield. When he and the other Argonauts arrived at the Field of Ares, they saw that Aeëtes's men had set an adamantine plow and a bronze yoke upon the ground. Jason noticed hoofprints nearby, clustering around a chasm in the earth; suddenly, from out of its darkness the bulls thundered forth, snorting plumes of fire from their nostrils. Jason grabbed one by the horn, neatly sidestepping the other. He dragged the bull to the yoke and forced his head into place. Then Jason turned towards the other bull, which was preparing to charge again; that one soon joined his companion. Distracted by the task at hand, Jason had not initially noticed how the flames from the bulls' nostrils danced harmlessly over his forearms. Now he saw, and marveled at what Medea could do.

With new assurance, he led the bulls to the plow. The adamantine plowshare was heavy and cut deeply into the rocky soil; without the strength that Medea's unguent had given him, Jason could not have completed the job and even with its help, he finished slowly. When he paused at the end of his labors to survey his work, he was shocked to discover that the first teeth he'd sown had already sprouted. Warriors were wriggling their bodies free of the soil. The spears they clutched in their hands grew alongside them, emerging like blades of wheat.

Jason prised a great boulder from the ground and, lifting it high above his head, lobbed it into the midst of those warriors who now stood, full grown, within the field. With a roar, they leapt upon one another; many were killed by their brothers' spears. Jason darted here and there, slaughtering others with his sword. The last-sown warriors, who had not yet fully emerged from the earth, were easy prey. Jason hacked them off flush with the ground, leaving their lower halves to rot within the soil from which they had sprung.

88
CLAIMING THE FLEECE

From the moment that Jason overpowered the first bull, Aeëtes knew that he had received help—and knew who had given it. Once Jason had thrown the boulder among the warriors, he set out for the palace to deal with his daughter.

But Hera had cast terror into Medea's heart as soon as Jason reached the field that morning. Medea barred the door of her chamber and opened the cabinets in which she kept all the medicines and poisons that she'd made from plants, as well as the notes that she'd kept during her years of study. Selecting the rarest and most important of these things, she tucked them inside her clothing and prepared to leave the palace. As a last-minute thought, she stopped at the room where her younger brother, Apsyrtus, was being cared for by his nanny. Explaining that she'd decided to take him to the spectacle, she led him away by the hand.

The city was nearly empty—everyone had gone to watch Jason—and she moved through it rapidly, despite being burdened by the parcels under her clothes and the child whom she'd begun to carry on her hip. She passed through the meadows to where the Argo lay anchored, reaching it just as the Argonauts were returning, victorious, from the Field of Ares.

"Friends! Save my brother and me from our father! And save yourselves! We must flee—*now*," she gasped, falling to her knees in supplication. "I can get you the fleece myself, if we move quickly!"

Jason helped her up. "Medea, I swear by Zeus and Hera that not only will I protect you if you help us, but I'll also make you my wife."

The Argonauts rowed up the Phasis until Medea directed them to stop. Jason and Medea disembarked onto a grassy bank where once, years before, the golden ram had landed with Phrixus on his back. They made their way to the sacred grove where the fleece still hung on an oak tree, placed there by Phrixus after he had sacrificed the ram to the gods in thanks for his salvation.

The dragon that guarded it coiled around the tree, its vast, sinuous bulk writhing like the murky swirls of smoke that rise from a resinous fire. When it noticed Jason and Medea, it rolled towards them, the hard scales of its belly rasping against the forest floor. Jason stood frozen by fear but Medea calmly stared at the dragon, willing herself not to blink, and began to chant in a soothing voice, calling on Sleep to descend upon the beast and on Hecate to help her with her work. Soon, the dragon's coils began to relax; its crested head continued to dart here and there, however. Dipping a sprig of juniper into a bottle that she took from her skirts, Medea sprinkled a potion upon the dragon's eyes. They closed, then, and the dragon crumpled to the ground.

Jason leapt forward to seize the fleece. Its lovely radiance threw a warm glow upon his face; as he moved, everything around him caught its brilliance and sparkled back. He draped it first over one shoulder and then over the other, stroking its warmth. Now he let it hang down his back, preening in its glory; now again he rolled it up tightly and hugged it, as if afraid that someone might snatch it away. Finally, Medea urged him to return to the Argo and they walked back to the bank.

Jason stood in the middle of the Argonauts, holding aloft the fleece. "We're going home, friends! We have the prize that we came for. But Aeëtes will surely come after us; put your backs into your work."

The Argonauts rowed vigorously and soon passed into the open waters of the Black Sea, where Hera dispatched a wind to blow them on their way. Aeëtes, however, had been quick in his pursuit and began to gain on them. As they neared the western coast of the sea where the Ister River empties its waters, it began to look as if all was lost; here, they could be easily caught.

And then some god cast an evil plan into Medea's mind. Going below, she lifted her small brother out of the hammock where he was dozing and carried him, still rubbing sleep from his eyes, above deck. She stood the boy in front of her and then, before the horrified eyes of the Argonauts, began to stab him, ignoring his terrified screams.

"I sacrifice this child on behalf of all of us!" she cried.

Some of the Argonauts made as if to stop her but Jason ordered them to fall back; they returned to their benches in a misery of pity. The murder, in any case, was so quickly committed that their interference would have been fruitless; what followed was slower and more horrible to watch. Medea butchered Apsyrtus's corpse, cutting off first his head, which she flung overboard towards her father's approaching ship, then his arms and legs and finally his torso, which followed the rest into the waves. She screamed across the water that if Aeëtes wished to bury his son properly he'd better move fast before the fish devoured the tender flesh.

However cruel and merciless he might be to others, Aeëtes loved his son. He stopped to gather the pieces of Apsyrtus from the sea. He buried them at a place nearby that he named Tomi, "The Cutting."

89
CIRCE AND THE PHAEACIANS

The Argonauts sat stunned and silent, unable to comprehend what they'd just witnessed. Finally, Orpheus began to play, haltingly at first but then with soothing rhythms. Medea and Jason went below deck and the rowers resumed their work.

The route home was complicated, as Phineus had warned. Zeus was outraged by what Medea had done and by Jason's failure to prevent it. He cursed the Argo, condemning it to wander the world. They sailed west on the Ister, south through the Adriatic Sea and then north again, skirting the coast of Italy, puzzled as to why the winds persisted in blowing them away from Iolcus.

Finally, Hera spoke to the Argonauts through the ship's figurehead, disclosing the cause of their problems and commanding Jason and Medea to seek purification for Apsyrtus's murder from Aeëtes's sister Circe, who lived on the island of Aeaea off the western coast of Italy. The gods eased their way by granting the Argo passage across Italy on the river Eridanus.

Medea had been hearing tales about Circe since she was a child. She lived alone, far from gods and mortals alike; decades might pass before anyone visited her island. She spent her time, like Medea, studying plants and their properties. This, combined with her mastery of ritual, enabled her to accomplish things that mortals could scarcely imagine; rumor had it that her island was populated by curious, hybrid creatures, the fruits of her strange experiments. The gods mocked the centuries of labor that Circe had put into her work—why should a daughter of Helios bother with such things?—but even the gods, on occasion, looked to her for help.

On the night before the Argo arrived in her harbor, Circe had a horrifying dream: the walls of her house dripped with blood and flames consumed the pharmacopeia of potions and elixirs that she had so carefully developed. She shuddered awake, her flesh twitching as if vermin swarmed over it. When day broke, she went to the seashore and immersed herself in the waves. She allowed the tide to carry away her old robes and dressed in new ones when she emerged. For a long time, she stood staring at the sea, trying to fathom what the dream had meant and hoping that her actions had averted whatever it portended.

It was there that Jason and Medea discovered her. She invited them to her home. When they reached the house, Jason and Medea refused the luxurious chairs towards which Circe gestured, and silently fell on their knees at the hearth, their heads bowed.

Circe understood then that they were seeking purification from murder. Obeying Zeus's law that such requests be honored, she performed the ritual, sacrificing a newborn piglet so that its blood might wash away the pollution that clung to their hands. She offered cakes and sober libations on their behalf to calm the anger of the Erinyes. Then she gestured for them to sit upon the chairs that they had earlier refused.

Throughout all of this, Medea had kept her head down, but now she met Circe's gaze and Circe saw the golden gleam in Medea's irises that marked all of Helios's descendants. Circe gasped and spoke to Medea in a language whose rhythms she had neither enunciated nor heard for a very long time. Medea replied, telling her aunt about all that had happened—except for the murder of Apsyrtus. This, however, Circe intuited on her own. She spoke.

"My brother is a brutal man and he isn't done with you yet. I pity you, Medea. Nonetheless, leave my house. Although I've cleansed you from your brother's blood, I can neither countenance what you have done nor forgive it."

Medea wept as Jason led her back to the ship: in grief, in remorse and in fear.

Hera watched the Argonauts depart from Aeaea and made preparations to ensure that they would reach the island of the Phaeacians, the next hospitable place on their way home. She dispatched Zephyr, the west wind, to see them on their way. She trusted Orpheus to get them safely past the island of the Sirens, but she prevailed upon Thetis and the other Nereids to guide them between the Wandering Rocks, the only route that allowed them to avoid the treacherous strait between Scylla, a ravenous monster, and Charybdis, a hungry whirlpool. Once these hazards were behind them, the Argonauts sailed past the meadows of Thrinacia, where Helios kept his herds, then east into the Ionian Sea and north to Sickle Island, where the splendid kingdom of Phaeacia lay. The place took its name from the sickle that Cronus had used to castrate his father, which he buried afterwards in the island's soil; the first Phaeacians had sprung from the drops of blood that clung to it. From this grim beginning grew a people who nonetheless were warm and gracious. The younger gods gave them a beautiful palace of bronze to live in, surrounded by marvelous fruit trees that provided apples, pears, figs, pomegranates and olives all year round.

King Alcinous and Queen Arete had just welcomed the Argonauts at the palace when the Colchian fleet sailed into their harbor. Aeëtes demanded that Alcinous hand over Medea and the fleece, threatening war if Alcinous did not. Alcinous was torn; to surrender a visitor ran counter to every principle by which his hospitable people lived, but war with Aeëtes was not to be undertaken lightly. Medea, meanwhile, implored Queen Arete to intervene on her behalf, pleading that her mistakes were those of an inexperienced girl. The queen took up her cause and urged Alcinous to protect her. After much thought, Alcinous declared that if Medea were still a virgin—still her father's daughter to control—she would be surrendered. If she had married Jason and now belonged to him, however, Alcinous would protect her.

Arete quickly sent a messenger to Medea with this news. Libations were poured; animals were sacrificed and a hasty marriage bed was prepared for Jason and Medea in a nearby cave. On its floor, Jason spread the fleece; on the fleece he consummated his marriage; on the fleece a virgin bled and became his wife.

90
HOME AGAIN

From Sickle Island they were blown to Libya, where they ran aground upon a vast ocean of sand that disappeared into the horizon. The Argonauts wandered the dunes like bloodless ghosts, wishing they'd already died in Colchis.

Then the nymphs of the place took pity on them and appeared to Jason as he slept in the searing heat of the day.

"When Amphitrite releases the chariot of Poseidon, carry your mother, who has nurtured you in her belly for so long, upon your shoulders," they said.

Jason sprang up from his nap and shared the puzzling message with his friends. As he was speaking, a huge horse with a golden mane galloped over the sands from the sea and disappeared into the distance. Peleus spoke with great excitement.

"Friends, that *horse* was Poseidon's chariot! Amphitrite has dispatched it in the direction in which we must now carry our mother— that means the Argo herself, as strange as that seems."

So the Argonauts hoisted the Argo onto their shoulders and carried her for twelve days and nights until they reached the waters of Lake Tritonis, which fed a river that emptied into the sea. Nearby they saw the Hesperides, who were lamenting the recent loss of three golden apples to Heracles. Nearby as well they saw a spring of fresh water that Heracles, when thirsty, had created by kicking at a rock. Some of the Argonauts excitedly set out to search for him then, hoping he was still nearby. Lynceus, however, whose eyes could see across great distances, dashed their hopes; he had just glimpsed Heracles far away, apples in hand, returning to Mycenae.

And so the Argonauts departed. Triton himself emerged from his lake to help them, taking hold of the Argo's keel and guiding her first into the river and then into the sea. After sailing north, they approached Crete and made ready to land, in order to replenish their provisions. This, however, proved to be difficult; many years before, Zeus had ordered Talus, a giant made of bronze, to guard the island. Three times each day, Talus patrolled its perimeter, lobbing boulders at any approaching ship.

Medea spoke to the Argonauts. "Listen! I know how to destroy this creature. Row us out of the range of his missiles and then keep the ship as steady as you can."

Drawing a fold of her dark robe up over her cheeks, she invoked the spirits of death that constantly prowl the earth—three times with prayers and three times with incantations. Then she willed herself to become a conduit for evil; from her eyes she shot forth a deadly stare while her teeth gnashed out destruction. Abruptly,

Talus stumbled and grazed his ankle against a stone. His bronze skin, stretched thin over the jutting bone, was torn. Ichor, which gave Talus life just as blood gives life to humans, gushed out upon the ground.

From Crete the Argo made a swift run to Iolcus. The Argonauts disembarked and dispersed, eager to return to their own homes. Jason strode to the palace, the Golden Fleece in his hands and Medea at his side, proud of his accomplishments and confident of his future.

But Pelias turned ashen when Jason's name was announced. He received the fleece that Jason so eagerly offered, but stammered out only the barest of niceties and told Jason to return the following day. When the next day came, Jason walked into an audience room packed with guards.

"I have realized, nephew," said Pelias, "that there are delicate *diplomatic* negotiations in progress at the moment that need the touch of an *older*, more *experienced* man. I cannot, in good conscience, give you the kingdom just yet. *Surely* you can wait a few weeks."

Weeks turned into months. Medea gave birth to a son. The couple wished to settle into their new life, but Jason had no formal standing in the city and Medea was thought to be rather peculiar; they sat at home, alone. More months went by. Medea bore another son. Jason lapsed into listless inertia, refusing advice even from Chiron, who journeyed down from Mount Pelion to speak with him. At last Medea decided to take matters into her own hands. She was on passingly friendly terms with the daughters of Pelias, who admired her extraordinary jewelry, which glowed with unfamiliar stones. One afternoon when Medea was entertaining them, she showed them her cabinet of medicinal plants and casually introduced the topic of Pelias's advancing age.

"It's such a shame that a great king like your father may not live to see the fruition of his plans," said Medea. "If only—well, never mind. I'm speaking out of turn, now."

They pressed her to finish her thought.

"I've got a drug that rejuvenates; we used it all the time in Colchis, but here in Greece it might not work."

Excited—more by the lure of mysterious rituals than filial affection—they pressed Medea further: couldn't it be tried out first on an animal? Feigning reluctance, Medea finally agreed. The next day, the daughters watched as Medea dropped herbs into a cauldron of boiling water. She slaughtered an old ram and butchered the meat with a deftness that made them gasp. She threw the pieces into the cauldron and out sprang a lamb, no older than a day.

Medea thanked them for the compliments they paid her, but declined to perform the ritual on Pelias herself. "I don't think he trusts me yet," she explained, and cautioned that if they decided to try it themselves, it was better not to tell him what they planned to do, lest he fearfully refuse the process. "Wait until he's asleep and then just do it," she said. "He'll thank you later!" Handing them a bundle of plants that she assured them would do the trick, Medea escorted her guests to the door and waved goodbye.

But the bundle lacked an essential ingredient. The girls slaughtered their father and threw his butchered body into the cauldron they had prepared, but all that emerged were bones and parboiled flesh. The people of Iolcus, horrified by what Medea had done, refused to put Jason on the ancestral throne that he'd anticipated for so long. Instead, they cast the entire family out beyond the city's borders.

91
MEDEA IN CORINTH

Generations earlier, Helios had set his son Aeëtes on the throne of Corinth, where he ruled for many years before his father moved him to the wealthier kingdom of Colchis. Medea hoped that, as Aeëtes's daughter, she might be welcome in Corinth and persuaded Jason that they should try their luck there. But local history remembered Aeëtes as a barbaric man; Corinth's current king, Creon, praised Jason as a famous hero but regarded Medea warily.

Jason ingratiated himself with Creon and quickly became the king's closest advisor, spending days in the throne room and nights in the banquet hall. His ability to read and manipulate other people's emotions, which he had honed during his quest for the Golden

Fleece, made him an invaluable confidant. It was only to be expected, therefore, that Creon would eventually seek to forge the closest of all alliances with the man he'd come to view as a son: one day, he announced that he had betrothed his daughter, Glauce, to Jason. Jason's existing "marriage" presented no obstacle, Creon declared: it had been contracted in a foreign place with a barbarian woman. Under Greek law, it was no marriage at all. Medea and her children would be banished from Corinth, he added, lest their presence cast a pall over his daughter's happiness.

Medea ranted and wept, lifting her hands to the gods. At one moment, she invoked the vows that she and Jason had made to one another; at the next, she called out to the father and brother whom she had betrayed. She clung pitiably to her children but then shoved them away and paced the floor, her soul bitten by a madness even sharper than that with which Aphrodite's iynx had once infected her. Yet while her soul was raging, a dreadful plan, unbidden, was taking root in her mind.

Jason, preening like a cat, spoke loftily of expedience.

"This is a *good* thing, Medea. You were nothing before—indeed, less than nothing, given the suspicion with which everyone regarded you. Now I'm making you the mother of sons who will be brothers to those I sire upon a princess. Think of the benefits our boys will reap! Wasn't I smart to befriend a king?"

"So *now* you're marrying a princess?" she replied. "I'm the daughter of a greater king than Creon—and the granddaughter of a god. Yet you didn't even tell me what you planned; I heard about it secondhand, in the most humiliating of ways. *I*, who rescued you in Colchis. *I*, whose skills won you the fleece! Greek poets sing about these things even now, and yet you discard me like rubbish."

"Face reality, Medea! It was Aphrodite and Hera who saved me; you were just their tool. And stop ranting: I've got everything figured out. I've got friends you can live with and money to keep you going; I'll send for the boys later on, when the time is right. I suspect that what you're really upset about deep down, like all women, is sex. Well, it's true that I've left your bed, but remember the advantages I've given you: if poets sing your praises, it's because I brought you out of that backwater into the civilized world."

Medea was silent for some moments before she spoke again, with an unexpected calmness in her voice. "You're right, Jason. But let's arrange for the boys to remain here. Send them to Glauce, carrying gifts from me, and ask her to plead with her father."

Jason shrugged, nodded and left.

Now Medea began to work, quickly and expertly. She took from her chest a golden robe that the daughters of Helios had woven, as fine as gossamer, and a golden crown that Hephaestus had forged. From her casket of drugs she selected noxious roots, twisted and dark, and lethal blooms, harvested with a ruthless sickle. Brewing a tincture, she rubbed it on her gifts and placed them in a box. She called her sons, taught them what to say to Glauce and sent them on their way. Then she sank trembling onto the floor, exulting in her coming victory but heartsick at what it would require of her.

In the palace, Glauce listened to the boys, smiled encouragingly and sent them home. She opened the box and gasped at what lay inside. Eagerly, she instructed her slaves to dress her in the robe and place the crown upon her head. Her mirror was the best that Corinth's smiths could make; few were its distortions and each one was a familiar friend. But as she stared at her reflection, ripples began to appear where she knew there should be no ripples; in the next moment, searing heat engulfed her. Her slaves screamed as their mistress's flesh began to melt. Creon ran to his child and enfolded her, crazily trying to remold her body as a potter refashions a collapsing vase, but the poison seized him, too, fusing together father and daughter.

Medea hugged her sons when they returned from the palace. Soon, she would be departing for a place they could not go. She knew that if she left them behind, the Corinthians would kill them in vengeance. It would be better, she had conceded with sorrow, to kill them herself. Would her lot be so much worse than that of other mothers? Women purchased their children with pain paid out to Eileithyia—or to Death himself. Then they fed the hungry things from their own bodies, unaccountably loving them all the more dearly. There followed a few years of smiles and sweetness and then the children departed: to war or to marriage beds.

Medea bathed her sons in warm water, singing the same songs she had sung a thousand times before. The younger one went into the tub first; he fell asleep before she had finished patting him dry. She slid her knife into his heart, wrapped his limp body in the towel and laid him in the bed. The older one took the same gentle road to Hades.

When the slave discovered Medea weeping over her sons, she ran to find Jason, but when he arrived Medea was gone, as were the boys' bodies. He rushed from the house, searching for them. Medea called down to him then from the air, where she stood in a blazing chariot drawn by dragons, sent for her by her grandfather Helios. The boys' corpses lay at her feet. Mad with grief, Jason begged to be allowed to bury his children.

"You'll never again touch them!" she said. "I'll bury them myself, in the sanctuary of Hera, where the Corinthians daren't harm them. As the years go around, Corinthian children will propitiate their ghosts and their mothers will pray that Hera be kinder to them than she was to me."

Then she was gone.

Jason, homeless once more, wandered from city to city and eventually made his way back to Iolcus, where he found the decaying hulk of the Argo. Curling up under her bow to escape the noonday sun, he jostled a rotting board, which fell on his head. That was Jason's death.

92
THE CALYDONIAN BOAR

Oeneus ruled Calydon, a settlement that lay in the fertile plain of the river Evenus. Dark-eyed Althaea bore him children, including the hero Meleager. One day, to celebrate the harvest, Oeneus prepared a splendid sacrifice and invited all the gods to partake. All but one, that was: in his haste, Oeneus forgot Artemis. While the other gods inhaled the delicious smoke that rose from the altar, Artemis sat alone on her golden throne, preparing a terrible vengeance.

Early the next morning, Oeneus's attendant shook him awake with dreadful news. An enormous boar, as large as a bull, had arrived overnight and was wreaking havoc. The beast had uprooted fruit trees, trampled fields of grain and killed lambs and calves before their mothers' startled eyes. The people looked to Oeneus for help.

After several of the kingdom's best huntsmen met their deaths at the boar's tusks, Oeneus instructed Meleager to seek the help of those with whom he had sailed on the Argo. In response to his plea, Jason, Euphemus, Echion, Admetus, Ancaeus, Laertes, Castor and Polydeuces, Nestor, Idas and Lynceus, Peleus, Eurytion, Acastus and Asclepius journeyed to Calydon. Other youths, hearing about the adventure, made their way to Calydon, as well: Amphiaraus, Iphicles, Theseus, Pirithous and two brothers of Althaea: Plexippus and Toxeus.

After some hesitation, Meleager also invited Atalanta, an excellent hunter. He was aware that she could be a distraction: although she dressed plainly and adorned herself with nothing more than the polished buckle that clasped her robe at one shoulder, her beauty announced itself. During the voyage of the Argo, many men had sought her favors, Meleager among them. She'd defended her resolute chastity with an obdurate stare and a studious caress of her hunting knife, dampening ardor before it burned too bright. Other men had resented her presence. Such an expedition, they said, was no place for any woman, whatever her skills.

The morning of the hunt dawned bright and humid; mist hung low among the trees, hindering sight. Some hunters stretched nets where they thought that the boar might appear; others unleashed their dogs, trusting more in canine noses than human eyes; still others slogged through the dank and sticky underbrush, trying to track the beast. Hours passed without success, but at midday, when the mist burned off, the hunters discovered the boar in a marshy dell. The dogs roused him and he fled like lightning. Behind the dogs, the hunters thrashed through reeds and brambles, bloodying their legs.

Finally, they cornered the boar in a rocky hollow. Echion hurled the first spear, which missed. Then Jason threw rashly, killing the best of the dogs. More spears followed, but none managed to penetrate the boar's tough hide. Striving to do better, Ancaeus ventured too close to boar's tusks and died, his entrails spilling out onto the ground.

And then Atalanta shot a brilliantly aimed arrow that pierced the soft skin beneath the beast's ear; he stumbled and stopped. Meleager seized the chance to launch his spear into the boar's unguarded back. The boar fell to its knees then, and died with a horrible grunt.

By rights the head and pelt belonged to Meleager, for he had thrown the fatal spear, but he gave them to Atalanta, whose arrow had afforded his opportunity. Some of the men applauded his gesture—the woman's shot had been truly remarkable. Others were aghast: there was something unchaste, they complained, in a woman bloodying herself with a trophy.

Meleager's uncles, Plexippus and Toxeus, were particularly appalled by their nephew's behavior and rebuked Atalanta for accepting his gifts. "Don't steal a hero's honors, girl! Your looks can get you only so far, and even then only among men whom you've already beguiled. If Meleager won't claim his trophies, then his family will." They snatched the head and pelt from where they lay at Atalanta's feet. This was more than Meleager could bear. Before he knew it, he had plunged his sword first into Plexippus's chest and then into Toxeus's. His uncles fell to the ground.

Word of her son's victory over the boar had reached Althaea quickly and she'd hastened to the household shrine to offer thanks. She was just returning to her loom when she saw the corpses of her brothers being carried in. She wailed in grief—until she learned who had killed them. Then, she dried her eyes and in the cold madness of anger plotted revenge.

Many years before, when Meleager was but a few moments old, Althaea had spotted three women standing near the hearth in her bedchamber. These were the Fates, who decided the length of every mortal's life. They'd thrown a log onto the fire and told Althaea, "Your son will live as long as this wood remains unconsumed," and then they'd vanished. Althaea leapt from her bed and pulled the log from the flames. She extinguished it carefully and hid it beneath tapestries stored in a chest, meticulously guarding her secret, and with it her son's life, for many years. Now she ran to her bedchamber and threw open the chest. Tossing the tapestries onto the floor, she seized the dry, brittle log and threw it onto the hearth. The flames crackled and attacked their new fuel eagerly. Far away, Meleager felt a fever slip through his veins and crawl into the tips of his fingers and toes. Suddenly, he fell to the forest floor, gasping out what little moisture remained to him. His soul, shriveled, fluttered down to the house of Hades.

Althaea, abruptly realizing that she now had neither son nor brothers, saw the folly of her actions. Untying her breastband, she looped it over a rafter of her bedchamber and hanged herself. Meleager's older sisters, who unceasingly lamented his death, were turned by Artemis into guinea fowl, *meleagrides*.

93
ATHENA'S CITY

When the world was new and the gods were dividing it up among themselves, Poseidon and Athena vied for a young city that lay in a fertile territory called Cecropia. Its king, Cecrops, was a creature born from Earth herself and, like many of Earth's children, he was oddly shaped: from his hips up he was a man, but where other men had legs, he had the coiling tail of an enormous snake.

Poseidon hastily laid claim to what he hoped would become his city by striking his trident into the bedrock of its acropolis, causing a spring of fresh water to gush forth—his gift to the local people. He made the mistake, however, of performing this miracle while he was all alone. Athena, with more foresight, called Cecrops to her side and then caused the first olive tree to spring forth from the soil—her gift to the people. When Zeus assembled the gods and commanded them to decide to whom the city should belong, Athena could call Cecrops as a witness to what she'd done but Poseidon could call no one. The gods awarded the city to Athena and she named it Athens.

Cecrops ruled over Athens for many years but left no heir; he was succeeded by Cranaus, a local man who was also a child of Earth. Cranaus was deposed by Amphictyon and Amphictyon was deposed by Erichthonius, yet another son of Earth, who'd been conceived when Hephaestus's seed fell upon the ground. Erichthonius was a man from his hips up but where other men had legs, he had the coiling tails of *two* enormous snakes.

Soon after Erichthonius was born, Earth had asked Athena to care for him. Athena nestled the baby snugly inside a basket, shut the lid firmly and delivered it to Cecrops's three daughters, Aglaurus, Herse and Pandrosus, for safekeeping. She told the girls to guard the basket carefully but never to look inside.

Curiosity ate away at the girls; one day, they lifted the lid and saw the peculiar baby sleeping inside. Athena, furious that the girls had disobeyed her, drove them mad and in their madness they leapt off the Acropolis to their deaths. Athena finished raising Erichthonius herself and made him king of her city, thus beginning a royal dynasty that descended from Earth and Hephaestus.

In the fifth generation of Erichthonius's descendants, Aegeus inherited the throne. His first wife died without bearing him children. When his second wife failed to bear children, too, Aegeus traveled to the Delphic Oracle to ask Apollo for help. The Pythia spoke forth from the tripod, channeling the god's response: "Do not loosen the foot of the wineskin until you reach home."

Puzzled, Aegeus looked at the wineskin his slave was carrying for him. The foot—which, once loosened, allowed the wine to pour forth—was tightly tied. Resolving to keep it so, but suspecting that Apollo had been speaking in riddles that he didn't understand, Aegeus started the journey home. Before he'd gone very far, it occurred to him that his clever friend Pittheus, the king of Troezen, might be able to decipher what Apollo meant. Aegeus made a detour to visit him. When Pittheus heard the oracle, he silently laughed to himself. "Foot" was common slang for "penis"; it was clear to him that the oracle was admonishing Aegeus not to have sex before reaching home because the god would enable him to sire a child upon the next woman with whom he slept.

Pittheus saw his chance to bind his small kingdom to Athens, the most powerful kingdom of all. After plying Aegeus with wine (Pittheus assured him that it was only the foot of his *own* wineskin that Apollo meant him to keep tied), Pittheus led him to the chamber of his daughter Aethra. Aegeus made love to her.

Poseidon saw his chance, too. After Aegeus left Aethra's bed, she had a dream that commanded her to walk to the seashore and wade into the water. Once there, she felt the waves embrace her with a surprisingly pleasant warmth and then swirl between her legs. She returned to her bedroom with a secret that she kept locked in her heart.

The next morning, Pittheus revealed the true meaning of Apollo's words to Aegeus and confessed what he'd done. Before he departed for home, Aegeus walked with Aethra to a nearby hillside. Heaving aside an enormous rock, he dug a hollow in the soil beneath, in which he deposited his sword and his sandals, wrapped in sealskin to protect them from moisture. Then he restored the rock to its place.

"If the child you've conceived is a boy and he grows strong enough to lift this rock, tell him who his father is and send him to Athens, with these proofs of his identity. Tell him to travel incognito, lest my enemies attempt to kill him."

The child was indeed a boy, whom Aethra named Theseus. Pittheus gave him everything that a royal child should have. He was tutored in rhetoric, ethics, philosophy and history. He was trained as an athlete to be strong, agile and enduring. He heard from traveling bards about the great heroes and developed a particular admiration for Heracles. And, he was given a proud sense of who his family was—at least on his mother's side.

One day, after the first signs of a beard had appeared on Theseus's face, Aethra asked him to walk with her to the hillside where, so many years before, she'd walked with Aegeus. She pointed to the rock—which by now was moss-covered and firmly sunk within the soil.

"Can you lift that?" she asked.

Theseus squatted and, bit by bit, nudged his fingers under the stone's edge. Slowly rising, he lifted it and then, toppling it over itself, sent it rolling down the slope. He picked up the sealskin package and unwrapped the sword and sandals.

"Who left these here, Mother?"

"Your father, Aegeus, the king of Athens," she said. "Now you must go to meet him and claim your birthright. But know this, too, Theseus: on the same night that Aegeus visited me, I was visited by Poseidon, as well. Only the gods know whose child you truly are."

Poseidon, watching the scene unfold from afar, smiled with satisfaction. The gods may have given the city to Athena, but he was sure that *his* son would soon be on its throne.

94
THESEUS TRAVELS TO ATHENS

As they walked back to the palace, Aethra began to talk of preparing a ship to carry Theseus to Athens, but Theseus cut her short.

"I'll go overland—along the coastal road through Epidauria, across the isthmus and the cliffs overlooking the Saronic Gulf, and from there to Athens."

"But, Theseus," she exclaimed, "monsters and brigands lurk around every bend of that blighted road!"

"If I want the Athenians to accept me as their ruler one day, Mother, then I should try, first, to rid the land of evils, as Heracles once did."

And so the next morning Theseus set out, wearing a crimson tunic that Aethra had woven with her own hands and a warm woolen cloak. A traveler's hat kept the sun off his face, Aegeus's sword hung at his hip and he carried a spear in his right hand. As the evening shadows crept across a lonely stretch of road, he spotted an odd figure: short, with bowed legs, but mighty in the chest and shoulders. He leaned on a large club as if it were a crutch.

This was Periphetes, a son of Hephaestus who lay in wait for unlucky travelers. He presented himself as pitiable until they drew near, and then lashed out with astonishing strength, clubbing them to death. If Theseus hadn't been well trained by Pittheus's boxing coaches, he would have fallen victim to the club as well, but he nimbly stepped aside as it came rushing down. Periphetes stumbled and fell to the ground, where Theseus's sword made an end of him. Theseus picked up the club, which he thought might serve him well in future adventures. He ate some of the food he'd brought along from the palace kitchen, rolled himself up in his cloak and slept.

Two days later, as Theseus approached the isthmus, he passed through a forest of pine trees—none of them tall enough to offer much shade but suffusing the air with the heavy scent of resin. This was the territory of Sinis, a son of Poseidon who had invented a ghastly amusement for which he kept two of the trees in constant readiness. Selecting a pair that grew close to one another, he pulled their tops down to the ground and tied them to stakes. Capturing a hapless traveler, Sinis bound him spread-eagle between the tree-tops and then cut the ropes so that the trees sprang up once more, tearing the traveler in half.

Theseus had expected to encounter Sinis, however, and emulating Heracles, inflicted upon the villain what he'd inflicted upon so many others: a terrible death between two pines. He anticipated his next opponents as well: the vicious sow of Crommyon, a child of Typhon and Echidna who destroyed crops and devoured local flocks, and Phaea, the depraved woman who tended the sow. Theseus chased them to the filthy farm where they dwelt and killed them both.

He continued his journey across the isthmus, keeping to the road that ran along the cliffs overlooking the gulf. As he approached the city of Megara, a man blocked his path.

"Wash my feet, traveler!" he demanded.

"Why should I?"

"Because I'm Sciron, the son of Poseidon, and I won't let you pass before you do."

Suspecting a trick, Theseus warily sat down on the stool that Sciron placed before his chair, close to the edge of the cliff. As he bent to pick up a sponge, he saw, from the corner of his eye, Sciron pulling back his foot, as if preparing to kick. In a flash, Theseus grabbed him by the calves and flipped him over the edge onto the rocks below. Peering down, he saw an enormous turtle ambling over to feed upon Sciron's body just as it had fed upon those of Sciron's victims.

The next day, Theseus arrived in Eleusis, where a man named Cercyon ran what he mockingly called a "wrestling school," compelling travelers to compete against him and killing those who lost. Theseus lifted Cercyon high above his head and dashed him to the ground. His brains spilled out upon the soil.

Athens lay only a half day's hike ahead now, but it was late afternoon when Theseus left Eleusis. As dusk fell, he was beginning to look for a place to make camp when a man stepped out of a house on a lonely stretch of road. He was peculiar looking: tall and pinched, with eyes that darted here and there while he spoke. His fingers darted here and there as well, nervously picking at his clothing.

His voice, however, was silky smooth: "Do you need a place to sleep, traveler? No one has ever slept in the house of Procrustes and complained of it afterwards!"

Theseus felt uneasy but nonetheless walked through the door, which Procrustes promptly closed and bolted. The only thing inside was a bed, which looked soft and inviting but was oddly equipped at each end with ropes and wheels. Through the straw strewn across the floor Theseus glimpsed rust-colored stains.

Procrustes spoke once more, his voice breaking into a cackle.

"Now, then! I have only one bed but I find that it fits every-one . . . one way or another. For if you're too long"—he dragged an axe out from under the bed—"I'll cut your legs till you fit. And if you're too short, well, my ropes will stretch you out nicely. Let's see how *you* fit, traveler!"

Then he dashed at Theseus. This was a more difficult fight than those Theseus had waged against Periphetes, Sinis and Sciron, for he lacked the advantage of surprise, and it was more difficult than that against Cercyon, for this opponent was a taller man. After a few minutes of hard work, however, Theseus prevailed. He threw Procrustes onto his own bed and, discovering that he was too long, hacked him off midshins.

95
A WICKED STEPMOTHER

Soon after starting out the next morning, Theseus came to the Cephisus River, where he was greeted by some priests of Demeter who were on their way to Eleusis. At Theseus's request, they purified him from the bloodguilt he had accumulated during his journey from Troezen. It was the first kindness that anyone had done him during his travels.

Aegeus had been hearing about the young stranger for some days. Reports had filtered into Athens about the deaths of Periphetes,

Sinis, Sciron and the sow and just that morning a messenger had brought news of the deaths of Cercyon and Procrustes, as well. On the one hand, Aegeus was grateful that someone had rid an important trade route of such outlaws; on the other hand, anyone who could do these things might present a threat to his throne.

Aegeus was an old man, now. Having heard nothing from Pittheus over the years, he'd given up hope that Aethra had conceived a son on the night he'd visited her. When, some time after that, his old acquaintance Medea had arrived in Athens seeking shelter, he'd accepted her both because the laws governing suppliants demanded that he do so and because she promised that her knowledge of drugs would enable him to sire the heir he so fervently desired.

His wife, nonetheless, died childless and in the years that followed, Aegeus fell increasingly under Medea's influence. Her beauty had something to do with this but even more powerful were the drugs that she put into his food. Aegeus grew steadily feebler in body, mind and resolve; people began to whisper that it was really Medea who ran the kingdom. Eventually, Medea became Aegeus's wife and bore him a son, Medus; her control over the king, and therefore Athens, seemed secure. But on the night before news of the stranger first reached the city, Medea had a terrible dream. Upon awakening, she sacrificed a sheep and consulted its entrails. The liver, still warm in her hands as she peered at it, told her everything she needed to know: she began to lay groundwork for the disposal of Theseus.

After being purified at the Cephisus, Theseus entered the city gates and walked past a new temple of Apollo, which lacked only the peak of its roof. When the workmen saw the young man, they whistled mockingly and called down flirtatious remarks—his hair, which had never yet been shorn, hung in braids down his back and the crimson tunic his mother had made for him was effeminate by Athenian standards. Smiling to himself, Theseus unyoked two oxen from a nearby cart and tossed the beasts over the roof where the workmen stood. Then he laughed and walked on. News of this escapade raced through Athens. Aegeus trembled all the more in fear of the stranger and Medea seethed with exasperation: disposing of Theseus would not be as easy as she'd hoped. She formulated new plans and convinced Aegeus to do as she wished.

The stranger presented himself at the palace that afternoon and was feasted that night. After dinner, a bard performed. The story that Aegeus had asked him to sing, at Medea's suggestion, was of Heracles's capture of the Cretan Bull.

When the story was over, Medea sighed.

"If only Heracles hadn't set that beast free! The bull wandered across the isthmus and has caused no end of trouble for our subjects in Marathon ever since—trampling their crops and killing their sheep."

Theseus felt a thrill run down his spine when he realized that he might perform the same labor as his favorite hero. "I'll capture the bull for you!" he declared.

"Wonderful!" exclaimed Medea, clapping her hands. "Perhaps after that," she continued coyly, "we'll finally learn who you are."

The task was quickly completed; as the bull charged him, Theseus grabbed a horn and wrestled him to the ground. Then Theseus rode the bull back to Athens, paraded him through the streets and sacrificed him at the new temple to Apollo where he had so recently tossed oxen into the air. Aegeus began to admire the young man. But Medea contrived another plan, to which Aegeus reluctantly agreed. That night at dinner, she mixed poison into a cup of wine and then handed it to Theseus.

Theseus, however, had decided that it was finally time to reveal his identity. Noticing that the slaves were bringing in the meat, he set down the cup that Medea had handed him and took from its scabbard the sword that he'd found under the rock in Troezen. With a flourish he cut off the choicest portion of the roast and served it to his father. Then he lifted his cup to toast Aegeus, who was gaping at the sword.

The king sprang up, startled into unaccustomed vigor. He knocked the cup from Theseus's hand, spilling the poisoned wine onto the floor, where it etched a hole in the marble. Medea screamed with fury, called for her son and spat out a command in the Colchian language. A fiery chariot drawn by dragons descended from the sky to carry Medea and Medus to Persia, where Medus later became king.

Aegeus and Theseus wept and embraced one another. When they were done rejoicing, however, Aegeus stepped back and looked somberly into his son's face.

"My child, you have arrived in Athens at a sad and troubling moment. This is the time of year when we must send seven of our young men and seven of our young women to Crete, to be devoured by the Minotaur."

96
A VOYAGE TO CRETE

From the neck down, the Minotaur had the body of a man but his head was that of a bull. He had been conceived when the great white bull—the very bull that was later captured by Heracles and then Theseus—mounted Pasiphaë, the wife of Minos, king of Crete.

Minos was so repulsed by the monster to which his wife had given birth that he commanded the inventor Daedalus to devise a prison from which the Minotaur could never escape. Daedalus designed the Labyrinth, a vast hall with tortuous passageways that made up a maze of great complexity. Through a trapdoor in its ceiling, Minos periodically threw animals down to the beast— sheep, goats and occasionally game that the hunters brought home. The indigestible bits of these creatures littered the Labyrinth's corridors.

Once a year the Minotaur received a heartier meal, when Minos forced fourteen young Athenians to enter the Labyrinth. There, they wandered in the dark until the Minotaur found them. This "tribute," as Minos called it, had started after his son, Androgeus, was murdered while visiting Athens to compete in athletic games. In grief-stricken rage, Minos attacked Athens with his powerful navy. Eventually, Aegeus was forced to accept a grisly compromise of annually sending fourteen young Athenians to feed the Minotaur in retribution for Androgeus's death.

When all of this had been explained to Theseus, he volunteered to be included in that year's contingent of victims. His victory over the bull had convinced him that he could overcome anything, including the bull's monstrous son. Aegeus objected, insisting that the victims were always chosen by lot, but Theseus asserted that because a king should always be the first to make a sacrifice for his city, so should a king's son be first to risk his life. Aegeus found it hard to disagree.

And so the next morning, Aegeus and Theseus walked to the harbor, where a dark-prowed ship, fitted with a mournful black sail, awaited the chosen youths. Their weeping families were assembled there to bid them goodbye. Mothers handed baskets of food to their children to sustain them on a voyage from which they would never return.

Aegeus, saying farewell to a son he had only just met, made a request.

"Theseus, if you do manage to escape with your life, change the sail on the ship before you return to Athens. I'll climb the Acropolis each day to watch for it; if the ship's sail is still black, I'll know you're dead, but if it's white, I'll rejoice."

Minos, as usual, had traveled to Athens to supervise operations. As soon as he surveyed the victims, desire for one of the young women, Eriboea, began to chafe at his heart. He decided to return to Crete on the Athenians' ship and seduce her. Once they were at sea, he stood behind Eriboea, caressing her cheeks with a calloused finger while whispering of love's delights in a deep, rumbling voice. She cried out to Theseus for help.

Theseus glowered with anger. "Minos, perhaps you're the son of Zeus, as you claim, but that doesn't give you the right to do as you like with Athenian women. *I* am the son of Poseidon and I won't tolerate it."

"Really?" replied Minos. "Let's see whose paternity holds up. If I'm the son of Zeus, let Zeus confirm it with a lightning bolt. And if Poseidon is *your* father, let him confirm it by helping you recover this ring." And with that, he pulled a golden ring from his finger and tossed it into the sea.

Immediately, Zeus split the sky with lightning and Theseus dove overboard. Straightaway, the currents carried him to the palace of Poseidon, where Amphitrite welcomed him. All around her danced the glorious daughters of Nereus with feet that were as supple as water itself and golden ribbons that rippled through their hair. Fish and octopuses and dolphins darted among them, iridescent in the shimmering light. Amphitrite wrapped a purple cloak around Theseus's shoulders and crowned him with a wreath of roses, which Aphrodite had given to her when she married Poseidon. Then she handed Theseus the ring that Minos had tossed into the sea.

The gods accomplish many things that no sane mortal would think possible. With the ring in his hand, Theseus shot to the surface and emerged right next to the ship, in spite of the fact that Minos had urged it onwards towards Crete. The women rejoiced, the men sang a victory chant and the sea itself resounded with praise. Minos ground his teeth in fury and urged the ship forward all the more, eager to watch Theseus disappear into the Labyrinth's gloom.

The sight of the Cretan harbor was overwhelming in its splendor. Daedalus had equipped it with strange devices to facilitate the provisioning of vessels. In back of those, he'd built tall buildings that gleamed with bronze and ivory; even the harbormaster's house was grand. From a balcony there, where she sat with the harbormaster's wife, Minos's daughter Ariadne saw the black-sailed ship arrive and watched the Athenians disembark. Theseus, who by now walked an easy grace born of confidence, intrigued her.

97
THE PRINCESS AND THE MINOTAUR

The Athenians were taken to a cave near the Labyrinth where they would be lodged and fed for a few days before they were led to the dim corridors of the maze. A stream of curious Cretans gathered in front of the cave's barred entrance to stare at the captives inside. Ariadne mingled among them to get a closer look at Theseus, who sat apart from the others with his chin in his hand and an abstracted look on his face. That evening she returned.

By then, she had learned that the year's quota of victims included the king's son, and surmised that he was the man who intrigued her. Now she peered into the cave and saw that he had not fallen into the same exhausted sleep as his companions. Quietly, she called to him and he walked over.

"You are a king's son," she said. "You could have avoided this fate—why are you here, throwing away your life?"

"A king rules best by making common cause with his subjects. The dynasties of kings who do not do so are brutal and short."

"A dead man cannot rule."

"If I defeat the Minotaur and return, I'll lead Athens to further greatness. If I fail and die, the sons of my father's brothers will topple first my father and then each other until one of them, bloody but victorious, seizes the throne and rules Athens as a tyrant. But strength alone cannot make a city strong—Athens will last for another generation and then it will be toppled, as well. Some things lie with the Fates; I can only act as I'm called to act."

"I'll come again tomorrow night," she promised, and returned to the palace.

In the morning, Ariadne hastened to Daedalus's workshop. She reasoned that the task Theseus faced could be divided into three challenges. He needed light inside the Labyrinth, he somehow had to kill the Minotaur and, once the Minotaur was dead, he needed to find his way back out of the Labyrinth again. She realized that she herself could address the first of these: among the palace's treasures was a crown forged by Hephaestus, encrusted with Indian opals that cast light into darkness. The second challenge could be addressed only by Theseus himself; it was up to him to figure out a way to overpower the Minotaur.

It was the third challenge that Ariadne wanted Daedalus to help her with and he did so with a remarkably simple device: a clew of thread. He told her to have Theseus tie one end of the thread to a pillar near the Labyrinth's entrance and then unroll it behind him as he made his way through the corridors. Once the Minotaur was dead, he need only wind the thread up again to find his way back out. That night, Ariadne delivered the crown and the clew to Theseus and instructed him in their use.

The following afternoon, the captives made the short journey to the Labyrinth, accompanied by the mournful wailing of flutes. The guards prodded them through its gloomy entrance, but most of them didn't go very far beyond that; Theseus had instructed them to stop after they'd made the first turning in the maze and wait silently until he returned.

Theseus tied the end of the thread around a pillar. Then he pulled the crown out from under his cloak, placed it on his head and began to advance with the help of its light. What it revealed was horrifying. Human bones and tattered bits of cloth were scattered here and there on the floor, as were piles of dung in varying states of decay. The place stank: not only of dung but also of the mold that grew on its clammy walls, the brackish water that dripped through its roof, and the bits of flesh that even the Minotaur had abandoned as too rank to eat. Flies swarmed everywhere.

Theseus had tried to prepare himself for what the Minotaur would look like, but when he turned a corner and finally saw him, Theseus was surprised by his appearance. The creature's body was massive but there was a flabbiness to it, like that of an athlete who has fallen into lassitude. The part of him that was human was covered by worm-gray flesh that sunlight never touched; the hide on his head was matted and dirty. His eyes brimmed with wretchedness—one could not say he was sad because sadness implied a yearning and the Minotaur had never had anything, or anyone, to yearn for. He had been cheerless from birth, the shameful product of a god's curse inflicted upon his mother.

The light from the crown, which bewildered the Minotaur, gave Theseus a moment's advantage. He darted up, grabbed the Minotaur by the horns and flipped him onto his back on the floor, using his own weight against him. Spanning his hands around the Minotaur's neck where it emerged from his chest—the creature was still a man, there, with a man's dimensions—Theseus strangled him.

He dragged the corpse to the front of the cave for Minos to find the next morning. By now, night had fallen and the guards had gone home, assuming that their job was over. The Athenians sprinted through empty streets to the harbor, where Ariadne was waiting aboard their ship, trusting that Theseus would triumph. Theseus quietly stove in the hulls of Crete's fastest vessels to hamper pursuit. Then he returned to his own ship and told the captain to depart. He didn't waste time changing the sail, assuming that they could do that when they stopped on Naxos the next day.

◄ THESEUS AND THE MINOTAUR

98
THESEUS BECOMES KING

The people of Naxos were celebrating a festival of Dionysus when the Athenians arrived and they invited the visitors to join them. The god was present and glimpsed Ariadne. Enthralled by her beauty, he resolved to make her his wife and asked for his sister Athena's help in arranging the matter.

Athena appeared to Theseus and announced that Ariadne was not fated to reach Athens; he and his comrades were to leave Naxos without her, immediately. Theseus wept at losing a woman whose bravery and resourcefulness he admired and whom he had hoped to marry, but he obeyed Athena and set sail. When Ariadne discovered that Theseus was gone, she wept as well, heartbroken and alarmed at the thought that she was now alone and far from home. Soon, however, Dionysus appeared at her side and gently escorted her to Olympus, where on that same day she became both a god's wife and a god herself.

The Athenians sailed northwards to Delos, where they stopped to make offerings to Apollo. Theseus cut off his long braids and laid them on the god's altar in thanks for protecting him throughout his boyhood. The other Athenians, still giddy with the joy of escaping death, invented a dance that imitated the twists and turns of the Labyrinth. The Delians admired the dancers' exuberant movements but thought they were imitating cranes; forever after, the Delians performed what they took to calling the crane dance in Apollo's honor each year.

Distracted by his sorrow at losing Ariadne, Theseus had forgotten to exchange his black sail for a white one before they left Naxos. He forgot again when leaving Delos. And so it happened that one day, when Aegeus climbed to the top of the Acropolis to watch for Theseus's return, he saw a black-sailed ship rising over the horizon. Grieving for a son he had so recently found, Aegeus leapt from the Acropolis to his death.

When Theseus learned what had happened, he was devastated by the loss of his father and guilt-ridden about the role that he'd played in bringing it about. He was also overwhelmed by the sudden responsibility of ruling the Athenians. Lacking trusted counselors to guide him, he drew on the lessons of his boyhood tutors to try to govern wisely. He unified the people of the city and the surrounding countryside into a single state that he named Attica and made it a democracy; the king, he declared, would be no more than the commander of Attica's army and the guardian of its laws. He encouraged people from other places to immigrate to Athens, promising that they would be given rights equal to those of native-born Athenians. In these and many other ways, Theseus made Athens the most admired city in Greece and himself its most admired citizen.

Pirithous, the king of the Lapiths, heard about Theseus's deeds and was determined to become his friend. He devised an unusual way to do this. He traveled to Marathon, where Theseus kept a herd of cattle, and drove some of them away. Theseus soon set off after the thief; when he drew near enough that Pirithous could be sure of making himself heard, Pirithous stopped, turned around and stretched out his hand. He promised to return Theseus's cattle and pay any penalty that Theseus might chose to levy. In return he asked only that the two of them should become friends.

Theseus laughed at Pirithous's ingenuity and clasped his hand. The two became constant companions, supporting one another through many adventures. Theseus helped Pirithous defeat the drunken centaurs who disrupted his wedding to Hippodamia and the two traveled together to Calydon to help kill the great boar. When Theseus decided to travel to Themiscyra, the city of the Amazons, in order to learn how the women ran their lives apart from men, it was a foregone conclusion that Pirithous would accompany him.

Northwards they sailed and then east to the Black Sea. When they reached the mouth of the Thermodon River, the captain quietly lay at anchor some distance from Themiscyra. Theseus and Pirithous rowed ashore and crept through the woods towards the city. They saw Amazons dressed in tight-fitting trousers and short tunics patrolling its walls. Each one carried a bow and a spear; quivers of arrows hung at their waists. The men decided to approach the gates, throw down their weapons and ask to be escorted to the queen. This worked—but the Amazons remembered what had happened when Heracles had visited their previous queen. They never left Theseus and Pirithous alone with the new one.

The new queen, like her predecessor, was named Hippolyta. Her red hair was crowned with a golden diadem upon which the smith had embossed stags with swirling antlers. Her pectoral collar of gold and turquoise depicted a war between monkeys and dragons and her golden belt was engraved with griffins. Tattoos of geometric designs danced up and down her bare arms.

Theseus and Pirithous talked with her about the lives of the Amazons: how they cared for their livestock and bred their horses; how they hunted, harvested and trained for warfare; how they chose their leaders and how they conceived children with the help of men who visited once a year. After many hours of such discussions, Hippolyta stood up and asked Theseus to show her his ship. When they reached the harbor, she ordered her guards to remain on shore and entered the rowboat without them. Once she was aboard the ship, she declared, "Theseus! I find I have fallen in love with you. Take me to Athens and I will bear you strong sons."

Shocked but fascinated, Theseus told the sailors to depart as quickly as possible. On shore, the Amazons, unable to comprehend what was happening, futilely launched arrows at the ship, then ran to their own vessels and prepared to rescue their queen.

99
A FATHER'S CURSE

The sleek ships of the Amazons arrived in Athens just behind that of Theseus. The Amazons, ignoring Hippolyta's insistence that she had sailed with Theseus of her own free will, waged war to recover her. Eventually, however, with the help of the Athenian army, Theseus, Pirithous and Hippolyta repelled the attack. The Amazons returned to Themiscyra and chose a new queen.

In spite of the immigration reforms that Theseus had enacted and his public declaration of admiration for Hippolyta, the Athenians refused to accept her as their queen or even as Theseus's legal wife: they could not imagine such a woman bringing anything but degeneracy into their city. She died a few years later, leaving behind a son, Hippolytus. Theseus, who treasured the boy, sent him to Troezen to be raised by Aethra and Pittheus, just as he himself had been raised. When he finished mourning Hippolyta, he negotiated a peace treaty with Deucalion, who had inherited the Cretan throne from his father, Minos, and married Deucalion's sister Phaedra, who bore him two more sons.

Hippolytus had a streak of asceticism that grew fiercer with time. Embracing chastity, he shunned the company of women and devoted himself so ardently to Artemis that he became her favorite companion. This proved to be his downfall. Aphrodite, offended by Hippolytus's rejection of her gifts, contrived a devious plan to destroy him. Seizing an occasion when he traveled to Athens, she infected Phaedra with a raging desire for him. Some months later, when Theseus and Phaedra paid a visit to Troezen, Aphrodite stoked the fires by ensuring that Hippolytus frequently crossed Phaedra's path.

Phaedra's desire burned so hot that she could scarcely eat or sleep; her old nurse, who had accompanied her to Athens at the time of her marriage, began to despair for her life. The palace slaves speculated that Phaedra had offended one of the gods who were known to send madness—Pan, Hecate or the Mother of the Gods. The nurse wondered, instead, whether her mistress's illness had been caused by Theseus's eye straying to another woman. In the course of probing Phaedra about that possibility, the nurse happened to speak Hippolytus's name.

Phaedra swooned at the sound of the syllables, which told the nurse everything she needed to know: a god far deadlier than Pan or Hecate was afflicting her mistress. Fearing for Phaedra's health, she offered to arrange a tryst. Phaedra refused; faithfulness to Theseus meant more to her than satisfying her lust—more, even, than her life. Well then, said the nurse, what about a charm to cure lovesickness? Would Phaedra allow her to arrange for that? Phaedra agreed and the nurse scurried away.

But the nurse, who knew a lot about the ways of women yet too little about the ways of the one whom she loved best, went straight to Hippolytus. After extracting an oath that he would repeat nothing of what she was about to say, she told him about Phaedra's illness and described some ways in which he might alleviate it.

"Women are vile," he spat, interrupting her, "like counterfeit coins that men trade from hand to hand, hoping that one—just one!—might prove true. And worst of all are the clever women, who weave webs of deceit such as this Cretan woman hoped to weave around my father. Only the oath that you extracted from me stops me from repeating to him every disgusting thing that you've been saying."

Phaedra, passing by the door, heard much of what Hippolytus said and realized that the nurse had betrayed her. Desperate to protect her good name and bitterly desperate, as well, to punish Hippolytus for his arrogant misogyny, she tied around her wrist a letter to Theseus in which she claimed that Hippolytus had raped her. And then, she hanged herself.

Theseus came home that afternoon to the sound of women wailing and found the body of his wife laid out upon her bed. He read Phaedra's letter and, maddened by grief, didn't pause to wonder whether its words were true. Poseidon, some years earlier, had given him a gift of three curses; Theseus rashly enacted one of them then by asking Poseidon to kill his son.

Hippolytus heard Theseus lamenting and hurried to the room. Speechless, he stared at Phaedra's corpse.

"Have you come to smirk at what you've done?" roared Theseus. "To parade your false chastity in front of a dead woman who knows the truth and the living man whom you betrayed? Get out of here—get out of Troezen! Go boast to fools elsewhere about the promise of virginity you made to Artemis and the purity of your body!"

"Father, I think I glimpse what has happened and I swear: no man on earth is chaster than I! And think for a moment: if I *did* wish to break my vow, why would I choose to do so with your wife? Would there be no other women for me to sleep with?"

"Don't spew sophistry at me—clever words won't help you now. Leave this house—leave your grandfather's kingdom!"

The gods act quickly, when they choose to. As Hippolytus drove his chariot north along the coastal road, a rumbling shook the ground. Waves frantically slapped the beach and then one rose so high that it blotted out the sky. When it thundered down again, it spit forth an enormous, savage bull. Panic seized Hippolytus's horses and in their frenzy they ran wild. The chariot crashed—axles, lynchpins and splintered wood flew through the air. Hippolytus, tangled in the reins, was dragged along behind his horses, his body breaking and his head banging against the stones.

His men carried him back to the palace, barely alive. Theseus taunted his son—Poseidon's strike, he claimed, proved the truth of Phaedra's words.

But suddenly, the sharp scent of the forest filled the room and in a seering blaze of light, Artemis arrived. She spoke.

"Theseus, your exultations revolt me. Learn how this came to pass, and be ashamed. Aphrodite, resenting your son's virginity, infected Phaedra with desire. She was faithful to you in heart as well as deed, but her nurse, a traitorous creature, told Hippolytus everything; in shame, your wife hanged herself. Your son had sworn to tell you nothing of this and he kept his oath. Thus, the snare contrived by Aphrodite caught its prey.

"The gods refrain from annulling one another's actions; otherwise, I would have intervened. Know, however, that I will avenge Hippolytus one day in a manner that makes Aphrodite weep. And know this, too, Hippolytus: I will command all the girls of Troezen to cut their hair in your honor on the eve of their weddings.

"Now I must go—human death is not for divine eyes. Hippolytus: forgive your father. Theseus: embrace your son a final time."

Her commands delivered, Artemis vanished.

It is natural for mortals to err when the gods conspire against them, but the gods impose high penalties, nonetheless. Theseus returned to Athens alone and never forgave himself for what he'd done. Artemis persuaded Asclepius to resurrect Hippolytus—a transgression for which Asclepius paid with his life. She conveyed the new Hippolytus to Italy; Theseus never knew that his son had returned from death.

100
NEW BRIDES

Finding themselves widowers after the deaths of Phaedra and Hip-podamia, Theseus and Pirithous decided to marry again. Resolving that their next wives would be truly exceptional, they vowed to wed daughters of Zeus. There were numerous candidates, thanks to Zeus's amorous nature.

Theseus chose first. He had heard—indeed, everyone had heard—that Helen, whom Zeus had fathered upon Leda, the queen of Sparta, was exceptionally beautiful. Helen was only seven years old at the time, but Theseus was determined to have her, and he reasoned that once he'd carried her home to Athens, he could leave her in the care of his mother, Aethra, until she came of age. And so Theseus and Pirithous slipped down to Sparta and seized Helen while she was dancing in honor of Artemis one day.

That being done, it was Pirithous's turn to select a bride. His choice was even more ambitious: he wanted to marry Persephone, the queen of the Underworld. His choice also violated more con-ventions. It was bad enough that Theseus had kidnapped a girl from Artemis's sanctuary, but Pirithous, a mortal, was seeking to marry a goddess whom her father had already given in marriage to another god.

Nevertheless, Theseus and Pirithous tied their traveling hats under their chins, picked up their walking sticks and set out on the path downwards. After they had convinced Charon to ferry them across the Acheron, they confronted a bigger challenge. How would they persuade Hades to relinquish the wife whom he had worked so hard to obtain? Pirithous believed that he had a claim to precedence: he was Persephone's half brother (they shared Zeus as a father, or so Pirithous's mother had told him), whereas Hades was only her uncle. He tried this argument out on the ghost of Me-leager, whom they chanced upon in one of Hades's antechambers. Meleager was shocked by the idea, but Pirithous's lofty confidence was undeterred.

When they reached Hades's audience room, they found him sprawled on his throne, a scepter in his left hand and a drinking cup in his right. Persephone stood next to him, holding a torch to help dispel the gloom.

After they had exchanged niceties, Pirithous cleared his throat and made his request. Persephone's eyes widened in surprise but otherwise nothing happened for a few moments. Literally nothing: the Erinyes stopped whipping their victims; the daughters of Danaus stood still, their pitchers in hand; the vultures lifted their heads from Tityus's abdomen and Tityus himself craned his neck, as far as his bonds would allow, to stare at Pirithous in disbelief. Everyone waited eagerly to find out what kind of punishment Hades would devise for two such arrogant transgressors as these.

But Hades only smiled. "Why of course," he replied to Pirithous. "I never thought of it that way. And, being an unusually continent god, I have had little experience with the variety of sexual pleasures that my brothers Zeus and Poseidon have long enjoyed. Perhaps a change would be good for me."

Persephone glanced at him but held her silence; only the skittish way in which she twiddled her torch, causing shadows to dance across the walls, betrayed her nervousness. She knew, all too well, that Hades was tricky and unpredictable.

Hades snapped his fingers and the strapping ghosts of two trireme rowers suddenly appeared. "Bring our guests some chairs—those *comfortable* chairs that we keep in the northernmost storeroom, I mean." Soon they returned, hauling two deliciously cushioned seats. Hades gestured to Theseus and Pirithous to sit down, while he mumbled about refreshments that would soon arrive.

And so the two friends sat. Immediately, a cloud of numbing forgetfulness fell over their minds. Before oblivion entirely set in, they tried to stand and flee, but they were caught fast by the gluey chairs, like flies in a spiderweb. The Erinyes nodded to one another, impressed. Yes, this was an appropriate punishment, indeed: Hades had subjected two guests who'd tried to steal his wife to an eternity of hospitality that they could not enjoy.

Sometime later, when Heracles arrived in the Underworld seeking Cerberus, he saw his friends still sitting motionless and mute in Hades's throne room. Realizing what had happened, he grasped Theseus's hand and gave a mighty pull. With a sound of tearing flesh, Theseus arose at last, leaving quite a bit of his rear end on the chair (forever after, Athenian men had unusually flat rear ends). But however hard he pulled, Heracles could not free Pirithous, and so Theseus had to leave him behind.

101
THE DEATH OF THESEUS

When Theseus returned to Athens, he discovered that his own marriage plans had collapsed, as well. While he was in the Underworld, Helen's brothers, Castor and Polydeuces, had attacked the city. Eventually, they'd found Helen living with Aethra in the neighboring village of Aphidnae and furiously demanded recompense from the Athenians.

Theseus also discovered that one of his cousins had deposed him. This was Menestheus, a demagogue with a golden tongue and a finely tuned ability to arouse people's indignation. He had put both talents to work as soon as Theseus disappeared. When he spoke to the nobles, he stirred up their smoldering resentment over having lost power when Theseus united all of Attica. "You've been treated as little more than slaves!" Menestheus cried to them. When he spoke to the masses, he reminded them that Theseus had replaced many of their ancestral rites with new ceremonies that were meant to unify Attica. And all of this had been done, Menestheus thundered to both groups, by a man who was a foreigner and an immigrant to their city. Then, when Castor and Polydeuces attacked Attica, Menestheus reminded everyone that it had been Theseus's kidnapping of Helen that led to that attack. Playing the diplomat, he persuaded the people to placate Castor and Polydeuces by offering them anything that it was in Athens's power to give. Having already obtained what they really wanted, Castor and Polydeuces asked only to be initiated into the mysteries of Demeter at Eleusis. As soon as that was done, the brothers departed for Sparta with not only Helen but also Aethra, whom they'd decided to take home as Helen's slave.

Such was the situation that greeted Theseus upon his return: his bride gone, his mother gone and Menestheus controlling his people. He tried to regain his authority but discovered that the nobles laughed at him contemptuously and the common people, spoiled by Menestheus's calculated indulgence of their desires, refused to be led. Giving up on regaining control of Athens for the moment, Theseus sent the sons whom Phaedra had borne him, Acamas and Demophon, away to an old friend in Euboea and then decamped for the island of Scyros, which was at that time ruled by Lycomedes. Theseus's ancestors had once owned estates on the island and he asked Lycomedes to restore the lands to him so that he might live there.

But Lycomedes, who feared a man of Theseus's vision and accomplishments, longed to rid himself of this unwelcome visitor. He invited Theseus to walk with him to the top of the island's highest cliff so that they might better survey the estates and discuss what was to be done. Once there, Lycomedes succeeded where Sciron had long ago failed and pushed Theseus over the cliff to his doom.

No one in Athens paid much attention to the news of Theseus's death; by then, Menestheus had done everything he could to erase his predecessor's memory. Eventually, however, the Athenians realized how good a man they'd lost and began to worship Theseus as a hero. Centuries later, when Miltiades was commanding the Athenians against the Persians at the Battle of Marathon, Theseus suddenly appeared on the battlefield and led them to victory.

When the war with the Persians was over, the Delphic Oracle commanded the Athenians to retrieve Theseus's bones from Scyros and give them honorable burial in Athens. Miltiades's son Cimon searched the island for Theseus's burial place. By and by, he noticed an eagle pecking and clawing at the dirt on top of a mound and commanded his men to dig. They uncovered a huge coffin that held the bones of an enormous man. A spear and a sword lay at his side. Cimon took the remains back to Athens where they were piously laid to rest in a tomb that became a place of sanctuary for runaway slaves and anyone else who was poor or abused.

Soon after becoming king of Athens, Menestheus departed for the Trojan War and died there in battle. Acamas and Demophon, who had traveled to Troy as part of the Euboean contingent, discovered their grandmother Aethra in an inner chamber of the palace after Troy fell and took her home to Athens. Demophon became the Athenians' new king.

102
THE BIRTH OF OEDIPUS

Cadmus of Thebes had lost most of his family because of Dionysus. Hera contrived to kill his daughter Semele because Semele was pregnant with the young god. Dionysus survived, nonetheless, and was nursed by Semele's sister Ino, who was killed by Hera as well. Now, Cadmus watched helplessly as what was left of his family was destroyed by Dionysus himself, who was enraged because Semele's sisters Autonoë and Agave and Agave's son Pentheus were refusing to accept Dionysus as a god. Dionysus maddened his aunts and drove them to tear Pentheus limb from limb.

Cadmus had honored and worshipped Dionysus, but the god proclaimed that for him, retribution had finally come due on an older transgression: the slaughter of an enormous snake that was the son of Ares. In punishment, Cadmus and his wife, Harmonia, would themselves be transformed into snakes and banished not only from Thebes but from all of Greece until, one day, they would return leading hordes of barbarians to ravage the land.

As soon as Dionysus had announced this, Cadmus began to change. His skin grew scaly and mottled; his legs fused together and he toppled forward. Harmonia lifted her husband from the ground and kissed his lips while they were still the lips she knew, yet even as she did so, she felt her own legs dissolving. As the new snakes slithered away, they heard Dionysus promise that someday, after the gods had pardoned them, they would be conveyed to the Island of the Blessed, where they would live together in pleasure forevermore. This, however, was a reward too remote in time and too vague in its details to be of much comfort.

Amphion, a son of Zeus, became the next king of Thebes. He left no heir: all of his sons and daughters had been killed by Artemis and Apollo after his wife, Niobe, boasted of being a better mother than Leto. The throne of Thebes passed to Polydorus, a son of Cadmus who had been just an infant when Dionysus destroyed the rest of his family. Marrying the granddaughter of one of the five original settlers of Thebes, Polydorus begot a son, Labdacus, who inherited the kingdom. Labdacus begot Laius, who in turn inherited the kingdom.

Once, when Laius was competing at the Nemean Games, he caught sight of Chrysippus, the son of King Pelops of Elis. Chrysippus carried his youthful limbs with grace. His skin, burnished by the sun and rubbed sleek with oil, gleamed like gold. Desire gripped Laius; he kidnapped Chrysippus and violated him—the first time that a man had raped a boy. Pelops recovered Chrysippus and prayed to the gods to punish Laius for what he'd done. Zeus listened and contrived a trap that would slowly close around Laius, his family and his city—a trap that Laius and his own son would not only be caught by but also, unwittingly, help to build.

Laius became betrothed to Jocasta, the daughter of a noble Theban family. Before the wedding, Laius traveled to Delphi to ask Apollo how he might ensure that his first child was a son. Apollo ignored that question and instead proclaimed, "Only by dying childless will you save your city!"

Obstinately, Laius returned to the oracle twice again, but twice again he heard, "Only by dying childless will you save your city!"

The marriage could not be called off; too much political capital had been invested in its negotiation. For many nights after its celebration, Laius left it unconsummated, to the bewilderment of his bride. There came a night, however, when Laius drank heavily at dinner and Jocasta saw her chance. Adorning herself in little more than translucent silks and the best Arabian perfumes, Jocasta drew Laius into her bed. Their son was conceived.

When Jocasta told Laius of her pregnancy, he was deeply alarmed and immediately departed for Delphi, hoping that Apollo might relent and give him a new, reassuring message. What the Pythia spoke forth this time, however, was even worse: "Your son shall kill his father and marry his mother."

Aghast, Laius returned and told Jocasta what Apollo had said. He decided that their son would be taken to the wilderness and abandoned as soon as he saw the light of day.

And so when the squalling baby arrived, still covered with the blood and vernix that he had worn into the world, he was placed in a pot and handed to one of the royal shepherds. Although, formally, Laius would be free from guilt (the pot, once it was covered, afforded the pretense that Laius was protecting the child), for good measure he had the hollows behind the child's ankles pierced and tied together with a rawhide thong, to hobble its vengeful ghost.

"Take this child to the highest ridge of Mount Cithaeron and leave him there," Laius ordered, as Jocasta wept inconsolably.

But the shepherd took pity on the child. Knowing that Polybus and Merope, the king and queen of Corinth, were barren, he smuggled the baby to another shepherd, who tended Polybus's flocks. The baby was carried into the Corinthian palace after dark and the next day it was announced that the queen had finally given birth to an heir. Indulging in a private joke, Polybus and Merope named him Oedipus—"Swollen Feet"—for the piercing of the poor baby's ankles had caused his feet to swell. Merope removed the thong and anointed the wounds with salve each day, until they healed.

Oedipus grew up in Corinth surrounded by doting parents, attentive coaches and dedicated tutors who prepared him to rule the kingdom one day. But the people of Corinth had been neither so blind nor so gullible as their king and queen had hoped. One night at a banquet, when Oedipus was nearly grown, a drunken nobleman referred to him as a bastard. Polybus denied this, but Oedipus, made uneasy by the nobleman's assuredness, set out the next morning to learn the truth.

103
A TROUBLING ORACLE

Oedipus walked to the harbor and arranged passage aboard a ship that was sailing to Cirrha, the port that served the Delphic Oracle. The next day, he hiked a road that zigzagged up Mount Parnassus, alongside mules that carried supplies to the town where the oracle's priests and their families lived. He paid an innkeeper for a meal and a place to sleep that night.

In the morning, he took his place among those requesting an audience with the Pythia. His royal status guaranteed preferential treatment; before the sun had reached its zenith, he was escorted across the porch of Apollo's temple and into its outer chamber. In the inner chamber, as Oedipus knew, the Pythia sat upon her tripod, awaiting Apollo's prophetic embrace. A fragrance wafted forth to meet his nose—sweet and musky, like peaches that in their ripeness have dropped to the grass, windfall for wasps. He knew then that the god was present.

The priest asked Oedipus for his question and Oedipus said, "Who are my real parents?" The priest walked to the inner chamber and quietly repeated it to the Pythia. After a few moments of silence, Oedipus heard dissonant moans, punctuated by gasping, gulping sobs, as if the Pythia was struggling against the voice that demanded to speak through her. Finally, across the still air of the temple came Apollo's dispassionate reply.

"You will kill your father and marry your mother."

The priests at Delphi possessed a practiced equanimity; over the centuries, they had heard Apollo say many remarkable things. They had learned to maintain their composure and escort inquirers out in a dignified manner. The god's pronouncement to Oedipus, however, left the priest bewildered. Before he could collect himself, Oedipus had unceremoniously run from the temple.

He fled the sanctuary and found himself on an eastward road that ran steeply up the mountain, as he blindly scrambled to put as much distance as he could between himself and what the Pythia had said and between himself and Corinth, to which he knew he could never return. He kept moving until the sun began to set and then found lodging with a farmer. The next day, he continued eastwards, with the vague idea of eventually reaching a seaport and leaving Greece altogether.

The road was curling through gnarled olive trees and knee-high grasses when he rounded a bend and reached a place where three roads met—the road he'd just taken from Delphi, a road north to Daulia and a road east to Thebes, on which a chariot, drawn by two horses, was approaching the intersection. The crimson-dyed leather of the horses' harnesses, gilded here and there to pick out embossed acanthus leaves, and the purple cloak of the man who rode behind the chariot's driver announced that the passenger was of royal bearing. His grizzled hair and beard suggested an older man—a king. In front of the chariot walked a herald. Three slaves walked behind.

They pulled up abruptly at the sight of Oedipus; the road was narrow, allowing little room for the travelers to pass one another.

"Get off the road!" commanded the herald. Oedipus, glancing at the thick tangle of grass that he would have to step into, didn't relish the idea. He wasn't looking for trouble, however, so he moved as far to the margin of the road as he could.

The chariot began to move forward again. The horses passed so close to Oedipus that he could smell the oil with which the stable-boy had rubbed their coats that morning, mixed with the odors of dust and lathery sweat. Then came the chariot itself. As its driver drew even with Oedipus, he grinned and gave Oedipus's shoulder a sharp push, hoping to topple the youth backwards into the grass. Oedipus shifted weight to keep his balance and then lashed out, striking the man with his fist. Suddenly, the grizzled man was there, too, beating Oedipus on the head with a horse goad.

For doing that, the grizzled man paid in full. Oedipus shoved his walking stick into the man's stomach and he tumbled backwards out of the chariot. White-hot with anger, Oedipus killed him then and there, right where he lay. Then he killed the driver, the herald and the slaves, who were cowering behind the motionless chariot.

Shocked by what he'd done, Oedipus sat down in the grass that had seemed so unappealing a moment before and drew a deep, shuddering breath. The emotions that washed over him were staggering; he struggled to decide what to do next. After a while, he stood and brushed off his clothing. He approached each of the corpses in turn: first the slaves, then the driver, then the herald and finally the grizzled man in the purple cloak. He dipped his finger in the blood of each, licked it and then spat it out again, to avert their angry ghosts.

He looked first at the road to Daulia and then at the road to Thebes. Cities full of people lay at the end of either one, and people were the last thing he wanted to see at the moment. He strode into the grass and kept walking, vanishing into the grove of olive trees.

104
A RIDDLE CONTEST

For some days, Oedipus lived rough, eating whatever he could catch or forage and rolling himself up in his cloak to sleep. Eventually, from atop a hill he glimpsed a footpath and decided it was time to continue his journey towards the sea. Descending, he set out eastwards once again.

He was passing through craggy hills when he encountered the strangest creature he had ever seen. She (he knew that the creature was female for her face was that of a lovely woman) was like a human from the neck up but had the body of a lion below; from her shoulders sprang the mighty wings of an eagle. She sat atop a short marble column at the mouth of a cave that opened into a hillside; this put her eyes unnervingly level with those of anyone who passed by.

She tilted her head to one side and observed Oedipus for a moment before she spoke. Her words came forth with difficulty, either because of some unfortunate confluence of the human and the feline where her vocal cords were lodged or because she purposefully aspired to turn speech into mere vibrations. An odor of corruption accompanied each syllable; Oedipus, trained in the etiquette of polite disregard, managed to resist stepping away from the stench, which was fortunate: on the other side of the path, the ground dropped off precipitously.

"Pause for a moment, traveler," she said, "and tell me where you're going."

"To wherever the path takes me and from there to the sea."

She settled herself more comfortably upon her column and sighed.

"Mine is a dreary existence; so few people pass my cave. I fill my time contriving puzzles for myself. It's astounding how far one's wits may travel even while one's body is compelled to be still."

Oedipus looked at her powerful wings and wondered why she was lying.

"Of all puzzles, I enjoy riddles most," she continued. "Humor me, stranger, and let us test our wits."

"As you wish."

"I'll go first. What can pass before the sun without making a shadow?"

"The wind, of course."

"Clever boy!" she purred, switching her tail back and forth. "Now fool *me*, if you can."

"If you feed it, it will live; if you give it water, it will die," he said, silently thanking his childhood tutors for giving him an eclectic education.

She smiled. "So simple! A fire. What about this, then, clever boy: slain, I slew the slayer, but even so, he did not go to Hades."

Oedipus thought for a moment. This was not among the riddles his tutors had taught him, but something tugged at his mind. Finally, it came to him. "The answer is the centaur Nessus," he said, "who was slain by Heracles but from whose blood, or so I have heard, a potion was made that put an end to Heracles's earthly existence; now Heracles is a god, they say."

She nodded and her tail began to switch more vigorously. After a moment he cleared his throat and spoke again. "In the field there grazes a calf who changes color thrice a day. White in the morning, red in the afternoon and black in the evening."

Her pupils constricted and the muscles in her hind legs tensed. Then she relaxed and laughed, and Oedipus saw that behind her pretty lips was a maw of needle-sharp teeth. "You mean to test my knowledge of what has happened far away, clever boy. That is the puzzle with which King Minos enticed the seer Polyidus. The answer that Polyidus gave was the blackberry: when it first appears on the bramble, it is white. Then it ripens to red and finally to black."

Now she crouched as if preparing to pounce and her voice became a sultry growl. "Listen, clever boy, to my very best riddle, which no one has ever managed to answer: what has a single voice but is four-footed and two-footed and three-footed?"

Oedipus stood quite still, sensing that whatever pretense of playfulness the game might have had when it started was over and that his life depended on his answer.

"It is a person," he said slowly, "who crawls on hands and knees as an infant, walks on two feet as an adult and leans on a cane when elderly."

Furious in defeat, the creature shrieked and sprang at Oedipus, but, thinking quickly, Oedipus stepped aside. She plummeted over the precipice and—either being too surprised to use her wings or choosing, in her shame, not to do so—was dashed upon the rocks below.

After peering over the edge to make sure that the monster was dead, Oedipus resumed his walk. The path eventually led to a road and that road led to the road to Thebes that he'd once intended to take. He reached the city at twilight and sat down in a tavern. After he had slaked his thirst, he asked the other men what they knew about the strange creature whom he'd met in the hills. Dumbfounded, they told him that she was the Sphinx, a daughter of Typhon and Echidna and a deadly plague upon the Thebans. It had been her custom to eat those wayfarers who could not solve her favorite riddle and, when wayfarers were scarce, to seize the Thebans' children.

"Creon, who has acted as regent since we lost our king some weeks ago, has offered the greatest of rewards to any man who kills the Sphinx: the hand of his sister Jocasta, our widowed queen, and a third of the kingdom, as well, in joint stewardship with Jocasta and himself. Stranger, present yourself to him."

Oedipus led a party to the base of the cliff where the Sphinx lay and they carried her body back to Thebes to show Creon. Satisfied, Creon married his sister to Oedipus.

105
REVELATIONS

The years passed. Oedipus took the lead in ruling Thebes and Thebes prospered. Jocasta bore him two sons and two daughters. But there came a day when the gods sent a terrible plague upon the city. Cattle died in the pastures, crops wilted in the fields and babies withered in their mothers' wombs. The flesh that mortals offered to the gods sputtered on sacrificial fires, rejected by those above. Thebes was a ship with rotting planks, foundering in a sea of miasma whose cause could not be discerned.

Oedipus dispatched Creon to Delphi to ask how they might save the city.

"Apollo speaks of a sleeping murder now awoken, of clotted blood that the Erinyes gleefully lick back to life," reported Creon upon his return. "Before you arrived, we had a king named Laius who was murdered while away from home. Apollo has revealed that his murderer now dwells among us. To end the plague that besets us, we must find that man and banish him from Thebes."

"Leave the matter to me—I'll avenge Laius as if he were my own father," said Oedipus.

But the tempers of kings obstruct their best designs. Oedipus called upon Tiresias, a seer of great skill, for advice. When Tiresias hobbled into the courtyard—relying, in his blindness and old age, on the third leg of the Sphinx's riddle—he refused to share what the gods had shown him, warning that it would lift one curse from Thebes only to burden the city with others that would be even heavier. Oedipus, vexed by the seer's recalcitrance, ranted and sneered until Tiresias's composure finally frayed away.

"King, I'll tell you this much: you're living in vile disgrace with those you love best, wallowing in depravity with a wife who is no wife. Have your slaves fetch a mirror: the killer of Laius is close at hand now, plowing his father's field and sowing unholy seed."

"Don't juggle words with *me*, seer; I rescued this city from the Sphinx by deciphering her riddle. The real flavor of the stew you're dishing out is unmistakable: Creon told you to frighten me—Creon wants the throne. Away with you!"

Once Tiresias was gone, Oedipus wasted no time in summoning Creon. After accusing him of bribing Tiresias to twist Apollo's message, Oedipus banished him from Thebes. Just then, however, Jocasta entered the room, having heard the voices of her husband and her brother raised in anger.

"Shame on you, Oedipus!" she said. "The king of a city should be tending to its welfare, not playing the petulant child. And you, too, Creon. Stop fighting!"

"But he's banishing me!"

"Because he and Tiresias are plotting against me!"

"Oedipus!" insisted Jocasta. "Don't be absurd. Lift my brother's banishment. Creon, go home and cool your tongue."

After Creon left, the queen turned to her husband and demanded to know what had happened. When Oedipus explained, Jocasta laughed. Seers and oracles were notoriously unreliable, she said; no sensible person believed in them. As proof, she told Oedipus that Apollo had once prophesied that Laius would be killed by his own son—a son who died in infancy on a lonely mountain. In truth, she continued, Laius had met his end many years later at the hands of a stranger, at a place where three roads met.

Fear seized Oedipus when he heard where Laius had died. He asked Jocasta what the king had looked like and with whom he'd traveled. Her answers wrapped an even tighter band of dread around his heart, but before he could learn more, a messenger arrived from Corinth, announcing that Polybus was dead; the Corinthian throne awaited Oedipus, if he wished to take it. Oedipus hesitated; although half of what he'd run away from now was gone—his father, dead, could no longer die at the hands of his son—the other half lay in wait for him as long as his mother, Merope, was still alive.

"Cast fear from your heart," the messenger said, "for I can tell you, assuredly, that Merope is not your mother. I myself received you as a newborn infant, your ankles cruelly pierced and bound, from the hands of a Theban shepherd. I gave you to Polybus and Merope to be raised as their son, but you share no blood with them."

"Oh gods, what have you done to us?" whispered Jocasta softly. Then, aloud, she begged her husband to cease investigating mysteries whose riddles he needn't solve. Oedipus, however, ignored her. He summoned the shepherd who had long ago passed an unwanted infant into the hands of a friend. With that, the last slats of Zeus's trap slid neatly into place, fulfilling Pelops's curse.

"Tell me," Oedipus asked the shepherd, "from whom did you receive the baby that you handed over to your friend, the baby whose injuries are still inscribed upon my ankles?"

The shepherd, who glimpsed the truth that was unfolding, begged to be excused from answering, but torture loosened his tongue. The baby, he said, had been handed to him by its parents, the king and the queen of Thebes, with instructions to abandon it on Mount Cithaeron. He, however, pitying the child, had found a home for it. Oedipus understood, then, who he was and how Apollo's oracles had inexorably found their fulfillment. Running into the palace, he sought Jocasta. When he reached her chamber, he found that she'd barred the doors; with a strength born of madness, he wrenched them from their hinges.

Inside he discovered her—his mother? his wife?—dangling from a twisted noose. Weeping, he cut her down and laid her gently on the floor, unwilling to approach the bed where they'd lain together in tenderness. He removed the pins that held her dress together, raised them high above his head and then plunged them into his eyes, ensuring that he would never again look upon a world whose laws he had so grossly transgressed. The blood ran down his cheeks and stained his beard, a grisly testament to the futility of trying to evade the gods' plans.

Once, Oedipus had stood upon the summit of achievement, but fate's waves finally submerged him. Count no one happy till they're dead; even the last hour may bring pain that obliterates all the blessings that came before.

106
THE THEBAN WAR

A few days later, Oedipus left Thebes so that the city might be cleansed of the pollution that clung to him and cured of the plague.

Before he departed, he cursed his sons, Eteocles and Polynices, who had been quick to take advantage of his blindness. They'd begun serving him the poorer cuts of meat, thinking he would never know the difference—but his mouth was not fooled. They'd dragged from the storerooms silver tables and golden goblets that had belonged to Cadmus. Oedipus, who regarded these as hallowed objects, had never allowed their use at common dinners. When he felt their shapes beneath his fingers, he could not contain his fury.

"May you die at one another's hands!" he cried out—and the gods took note.

After he left Thebes, Oedipus wandered the land with his daughters, Antigone and Ismene, to guide him. Eventually, they came to an Athenian village called Colonus, where they were received by Theseus. In this place there was a grove sacred to mysterious goddesses called the Semnai Theai. A great clap of thunder sounded from beneath the ground there, announcing to Oedipus that the thread of his life was about to break. He wept and embraced his daughters until a fearsome voice called out, "Oedipus, why do you tarry? We are waiting for you!" Leaning on Theseus's arm, Oedipus walked into the grove and vanished from sight, escaping the mortal world of pain and grief. Forevermore, in gratitude for Theseus's kindness, his spirit protected Athens from its enemies.

Eteocles and Polynices squabbled over their patrimony. Eventually, they came to a grudging agreement: Eteocles would become the king of Thebes and Polynices would leave the city, taking most of Oedipus's wealth with him. Among the treasures that he carried away was the marvelous golden necklace, as sinuous as a snake, that Hephaestus had given to Harmonia as a wedding present many years before. Hephaestus had forged his hatred of Harmonia's father into every link of it, ensuring that the necklace brought tragedy to all who touched it.

As Polynices wandered in exile, never at home wherever he was, he came to feel that he'd been cheated. Late one night, he arrived in Argos, hoping to convince King Adrastus to help him regain the throne of Thebes. He was hungry, tired and soaked by the rain that had been coming down all day. The boar's pelt that he wore around his shoulders was sodden and heavy. The guards refused to wake the sleeping king to announce the visitor, but feeling sorry for the shivering man, they allowed him to bed down on the porch. Soon, another traveler arrived: Tydeus, the exiled son of King Oeneus of Calydon. The lion's pelt that Tydeus wore around his own shoulders was even more bedraggled than that of Polynices's boar.

There was only one pallet of straw to sleep on and the two men argued over it so loudly that Adrastus awoke. When he stepped onto the porch to find out what was causing all the noise, he saw in a flash that he could at last obey a puzzling oracle that Apollo had once delivered, commanding him to marry his two daughters to a battling boar and lion. The marriages took place the following day.

Adrastus promised his new sons-in-law that he would mobilize armies to restore them to their kingdoms. He started with Thebes. Gathering the best warriors that Argos and its allies had to offer, he mustered seven companies, to be led by Polynices, Tydeus and five other captains. One of these was Capaneus, an arrogant man who'd been heard to boast that not even Zeus's lightning could stop him. Another was Eteoclus, who contemptuously declared to anyone who cared to listen that he could beat Ares himself. Hippomedon prided himself on his beautiful armor, crafted to hug his body. Young, handsome Parthenopaeus, the son of Atalanta, came carrying a shield that he'd designed to provoke the enemy: on it was embossed the ghastly Sphinx, snatching a Theban in her dreadful claws.

The seventh captain was Amphiaraus, a seer of great renown, descended from Melampus. After Adrastus had summoned him, Amphiaraus saw seven eagles in the skies, with talons sharp as razors, attack a circle of seven swans. The swans were ripped to shreds, but the eagles fell to earth as well, destroyed by the sudden heat of the sun and by thunder from the clouds. Amphiaraus knew then that the gods would not permit the Argive captains to return from Thebes.

Yet he had no choice but to fight. Amphiaraus's wife, Eriphyle, was Adrastus's sister and the two men, who often argued, had long ago agreed that she would settle any disputes between them. Learning this from Adrastus, Polynices had slyly used Harmonia's necklace to bribe Eriphyle. When Amphiaraus defied Adrastus's command to fight, Eriphyle caressed the gold that newly coiled around her neck and told her husband to join the expedition.

The wall surrounding Thebes had seven gates, as befitted one of the largest cities in the world. Adrastus ordered each captain to lead the charge against one of these; Eteocles, in turn, dispatched the best of his warriors to defend each. At Electra's Gate, Capaneus faced Polyphontes, a courageous Theban warrior. Before Polyphontes could strike a single blow, however, Zeus smote Capaneus with the very lightning that he'd mocked. Creon's son Megareus fought Eteoclus at the Gate of Neïs; Megareus's sword made short work of the insolent Argive. At the gate next to a temple of Athena, Hyperbius's spear pierced Hippomedon's stylish armor and skewered the heart behind it. At the Northern Gate, Hyperbius's brother Actor, enraged by Parthenopaeus's shield, hurled a javelin through both the Sphinx and Parthenopaeus; Parthenopaeus died on the spot.

Tydeus, flaunting bells on his shield and plumes on his helmet, fought Melanippus at the Proetid Gate and was fatally wounded. But Tydeus was a favorite of Athena's; when she saw him fall, she hurried off to fetch a drug that would not only preserve his life but also immortalize him. While she was gone, however, Amphiaraus slew Melanippus and rolled his severed head across the ground to where Tydeus lay dying in the dust. When Athena returned, she saw her favorite feasting on his killer's brains, a scarlet smudge around his lips. Horrified, she rushed to Athens where she purified herself of what she'd seen in the Ilissus River, leaving Tydeus to die.

Amphiaraus fled from Periclymenus at the Homoloian Gate, hoping to escape what the Fates had planned for him, but Periclymenus overtook him and raised his spear to strike. Suddenly, the earth split open, swallowing Amphiaraus, his horses, the chariot and its driver in a single gulp. Swift as thought, Zeus transported Amphiaraus to a wooded glen near Oropus, where forever after, from under the earth, the seer spoke prophecies to mortals and healed the sick.

Eteocles chose to defend the High Gate himself, knowing that this was where his brother would attack. The two fought furiously, driven by the irrational rage that only siblings can generate. At first, their swords flashed here and there erratically, to little effect. But then a lucky thrust of Polynices's blade pierced Eteocles's groin, just below his corselet. Eteocles gasped and struggled to remain standing—until some god put an evil plan into his head. Falling to the ground, he lay as still as death until his brother approached to strip the armor from his corpse. Using his last bit of strength, Eteocles darted upwards and drove his sword through his brother's heart. Then he fell, too, truly dead at last.

The Erinyes drank deeply from the mingled blood of Oedipus's sons. Never sated, however, they licked their lips in anticipation of the drama's next act.

107
ANTIGONE

Adrastus fled the battle on the back of his divine horse Arion, leaving behind his comrades' bodies. Once home, he dispatched an embassy to retrieve them, but Creon refused the request. Spurning the gods' laws as well as human decency, he ordained that the Argive dead would lie unburied on the plain outside the city, a feast for Theban birds and beasts.

Adrastus's pleas continued to fall upon deaf ears. Finally, the mothers of the slain journeyed to Eleusis, where Theseus's mother, Aethra, was sacrificing to Demeter. With her help, they persuaded Theseus to lay siege to Thebes until Creon relented. With his own hands, Theseus washed and anointed the warriors' bodies and then brought them back to Eleusis, where he burned them with full honors.

Except for one. Creon adamantly refused to surrender the body of Polynices, who'd been, he claimed, a traitor to the city that had nurtured him since infancy. Eteocles received a hero's funeral, but Polynices rotted on the dusty plain under the watchful eyes of Creon's guards, lest someone bury him and grant passage to his weary soul, which wandered restlessly between life and death. Indeed, anyone who showed mercy to Polynices's corpse, Creon decreed, would join him in death.

Ismene and Antigone wept together for their brothers but were torn asunder by Creon's announcement. Ismene, praying that the dead would forgive her, trembled at the very thought of defying a king's orders. Antigone, however, held that nothing could be worse than abandoning her brother in his last and greatest moment of need. And so it was that the next day, a guard reported to Creon that, during the night, someone, somehow, had sprinkled dust upon Polynices's corpse—mere handfuls, but enough to serve the ritual's demands. The guards had brushed the dust away, leaving the corpse to once more grimace at the unforgiving sun. Then, sitting upwind from the stench, they'd resumed their careful watch until an uncanny whirlwind arose, clogging the air with dirt and swirling leaves. When it stopped, they saw Antigone crouching over her brother, pouring libations from a bronze urn. A new cloak of dust covered his body. Now, they delivered Antigone to Creon.

"You defied me?" he thundered.

"No mortal can override the gods' eternal laws—not yesterday, not today, not tomorrow!" she replied. "We owe honor and burial to *all* the dead but I owe it to my brother before all others. If I'd lost a husband or a child, I could get another, but because my parents are dead, I can never get another brother. If by paying him final honors I die myself, so be it! I'll embrace him in the Underworld, having done what I know to be right."

"Your insolence astounds me! Go, then, wallow in death among the ghosts you love so dearly. No woman will get the better of *me* while I live."

Ismene begged Creon to spare Antigone, appealing to his love for his son Haemon, to whom Antigone was betrothed. Surely Creon could forgive his future daughter-in-law? Creon refused—he would find a more obedient field for Haemon to plow, he said. Haemon himself begged his father to relent, invoking political expediency—Creon's own accustomed justification for unpalatable decisions. The people had risen up in support of Antigone, Haemon told his father; if Creon yielded to their wishes, his reign would be more secure. Nonetheless, Creon refused. Even when Haemon resolved to join Antigone in death, Creon refused, rebuking his son as if he were a petulant child.

Antigone was taken to a cave outside the city. Creon handed her a flask of water and a bowl of food—token sustenance that freed him from guilt—and then commanded his men to block the cave's entrance with stones too large for her to lift. As they did so, Antigone stood staunch, continuing to meet the gaze of the gathered people until they could no longer see her.

When Creon returned to the city, the seer Tiresias met him at the High Gate.

"I tell you, Creon, you're teetering on a razor's edge! I went this morning to the place where I listen for the birds' messages each day and heard maddened screeching, each bird tearing at the others. From there, I hastened to the city's altar and made sacrifices to appease the gods, but the fire refused to consume the meat; its greasy fat dripped onto the coals, filling the air with a suffocating stench. The gods are furious! But if you release the girl and bury her brother, you may yet win their forgiveness."

"Don't tell me how you think the gods feel, seer. I won't govern according to your religious fantasies!"

"Listen! You've confused the upper and the lower worlds! You've left the dead unburied, robbing Hades of his kingdom's rightful citizen, and you've shut the living in a tomb, robbing the Fates of their right to determine the length of her life. Think, Creon, lest the Erinyes who lurk in your family's house soon taste its blood again."

Creon faltered then and fell silent. The gathering crowds drew closer, urging him to undo what he'd done. Finally, he drove to the plain where Polynices still lay, or at least those parts of him that the birds and dogs had not devoured. Praying to the gods of the Underworld, Creon bathed the poor remnants as best he could, burned them and heaped a mound on top. Then he hurried to the cave. As he drew near, he heard the voice of his son lamenting and saw that some of the stones before the entrance had been removed. Scrambling over those that remained, Creon entered the cave.

Inside, dim rays of light filtered through shafts in the cave's roof, casting monstrous shadows. Creon stumbled in the direction of his son's voice. He rounded an outcropping of rock and saw Antigone's corpse, hanging limp from her linen veil. Haemon was kneeling on the ground beside it, encircling her waist with his arms and weeping. Tears rushed to Creon's eyes, as well; he called out to Haemon, who turned around. Enraged, Haemon spat in his father's face and then, pulling his sword from its scabbard, lunged at him. Creon shrank back, evading the blade. Haemon drove it into his own side instead, then, and died at Antigone's feet.

The messengers who had traveled with the king returned to Thebes more swiftly than Creon did, bearing their sorrowful news. When the king entered the palace courtyard, he found his wife, Eurydice, lying dead before the gods' altar. She had thrust a knife into her own abdomen, piercing her liver. As she died, she'd cursed Creon for murdering their son.

When the sons of those who had fallen at the gates of Thebes were grown, they avenged their fathers' deaths by attacking Thebes again, led by Thersander, whom Adrastus's daughter Argia had borne to Polynices after his death. They conquered Thebes and put Thersander on the throne where Cadmus had once sat.

The Theban Wars were the greatest that the Greeks had ever fought—but a greater one was soon to come.

THE TROJAN WAR

THE PLAN OF ZEUS SPILLS THE BLOOD OF MANY MORTALS

◄ PELEUS WRESTLES WITH THETIS

108
PELEUS AND THETIS

Zeus courted the nymph Aegina, daughter of the river god Asopus, and spirited her away to the island of Oenone, which he renamed Aegina after they made love. When the months came round, Aegina gave birth to a son, Aeacus, whom Zeus set upon the island's throne. Aeacus married Endeis and fathered two sons, Peleus and Telamon. Later, Aeacus fell in love with the sea nymph Psamathe and she bore him Phocus, whom Aeacus raised in the palace alongside the sons of his marriage.

Endeis resented this bastard child and endlessly nagged her own sons to kill him. One day, Peleus and Telamon finally contrived to do so while the three of them were practicing with the discus. A slip of the hand—afterwards, no one could say whether it had been Peleus's hand or Telamon's—sent a discus into Phocus's forehead. He crumpled to the ground, like some flower crushed by a peevish child.

When Aeacus found out what Peleus and Telamon had done, he banished them from Aegina. Telamon went to Salamis and Peleus to the city of Phthia, in Thessaly, where he was received by King Eurytion. After Eurytion had purified Peleus of his brother's murder, he gave him the hand of his daughter Antigone and a third of his kingdom to rule.

But Peleus's troubles were far from over. While Peleus and Eurytion were helping to hunt the Calydonian Boar, Peleus accidentally killed his father-in-law. Once again, he needed to seek purification from some sympathetic king. This time, he went to the city of Iolcus, where Acastus, the son of Pelias, now ruled. Acastus performed the necessary rituals, but before Peleus was able to set out for home, Acastus's wife, Astydamia, attempted to seduce him. Having failed, she vengefully accused him of rape. Peleus was eventually exonerated, but Astydamia, embittered by the bile of anger, sent a letter to Antigone claiming that Peleus was about to set her aside in order to marry Astydamia's daughter.

In grief, Antigone hanged herself and Peleus returned to Phthia a lonely man.

Soon, however, the gods had devised another plan for him. Many years earlier, it had been prophesied that one day, Zeus would fall in love with a female destined to bear a son stronger than his own father. Only Themis and her son Prometheus knew who this female was, and it was to obtain this information that Zeus had finally allowed Heracles to release Prometheus from the cliff to which he had been fettered for so long. And just in time: the dangerous female, Prometheus revealed, was the Nereid Thetis, whose sloe-eyed gaze had recently begun to beguile Zeus. In hopes of restraining himself before it was too late, Zeus decided to marry Thetis off to a mortal man (no god dared risk such a union) and Peleus was the ideal candidate: well-born enough to be an honorable husband for a goddess and with a history that would make it hard for him to find any mortal man who was willing to become his father-in-law.

Zeus told Peleus to fetch his bride from the Thessalian cove where she was accustomed to sun herself each day. At this point, Peleus's former teacher Chiron came forward to advise him.

"Thetis will not want to be caught, and like all sea gods, she is able to change her form rapidly into whatever she wishes. She will use that skill to try to elude you. Hold tight, Peleus, whatever pain you may feel and whatever fright may seize you!"

The next day, as the warmth of the sun settled over the cove, Thetis walked out of the sea in robes that shimmered blue and green under a cloudless sky. Leaping from behind a rock, Peleus wrapped his arms tightly around her. Thetis struggled and twisted and as she did, Peleus felt her body grow cold. She grew longer and heavier; her ears and nose disappeared and her garments fused with her flesh. Thetis became an enormous serpent, strong, sinuous and vile.

But Peleus held tight. He felt the serpent's scales grow warm and its flesh begin to throb. Suddenly, four legs burst through its clammy skin, ending in deadly claws. Distracted by this marvel, Peleus turned away from the serpent's face for a moment. When he looked again, he was met by a lion's ravening jaws.

Yet Peleus held tight. Heat began to suffuse his body and his ears caught the crackle of fire. Quickly shutting his eyes, he ordered his arms to remain fixed against the flames that they were suddenly hugging. Just when he thought that they could hold no longer, the fire grew wet and spilled through his fingers; Thetis was dissolving herself back into the element from which she'd once been born. Desperate, Peleus flung himself upon the damp sand through which she was trickling. Scooping it into a mound, he embraced what was left of her.

Thetis surrendered, then. She was adept at many other transformations—squid, panther, tree, bird—but she found herself moved by Peleus's constancy. Resuming the shape in which he'd first glimpsed her, Thetis gave him her hand.

Their wedding was a splendid affair, held outside of Chiron's cave on Mount Pelion. The gods arrived in a procession led by Iris. First came Hestia, leaving her hearth for the occasion, then Demeter and Leto, accompanied by Chiron's wife, Chariclo, ready to lay out the feast. Next came Dionysus, who carried a golden amphora as his gift for the couple, with Hebe and Heracles at his side. Chiron followed with wild game for the table. Themis, setting aside her usual solemnity, laughed with delight as she prepared to preside over the wedding.

Zeus escorted Hera, who carried the bridal torch. Amphitrite and Poseidon arrived in a chariot drawn by Xanthus and Balius, immortal horses born of the wind, which were their gift to the couple. Ares and Aphrodite, Apollo and Artemis, Hermes and Eileithyia came next. Nereus, the father of the bride, brought salt to flavor the feast. The Graces, Seasons and Fates danced to the Muses' songs. Hephaestus lumbered in on a donkey.

One god alone had not been invited: Eris, whose rightful portion, assigned at the beginning of time, was to rejoice in strife. Pale with envy and anger, she peered at the party from the surrounding forest. When it was well underway, she stole to the edge of the crowd and rolled a golden apple into its midst. Thetis, at whose toes it stopped, picked it up and read aloud the inscription it bore.

"For the Fairest."

109
THE JUDGMENT OF PARIS

Zeus was fascinated by the scene unfolding before his eyes. Years before, he'd set a certain plan in motion but he hadn't known how its details would play out—or rather, that was to say, how the Fates would make its details play out.

It had started when Earth came to him complaining that the tribe of mortals crawling over her body had burgeoned so greatly that its weight had become unbearable. She begged Zeus to find a way to relieve her and he turned to Themis, his closest confidante, for advice. After considering the matter carefully, Themis declared that the best plan was to thin the population through a series of wars. The first was the Theban War, which brought about many deaths. When the sons of the seven slain attackers assailed Thebes again, there were more deaths. Earth stretched and sighed with relief. But it wasn't long before the population increased once more, becoming even larger than before. Earth groaned again, this time more urgently.

Some years earlier, having foreseen this problem, Themis had advised Zeus to seduce Leda, the wife of King Tyndareus of Sparta, and sire upon her an astonishingly beautiful daughter, Helen. Now Themis explained to Zeus that the birth of Helen had provided one of two things necessary to launch the next, and greatest, war. It was in order to provide the other requisite that Themis and her son Prometheus had advised Zeus to give Thetis in marriage to Peleus.

And that was how Zeus had come to be reclining at the wedding feast when Eris rolled her golden apple into the crowd. His spine tingled when he saw it; he suspected that this was the beginning of what would be a most interesting series of spectacles. When Thetis read out the inscription, he knew he was right. To no one's surprise, three goddesses each claimed to be the apple's rightful recipient: Zeus's wife, Hera; his daughter Athena; and Aphrodite, who lingered mysteriously on an outer branch of the gods' genealogical tree but who was the most powerful of them all. The three goddesses looked at Zeus expectantly, assuming that he'd be the one to decide to whom the apple belonged.

Zeus wasn't that stupid, however. Casting about for a mortal whom he didn't mind putting in harm's way, his thoughts drifted to Paris, a young prince of the Trojan royal family. When Paris's mother, Queen Hecabe, was pregnant with him, she'd dreamt that she gave birth to a torch that burned down Troy. The seers in the palace interpreted the dream and told her husband, Priam, that to protect the city, he must kill the child as soon as it was born. Priam handed the baby to a slave who left him to die on the slopes of Mount Ida, but the baby was found by a she-bear who nursed him until he was discovered by shepherds. Later, the royal family had learned that Paris was still alive and, ignoring the horrified warnings of the seers, welcomed him home.

Even as a prince, Paris preferred to spend his time alone with his flocks in mountain pastures. One day, he was reclining beneath a tree as the sun passed through its zenith when he saw coming towards him what he took to be one of the hallucinations with which the midday demons tempted shepherds into danger. A young man with a traveler's hat and oddly styled sandals was escorting three women. The first of them walked assuredly, as if in procession, a paragon of decorous female beauty. Her sleek hair was pulled back tightly, accentuating the clean delicacy of her jawline. A crenellated crown sat atop her head. The second one strode behind the first with visible impatience but took care, nonetheless, to stay in formation. She had pushed back the helmet she wore on her head, revealing straight brows above gray eyes. The third one kept well behind the second so as to showcase the languorous movements of her body. Her luxuriant hair curled around her face as if each strand strove to kiss her flesh.

The man in the traveler's hat held out a hand in which something golden was nestled and spoke. "I am Hermes, dispatched by Zeus to bid you, Paris, to award this apple to whichever goddess you judge to be the fairest. This is Hera, this is Athena and this is Aphrodite."

Paris goggled, too stunned to speak. The situation became even more bewildering a moment later when Hermes instructed the goddesses to undress so that their judge might appraise them more fully. Hera turned away while she unpinned her purple robe, maintaining propriety for as long as she could before turning back towards Paris again—perfect in posture, feet together, hands on her hips. Athena glared at Paris defiantly, unbuckled her corselet and then unceremoniously let her robe fall away to reveal the lean flanks and taut belly of a virgin. Aphrodite seemed to struggle with the pins that fastened her embroidered robe—first one shoulder was revealed, then another and then finally, all at once, the silk shimmered to the ground after momentarily catching on her nipples. She shifted her weight onto one leg, causing its hip to jut up invitingly; a small but delicious fold of flesh appeared at her waist. Her elegant hands darted to cover that part of her that modesty demanded she cover, but in doing so drew attention to it all the more.

Athena realized that the game had just moved onto a field where Aphrodite had a distinct advantage. Quickly, she declared, "Choose me, Paris, and I'll make you the general of the greatest army in Phrygia!"

Hera blurted out, "Choose me and I'll make you the ruler of all Greece and Asia!"

Aphrodite spoke. "If you like what you see here," she said, rippling her body a bit, "then award the apple to me. I'll give you the woman who, in all the world, looks most like what you're gazing at now: Helen of Sparta, the daughter of Zeus."

Paris handed the apple to Aphrodite.

110
A PROMISE COMES DUE

Already as a child, Helen was extraordinarily beautiful.

When she was seven, Theseus had kidnapped her, planning to keep her in Athens until she was old enough to marry. Her brothers, Castor and Polydeuces, had to rescue her. When she was fourteen, all the princes of Greece had come to Sparta to ask for her hand. Her stepfather, Tyndareus, foresaw trouble: his choice, whoever it might be, would leave many other suitors angry. A sage man, he declared that he would allow Helen herself to choose her husband. Before she did so, however, he made her suitors swear that, should Helen ever again be abducted, all of them would help her husband retrieve her. Helen chose Menelaus, the son of Atreus and the younger brother of King Agamemnon of Mycenae, who had recently married Helen's sister, Clytemnestra. The marriage was a happy one and soon Helen bore Menelaus a daughter, Hermione. When Tyndareus died, Menelaus became king.

One day, a Phrygian ship arrived in the harbor of Gytheum on the southern coast of Greece. Soon, an embassy from Troy, led by Paris, presented itself at the Spartan palace; Aphrodite made sure that it was invited to stay.

The Phrygians were entertained lavishly and Paris, in turn, presented wonderful gifts to Menelaus and Helen. To Menelaus he gave gold and silver drinking cups engraved with griffins and bronze cauldrons on whose rims perched Sirens that looked as if they were about to sing. To Helen he gave patterned robes, a necklace delicately strung with golden acorns and earrings from which garnets dangled like clusters of grapes. Helen and Menelaus were overwhelmed by the generosity of their guest and invited him to stay longer.

On the tenth day of Paris's visit, Menelaus departed for his grandfather's funeral on Crete, bidding his guests to continue feasting. The day after that, relying on Aphrodite for help, Paris smuggled Helen out of the palace and down to Gytheum, where he carried her aboard his waiting ship.

The voyage was difficult; the winds blew the ship off course, first to Sidon and then to Canopus. After many days, the travelers arrived in Troy and Helen stepped onto its soil, bringing death as a dowry to her new city and its people.

When Menelaus returned to discover what had happened, he sent messengers to Helen's other suitors, reminding them of their oath and instructing them to assemble with their troops at Aulis, on the eastern coast of Greece. Among them were Ajax of Salamis, the son of Peleus's brother Telamon; Ajax of Locris, a small but powerful man; Nestor of Pylos, a wise advisor, and his sons; Philoctetes of Meliboea in Thessaly, a great archer who had inherited the bow of Heracles; Philoctetes's cousin, Protesilaus, who left a new bride behind at home; Palamedes of Euboea, who was the first to arrange letters into an alphabet; and Podalirius and

Machaon, sons of Asclepius who were excellent healers. Some of those who'd fought in the second Theban War came as well: Diomedes, the son of Tydeus; Sthenelus, the son of Capaneus; and Thersander, the son of Polynices. Agamemnon, because he was king of the most powerful Greek city, was the high commander of them all.

Other former suitors of Helen's came less willingly. Odysseus of Ithaca had long since married Helen's cousin Penelope and settled down happily. A shrewd man, he thought carefully about how to avoid keeping his promise. When he heard that the Greek leaders had landed on Ithaca to collect him, he yoked an ass and an ox together and began to plow the sand on the seashore, casting salt into the furrows so that, he said, the sea might always be salty. Most of the leaders concluded that Odysseus was hopelessly insane and turned to leave, but Palamedes—who was a shrewd man himself—seized Odysseus's infant son, Telemachus, from Penelope's arms and laid him in the path of the sharp plowshare. Odysseus swerved to avoid the baby, thus proving himself sane, and was forced to depart for Troy. Later, he paid Palamedes back by planting evidence in his tent that suggested he was conspiring with the Trojans. Palamedes was stoned to death by the Greek soldiers.

Achilles, the son of Peleus and Thetis, was eager to fight. His mother, however, fearing for his life, dressed him in women's clothes and hid him on the island of Scyros among the many daughters of King Lycomedes. Odysseus and Diomedes heard rumors of this and prepared a trap. Sailing to Scyros, they carried a tray of gifts for Lycomedes's daughters into the women's quarters—silks, necklaces, earrings—in the middle of which they'd placed a fine sword. When one of the girls seized the sword and brandished it through the air, they knew they had their man. Tearing the robes from Achilles's body, they carried him off to Troy, where he was destined to die. Achilles's old tutor, Phoenix, went with him, as did the Myrmidons, soldiers whom Zeus had created for Achilles's grandfather Aeacus from a colony of diligent ants. The most important member of Achilles's contingent, however, was Patroclus, a cousin whom Peleus had taken in as a boy and raised alongside Achilles. The bond between the two young men was stronger than brotherhood, stronger than friendship—either would have gladly died for the other.

When more than a thousand ships had assembled at Aulis, the Greeks set out across the sea. They landed at Teuthrania on the coast of Mysia and, mistaking it for Troy, attacked. Many were killed in the battle that followed, including Thersander, who never again strode through the gates of Thebes. The Greeks limped back to Aulis to regroup, but it would be many days before they once again departed for Troy.

111
IPHIGENIA

Some weeks later, Clytemnestra and her daughter Iphigenia traveled to Aulis, too. Their journey had been a long one, over bumpy roads and rutted paths. On the first night, they'd stayed in Corinth, with a family to whom they had old ties of friendship, and on the second night with another family in Eleusis. The third night had found them sheltering in the countryside between Tanagra and Aulis, the male slaves standing guard around the wagons until daybreak. In the morning, Iphigenia's own slaves bathed her, under the careful eye of her mother. They dressed her in the second-best finery that Mycenae's storerooms had been able to disgorge a few days earlier, after Clytemnestra had received a letter from her husband, Agamemnon. The best finery was still in the wagon, packed away in lavender for a wedding soon to come.

Agamemnon's letter said that Achilles—the best of the Greek warriors, the son of Thetis and Peleus, young and handsome—wished to join the blood of his family to that of their own before the army sailed for Troy. Agamemnon told his wife to send their daughter, who was now fourteen and ripe for marriage, to Aulis, where the fleet was assembled. He said nothing about Clytemnestra's accompanying her, but it was the prerogative of the bride's mother to place the wedding wreath upon her daughter's head and so Clytemnestra made the journey, too, taking along Orestes, her youngest child.

The final leg brought them close to the foot soldiers' camp on the beach, at the hour when the noonday sun was beating down.

Some of the soldiers were wading in the shallows; others were leading their captains' horses into the water to be cooled. All of them
were weary—of bad food, of rationed wine, of inactivity. Aching
for the war that their leaders had promised them, they festered in
idleness, for the winds that could carry them to Troy had not blown
since the moment, weeks earlier, when Zeus dispatched his eagles to
deliver a portent. The birds swept down from the clouds and seized
a sprinting hare, her belly bursting with nine babies still unborn.

"For nine years, you will fight fruitlessly before Troy's gates, but
in the tenth you will be victorious," declared Calchas the seer, as
the eagles feasted on the mother and her fetuses.

The portent had arrived unbidden, but Artemis, sickened by the
birds' banquet, had nonetheless directed her anger at its recipients:
she stopped the winds and stranded the fleet in Aulis. Then Calchas
sacrificed a bull, peered at the liver and spat out a second message.
Artemis, he said, demanded an expiatory sacrifice in exchange for
the winds, and the victim she required was the eldest daughter of
the army's general.

For many days Agamemnon refused to comply, but the dead air,
lying plague-like upon the men, finally forced his hand. Weeping,
he devised a lying letter to his wife to draw the victim near. Two
days later, he wrote another, secret letter that revoked the first,
but the slave to whom he entrusted it had been captured by Odysseus's spies before he'd even left the camp. Now Agamemnon
looked through the window of the shepherd's hut that served as
his headquarters and saw Iphigenia running towards the door. The
roundness of childhood lingered on her face, framed by hair that
had recently been shorn and dedicated to Artemis in hopes of safe
passage through adolescence.

"Father!" she cried, hugging him tightly. "Am I still your favorite
child?" Agamemnon saw Clytemnestra striding forward, too, holding Orestes on her hip, and his heart, already broken, broke again
at the thought of what they would now have to witness. After
giving his wife the most perfunctory of kisses, he left, pleading
duties among his men.

Sometimes the Fates, efficient in their cruelty, contrive to smite
two lives at once. Achilles, who knew nothing about the role that

he'd played in Agamemnon's lie, arrived at the hut shortly after Agamemnon departed. Seeking the leader of the army, he found Clytemnestra instead, who warmly clasped his hand and called him son-in-law, while giggling slaves rushed to hide a girl from his eyes. In fits and starts, Clytemnestra and Achilles built a picture from the separate pieces they held: Iphigenia was destined not to marry in Aulis but to die there and it was Achilles's name that had endorsed the deception that lured her to her death.

Iphigenia bolted then like a frightened foal, scrambling and slipping through forests and meadows, tearing her fine clothes on brambles and rocks. As the full moon rose in the sky, soldiers were sent to hunt her down; an hour later, they brought her to her father's hut, where Clytemnestra had been pleading for her daughter's life.

"When the blood of our daughter flows out onto the altar, Husband, where will you direct your gaze? At her throat, gushing red like that of a sacrificed heifer? At your brother Menelaus, waiting to launch a thousand ships to retrieve a single whore? What has Iphigenia to do with my slut of a sister, anyway? Helen left her own daughter behind when lust carried her to Troy—let Menelaus spill *her* blood to please Artemis.

"And what tale shall I take home to Iphigenia's sisters?" she continued. "What picture of a father's love shall I offer them? Make no mistake, Agamemnon: if you kill our child, you set us all on a path to destruction; the pain will not cease with a single slash of the knife. Think about the sorrowful welcome that will await you if you return from Troy. Think, Husband, and spare our daughter's life!"

Achilles argued with Agamemnon as well, swearing to protect the girl whom his name had betrayed, even if it meant his own death in Aulis at the spears of his own men.

But every mortal is born to a particular grief; no other hand can lift it. As Iphigenia listened to others bartering with her life, she reached her own decision. "I will die as Artemis demands. Achilles's blood shall not be wasted for me, nor shall my father's. I am destined to die here for reasons that the gods, in their obscurity, do not disclose. The only choice I can make lies in how I go to my death, and I choose to so in a way that befits the honor of my family. Be strengthened by my blood; cross the sea to do what you must do."

At dawn, Iphigenia placed upon her head a wreath of flowers that the slaves had plaited for her wedding. She embraced her mother and begged her not to hate her father. She kissed Orestes. And then, on Agamemnon's arm, she ascended the hill on which Artemis's altar stood.

Calchas waited there, his black robes flapping like a crow's wings in the breeze that was beginning to blow. As Iphigenia reached the altar, the wind blew harder; smoke from the fire blossomed out to fill the empty air. Coughing in the haze, Agamemnon lost his daughter's arm. His eyes pricked with tears; he was never sure of what he saw, moments later, when Calchas's knife slashed down.

Below on the shore, the sails began to slap in the wind.

112
PROTESILAUS AND LAODAMIA

The fresh winds carried the Greek ships quickly to Troy. As they approached the beach, Achilles eagerly strapped on his armor and gathered up his weapons, preparing to leap into the shallows as soon as he heard his ship's hull scraping against the sand. But then his mother, invisible to everyone but him, wrapped her arms around his shoulders and whispered in his ear. It had been foretold, said Thetis, that the first Greek to touch Trojan soil would also be the first to die.

Frustrated but obedient, Achilles held back until he saw someone else—it happened to be Protesilaus—running up the shingle towards the waiting Trojans. Initially, everything went well; Protesilaus killed each man whom he confronted. Achilles began to wonder whether his mother's warning had been just another of her devices to keep him out of combat. He started up the shingle himself, leading his men. Then he saw a tall man with a glinting helmet engage Protesilaus. The struggle was brief; Protesilaus soon crumpled to the ground, becoming the first of many Greeks to die at Troy and the first to die at the hands of Hector, King Priam's son and Troy's greatest warrior.

The Greeks mourned Protesilaus grandly, burning his body atop a towering pyre along with numerous gifts meant to comfort his soul in the Underworld. They sent his bones back to his wife, Laodamia, whom he had married only the day before departing for Aulis.

Numb with grief, Laodamia lopped off her hair and tore at her cheeks. Locked in a solitary prison of sorrow, she no longer cared for the world and its realities. The food that her attendants entreated her to eat was tasteless; the possets they offered were unappealing. Her body grew thin and her face wan. But then one morning, she devoured her breakfast hungrily. The day after that, she smiled, and on the third day, there was a gleam in her eye. Her attendants eventually discovered the reason: Laodamia had ordered one of the palace artisans to craft a life-size statue of Protesilaus from the finest beeswax. Every night, she took the statue to bed, delighting in the warmth that each part returned to her ardent caresses.

The gods looked down with astonishment and pity. Zeus commanded Hermes to escort Protesilaus back from Hades so that he might spend one last day with Laodamia before returning to the Underworld forever. Hermes tidied Protesilaus up, putting flesh on his gaunt frame and color into his gray skin, until he looked like the same handsome youth whom Laodamia had married.

Laodamia was overjoyed by her husband's return, even after she learned that their time together would be brief. The two lay in each others' arms while the sun and the moon crossed the sky—and then, when his time was up, Protesilaus simply vanished from the bed. Stricken with a new grief that was much sharper than the first, and no longer able to find happiness with her rigid statue, Laodamia killed herself. The gods sighed; in their unaccustomed kindness, they had clumsily miscalculated the human heart.

At Troy the skirmishes continued, filling the plain in front of the city with corpses, most of which were Trojan. The Greek leaders decided to send an embassy to Priam, offering to cease hostilities if he would surrender Helen. Odysseus and Menelaus set out carrying a staff that announced their peaceful intentions.

Some god contrived that as the two approached the city, they encountered Antenor, a prudent man of moderation. Antenor

welcomed them into his home and encouraged them in their mission. After the guests had eaten and drunk, Antenor and his sons
escorted them to the palace, protecting them from attack. Years
later, when the Greeks conquered Troy and were preparing to sack
it, Odysseus hung a leopard skin on the door of Antenor's house,
signaling that it and its inhabitants were to remain untouched.

With impassioned words, Menelaus pleaded for justice to Priam
and the Trojan leaders, imploring them to expunge Paris's insolent
deed by returning Helen—but the Trojans remained unmoved and
the Greeks returned to camp unsuccessful.

And so the war continued. Each day, Queen Hecabe watched
her older sons depart for the battlefield and prayed for their safety.
Desperate to safeguard the life of at least one of them, she sent the
youngest, Polydorus, away to live with King Polymestor of Thrace
until the war was over. On the Greek side, the army's hunger demanded raids upon the countryside surrounding Troy, two of which
rippled out to doom Greeks and Trojans alike. In the ninth year of
the war, Achilles and his Myrmidons sacked the town of Lyrnessus,
seizing among their spoils Briseis, the daughter of Brises, a priest
of Apollo. She was newly married, but Achilles slaughtered her
husband and took her for his own bed. When the Greeks raided the
nearby village of Thebes, Agamemnon received among his spoils
Chryseis, the daughter of Chryses, another priest of Apollo, and
took her for his bed.

Briseis and Chryseis had no status of their own but they conferred immense status upon the men to whom they had been given
as prizes. And by their very existence, they would cause the deaths
of Patroclus, Hector and Achilles.

113
AGAMEMNON AND ACHILLES

Soon after the sack of Thebes, Chryses arrived at the Greek camp
to ransom his daughter, bearing many gifts. In his hand was a
golden staff wound with ribbons, marking him as Apollo's priest.

But Agamemnon refused to return Chryseis, whatever her father might offer. He intended to carry her back to Mycenae when

the war was over, where she would weave cloth for his household during the day and provide pleasure in his bed at night—she would be much better at that than Clytemnestra, he chortled. Angry and heartbroken, Chryses left. As he returned to his ship, he lifted his hands to Apollo and prayed.

"Hear me, God of the Silver Bow! If it pleased you when I put a roof on your temple or burned the thigh pieces of goats and bulls for you, then make the Greeks pay for what they've done to me!"

Apollo listened. Slinging his quiver over his shoulder, he fell upon the Greek camp like a dark shadow. With his great bow he shot the mules and the dogs and then the men themselves, infecting them with a terrible plague. For nine days, the corpse fires burned continuously. On the tenth day, Achilles called the Greeks together and asked Calchas the seer which god had sent the plague, and why— had they omitted some sacrifice or forgotten some vow they'd made? Calchas replied that the plague was Apollo's work, a punishment for refusing to allow Chryses to ransom his daughter.

The Greek leaders commanded Agamemnon to surrender the woman. Enraged, he demanded another woman to replace her, but was told that all of the women had been apportioned. He bellowed about his honor—why should Ajax or Odysseus or Achilles or anyone else have a woman in his bed, he asked, while he, the general of the army, slept alone? If a spare woman wasn't to be had, he'd take someone else's, he thundered.

Achilles's temper goaded him to speak then, when silence would have been wiser. "You shameless, greedy cur! You're nothing but a pot-bellied drunk with a dog's eyes and the quivering heart of a deer! I'm here for *your* sake—yours and that brother of yours. It wasn't *my* wife the Trojans stole, and yet I fight harder than anyone else, while you two skim off the best of the spoils. Push me further and I swear I'll go home."

Agamemnon had always disliked Achilles—an arrogant youth, smug in his warcraft and far too proud of his handsome appearance. So he smiled and said, "Fine! Stay or leave as you choose. Either way, Briseis will be in *my* bed tonight."

Achilles drew his sword then, but before he could use it, Athena yanked his long blond hair so hard that he spun around. Athena made herself visible to Achilles alone and glared at him with steely eyes.

"Stop!" she hissed. "Control yourself now and you'll receive three times as many gifts later. Roar all you want—but don't kill Agamemnon."

Achilles's sword went back in its sheath. Soon, the assembly dispersed. Chryseis was sent home to her father and Agamemnon's heralds escorted Briseis to Agamemnon's shelter. Achilles walked to the beach and looked out over the gray waves, weeping with anger and stretching out his hands to his mother. Thetis rose from the sea and stood at her son's side, stroking his hair and listening to his troubles. By the time they parted, he had resolved to abstain from the war until the Greeks restored Briseis and paid him the honor he was due.

Thetis had her own part to play in this plan. Waiting until she saw Zeus sitting apart from the other gods, she hurried to join him, touching his knees and his chin in the manner of a suppliant. "Zeus," she said, "if ever I've pleased you in word or deed, help me now. Give honor to my son, who is destined to die young—honor that Agamemnon has stolen. Infuse strength into the Trojan army until the Greeks beg Achilles to return to battle and restore his prize."

Zeus was silent for a long time before speaking. "Thetis, what you're asking me to do will infuriate Hera—she's hated the Trojans ever since she lost that beauty contest. Nevertheless, I'll find a way to accomplish it." Then he solemnly nodded his head, making his promise irrevocable. He spoke to her softly. "Leave quickly, now, before Hera sees the two of us together."

All night long, as he lay next to his wife, Zeus contemplated how best to achieve what he had promised to Thetis. Just before dawn, he rose and summoned an evil dream. Commanding it to assume the shape of Nestor, the Greeks' most trusted advisor, he taught it what to say and then dispatched it to Agamemnon's shelter. The dream stood by Agamemnon's head and announced, in Nestor's voice, that he carried a message from Zeus: the gods had decided it was time for Troy to fall. The Greeks must strike immediately.

The dream departed and Agamemnon awoke, rejoicing in things that were not true. Under his command, the Greeks swept across the plain towards Troy—thousands of men, making Earth groan beneath their hammering feet. Hector led the Trojans out to meet them, raising a cacophonous din. But as the armies drew near to one another, Paris suddenly leapt between them. A leopard's skin was draped across his shoulders and he clutched a bow, a sword and several javelins in his hands. He challenged the Greeks to choose a champion to fight against him in single combat, with the outcome to settle the war. Menelaus immediately stepped forward, like a hungry lion spotting a goat. Green fear seized Paris then and he shrank back.

Hector rebuked him scornfully. "Paris-the-Worthless! Always so stylish and good with the ladies but a complete failure at everything else. How I wish you'd never been born! But there's no changing that, so stop embarrassing us: face the man whose wife you stole."

Paris threw his spear first, but the bronze point crumpled harmlessly against Menelaus's shield. Then Menelaus threw: his spear pierced Paris's shield, corselet and tunic, but stopped short of the flesh. Bellowing with frustration, Menelaus pounded his sword against Paris's helmet until the blade broke. Exasperated, he grabbed the crest of the helmet itself and spun Paris around in circles, dragging him over the ground. The helmet's strap cut deeply into Paris's soft throat; he would have been strangled had not Aphrodite, who was keeping watch, caused the strap to break. And then suddenly, Paris vanished from sight.

114
HERA DECEIVES ZEUS

Paris found himself in his perfumed bedroom back in the palace. Helen soon arrived, looking sullen. Moments before, she'd been standing atop the city wall, watching the duel alongside Priam, when Aphrodite, disguised as an elderly wool-worker, had abruptly summoned her to Paris's side. Helen, who was in no mood to comfort a man who had become a laughingstock, resisted the summons, although she knew full well who the elderly wool-worker really was: Aphrodite's firm breasts and radiant skin had given her away. In the end, however, Aphrodite prevailed: she marched Helen home, dragged an armchair over next to the one in which Paris slumped, and ordered Helen to sit down.

Aphrodite couldn't control Helen's tongue, however, and Helen had plenty to say, none of which was comforting. Paris shrugged off her words—this time the gods who liked Menelaus had contrived to make him look good, but another time, he reasoned, his own gods would do the same. Meanwhile, he murmured to Helen, as long as they found themselves together there in the bedroom, how about mingling in love? He yearned for her body as intensely as if they were about to lie together for the first time. In spite of herself, Helen smiled and allowed him to lead her to bed.

The soldiers watching the duel had been dumbfounded by Paris's disappearance. Agamemnon declared that Menelaus had won by default, given that his opponent had left the field, but the Trojans disagreed. The deadlock was finally broken by the gods: Zeus dispatched Athena, disguised as a Trojan soldier, to persuade the Lycian archer Pandarus, an ally of the Trojans, to take a shot at Menelaus. Soon, the war was raging once more.

In spite of Zeus's promise to Thetis, the Trojans bore the brunt of it. As things got worse, Hector sprinted back to the palace to ask his mother to pray to Athena for help. Queen Hecabe carried rich gifts to Athena's temple, including a robe that glimmered like a star, which Hecabe laid across the knees of Athena's statue. The goddess ignored the gift, however, spurning the queen's prayers.

Before Hector returned to the battle, he stopped to see his wife, Andromache, and their little son, Astyanax. Andromache clung to her husband and wept.

"Beloved husband, your own excellence will be your death, for every Greek longs to kill you! What will become of me, then? Achilles slaughtered my father and seven brothers when the Greeks sacked Thebes; my mother died soon after. You're all that remains to me—you're my father, mother, brother and husband all rolled into one! Be careful, my love—you needn't always fight at the front."

"Andromache, I know in my heart that Troy is doomed to fall, eventually," Hector replied. "I'd rather die now, trying to defend it, than live long enough to hear you weeping when a Greek man drags you away."

He held out his arms to Astyanax then, who screamed in fright at the horsehair crest on his father's helmet, which nodded and bobbed like some living thing. Hector removed his helmet and placed it on the ground. Taking his son in his arms, he kissed him and tossed him into the air to make him laugh. He prayed to the gods that Astyanax would grow up to be a better warrior than his father and then strode through the city's gates onto the plain.

Aphrodite's rescue of Paris had been just one of many instances of the gods' constant meddling in the war, which sent ripples through the ranks of mortals and immortals alike. Athena endowed Diomedes with the ability to discern the gods as they moved about the battlefield; when Aphrodite swooped in to save her son Aeneas from Diomedes's spear, Diomedes, grinning wickedly, inflicted a wound upon Aphrodite's own divine flesh. With a shriek, Aphrodite dropped Aeneas and fled. Luckily, Apollo was near enough to rescue Aeneas and carried him away to be healed, leaving a simulacrum behind so that the other warriors wouldn't know that Aeneas was gone.

Zeus realized that he had to put an end to episodes like these if he was going to keep his promise to Thetis and temporarily sway the war in the Trojans' favor. He commanded the gods to abstain from the war and for a while they did; Zeus was free to arrange things as he wished and the Trojans flourished. Hera, however, came up with a devious plan that would enable the Greeks to rally. Retreating to her chamber, she bathed her graceful body in ambrosia and anointed it with sweet oil. She dressed in an exquisite robe that Athena herself had woven and cinched it with a sash from which one hundred tassels hung, rippling over her hips whenever she moved. From her ears she dangled glittering jewels and all around herself she draped a diaphanous veil.

For the crowning touch, she approached Aphrodite. "My dear, could you help me with something? I know we're on opposite sides of this silly war, but I really need your expertise."

"Of course! I'll do whatever I can."

Lying skillfully, Hera continued. "Our ancestors Ocean and Tethys have had a spat and no longer share the same bed. It's a sad situation and I'm trying to patch things up. You're the expert in persuasion; do you have something that would help me convince them to set aside their rancor?"

Aphrodite untied the band that bound up her breasts, upon which were embroidered charms and beguilements that would melt the heart of even the most unyielding person. She placed it in Hera's hands. "Take this and wear it. You'll be able to persuade anyone to do whatever you please."

Hera smiled her thanks to Aphrodite and then, binding the band beneath her own breasts, smiled once more, secretly to herself. She hurried away to where Sleep was lounging on Lemnos and persuaded him to help her by promising to give him Pasithea, the youngest of the Graces, as his wife. Together they flew to Mount Ida, where Zeus was looking down upon the war. Sleep disguised himself as a bird and hid in a pine tree while Hera approached her husband. When Zeus saw her, desire overwhelmed his heart as powerfully as it had on the day, long ago, that they had first mingled in love.

"Darling," said Hera, "I'm just off to visit Ocean and Tethys to try to settle their quarrel."

He reached up and pulled her down onto his lap. "Put that off a bit, my love, and lie down with me now; I've never felt as much desire for any goddess or mortal woman as I now feel for you! Not when I made love to Dia, the wife of Ixion, who bore me Pirithous; or Danaë, the daughter of Acrisius, who bore me Perseus; or Europa, the daughter of Phoenix, who bore me Minos and Rhadamanthys. Nor when I made love to Semele or Alcmene, who bore me Dionysus and Heracles; or Demeter of the beautiful hair; or Leto—nor even when I made love to you yourself!"

"Why, Zeus! I'm blushing! But anyone could see us here; let's go back to our bedroom."

"I've got a better idea," replied Zeus, waving a hand through the air. "There; I've created a golden cloud around us. Not even Helios could see us now."

The two lay down upon fresh grass and flowers that Earth sent up to cushion their bodies. The golden cloud cast a soft, shimmering dew upon their bodies as they made love.

115
ACHILLES AND PATROCLUS

A little while later, from the tree where he lurked, Sleep cast a postcoital nap over Zeus. When her husband's eyes were safely shut, Hera instructed Sleep to fly to Poseidon and tell him to rouse the Greeks. Poseidon led the Greeks into battle with a voice that boomed above the brazen din, brandishing an enormous sword that flashed in the sunlight. Infused with new courage, Telamonian Ajax threw a boulder at Hector's chest and knocked him senseless to the ground. Hector's friends managed to carry him to safety but in his absence, the Trojans faltered.

When Zeus awoke and saw what was happening, he glared at Hera. "Have you forgotten, Wife, that time I punished you for persecuting Heracles by tying anvils to your feet and hanging you from the heavens? The other gods pitied you, but no one dared to set you free. If you ever deceive me again, you'll get more of the same."

"Poseidon did all of this by himself!" cried Hera in a panicky voice.

Zeus ignored her lie. "Help me put things right. Fly to Olympus. Send Iris and Apollo back to me here, so that I can dispatch Iris to order Poseidon off the battlefield and Apollo to breathe strength into Hector."

Then he softened his tone. "And Hera, stop worrying. I've got a plan. Hector will kill Patroclus after Patroclus kills my own dear son Sarpedon. Then Achilles, grieving furiously for his friend, will kill Hector. Eventually, the Greeks will destroy Troy—but only after they've restored Achilles's stolen honor."

Hera did as Zeus commanded and Iris and Apollo soon departed on their errands. Apollo found Hector in Priam's palace. Gliding close to him, Apollo asked, "Why are you just sitting here, Hector?"

Hector looked up and stammered in astonishment. "Whoever you are, you must be a god! But if so, don't you already know that Ajax nearly killed me?"

"I am Apollo, who has protected you and your city during these many years of war. Listen to me now: injured or not, you must get up. Lead your troops to the Greek ships and set them ablaze. Fear not; I will be with you."

Then Apollo breathed strength into Hector and Hector raced off to marshal his men. Cloaked in mist, Apollo strode across the plain in front of them, howling and shaking the aegis that Zeus had lent to him, a fearsome device that cast terror into the hearts of the Greeks. Quickly, the Trojans fought their way to the trench that the Greeks had dug in front of their encampment and then swarmed across a makeshift bridge that Apollo created by kicking dirt into the gap. They pressed onwards towards the ships. Patroclus saw what was happening and sprinted to Achilles's shelter.

Achilles had remained obdurate in his refusal to fight. Only the day before, Agamemnon had dispatched Phoenix, Telamonian Ajax and Odysseus, the most persuasive speaker of the Greeks, to offer an apology on his behalf, hoping that Achilles would relent. The three told Achilles that if he returned to battle, Agamemnon would give him tripods, cauldrons, gold, horses, captive women, one of Agamemnon's own daughters as a wife once they were home again—and Briseis, with whom, Agamemnon swore, he'd never slept. Yet Achilles obstinately insisted that he would not stir himself to fight unless the Trojans were about to burn the Myrmidons' ships. Now that moment was surely drawing near, thought Patroclus, but when he told Achilles that the Trojans were closing in on the Greek ships, Achilles merely shrugged; until they approached his own ships, he didn't care.

Patroclus groaned in frustration. "I hope I'm never possessed by such inhuman wrath as possesses you now! If you completely refuse to help your friends, then at least let me put on your armor and lead forth the Myrmidons, so that the Trojans think you've returned. If they're frightened, they may fall back."

Achilles replied. "You can wear my armor long enough to save the ships. But listen: as soon you've done that, return! Don't be tempted to fight the Trojans any further; Apollo will crush you. Wait till the day when you and I can topple the walls of Troy together."

Patroclus eagerly donned Achilles's gleaming armor, which the gods had given to Peleus as a wedding present. Across his chest he slung his friend's great shield and silver-studded sword. He mounted Achilles's chariot, drawn by the immortal horses Xanthus and Balius, whom Poseidon and Amphitrite had given to Peleus and Thetis as a wedding gift, with a third, mortal horse, Pedasus, harnassed alongside them. When everything was ready, Achilles poured a libation and prayed for Patroclus's safe return. He bid his friend farewell.

Just as Patroclus was leading the Myrmidons into battle, the Trojans reached the ships and kindled one—it happened to be the one on which the ill-fated Protesilaus had sailed. They were preparing to burn others when they glimpsed an approaching warrior whom they took to be Achilles. Desperately afraid, the men dropped their torches and fled. Patroclus raced to the burning ship, killed the man who had set it ablaze and quenched the flames. He should have returned to Achilles then, but bloodlust blurred his wits. Spines were severed, teeth shattered, eyes skewered, lungs punctured and livers ripped apart as Patroclus advanced across the field—many Trojans died at his hands.

Then Patroclus confronted Sarpedon. High above the battle, Zeus turned to Hera. "My heart breaks at the thought that Sarpedon must die, Hera. Perhaps I should snatch him up and transport him home to Lycia."

"But Zeus! You know you can't do that—every mortal is fated to die at a particular time. And if you *did* save Sarpedon, the other gods would clamor for the same privilege—what then? Will no mortal whom a god loves ever have to die? The best thing you can do is to give Sarpedon an honorable passing. Send Sleep and Death to carry his body back to Lycia, where he'll be properly mourned."

Zeus did as Hera counseled—but he wept tears of blood onto the battlefield as he watched his son fall.

Insatiable, Patroclus continued across the plain like a lion in a sheepfold, counting nothing impossible and leaving a trail of bloody corpses behind him. All the while, however, Apollo was lying in wait, calculating the moment of Patroclus's death and orchestrating its manner. Shrouded in mist, the god flicked his finger against Patroclus's helmet—a marvelous, frightening, four-horned thing. It tumbled from Patroclus's head and clattered beneath the horses, its plumes defiled by dust. Apollo shook loose Patroclus's shield and spear, too, and caused his corselet to clatter to the ground.

Naked and dazed, Patroclus stood blinking in his sudden vulnerability. Euphorbus pierced him between the shoulders with a javelin and then dashed back into the ranks, afraid of Patroclus even after he'd been injured. Then Hector strode forward and drove a spear straight through Patroclus's belly.

"Fool!" he laughed. "The vultures will eat you now and Achilles can't do a thing about it. I, Hector, have killed you!"

"No," gasped Patroclus. "Fate and Leto's son and Euphorbus killed me—you've merely finished me off. And mark this, Hector: you'll die soon, too, at Achilles's hands." His soul fluttered free of his body then, leaving it limp, but Hector replied to him anyway.

"Who knows? I might kill Achilles, instead!" Then, placing his foot on Patroclus's corpse and giving a mighty yank, Hector retrieved his spear.

116
ACHILLES AND HECTOR

The Greeks rushed in to protect Patroclus's body and the glorious armor it wore, but Hector managed to snatch the armor and then fought hard for the body as well. He relished the thought of impaling Patroclus's head on a stake in front of the city and throwing the rest of him to the dogs. After many weary hours of guarding the body but not being able to carry it off the field, the Greeks sent word to Achilles that Patroclus had been slain and begged for his help.

When Achilles heard the terrible news, he rubbed dust into his hair and beat his fists against the ground. His wails of grief were so profound that they reached his mother, deep beneath the waves. Thetis walked from the sea and sat beside her son. Gently taking his face between her hands, she looked into his eyes.

"Achilles, you know the Fates have decreed that if you kill Hector, you, too, must die here, far away from home. Since your heart cannot be turned aside from avenging your friend, I must prepare myself for that sorrow. But don't go into battle with nothing to shield you; I'll ask Hephaestus, whom long ago I nurtured after his mother tossed him into the sea, to make you new armor." And Thetis ascended to Olympus, where Hephaestus kept his forge.

When his mother had departed, Achilles strode to the border of the Greek camp and bellowed mightily, casting terror into the hearts of the Trojans and driving them away from Patroclus's body. The Greeks carried the corpse to Achilles's shelter, where they washed the clotted blood from its skin, anointed it with fragrant oils and wrapped it in fine linen to prepare it for the pyre. Achilles, however, refused to burn it until Hector had paid with his life. Pitying the poor corpse, Thetis infused it with divine ambrosia and nectar, to prevent the flies from breeding maggots in its wounds. Then she spoke again to her son.

"Before you go into battle, child, you must unite the Greeks by setting aside your anger at Agamemnon. Summon an assembly and let the men watch the two of you make peace."

Achilles obeyed his mother, striding up and down the seashore to call the men together. When all were assembled, he spoke. "How I wish, Agamemnon, that Artemis had killed Briseis before I sacked her city and took her captive! She's turned us against one another and, by doing so, has caused the deaths of many Greeks. It's time for us to end this quarrel."

"I'll apologize to you, Achilles, but it wasn't really me who caused the problem," answered Agamemnon. "It was Zeus and Fate and an Erinys who crept through the mist. *They* misled me—how could any mortal fight against such gods? Delusion is the daughter of Zeus, flitting through the air, sifting madness onto all of us below. Nonetheless, as a token of my regret, accept all the gifts that I offered yesterday, and Briseis, as well."

When Achilles saw that the gifts and Briseis had been brought to his shelter, he prepared for battle. He donned the new armor that his mother had brought from Hephaestus, gleaming with bronze and tin and silver and gold. The new shield was especially wondrous, for on it Hephaestus had pictured all the things of the cosmos. Constellations gazed down upon marriages and quarrels, judgments and wars. Men departed for battle while their wives and children watched from parapets. Shepherds played their pipes while marauders prepared to steal the flocks and kill their keepers;

Death was already dragging one man away by the feet and tightening his grip on another. Farmers tilled the earth and men and women harvested grapes that hung heavy on the vines. Hephaestus also showed the dancing floor that Daedalus once had made for Ariadne, on which nimble young men and beautiful girls circled in their steps. Around the edge of the shield, embracing everything else, swirled the stream of Ocean.

After Achilles had gazed upon this wonder, he went to his chariot and spoke to his immortal horses, urging them to bring him home more safely than they'd brought Patroclus. Xanthus bowed his head so deeply that his mane swept the dirt. "Achilles," he replied, "it wasn't our fault that Patroclus was slain—it was Apollo who arranged his death. We'll bring you home safely this time, but beware: even now Fate and a god and a mortal man are orchestrating your death, too."

"Why bother to foretell my death, Xanthus?" said Achilles. "I know I'm destined to die here. Until I do, though, I'll pound the Trojans into the ground." Then he mounted his chariot and rode onto the plain.

The battle was hard-fought. Achilles alone killed so many men that the great Scamander River became clogged by the corpses he tossed into its stream. Rearing up like an enraged bull, the river swept Achilles into its waters, where eddies whirled him here and there among the bodies of the men he'd killed. He would have drowned then, if Hephaestus hadn't cast fire upon the river, boiling its waters until Scamander relented and released Achilles.

As the day drew to a close, the Greeks finally managed to chase the Trojans to the walls of their city. Priam ordered the gates to be opened briefly to admit the fleeing troops, but Hector refused to take shelter, intending to negotiate a truce with Achilles. When the two came face to face, however, Hector trembled at the eerie radiance that shone from the armor Hephaestus had made. He turned and ran and Achilles ran after him.

Three times they circled the walls of Troy, a great warrior fleeing from an even greater one, while the gods watched the spectacle. As they were circling for the fourth time, Zeus took out his golden scales and balanced their shimmering pans. He placed the fate of Hector in one and the fate of Achilles in the other; Hector's pan sank. In a flash, Athena descended to Hector then, disguised as his brother Deiphobus, and urged him to turn and confront Achilles.

And suspecting nothing, Hector did so. "Achilles, one of us must kill the other, now. Let's swear an oath by the gods that whichever one of us dies, the other will give his body back to his people to be lamented and buried."

Achilles stared at the man who was wearing the armor that Patroclus had worn only the day before, that he himself had worn, and that his father had worn before him. "*Agree?*" he spat. "There can be no agreements between men and animals!" He drove his spear through what he knew to be the armor's weakest point, where the collarbone met the throat. It went all the way through Hector's neck, but it did not pierce his windpipe, allowing him to speak a little longer.

"I beg you, by your life and by your parents' lives—don't throw my body to the dogs!" he gasped. "Accept the gifts that my father will offer so that the Trojans can burn my body. Let me cross into Hades, or I'll bring the gods' curse down upon you!"

"I'd like to tear off your flesh with my own teeth and swallow it down raw! Not even if your father offers me your weight in gold will I return your body!"

"Your savagery revolts the gods, Achilles! Soon, Paris and Apollo will avenge me by killing you at the Scaean Gate," said Hector. Then darkness fell upon his eyes and his soul fluttered away. Achilles stripped the armor from Hector's body and invited the other Greeks to drive their spears into Hector's flesh. When everyone had done so, Achilles pierced the corpse's heels, threaded them with a thong and tied the body to the back of his chariot, so that Hector's head would thump against the road as he drove back to the Greek camp and Hector's black hair, which had been so beautiful, would trail through the dust.

117
ACHILLES AND PRIAM

Hector's parents had watched all of this unfold from atop the city walls. When Achilles's spear pierced Hector's neck, Hecabe shrieked and clawed her cheeks. Priam hurried down to the great gate and tried to open it, meaning to rush to his son's side, but the guards restrained him. All across the wall, wherever people had gathered to watch the battle, there was weeping and lamenting.

Andromache was sitting inside at her loom, weaving flowers into crimson cloth for a cloak. She had just ordered her women to heat water for Hector's evening bath when the sound of lamentation chilled her heart. She raced to Hecabe's side, arriving just in time to see her husband's head bouncing over the stony ground behind Achilles's chariot, nodding this way and that. The jaw, loosened by death, gaped open as if struggling to speak.

"Ah, Hector," she cried, "it would have been better by far if neither of us had ever been born! Now you're flying down to Hades, leaving behind a fatherless son. Poor Astyanax—you used to hold him on your lap and feed him the best morsels from the table. Now, it will be dogs and maggots whom you feed!"

Achilles reached the Greek camp as evening was falling. Untying Hector's body, he dragged it over to the bier upon which Patroclus lay, hoping to please the spirit of the dead. Then he walked along the beach, grieving for his friend. When he finally dropped onto the sand and fell asleep, the ghost of Patroclus appeared to him, as handsome as he'd been when he was alive and speaking with the same voice.

"You're neglecting me, Achilles! If you truly love me, burn me quickly now, so that I can enter Hades's kingdom. The other ghosts prevent me from crossing the great river that separates the living from the dead and I wander restlessly along its murky banks. Burn me, and place my bones in the golden amphora that Dionysus gave your parents, which will some day hold your bones, too. That way, we'll lie together again in death."

Achilles reached out to embrace Patroclus, but the ghost gave a shrill cry and vanished like smoke into the air. Achilles awoke, amazed that even in death his friend should look so unchanged.

The next day, Achilles did as Patroclus had asked. Mules hauled timber for a great pyre upon which Patroclus's body was placed. On top of it, each man laid a lock of his own hair, covering the body like a blanket. Achilles cut a lock that he had left unshorn since birth, having meant to dedicate it one day to the river that flowed through Phthia. Knowing now that he would never see that river again, he gave the lock to Patroclus instead.

Achilles slit the throats of Patroclus's dogs and horses as well as those of twelve Trojan boys whom the Greeks had taken captive and then laid their bodies on the pyre, company for Patroclus's ghost. When the flames had consumed all of this and wine had quenched the flames, the Greeks competed in games to honor the dead. But still, each day, Achilles wept for his friend and each day, he tied Hector's body to his chariot and dragged it around Patroclus's tomb.

The gods protected the poor corpse, staving off decay and shielding it from the withering rays of the sun. After twelve days, however, they agreed that it must be returned to Troy for burial. Thetis told Achilles to allow Priam to ransom it and Zeus dispatched Iris to send Priam to Achilles's shelter. Iris found Priam in the palace courtyard, sitting among his remaining sons. In his grief, he had befouled himself, smearing dung onto his body and robes, but when he heard what Iris had come to say, he bathed and put on fresh clothes. He ordered his sons to prepare his mule cart and hurried to his wife's chamber with the news.

"Have you lost your mind?" Hecabe asked him, when she heard his plan. "How can you put yourself in the hands of a man who has slaughtered so many of our sons? You'll be next, Priam! Oh, how I wish I could sink my teeth into Achilles's liver and chew it up!"

"But I *must* go, Hecabe—a god has ordered me to. No one knows the appointed hour of their death; if I'm fated to be slain by Achilles, at least I'll die next to Hector's body."

Priam set out for the Greek camp with the ransom in his cart—gold, weapons and beautiful robes that his daughters and daughters-in-law had woven. When he was halfway there, a slender young man approached him, carrying a staff that flickered oddly in the twilight, as if serpents were twining around it. The stranger accompanied Priam to the Greek camp, where he cast sleep upon the eyes of the sentries, pushed open the gates and escorted Priam to the door of Achilles's shelter. Then he spoke.

"I am Hermes, sent by my father to guide and protect you, Priam. Enter Achilles's shelter now, and approach him as a suppliant."

Priam did as Hermes ordered. He knelt to clasp Achilles's knees and kissed the calloused hands that had slaughtered his sons. "Pity me, Achilles!" he said. "Think of your father, who like me endures a sorrowful old age apart from the son he loves. Peleus can hope to see you again one day, but my only hope, now, is to see my dear son properly lamented and dispatched on his journey to Hades. Accept the ransom I have brought, I beg you, and give me back my son."

Achilles marveled that so frail a man had dared to make the journey to the Greeks' camp; it stirred in him a longing for his own father, far away. The two enemies wept together then, each one thinking of those whom he had lost and those who would soon lose him. After a while, Achilles spoke. "We must stop weeping, King; lamentation is pointless. There are two urns that sit on Zeus's doorstep—one is an urn of evils and the other an urn of blessings. If Zeus hates a mortal, he takes and gives from only the first urn. If Zeus likes a mortal, he takes and gives from both. But for no mortal—not even for my father, who married one of the gods—does Zeus take and give from the second urn alone. Such is human life. Now, let my men bring in the ransom so that I can give you back your son."

While the gifts were being carried in, Achilles's slaves gently washed and anointed Hector's body, so that Priam would not see its wounds. They wrapped it in linen and placed it in the wagon beneath an intricately woven robe. Then Achilles invited Priam to dine.

"Even Niobe ate as she wept for her children," he said to encourage the king. "Apollo and Artemis killed them to punish Niobe for bragging that she was a better mother than Leto, and for nine days the children lay on the palace floor, unburied. Nonetheless, Niobe remembered to eat, even as she wept. You and I must eat, too, although we are burdened by grief."

When supper was over, Priam asked for a place to sleep before he returned to Troy in the morning. Achilles ordered his men to make up a bed on the porch of his shelter, with warm fleeces and soft blankets. But Priam had no sooner closed his eyes than Hermes stood beside him once more and spoke to him in urgent tones.

"Come! Quickly now! You've spent a lot to obtain Hector's corpse—how much more would your remaining sons have to pay to get *you* back, if Agamemnon or some other Greek catches you here? Let's go while the darkness still cloaks us."

The man and the god slipped from the Greek camp and traveled together until dawn, when they crossed the Scamander. His job done, Hermes vanished and returned to Olympus.

118
THE DEATHS OF ACHILLES AND AJAX

Achilles had asked Priam how many days it would take the Trojans to mourn Hector. Priam had answered eleven, and for that period of time, Achilles kept back the Greeks. For nine of those days, the Trojan mules and oxen hauled timber for Hector's pyre. On the tenth, the Trojans laid Hector's body atop it, with gifts to ease his journey. When the great pyre at last was lit, fire blossomed into the sky. Afterwards, the Trojans gathered Hector's bones and wrapped them in soft purple robes. They placed the bones in a golden casket and laid the casket in a tomb.

On the twelfth day, the battle resumed. With Hector gone, the Trojans summoned more allies to help defend their city. Penthesilea, a fierce, intrepid daughter of Ares, arrived with a troop of Amazons. She slew numerous Greeks before Achilles shot an arrow into her breast. After he had stripped her armor, he looked upon her loveliness and wept at what he had destroyed. Memnon, the beautiful son of Dawn, arrived from Ethiopia wearing armor that Hephaestus had forged for him, as marvelous as that he'd made for Achilles. Once again, Zeus placed Achilles's fate in his golden scales and once again, the other fate proved heavier; Memnon fell to Achilles's spear.

Achilles seemed to be invincible. All this time, however, the Fates were inexorably drawing him closer to death, cackling at the cleverness of the plan they were devising—for killing Achilles was a test to challenge the ablest of contrivers. Moments after Achilles was born, Thetis had risen from her bed and carried him to the Styx, knowing that the river's waters would make his mortal flesh as impenetrable as that of the gods. Gently holding Achilles upside down by his right ankle, Thetis dipped him into the river's water, so quickly and deftly that he never even cried.

Thetis knew that Achilles had been fated to die at Troy but she allowed herself to hope that the Fates might be confounded, just once, thanks to what she'd done. Each time that Achilles returned safely from battle, her hope grew stronger. But the day dawned when the Fates' scheme came to fruition. Achilles led the Myrmidons all the way to the Scaean Gate and, tasting victory, boasted that he would single-handedly bring down the walls of Troy. He turned to find himself confronting Paris—the seducer, the peacock, the coward—surely an easy foe to defeat. Except that Paris wasn't really Paris. Apollo, offended by Achilles's swaggering boast, had abruptly plucked Paris off the battlefield and taken on his form.

Apollo, who knew all things present, future and past, was well aware of what Thetis had done when Achilles was newly born. He was also aware that there was a small spot at the back of Achilles's right ankle that Thetis's fingers had inadvertently kept dry and that was therefore vulnerable. Apollo took careful aim at this spot and let fly his arrow. It pierced its target. Achilles sank to his knees with a cry of astonishment. Moments later, his soul fluttered from his body.

The field fell silent. Everyone was amazed by what they'd just seen: the worst of the Trojans had slain the best of the Greeks! Glaucus, a Lycian ally of the Trojans, broke the spell by darting forward to strip the body of its glorious armor, but Glaucus quickly died on the spear of Telamonian Ajax. Achilles, and his armor, were carried safely back to the Greek camp.

The funeral was magnificent. The voices of the Nereids, who joined Thetis in mourning her son, keened eerily along the seashore. The Muses sang a dirge of such unbearable grief that mortals wept and shore grasses bent their heads to the sand. For seventeen days, the mourning continued; on the eighteenth day, the pyre was lit. When it had done its work, the Greeks gathered Achilles's bones, anointed them with wine and oil and placed them in the golden amphora that already held Patroclus's bones. Over the amphora they heaped a mound of earth that rose so high above the plain that it was visible to sailors at sea.

Then they held funeral games in Achilles's honor, with splendid prizes provided by the gods. This was the beginning of the end of Telamonian Ajax, for the Greek leaders decided that, in addition to the prizes awarded in individual events, Achilles's armor would be given to the warrior whom they judged to be the bravest. Alone of all the Greeks, Odysseus and Ajax presented themselves as contestants. In a secret vote, the leaders chose Odysseus.

Humiliated, Ajax descended into wrathful madness. That night, he struck out against the leaders who had robbed him of his prize, beating them, whipping them and killing several, including Agamemnon and Menelaus. He bound Odysseus and dragged him back to his shelter to kill later, at his leisure.

Or such, at least, was Ajax's delusion. When he began his murderous rampage, Athena had cast a mist over his eyes and steered him towards the sheep and cows that the Greeks kept penned nearby. The poor animals bleated and bellowed in distress as Ajax pummeled them with the flat of his sword and then slit their throats with its edge. The next morning, when Athena cleared the mist from Ajax's eyes, he found himself covered by the blood of butchered animals. A wounded ram was trussed up in the corner of his shelter, where he thought he'd left Odysseus.

His shame was profound, beyond expunging. That night, he planted upright in the sand a sword that Hector had once given him in admiration of his warcraft, and cast himself sideways upon its blade, piercing his heart through the soft flesh under his arm.

Agamemnon and Menelaus forbade the Greeks to bury Ajax, but Odysseus spoke out against them, arguing that anger must not be carried past the limit set by death. Ajax was denied the glory of a pyre, but he was buried, at least, beneath the earth.

119
NEOPTOLEMUS AND PHILOCTETES

The war continued. Calchas took the omens and announced that the Greeks would not be able to capture the city without the help of Helenus, a son of Priam and the best of the Trojan warriors now that Hector was dead. It wasn't Helenus's warcraft that made him indispensable, however. When Helenus was a child, he'd fallen asleep in the temple of Apollo. Snakes visited him that night and licked his ears, giving him the ability to learn what other mortals didn't know. Calchas had discerned that Helenus—and Helenus alone—knew what had to happen before Troy would fall.

And so Odysseus ambushed Helenus and marched him back to the Greek camp. Understanding that Troy was doomed, Helenus bargained with the leaders: he'd reveal what he knew if they swore to spare him when the city fell. When they'd done so, Helenus told them three things. The first was that Neoptolemus, a son whom Achilles had fathered during the time he spent among King Lyco-medes's daughters, had to be fetched from the island of Scyros. Odysseus and Phoenix made the journey and found Neoptolemus eager to finish what his father had begun. Ignoring the pleas of his mother and grandfather, the young man accompanied them back to Troy.

The second thing the Greeks needed, said Helenus, was the great bow that had once belonged to Heracles—the very bow, in fact, with which Heracles himself had once conquered Troy after Priam's father, Laomedon, had cheated him of promised wages. Obtaining this bow would require not only a journey but careful strategizing, for the bow had a complicated history. When Heracles had real-ized that he'd been fatally poisoned by the gall of the Hydra, he'd climbed upon a pyre and begged his companions to burn him alive before he went mad and killed them all. Only Philoctetes had been loyal enough to light the fire and with Heracles's last breath, he had commanded his son to give Philoctetes his bow and arrows. Philoctetes carried these with him when he sailed for Troy, leading a contigent from his kingdom in Thessaly.

Philoctetes's journey had been interrupted, however. Midway across the Aegean, when the fleet paused to sacrifice to Apollo, Philoctetes was bitten on the foot by a viper that lurked near the altar. The wound festered and stank; soon, no one could bear to be near Philoctetes and no sacrifices could be made to the gods, so vile was the ooze that dripped from his wound and so ill-omened were his ghastly cries of pain. One night, after Philoctetes had fallen into an exhausted sleep, Agamemnon, Menelaus and Odysseus had lifted him into a small boat and ordered some of the men to row him ashore to a deserted part of Lemnos and leave him there, with nothing more than a handful of food and the great bow. For nine years, Philoctetes survived there alone. Winter and summer, a cave was his home and a pallet of leaves was his bed. The bow doubled as a way of supplementing his meager diet with small game and as a crutch with which he dragged himself from place to place.

Now Odysseus set out to obtain that bow, taking Neoptolemus along as bait for the trap he'd devised. Achilles and Philoctetes had been dear to one another; Odysseus wagered that Achilles's son would be the one Greek whom Philoctetes might trust. He carefully coached Neoptolemus in the part he was to play. He must pretend to be on his way home from Troy, having left the war in anger over the Greek leaders' awarding of his father's armor to Odysseus. A shared hatred of the leaders, Odysseus wagered, would help to forge a bond of friendship between the two men. Then, Neoptolemus was to lure Philoctetes aboard his ship by falsely promising to take him back to Thessaly.

But the ruse foundered. Neoptolemus won Philoctetes's confidence—indeed, Philoctetes gave Neoptolemus the great bow to guard while he slept—but Neoptolemus, who was too young to carry out deceit with a light heart, faltered and confessed the truth. Odysseus emerged from his hiding place, then, and tried to force Philoctetes aboard ship, but Philoctetes would not go. And Neoptolemus, refusing to abandon Philoctetes, prepared to defend him against Odysseus.

Suddenly, Heracles descended from the heavens. He ordered Philoctetes to go to Troy, carrying the great bow, and commanded Neoptolemus to accompany him. There, Heracles promised, Asclepius himself would heal Philoctetes's wound. Once cured, Heracles continued, Philoctetes would avenge Achilles by slaying Paris and himself be judged the best of the Greek warriors. Sweeping across the battlefield together, Achilles's son and Achilles's friend would turn the war in the Greeks' favor. Philoctetes and Neoptolemus obediently sailed to Troy and everything that Heracles foretold came to pass.

The third thing that Helenus told the Greeks they must do to win the war was to steal the Palladium, an ancient image of Athena that had fallen from the sky soon after Troy was founded. For many years, it had served as a talisman, protecting the city. Odysseus volunteered to sneak into Troy and get the lay of the land, so that they might come up with a scheme. He ordered his slaves to beat him savagely until his body was pitiably bruised and then he dressed himself in shabby rags. Limping through the city gates disguised as a beggar, he peered around with his sly eyes.

But other eyes were sly as well. Helen spotted Odysseus hobbling through the city and invited him back to her rooms to receive alms. Once there, she confronted him with his true identity. Swearing that she wished nothing more than to escape from Troy and return to Greece, she helped him concoct a way to steal the Palladium. That night, Odysseus and Diomedes crept into Troy through its sewer system and did just that.

Having met all three of the requirements that Helenus had revealed, the Greeks were finally poised to conquer Troy. Nonetheless, the war dragged on. The leaders realized that some final stratagem was necessary.

120
THE HORSE

There was almost no light in the belly of the great horse; the workmen had joined the planks together exceedingly well. That wasn't really surprising, Menelaus mused, given that they were shipbuilders by trade, brought along on this blighted quest to service the fleet and only pressed into other tasks as the years wore on. They'd been keen to put their real talents to work when Odysseus came up with his idea.

Menelaus peered through the gloom towards the spot where he thought Odysseus had been sitting when the final panel was put into place, cutting off the sun. He imagined that he saw the faint gleam of two eyes peering back, but he knew that more than a day of darkness had skewed his internal compass; he might really be looking at any of the other leaders who'd been sealed up in there with him, or at nothing at all. Fatigue had diminished all of his senses but one: the smell of fear and sweat and worse than fear and sweat was more oppressive than the darkness itself.

Now and then, he'd been able to hear what was going on outside. First, it had been the Trojans, discovering the horse where the Greeks had left it on the beach. "A gift for some god?" they wondered. "A war engine?" "Why didn't they take it with them?" "Too big to drag onto a ship, I guess." And then Sinon, the collaborator whom the Greeks had beaten to look as pitiable as possible, emerged from the bushes and spoke the words they'd coached him to say. "The Greek leaders—those bastards!—left it as a sacrifice for Athena, in hopes of a safe return home. They meant to offer *me* as a sacrifice, too, but I escaped. They hoped it would be too large for you to pull into your own city, stealing their luck."

Murmurs of a debate followed, and then suddenly the sickening thud of a spear hitting the horse's flank. "I fear Greeks even when they come bearing gifts!" shouted a resonant voice. The man—it sounded like the one named Laocoön, Menelaus thought, whom he'd heard shouting commands on the battlefield over the years— was met with jeers of derision from some people and cries of support from others. Then all at once there were horrified screams. Menelaus heard voices shouting, "Sea!" and "Serpents!" Laocoön cried, "My sons!" his voice carrying above the others until it suddenly dissolved into an inarticulate, high-pitched shriek. It reminded Menelaus of the noises that he'd sometimes heard mangled men making on the battlefield. The crowd fell silent.

When the debate resumed, the conversation was so halting and muted that Menelaus couldn't hear much of what was being said. Eventually, the horse lurched forward and they were traveling: through the city gates, he hoped, and not towards some cliff over which the horse would be pushed with all of them still inside. Finally, the rumble of wheels on paving stones reassured him and shortly after that the front of the thing pitched upwards—the men inside had to brace themselves, lest they slide towards the tail and give the game away with clattering armor. Hinges creaked and the horse, with its secret cargo, passed into Troy.

That night, the Trojans celebrated what they assumed was their good fortune. After ten years of grief and deprivation, of too many funerals and too little food, the ghastly war was finally over. They sang and danced and ate and drank, depleting their carefully rationed stores. They brought out the goats that the city still kept, retained past their prime for the small bits of milk and cheese they could produce, and sacrificed them on the altars of the gods. They draped fillets of wool around the neck of the great horse and burned incense at its base as if it, too, were a god.

The men inside the horse waited silently, except for a terrible moment when some god drove Helen to approach the door that was hidden in the horse's belly, exactly as if she knew it was there. Cunningly, she called out to each of the leaders with the voice of his wife. It was a near thing; her imitations were so good that some of the men began to quietly weep. Those who sat next to them pinched their comrades' arms painfully until the longing passed. Eventually, Helen laughed and walked away.

Later, when all the Trojans were asleep, Sinon crept to the horse and rapped a tattoo on its leg. Menelaus opened the door and shinnied down a rope onto Troy's acropolis. The other leaders followed him, Odysseus slinking down last of all. Sinon strolled to the gate, which still stood open, hiked to the beach and used a torch to signal to the fleet, lurking just in back of the island of Tenedos. In the darkness, they rowed back to Troy.

Slaughtering the Trojan men wasn't hard; many of them had passed out drunk after the celebration. Dealing with the royal family had taken some time, however, as had collecting the other women and children.

One person continued to elude discovery. Menelaus had thought many times about what to do with Helen once he'd found her, and had concluded that it was best to kill her there in Troy. He couldn't imagine resuming their life together, side by side on Spartan thrones. Better no queen at all than a queen whom his subjects would snicker about. He didn't want her raising their daughter, who must be eleven or twelve by now, either; what kind of role model would she be? Indeed, even allowing Helen back into the house would hurt the girl's chances of marrying well.

And then he turned a corner in the palace's labyrinthine corridors and saw her. It was unmistakably her—she had scarcely aged a day, although her beauty had a slightly tarnished look. But perhaps, he thought, that was just the effect of her barbarically splendid surroundings, which struck him as tawdry. Unbidden, a picture came to his mind of another Helen, sitting in the courtyard at home, laughing in the sun. He shook himself and pulled off his helmet so that she could see who he was. He drew his sword and stared at her.

She stood and met his gaze defiantly, lifting her chin. Then she calmly released the pins that held her chiton together at the shoulders. The soft wool fell to her waist, revealing her breasts—still firm and perfectly shaped, still impossibly youthful after all this time. His mind went blank and his sword dropped from his hand, clattering on the floor.

She spoke. "Home now, Husband?"

121
THE TROJAN WOMEN

When the Greeks poured into Troy, King Priam died clinging to the altar of Zeus, his blood spattering across his wife's robes. It was Neoptolemus who slew the old man, ignoring his pleas for mercy. Hecabe sobbed as Neoptolemus's men dragged her away to the hut where the Greeks were collecting the women of the royal family.

Priam's daughter Cassandra had sought asylum, too, racing to Athena's temple and clutching the goddess's statue. Apollo had pursued Cassandra once, wooing her with the gift of second sight, but when she remained obstinate in her virginity, he blighted that gift, cursing Cassandra so that no one would ever believe her predictions. She had foreseen the destruction that her brother Paris would bring to her city and had scried what lurked in the belly of the horse, but her warnings had evaporated, like aimless smoke in the wind, as soon as they were spoken.

Now, Locrian Ajax found Cassandra crouching in Athena's temple and ripped the robes from her body even as she clutched Athena's stony statue. Enraged by Cassandra's resistance, Ajax grabbed her thighs and pulled, until at last her arms let loose. Dragging her naked to the floor, he raped her, while his men looked on. The statue, appalled by what it was witnessing, turned its eyes upwards towards the heavens.

When Ajax had finished, his men marched Cassandra to the hut where her mother and the other royal women had been gathered. Each was to be given to one of the Greek leaders to be used as he pleased: as a wool-worker, a farm laborer, or a bedmate. It was announced that Cassandra would sail home with Agamemnon to Mycenae, to lie in his brutish embrace. Apollo's gift, cruel in its tenacity, took hold of her then. She raved of what she saw waiting there: death and death and death again, until Athena finally staunched the dark flow of blood.

Hecabe wept—for herself, for Cassandra and for the other women who huddled together in the gray dawn. The men continued their deliberations, divvying up the other women, now that Agamemnon had taken his pick. It was Neoptolemus's men who came for Andromache, who was standing in a corner with Astyanax in her arms. Accompanying them was the Greek herald Talthybius, his head unaccountably bowed. Over the course of the war, he'd earned a reputation among the Trojans as a decent man; his uncharacteristic posture filled Andomache with dread.

When he reached her, Talthybius lifted his head and told her that Astyanax would not be going with her to Phthia. She cried out in panic; was he to grow up without her, a slave in another house? Worse than that, he told her softly. Neoptolemus had decreed that Hector's son—simply because he was Hector's son—would be hurled from the walls of Troy to his death below.

Andromache clung frantically to Astyanax then, this little sheaf of wheat, this flower that she'd borne, the last of anyone she loved. Talthybius laid gentle hands upon the boy; it would be easier for the child, he said, if she remained calm. In numbness she kissed Astyanax's sweet head and forced herself to release him. Whimpering and peering back at his mother in puzzlement, he was carried away in Talthybius's arms. Neoptolemus's men led Andromache to his ship, mercifully far from sights and sounds at the city walls. Andromache begged her new master to allow the child a decent burial and Neoptolemus shrugged his acquiescence. When Astyanax was dead,

Talthybius retrieved the small body, washed the dirt from its wounds and carried it to Hecabe. Neoptolemus gave Talthybius royal robes from his share of the spoils, in which to wrap Astyanax's body, and Hector's great shield, in which to nestle him in lieu of a coffin. The Greek soldiers hastily dug a grave and buried the boy on the plain where his father had fought.

One of Hecabe's daughters had not yet been brought to the hut: Polyxena, the youngest and most beautiful. Hecabe asked Talthybius where she was. Had she already been allotted to one of the Greeks? Would there be a chance to say goodbye?

He paused before explaining. When the Greek leaders had begun to allot the spoils, a great shout had been heard from the mound under which the bones of Achilles and Patroclus lay together. They'd looked up to see the ghost of Achilles standing atop it, glaring at them, demanding his share and threatening to stop the homeward winds if he didn't receive it. They offered him gold and cauldrons and tripods and robes; they offered to sacrifice more horses and dogs, but he demanded a woman, like the rest of them—he demanded Polyxena, the pick of Priam's daughters.

Polyxena was carried captive to the mound, but begged to die honorably as what she was: a princess of Troy. Neoptolemus commanded the men to release her and she knelt in front of him, letting her robe fall to the waist so that he might better kill her. Neoptolemus had gazed at the girl's loveliness and hesitated—but then he remembered his father and slit her throat. When Hecabe heard of this, she collapsed. Talthybius pulled her to her feet and told her she must go now; she had been allotted to Odysseus.

Hecabe never made it to Ithaca, however. Soon after leaving Troy, Odysseus stopped in the Thracian Chersonese, where Polymestor was king. Hecabe had entrusted her youngest son, Polydorus, to Polymestor's care when it became clear that Troy was doomed, along with some of Troy's wealth. But when Polymestor heard that Troy had fallen, he murdered the boy and seized the treasure for himself. Hecabe avenged Polydorus's death by killing Polymestor's children before his eyes and then blinding him. When Odysseus's ships were out at sea again, the gods turned Hecabe into a dog and drove her to leap overboard. She drowned beneath the waves.

A few Trojan men escaped death. Helenus had been spared, as had Antenor and his sons. On the night that Troy burned, Aeneas had quickly gathered his family and fled the city, carrying his lame father, Anchises, on his back, leading his small son, Ascanius, with one hand and clutching statuettes of his family's gods with the other. His wife, Creusa, scurried behind him but was lost in the smoke and turmoil as they escaped. The trio, along with a few other Trojan men, set sail to find a new home. Anchises died on the voyage, but Aeneas and Ascanius eventually made it to Italy and prepared the way for the founding of Rome.

THE RETURNS

SURPRISES AWAIT THE GREEKS ON THEIR JOURNEYS HOME

122
ATREUS AND THYESTES

The family tree of Agamemnon and Menelaus had a diseased trunk from which grew twisted branches with blighted fruit. Tantalus, who lurked in its roots, had dismembered and boiled his son Pelops in a cauldron to test the gods' omniscience. The gods, knowing quite well what was in the stew that Tantalus had set before them, condemned him to everlasting punishment in Tartarus.

Clotho diligently fished all the pieces of Pelops out of the broth and reconstituted the boy, but because his father's blood still ran in his veins, Pelops grew into a corrupt and ruthless man. One of his crimes afflicted his family for generations to come. Pelops murdered the charioteer Myrtilus, and as Myrtilus died, he spat out a curse against Pelops and all his descendants.

It soon took effect. Pelops had an illegitimate son named Chrysippus, born of a youthful affair. When Pelops married Hippodamia, he told her to raise Chrysippus alongside her own children. With a stepmother's jealousy, Hippodamia begrudged Chrysippus his very existence. She persuaded the two oldest of her sons, Atreus and Thyestes, to murder their half brother. Atreus and Thyestes lured Chrysippus to an outlying part of the palace yard where there was a long-forgotten well. The wooden cover over its opening had rotted; it was but a moment's work for Atreus and Thyestes to pry it off. They dared Chrysippus to lean over the edge and peer down— and then each one grabbed a leg, lifted him up and dropped him in. The splash when Chrysippus hit the water sent a thrill down their spines. They ran away as fast as they could, ignoring his cries for help and savoring the taste of murder.

When Pelops discovered what Atreus and Thyestes had done, he banished them from the kingdom, laying yet another curse upon them and their descendants. They took refuge in Mycenae, the city that Perseus had founded. Their sister Nicippe had married Perseus's son Sthenelus, who inherited the throne, but by the time Atreus and Thyestes arrived, Sthenelus had died, leaving his son Eurystheus to rule. Eventually, after the sons of Heracles killed Eurystheus and his sons, the Mycenaeans looked to Atreus and Thyestes for leadership—but which brother would become king?

Hermes, who was the father of Myrtilus, spotted an opportunity to nudge his son's curse into action once more. He sent a glittering golden ram down to Mycenae, a wonder to behold. Atreus covetously snatched it away and, jealous lest anyone else ever possess it, secretly throttled it. He crammed its gleaming body into a chest that he hid deep within the vaults beneath his house.

Thyestes, who had always suspected that his brother would try to cheat him out of something, someday, had prudently laid a foundation for revenge by seducing Atreus's wife, Aerope. One night, while lying in her lover's arms, Aerope told Thyestes about the ram's corpse that her husband had locked away. With soft kisses and ardent caresses, Thyestes persuaded Aerope to give it to him. Soon afterwards, when the leading men of Mycenae met to choose a leader, Thyestes said, "Brother, would you not agree that whichever one of us could find and capture that wonderful golden ram would be the better man to lead this city?"

"Why yes, of course," chortled Atreus, confident of success.

Each of the brothers ran home. Atreus opened his chest to find it empty; Thyestes returned to the council meeting with the ram's corpse in his arms and was made king.

Some time later, Atreus invited Thyestes to dinner—brothers should mend fences, he said. It was a carefully prepared meal—in fact, Atreus had prepared it himself. With figs and honeycombs, he had enticed his young nephews into the cellar where once he'd kept the ram. He stabbed them there, their cries of "Uncle!" echoing against the walls. Butchering their bodies with a talent that would have made his grandfather proud, Atreus boiled and roasted every bit of them except their heads and hands. Carefully abstaining from the feast himself, he sat and watched Thyestes enjoy his meal.

"Ah, that was delicious! Such unusual piquancy—was it lamb? Ox? Surely not goat?" asked Thyestes.

Atreus held up his finger, signaling Thyestes to wait. He left the room and returned with a covered platter. Lifting the lid, he exhibited the sad remains of his victims. Thyestes leapt up so abruptly that he knocked the table over, spilling the last of the dreadful stew upon the floor. Screaming a new curse against his brother and all *his* descendants, he ran from the room, vomiting up chunks of his children as he fled the kingdom. Helios, looking down upon the scene in horror, pulled short his reins and brought his horses to a halt. Wheeling round, he drove the horses back on their accustomed path, and the sun, for the first time since the cosmos began, set in the east that night.

Thyestes lay low in Sicyon with his daughter Pelopia. He'd swept her along in his flight, remembering an old oracle that he once received: if he were to father a child upon his daughter, that child would grow up to avenge him. On the first night of their journey, he raped her, urged on by the murmuration of her brothers' ghosts. He named the child whom she bore Aegisthus.

Atreus, ignoring his brother's curse, settled happily into the kingdom that was now his and raised his own sons, Menelaus and Agamemnon. One day, many years later, when Atreus was performing a sacrifice on the shore, Aegisthus sprang out from the tall grass and slew him. Now, it was Menelaus and Agamemnon who fled the kingdom as Thyestes regained power. Taking shelter with King Tyndareus of Sparta, they wooed his daughters. Helen, for whose hand all the men in Greece had competed, chose Menelaus as her husband, with her father's blessing. Agamemnon wed Clytemnestra.

With Tyndareus's army backing him, Agamemnon routed Thyestes and Aegisthus from Mycenae and took the throne for himself. When Tyndareus died, leaving no sons behind him, Menelaus inherited the throne of Sparta. Laden with three generations of curses, the brothers began their kingships.

123
AGAMEMNON'S RETURN

Agamemnon's journey back from Troy had been difficult. As the Greek ships were passing the Gyrian rocks, a storm came up. Agamemnon saw the ship carrying Locrian Ajax splinter on the cliffs and watched the Aegean blossom with corpses. Poseidon nudged

Ajax towards a plank that carried him to land, but Ajax was stupid enough to boast, then, that he'd escaped death all on his own. For that, Poseidon's trident split the rock on which Ajax stood, plunging him into the depths of the sea. Agamemnon surely would have perished as well if Hera—who was still crowing at the destruction of Troy—hadn't saved him. Here he was now, home at last, climbing the hill to the citadel of Mycenae. He drove his chariot through the Lion Gate and between the massive bulwarks, then found himself facing the palace.

For the first time in years, he felt afraid. Ten years had not erased the image he carried of Clytemnestra as he'd last seen her, sitting in the back of a wagon with Orestes on her lap, riding away from Aulis. Her black hair whipped across her face in the wind that had sharply risen; her dark eyes pierced his soul like skewers. He'd never meant for her to be there when their daughter was sacrificed. The plan that had dimly formed itself in his frantic mind involved writing to her once they were in Troy with some sort of lie to cover Iphigenia's death—an accident? An illness? With a little luck and some heavy threatening of the men, Clytemnestra might never have heard the real story, never imagined the cold knife slicing her child's throat.

Now, he could see her standing in front of the palace, imposing even at a distance. The heavy gold with which she'd thickly encircled her arms and adorned her neck threw out a light that momentarily hurt his eyes as he emerged from the bulwark's shade. Bedecked as for a celebration, she awaited him. Well, he thought, perhaps ten years had cooled Clytemnestra's anger, given her a chance to consider what bigger issues had been at stake—what their daughter's life had purchased for the Greeks. Wasn't that why the gods had given suffering to mortals—so that they might learn?

As he got closer, the slaves who stood behind her moved forward and unrolled a crimson textile upon the ground, an expensive thing dyed deep with the ooze of sea creatures. Even in the grandeur of Mycenae's wealth, it struck a note of barbarian luxury. It was the sort of thing he'd dragged from the storerooms of the Trojan palace and burned, just for the pleasure of destroying beauty. He stepped down from the chariot and approached it, but stopped short of its edge and stared at Clytemnestra on its opposite shore.

"Welcome, Husband!" she said. "Tread the scarlet path into my arms! How many times have I despaired of this day arriving! How many times did my slaves cut me down from nooses that I'd fashioned in my misery! How many times in my dreams did I see your body sliced with holes like a fishing net! Now, my heart's unsleeping desire soon will be fulfilled!"

"Like my absence, Clytemnestra, your welcome is excessive," Agamemnon replied. "Surely you don't expect me to tempt the gods' anger by walking across something that only the foot of Zeus should touch?"

"The people have long awaited the return of their king; it is right for you to remind them who it is that brings wealth to this land. He who is not envied will not be respected! Yield, Husband, and walk upon this symbol that I wove in hopes of your return."

Agamemnon shrugged in acquiescence to her wishes, but stooped to remove his boots, hoping to at least dampen divine wrath. Trampling upon splendor, he entered his palace barefoot.

Lingering in the courtyard, surrounded by the household slaves, was Priam's daughter Cassandra, the seer, brought home among Agamemnon's spoils. She shivered now, although the sun was hot, and crumpled to her knees on the pavement. Staring blankly at its stones, she spoke. "This is a house that the gods hate, a house that reeks of kindred blood. Children wail for the flesh that their father ate, stretching out hands in which they clutch their own entrails, dark with portents for me to read."

She shivered again and looked up at the crowd of slaves. "Have I spoken truly? Have I scried the tangled evil hidden in this house? Listen! Act quickly! Even now, I tell you, I see a bitch who fawned upon her master but now prepares to strike like a viper; even now, I say, I see a wolf preparing to lick up blood." Rising then, she followed Agamemnon into the palace but paused at the lintel and spoke again to the slaves. "You ignore my warnings; that is Apollo's curse upon me. I know that I walk to my own doom now—there is no escaping it—but I promise you: vengeance will come."

Moments later, Agamemnon's voice bellowed out from within, crying for help. The slaves, distressed, gabbled among themselves, unable to act. Then, the great doors of the palace were thrown open, and they saw Clytemnestra standing exultant above the bodies of Agamemnon and Cassandra, a bloody axe in her hand.

"The thing is done—a man's deed, they'll say, but it was done in a woman's way. *I* wove the textile that he stepped on, inviting the gods' anger. And then *I*, like a good wife, bathed him. *I*, like a good wife, held out clean robes when he rose from the water, and while he struggled, wet in the fabric, I struck and struck and struck again! I struck her, too, this foreign thing that he brought home for his bed. My child waited ten years for justice; now, at last, my mother's heart beats clean and strong."

From the shadows behind Clytemnestra stepped Aegisthus, wiping the spattered blood from his face. He smiled. The ghosts of his father and brothers had been laid to rest by the day's work, too. Now, he could rule the kingdom that was rightly his.

124
ORESTES'S RETURN

For years, Aegisthus had played a careful game. Pleading frailty, he'd stayed home from the war in which other Greek men sought their glory, waiting for Agamemnon to depart so that he could seduce Clytemnestra and lurk like a spider, waiting for his chance to seize the throne. The sacrifice of Iphigenia had been an unexpected boon: Clytemnestra practically jumped into his arms, so eager was she to join forces with anyone who hated Agamemnon as much as she did. And she'd been a surprisingly resourceful ally, contriving tricks that never would have occurred to him. It had been immensely satisfying to watch a man who survived for ten years on the Trojan battlefield die in his own bathtub, trapped by something as trifling as fabric! Best of all, she'd taken the lead in the actual murder, striking her husband with a fury that alarmed Aegisthus even as it delighted him.

Aegisthus assumed he was safe now, although there was one loose end that nagged him during his darker moments. Orestes had disappeared on the day that Agamemnon died. Aegisthus suspected that Electra, Orestes's older sister, had orchestrated that;

she'd been a problem ever since Aegisthus moved in with Clytemnestra, thwarting their plans whenever she could. After Agamemnon's death, she'd become worse, wailing at his grave and stirring up rebellion in anyone who would listen to her. By now, she was years past the age when normal girls were married—a frustrated virgin whose constant anger had begun to make her look pinched and haggard. He wondered what was keeping her alive.

What sustained Electra was the hope that Orestes would one day return. When Aegisthus crept into her mother's bed, Electra knew that her father's life was in danger and that after he was gone, her brother would be murdered as well. With the help of Orestes's tutor, she made plans to protect him. As soon as Agamemnon was dead, the tutor seized Orestes's hand and ran from the palace. Days later, they reached Phocis, where they were welcomed by King Strophius, a friend of Agamemnon's. He raised Orestes alongside his own son, Pylades; the two became as close as brothers. Years passed without anyone in Mycenae hearing anything of Orestes.

But the gods' plans flout mortal expectations. One day, Electra arrived at her father's grave to discover a freshly cut hank of hair lying upon it—fit offering for the dead—whose hue and texture matched her own. As she stood bewildered, two men stepped out from the trees: Orestes and Pylades, newly arrived. Speaking from his Delphic Oracle, Apollo had commanded Orestes to avenge his father's death, even at the cost of slaying his own mother. Should he refuse, Apollo continued, the foul poison of the dead would seep up through the ground, infecting Orestes's flesh with leprous fur and deranging his mind with raving madness. Polluted, he would be banished from communal feasts and excluded from the altars of the gods—dishonored, unloved, driven from place to place until he died.

Quickly, the three devised a plan, praying for help to the ghost of Agamemnon and to Hermes, who protects the dead. Electra would return home and keep Clytemnestra occupied until the crucial moment arrived. Orestes and Pylades would present themselves as travelers bringing news of Orestes's death; when Aegisthus received them in the throne room, they would kill him. Then it would be Clytemnestra's turn.

"How very *sad*," sighed Aegisthus, swallowing a smile when the two travelers announced their news. "Another mis*fortune* for this most un*fortunate* of houses!" He turned to reach for a cup of wine then and the two strangers leapt upon him. The work was fast and dirty.

The slaves cried out for Clytemnestra, who came running, demanding to know why they were making such noise.

"The dead have risen and are bringing death!"

"You speak in riddles, but I think I can decipher them. Bring me my axe!"

Before it could be fetched, however, Orestes threw open the door.

"Your turn, Mother. Come lie down with your lover."

"Wait, child! Would you really murder the one who gave you life?" Clytemnestra released the pins that held her chiton together at the shoulders and allowed the fabric to fall to her waist. "Take pity on these breasts that once nursed you, a drowsing baby."

Orestes faltered and allowed his sword to drop to his side. Pylades, however, urged him on. "Remember Apollo's oracle: avenge your father or suffer his curse!"

"And what about a mother's curse?" hissed Clytemnestra. "The creatures that my curse calls up will rip you to pieces like dogs."

Orestes trembled under the weight of his choice. Finally, he spoke. "You slaughtered one whom it was wrong for you to kill, Mother. Now, you must die at the hand of one who should not kill you." He slashed out and Clytemnestra fell atop Aegisthus in a grotesque embrace. Pylades gently took the bloody sword from his friend's hand.

"Come, now, Orestes. Apollo commanded you to return to Delphi to be purified after this was done. Place upon your head a laurel wreath and take in your hand a laurel branch, which will mark you as the god's suppliant; thus equipped, you'll travel safe from harm."

But Orestes, staring blankly ahead, ignored his friend and began to scream. "God help me, they're here already—filthy women with oozing eyes and snakes for hair! They're licking their lips, thirsty for my blood!"

Orestes pointed at the monsters, but Pylades could see nothing. Finally, he tugged his sobbing friend out of the palace and led him down the hill. In the meadow below, he broke branches from a laurel tree to fashion what Orestes needed and then pushed him onto the road towards Delphi, down which they had traveled together only the day before. Returning to the palace, he kept a promise that he'd made to Orestes by marrying Electra.

125
A TRIAL IN ATHENS

Orestes arrived in Delphi mad-eyed, hungry, unkempt, and struggled up the mountain as dawn was breaking. He ran through the portico of Apollo's temple and into the inner sanctum. There he found the omphalos, the stone that Cronus had once been given to swallow instead of the infant Zeus. After Cronus had vomited it up, Zeus placed it in Delphi to mark the spot that was the navel of the world, the very center of the cosmos. Orestes raced to it now and wrapped his arms around it; as long as he was touching it, nothing would dare to harm him. He did so just in time: moments later, the vile creatures who had pursued him from Mycenae clattered into the temple, gnashing their teeth in frustration. When they saw him at the omphalos, they settled down to wait. Sooner or later, they knew, Orestes would fall asleep and let go of the stone.

These creatures were the Erinyes, generated in the early days of the cosmos when bloody drops from Sky's castrated genitals had fallen upon Earth and impregnated her. It was their responsibility, and their pleasure, to punish people who had betrayed the bonds of blood. Clytemnestra's curse had called them into action; now, they looked forward to hounding Orestes into madness and then death. When Apollo's priestess arrived to open the temple that morning, she saw them squatting near the god's altar and called to Apollo for help. He soon arrived, a piglet under his arm and Hermes at his side. Apollo cast sleep upon the Erinyes' eyes and then spoke to Orestes.

"I've overpowered these repulsive old maids, but that won't last forever. Quickly now—sit here before me. *With the blood of this piglet whose throat I slit above your head, I purify you from the murder of your mother*. Good. For everyone except the Erinyes, that suffices to make you clean. Run to Athens as fast as you can, now, and throw yourself upon the mercy of my sister Athena; ask her for further help. And you, Hermes: accompany Orestes and look after him. Guide his way and make sure that his Zeus-given rights as a suppliant are not violated."

As soon as Orestes left the temple, Clytemnestra's ghost filtered up through a crack in its floor. Blood still trickled through her winding sheet and her face was smudged with the dirt of a hasty burial. Unavenged, she was prevented from entering Hades, condemned to wander restlessly between life and death. Now, her ghost reproached the Erinyes and mocked them for being so easily overcome by Apollo. In their sleep, the Erinyes snorted and whimpered at her words until at last they awoke and discovered that their prey had escaped. They ranted then about Apollo and Hermes, complaining that the younger gods had no respect for the rights distributed at the beginning of time, when Earth had freed herself from her husband's heavy embrace and entrusted them with protecting the bonds of common blood.

Then the Erinyes sped to Athens, where they found Orestes alone on the Acropolis, clinging to Athena's statue just as he had clung to the omphalos. Cackling with glee, they circled him in a frenzied dance, singing a spell that would scatter his wits and rot his body. They sang of their right to protect the privileges of parents and siblings, even if doing so meant the downfall of a family. They sang of their right to enforce justice, even at the cost of mercy and compassion. They sang of beheadings, of stonings, of castrations and impalements. And they sighed happily in anticipation of the feast they would enjoy when Orestes finally became theirs. But then Athena arrived and abruptly put an end to their rejoicing. After listening both to Orestes and to the Erinyes, she spoke.

"Orestes is my suppliant, whom I must protect, but the Erinyes protect relationships that deserve respect, as well. Even I, a god, cannot on my own devise an easy solution to this dilemma. Therefore, I will convene what shall hereafter be known as a trial:

twelve of my citizens will listen to each argument and judge between them."

Apollo arrived just as the trial began. He suggested to Athena that, because it had been his oracle that commanded Orestes to kill Clytemnestra, he should defend the actions for which Orestes was held accountable. Athena nodded her permission.

The Erinyes put their case first, insisting that a child had a stronger debt to its mother than its father because the child grew within the mother's very body. If a child must choose between its parents, the mother should come first. Then Apollo spoke, advancing a different view. The mother, he claimed, was really no parent at all, but only a vessel into which the true parent, the father, injected the seed from which the child grew. As proof, he gestured towards Athena, born from her father's head without the help of any mother—or so Apollo claimed, blithely excising Metis from the story.

The jury was split, leaving Athena to cast the deciding vote. She did so in Orestes's favor, endorsing Apollo's statement about the precedence of fatherhood. Orestes thanked the gods and began his journey home to Mycenae, a free man. The Erinyes, however, planted themselves firmly on the Acropolis and refused to leave. Furious with Athena's decision, they swore to poison her city, blighting its crops, its animals and its people until everything withered and died.

Athena looked studiously at her fingernails and spoke to the Erinyes in a measured tone. "I'm the only child of Zeus who knows where he keeps the keys to his cabinet of thunderbolts—need I say more, ladies?" Then she raised her gaze to meet their eyes. "But surely I needn't go that far. Let's make a deal: if you sink into the earth right here and settle into a shrine that I've prepared for you beneath my city, I'll guarantee that Athens will never forget how kind you can be, when you choose to. Gifts will grace your altars whenever a marriage takes place or a child is born. You'd still be able to smite people when you really need to, but wouldn't it be nice to be . . . nice?"

"You mean that we'd be honored, worshipped, even revered?"

"If you bless my people, yes. In fact, instead of Erinyes, we'll call you Semnai—'Revered' goddesses."

The Erinyes looked at one another and slowly nodded their snaky heads. Dissolving into the bedrock of the Acropolis, the Semnai descended into their new home.

126
HELEN AND MENELAUS

Agamemnon and Menelaus parted ways as the Greek fleet left Troy, each of them sailing home alone with his own ships. Menelaus was blown here and there across the sea before finally reaching Sparta eight years after the war had ended. Many were the remarkable things that he saw on this voyage and many were the wonderful gifts that he received from the people he met. None, however, was more marvelous than that which he received in Egypt.

When Menelaus's ships limped into port at Canopus, near the mouth of the Nile, they had been at sea many days. He was greeted by Thon, the warden of the port, who invited Menelaus and Helen to stay with him that night while Menelaus's men repaired the ships and took on provisions. Thon's wife, Polydamna, ordered the cooks to prepare a feast of roasted ox, heron delicately seasoned with cumin and all manner of fruits preserved in honey. They were given something called beer to drink. Menelaus thought it fell far short of wine but consumed it with as much enthusiasm as he could muster. They dined in a room brightly lit by lamps that shone on colorful frescoes like those that Menelaus had once seen at Knossos: boys leapt over the backs of great-horned bulls with what looked to be astonishing audacity and agility.

Throughout dinner, Thon stared at Helen. That in itself wasn't surprising—men always did that—but Thon stared with the dissecting intensity of those who made it their business to study insects and fish and other curiosities of the world, as if he were memorizing Helen's distinctive qualities in order to measure them against something else. It made Menelaus uneasy; he hurried them away from the meal as soon as he decently could, pleading fatigue. The next morning, they left just after daybreak, Menelaus muttering quick, formulaic thanks and leaving their host standing open-mouthed beneath his portico.

The ships made it as far as the island of Pharos that afternoon before the wind suddenly disappeared. For twenty days, they were stranded there. Menelaus began to remember another becalming, years earlier, at Aulis. They'd had to sacrifice his niece Iphigenia to raise the winds, then—a grim affair, although he'd once heard his brother, when drunk, stammering through his tears that just before the knife fell, the girl had disappeared. On another occasion, he'd overheard two seers whispering that Iphigenia had become some sort of companion to Artemis—perhaps had even become the goddess Hecate. Well, who could know the truth, if the gods chose not to reveal it? He only hoped his men wouldn't remember the sacrifice of Iphigenia and take it into their heads that the single woman they had with them this time—Helen—should be sacrificed as well.

And then while walking on the shore one afternoon, considering his plight, he was confronted by a creature who announced herself to be the sea nymph Eidothea. She said that her father, Proteus, could tell Menelaus how to bring back the wind. Menelaus would have to capture him first, but she would tell him how to do so. The next day, she bid Menelaus and three of his men to lie down on the sand underneath the pelts of four seals she'd just flayed. They sprawled there in the heat for hours—the stench of the pelts would have been unbearable had Eidothea not smeared ambrosia under the men's noses—until Proteus finally appeared.

Like all sea gods, Proteus could change form with remarkable skill. Eidothea had instructed Menelaus to grab him quickly and hang on tight, whatever he saw and felt. So when Proteus crawled out of the sea, Menelaus lunged out from under his pelt and held fast, embracing a roaring lion, a writhing snake, a mighty boar, rippling water and a leafy tree. Finally, Proteus resumed his own form.

"Son-in-law of Zeus," he said, "you have offended the gods. Go back to Canopus and sacrifice a hecatomb of cattle. Then, you will receive what you need to return home."

Thon seemed oddly unsurprised when they turned up again, and insisted that Menelaus and Helen stay with him once more.

At dinner that night, Menelaus politely drank the beer and listened to Thon, who, prompted by Menelaus's tale of Proteus, discoursed learnedly about the variety of creatures the world contained: centaurs, satyrs, empousai and more.

"And then," he continued, "there is the eidolon, the thing that seems to be there but is not, the false creature, the mimic of that which lives but that does not live itself."

"A sort of god you mean?" asked Menelaus, wearily.

"Not a god; a thing *made* by the gods to deceive mortals. Like the thing reclining next to you."

"Sir, you've gone too far in your jests—you insult my wife."

"But *that* is not your wife. *This* is your wife."

A woman walked through a doorway from some inner chamber. She was like the woman Menelaus had reclaimed at Troy, but more so: more beautiful, more graceful, with more warmth in her smile and much more modesty in her carriage. Menelaus turned back to look at the Helen who reclined next to him only to discover that she was gone.

"You are surprised," said Thon. "Let me explain.

"When Earth began to feel burdened by the weight of the mortals walking upon her, she complained to Zeus. He contrived the Theban Wars, which killed many, lessening Earth's load. But soon Earth complained again. Having foreseen this, the Fates had driven Zeus to sire upon Leda a daughter whose face would launch a thousand ships, engendering a yet greater war.

"But because she was his daughter, he wished her to remain chaste. So he made this *thing*, this eidolon, that he allowed Paris to take to Troy. The real Helen—your Helen—has been here with me all this time, waiting for you to find her."

Helen took Menelaus's hand. "I've missed you, Husband."

"Tomorrow," continued Thon, "perform your hecatomb—a hecatomb of thanks, now—and then depart. I think the winds will be with you."

Many years later, when Menelaus grew old, the gods carried him to Elysium, where gentle breezes blew eternally and where Peleus, Cadmus and many other heroes dwelt. There he lived forever, alongside Helen, the daughter of Zeus.

127
NEOPTOLEMUS'S RETURN

Neoptolemus did not sail home like the other Greeks. The night before he was due to depart, his grandmother Thetis emerged from the waves and warned him against it, foreseeing the misfortunes that would befall the Greek ships. She urged him, instead, to lead the Myrmidons home by an overland route.

And so Neoptolemus and his men set out on horseback, pulling wagons that groaned with gold, weapons and other spoils of war. With him were the Trojan seer Helenus and, as his special war prize, Hector's widow, Andromache. Nine months later, just as they arrived in Molossia, Andromache delivered the first of three sons whom she bore to Neoptolemus. Neoptolemus liked the look of the place and decided to settle there. Soon, he had become king. When old Phoenix died, Neoptolemus was able to bury him among the Molossians in a grand style, as his father would have wished.

He thought about what to do next. Back when the Greek leaders had been trying to convince Neoptolemus to enter the war, Menelaus had promised to give him Hermione, the daughter whom Helen had borne to him. By the time that Menelaus and Helen reached home, Hermione was ripe for marriage—indeed, some people whispered that she was overripe. Neoptolemus had her brought to Molossia and married her there.

Several years passed without Hermione conceiving a child. Determined to have a legitimate heir, Neoptolemus set out once more, this time to seek Apollo's advice in Delphi. He and his men carried with them the best of the Trojan spoils, hoping to please the god: bronze tripods, gold and silver jewelry, exquisite vases and finely woven robes.

They arrived in Delphi on the fourth of the month—three days before Apollo would speak through the Pythia's mouth—and set up camp near the village below the sanctuary. Neoptolemus sent his men ahead to the temple with the gifts, to ensure that Apollo's priests would grant him an audience with the god. Just before dawn on the seventh, Neoptolemus climbed the zigzagging road to the temple. On either side were treasuries that rich cities had built to display their gifts to the god—vast wealth held captive behind iron grilles. He gawked and wondered for a moment whether his Trojan spoils would suffice to please Apollo.

The area around the temple was busy with preparations for the day's ceremonies. Some slaves were sweeping the marble porch and carrying fresh laurel branches into the fragrant chamber. Others were clearing out accumulations of the small, cheap gifts that ordinary visitors left for the god—bronze drinking cups and, from visitors who were poorer, clay replicas of bronze drinking cups. The younger priests peddled sacred cakes: the first offering that every inquirer had to make to Apollo. Local herdsmen sold sheep and goats: the second offering, to be sacrificed on the god's altar.

The temple itself was more elaborately beautiful than anything Neoptolemus had ever seen, even in Troy. It glowed with pictures that had been sculpted and painted by hands more skillful than those of any mortal: here he saw Heracles beheading the Hydra with a gleaming sickle; there he saw Bellerophon on Pegasus, sweeping down to kill the Chimera; elsewhere the gods were battling snake-legged Gigantes. From the pediment, six golden birds with the faces of women smiled down with parted lips, as if they were about to sing. There was no rest for his eye: every surface shimmered and seduced the gaze.

Different things constrain each mortal's fate. While Neoptolemus waited to be called forward, the gods' plan unfurled. It was destined that a descendant of Aeacus should remain forever in Delphi's sanctuary, supervising processions rich in sacrifices from his place below the earth, and Apollo now reached out to lay the yoke of necessity upon Neoptolemus's neck. A young priest gestured for Neoptolemus to approach the altar, where an older priest was apportioning the flesh of the sheep that Neoptolemus had bought that morning: some for the god, some for the priests and some for Neoptolemus to carry away and eat with his men. But the priest wielded his knife with a greedy hand; neither the donor nor the god was likely to get a full share. Neoptolemus reached for the man's wrist, meaning to stop him, but the priest lashed out, gluttony clouding his senses. Neoptolemus crumpled to the floor, a fresh offering to the god.

The people of Delphi were horrified. They buried Neoptolemus near the temple and built a shrine above his grave. There, as the seasons rolled around each year, they sacrificed an animal to feed his ghost.

Neoptolemus's men returned to Molossia with the news of his death. The instructions he had left behind commanded Helenus to wed Andromache and assume the kingship; the two ruled there happily, making their city into a new Troy. They welcomed their kinsman Aeneas when he passed through on his way to Italy. Hermione returned to Sparta and married her cousin Orestes. Becoming pregnant at last, she bore him a son, Tisamenus, in whom was mingled the blood of both of Leda's daughters and both of Atreus's sons.

128
ODYSSEUS AND TELEMACHUS

Odysseus sailed from Troy with the other Greeks, but he was still wandering the seas long after everyone else had reached home. For ten years, the waves buffeted him here and there, hurling him towards strange peoples and terrible monsters. One by one, his companions were lost; when he finally reached Ithaca, he did so alone.

It was Odysseus himself who brought on much of what he suffered. He was a complicated man: shrewd, resourceful and resolute in the face of challenges, but burdened by pride and greed. Soon after Odysseus left Troy, his rash boasting had kindled the fury of Poseidon, who marshaled all the sea's forces to prevent him from reaching home. The other gods pitied Odysseus, Athena most of all. One day, when Poseidon was absent from Olympus, having gone to Ethiopia to receive sacrifices, Athena seized the chance to plead with Zeus on Odysseus's behalf. The gods had been discussing the latest sensation among mortals: Orestes had returned to Mycenae and avenged his father's murder by killing his mother, Clytemnestra, and her lover, Aegisthus.

"Aegisthus was a fool," said Zeus. "Mortals like to blame us for their troubles, but here's a case where we did everything we could to avert disaster. We sent Hermes down to tell Aegisthus not to seduce Clytemnestra or murder Agamemnon, but he didn't listen; now, he's paid the price at the hands of Agamemnon's son."

"But what about those who *do* respect our laws and honor us with sacrifices?" exclaimed Athena. "Why must *they* suffer? Odysseus burned many thigh pieces for us at Troy, yet now he's been languishing for seven years on the island of Ogygia, trapped by Calypso, who wants him for a husband. He pines for even a glimpse of the smoke rising from hearth fires on Ithaca. Have you forgotten him, Father?"

"Of course not—I've just not wanted to offend Poseidon, who still hates Odysseus bitterly. But it's time for Odysseus to go home; Poseidon must accept that."

Athena's gray eyes glinted. "Let me go to Ithaca now, to rouse Odysseus's son to do what must be done before his father returns. And Father—send Hermes to tell Calypso to let Odysseus go."

Zeus had scarcely nodded agreement before Athena was tying on her golden sandals. She sped down Olympus and then flew over land and sea to Ithaca, where she assumed the form of Mentes, a Taphian trader who was an old friend of Odysseus. She found Odysseus's house swarming with young noblemen from Ithaca and neighboring kingdoms. For years, they'd gathered there, frittering away their time in hopes of winning Odysseus's wife, Penelope. Each day, they crowded into the great hall of Odysseus's palace, where they lounged on cushioned chairs—drinking, playing checkers and consuming the flesh of Odysseus's herds. Athena spotted Odysseus's son, Telemachus, sitting among them, despondent. When the suitors had first started to call, he'd been too young to object. Now, he was twenty years old; Athena intended to stir in him a determination that would prepare him to fight alongside Odysseus when he returned.

When Athena entered the hall disguised as Mentes, Telemachus rose to welcome his visitor. He carried a comfortable chair to a corner, well away from the suitors' noise, and spread upon it an embroidered cloth before inviting his visitor to sit down. A slave fetched a jug of water so that Mentes could wash his hands. Others brought bread, meat and wine. After Mentes had eaten, he asked

Telemachus who the young men were and why they'd gathered. When he heard the answer, he was outraged.

"Telemachus, allow me, as an old friend of your father's, to advise you. Hire a sturdy, twenty-oared ship and visit Nestor and Menelaus, who may have news of Odysseus. If you hear that he's nearly home, then bide your time. The two of you can rid the house of these parasites together. But if they tell you that Odysseus is dead, build a tomb and honor him with a fine funeral. Give your mother to a new husband and then calculate how you might best kill the remaining suitors—openly or through guile. Perhaps you've heard about the glory that Orestes won by avenging his father's murder? You, too, must win glory through your actions."

Telemachus thanked Mentes and urged him to stay, but the disguised goddess flew away like a bird, astonishing Telemachus. When he realized that his visitor had been divine, courage filled his heart.

Soon, the bard struck up a song to entertain the suitors, narrating the Greeks' departure from Troy. Penelope hastened down from her chamber then, weeping behind her shimmering veil, and begged him to sing something different—something that wouldn't remind her of Odysseus. But Telemachus rebuked his mother; as long as his father was absent, he said, he was master and such matters were his to decide. She should return to her loom. Stunned by her son's new resolve, Penelope went back to her chamber and wept for Odysseus until Athena cast sweet sleep upon her eyes.

The next morning, Telemachus summoned the noblemen of Ithaca to meet him in the place of public assembly. Once they'd gathered, he denounced the suitors for devouring the household's wealth and reproached the noblemen for standing by as they did so. Antinous, the most insolent of the suitors, laughed scornfully.

"Don't blame *us*, boy. It's your mother's fault that we're still here, eating your pigs and cows. In the beginning, she promised us she'd choose a husband when she finished weaving a shroud for old Laertes. Three years passed without her finishing the thing and then one of her slaves told us why: each night she'd been unraveling all the rows she'd woven during the day! Well, Penelope's clever, but we caught her—and we're not leaving till she marries one of us."

"I won't force my mother to marry, Antinous—the Erinyes would surely hound me for that. No—tomorrow I'm leaving for Pylos and Sparta, to gather news about my father. When I return, I'll know how best to deal with any unwanted guests who are still in my house."

The nobleman Mentor stood up, then, addressing the men of the city. "Telemachus is right, friends; we never should have tolerated the atrocious way these men have pillaged Odysseus's house. Shame on us!"

And so the discussion continued, without resolution, until the crowd dispersed. Telemachus walked to the shore and prayed to Athena for help. She came to him disguised as Mentor, and offered to arrange for a ship, if Telemachus would see to its provisioning.

Telemachus went home and spoke with Eurycleia, an old female slave who had once been his nurse and his father's nurse before that. Now, in her old age, she kept the keys to the household's storerooms. Together, the two prepared food for the voyage. Then Telemachus left to meet Mentor where the ship lay ready—having exacted an oath from Eurycleia that she wouldn't tell Penelope that he'd left.

129
NESTOR AND MENELAUS

Zephyr whistled up a tailwind that sent the ship scudding over the sea to Pylos. When Telemachus and his shipmates arrived, they found Nestor and his men on the beach, sacrificing forty-nine black bulls to Poseidon. Telemachus hung back, unsure of what to say or do.

"There's no reason to be shy," said Athena, who was still disguised as Mentor. "Approach Nestor and ask him about your father. Your own instincts are good and the gods will help you, too."

Nestor and his son Pisistratus welcomed the strangers, spreading soft fleeces upon the sand so that they could recline. Pisistratus brought them plates of tender giblets and asked Mentor to pour out the first libation to Poseidon, handing the disguised Athena a golden goblet of wine. Athena made the libation and prayed that

Poseidon would grant fame and riches to the Pylians and success to the mission on which they themselves had come—but knowing full well that she, not her uncle, would be the one who answered those prayers.

When the feast was over, Telemachus introduced himself. Nestor wept at meeting the son of Odysseus, who had been very dear to him, but he had no news to share. He explained that Menelaus and Agamemnon had quarreled bitterly as the Greek fleet prepared to leave Troy and that this had split the other leaders' loyalties. Nestor sailed away when Menelaus did, but Odysseus stayed behind with Agamemnon's contingent. That was the last Nestor had seen of him.

"By the way," said Nestor, "have you heard about Agamemnon's terrible homecoming? What a treacherous man Aegisthus turned out to be! Now he's paid for it; Orestes killed him and dumped his body outside the city, to be eaten by birds and dogs. But what's this I've been hearing about suitors overrunning your house, Telemachus? Why do you tolerate it—are you waiting for Odysseus to return? That might never happen! Ah, well, if only Athena loved you the way she loved your father: she'd help you cleanse your house."

"Perhaps she does love Telemachus," interjected Mentor. "And let's not give up on Odysseus; a god can easily save anyone she chooses to. I'd rather see Odysseus return in his own good time and survive than return early and be slaughtered, like Agamemnon."

"Maybe Menelaus will be able to tell me something," said Telemachus. "Could you lend me a chariot to travel to Sparta?"

Pisistratus leapt up eagerly. "Let me escort him, Father!" Nestor nodded in agreement.

Night had fallen while they were talking; Nestor told his stablehands to prepare a chariot for the morning and ordered his female slaves to make up soft beds for his guests. Mentor explained that he preferred to sleep on the ship and stood up to leave, but as he walked away, he turned into a bird and disappeared into the starry sky, astonishing everyone. "Telemachus!" cried Nestor. "I think that was Athena *herself*! She surely *does* love you! You'll be a great hero, like your father!"

When the sun rose, Telemachus and Pisistratus set out for Sparta and slept that night at the home of a friend. On the following day, they reached Sparta just as evening fell. They found Menelaus hosting a wedding feast for his daughter, Hermione, who was departing for Molossia to marry Neoptolemus. The guests were already present—eating and singing and dancing—but when two new visitors arrived, Menelaus welcomed them to the feast. Telemachus and Pisistratus gazed around as they ate, admiring the many beautiful things that filled Menelaus's house.

"Ah, but all those things were paid for with pain," sighed Menelaus. "The winds buffeted me here and there after I left Troy, making me the unintended guest of kings who sent me on my way with the gifts you now admire. I'd rather have reached home in time to save my brother. How I miss Agamemnon! How I miss all the men who fought with me at Troy! Most of all, though, I miss Odysseus—such a hard-working man, and so clever!"

Tears began to roll down Telemachus's cheeks as he listened to these words. Bewildered, Menelaus fell silent.

Just then, with uncanny timing, Helen descended from her chamber.

"Who are these new guests, Husband? I've never seen anyone who looked so much like Odysseus as this young man; might he be Telemachus, who was just a baby when his father went to war?"

Telemachus wept even harder then, covering his face with his cloak. Pisistratus introduced himself and his companion, making Menelaus and Helen weep, too, as they remembered Nestor, Odysseus and other absent friends. But while the men continued to weep, Helen dried her eyes and took charge of the wine, mixing into it nepenthe, a drug that could numb even the gravest of heartaches. She had acquired it from Polydamna, the wife of Thon, when she stayed in Egypt, a land whose soil nurtured many drugs, both good and evil. Soon, the nepenthe was cradling each of them softly in its spell. They went to bed and enjoyed the sweet oblivion of sleep.

In the morning, Menelaus and Telemachus talked again, and Telemachus learned what the sea god Proteus had told Menelaus about Odysseus, after Menelaus had captured him as he lay among his seals on the island of Pharos two years earlier. Odysseus was still alive then, Proteus had said; he'd seen him standing on the shore of Calypso's island, gazing towards Ithaca.

"So cheer up, Telemachus," concluded Menelaus. "If I know your father, he'll still reach home. Now: stay here with us a little longer and enjoy yourself." Athena, however, had appeared to Telemachus in a dream the previous night and urged him to return home, so he thanked Menelaus and departed for Pylos with Pisistratus. From there, he and Mentor set sail for Ithaca.

Danger lay in wait for them. When the suitors heard that Telemachus had gone in search of news about his father, Antinous had hired a boat and lurked in the strait between Ithaca and Cephalonia, expecting to catch Telemachus on his way home and murder him. If Athena hadn't warned Telemachus to take a different route, he surely would have been killed.

130
CALYPSO

A few days after Athena went to Ithaca to help Telemachus, Hermes strapped on his own golden sandals and picked up his wand. Gleaming in the sunlight, he plunged from Olympus into the sea, darting in and out of the waves like a gull catching fish.

At last he came to the island of Ogygia. The air was filled with the fragrance of pine and cypress and citrus trees. Calypso was in her cave, where bright flames leapt on the hearth. She sang while she passed a golden bobbin back and forth through the warp of the cloth she was weaving. A grapevine, heavy with fruit, curled around the entrance to the cave and nearby were four springs, sparkling with waters that poured into a single stream. Soft meadows bloomed with parsley and violets. Birds darted here and there on their own business—owls and hawks and long-beaked seabirds. Even Hermes, a god, gazed around in wonder and delight.

As soon as Hermes entered her cave, Calypso knew who he was—for the gods always recognize one another, however far apart they may live.

"You're always welcome here, Hermes," said Calypso, "but why have you come? It's been a very long time since your last visit."

"If you're truly a goddess, then I'm sure you already know the answer: Zeus sent me. I'd never cross such an endless stretch of sea of my own volition. He commands you to let Odysseus return home."

Calypso trembled with exasperation. "You gods! You bed any mortal you please, but when a goddess does the same, you begrudge us our pleasures. I saved Odysseus when he drifted to my island and I've cared for him ever since; I should be allowed to keep him! But I know I'm wasting my breath; Zeus always gets his way."

Calypso walked to the beach where Odysseus stood weeping as he gazed over the water towards Ithaca, as he did every day. When she told him he could leave, he suspected a trick; only after she swore the gods' great oath by the River Styx did he trust her. Even then, she tried to dissuade him from departing, offering to make him immortal just as she had offered many times before. She couldn't understand why he persisted in longing for a brief life beside a wife whose body, even in its youth, couldn't have equaled the beauty of her own.

That night, Calypso welcomed Odysseus to her bed for the last time. In the morning, she gave him tools and told him to make a raft. She led him to a place where the island's trees grew tallest, twenty of which he felled and planed into planks. Then, drilling the planks, he skillfully joined them together with pegs and cords. He made a rudder and raised a mast, attaching to its yardarm a sail made from cloth that Calypso had woven. When the raft was finished, Calypso provisioned it and told Odysseus how to reach the island of the Phaeacians, who would carry him home.

On Odysseus's eighteenth day at sea, just as Phaeacia rose on the horizon, Poseidon caught sight of the raft as he traveled home from Ethiopia. Seething with fury, he stirred the sea with his trident and gathered the clouds together into fog. The sea threw the raft here and there in the sudden darkness: the mast snapped and the rudder was lost. Mighty waves crashed down upon Odysseus; he began to wish that he had died at Troy. But then divine Leucothea, who had once been Cadmus's daughter Ino, noticed his distress and rose from the waves to speak to him.

"Poor mortal—why does Poseidon hate you so? Here; you look like a sensible man: listen to me carefully now. Take my veil. Strip naked and tie it across your chest and under your arms. Then abandon what is left of your raft; the veil will buoy you up while you swim to Phaeacia. When you reach land, return the veil by throwing it into the sea—but don't look back!" Then Leucothea darted beneath the waves again.

Odysseus was stunned and confused. Help from a goddess would be a marvelous thing, but what if she were tricking him? Should he desert his raft as she commanded, or stick it out where he was and hope for the best? Then, all at once, Poseidon mustered the greatest wave of all, which smashed the raft to bits. Odysseus dragged himself onto a bobbing plank, stripped off his clothes and bound the veil around his chest. Diving into the sea, he rode the swell, kept aloft by the divine cloth.

For two days and nights, he drifted. On the third day, he spotted sheer cliffs and sharp crags—no place to come ashore. A great wave threw him forward and he escaped death by grabbing onto a rock and clinging there, but then the surf rushed back and tore him from his perch. He would have died then had Athena not given him the idea to swim across the current until he spotted a river's gentle mouth. He prayed to the river god for help, and the god listened. Odysseus scrambled ashore—bruised, naked and crusted with brine. He threw Leucothea's veil into the river's mouth and the current swept it into her hands.

Odysseus knelt to kiss the earth and then burrowed beneath two bushes that had grown together. He fell into an exhausted sleep.

131
THE PRINCESS AND THE CASTAWAY

As Odysseus slept beneath the bushes, Athena hurried to Phaeacia and slipped like a whisper into the bedroom of Nausicaa, the daughter of King Alcinous and Queen Arete. She took on the appearance of Nausicaa's best friend and spoke to her in a dream.

"Nausicaa! Your lovely clothes lie all over your room in dirty heaps! Any day now a handsome man will ask for your hand and you'll have nothing nice to wear at your own wedding. Get up! Borrow your father's mule cart and go to the pools near the shore to wash your things." Then the dream vanished and Nausicaa awoke.

She was embarrassed to admit to her father that she'd been dreaming about marriage, so instead she said, "Father, I've noticed that your clothes need to be washed—you can't meet your counselors looking scruffy! And then there are my brothers, who always want clean outfits when they go dancing. There are a lot of clothes to take to the washing pools down at the shore, in fact; can I borrow the mule cart and go?"

Alcinous smiled to himself, guessing what was really on his daughter's mind, and told his slaves to prepare the cart. Queen Arete packed a picnic for Nausicaa and her slaves—wine and cheese and olives—and off they went, Nausicaa holding the reins. When the girls had washed the clothes and spread them on the shingle to dry, they amused themselves by playing catch. Athena, who had waited for this moment, swatted their ball into an eddying pool. Chagrined, they cried out, waking Odysseus. He peered through the bushes and wondered what to do. What kind of place was this? Were these mortal girls he saw, or nymphs and goddesses who would hold him captive, like Calypso? One thing was clear: he'd get no help by hiding. Ripping off a leafy branch to hold in front of his groin, he took a deep breath and emerged, naked and caked with brine. The slaves shrieked and ran away, but Nausicaa stood still; Athena had put courage in her heart.

"Lady," said Odysseus, "are you human or divine? Certainly, you look like Artemis, but if you're human, your parents are lucky and your husband will be lucky, too; I'm filled with wonder when I gaze at you. I'm desperate for help; I came here from Ogygia, driven by storm winds for twenty days. Pity me, I beg you. Give me some rags to wear and tell me where I might find food."

"Sir, my people have always been kind to strangers," replied Nausicaa. "Here, help yourself to some olives and cheese. Then, slough the brine off your skin and put on this tunic, the work of my mother's hands, freshly washed."

After Odysseus had bathed and dressed, Athena made him seem bigger and sturdier and caused his hair to curl handsomely around his face. Nausicaa was stunned by the stranger's godlike appearance, and began to imagine what it would be like to be his wife. She came up with a plan to make her parents like him.

"Follow us, sir, as far as the edge of town and then fall back and wait a bit in Athena's grove—people would gossip if they saw us together. Make your way to my father's palace—you can't miss it. When you're shown in, supplicate my mother first, as she sits spinning wool into yarn; if she likes you, so will my father."

They walked together to Athena's grove and then parted company. Soon, Athena herself arrived, disguised as a little girl, and led Odysseus to the palace, casting a mist around the two of them so that they might travel invisibly. As they walked, she told him the history of the Phaeacians, descendants of Poseidon whom the god had blessed with wonderful seafaring skills and ships that traveled with extraordinary speed. When they drew near to the palace, which was made from polished bronze, Odysseus marveled at its radiance. As he got closer, he noticed it was outfitted with clever devices invented by Hephaestus: gold and silver dogs guarded its threshold and golden boys untiringly held torches to light the way. He passed through gleaming doors and found the king and queen entertaining the nobles at a feast. As he knelt to embrace Arete's knees, Athena suddenly swept away the mist that had cloaked him, astonishing everyone.

"Queen Arete," he said, "may the gods bless you, your husband and your children! As a shipwrecked traveler, I beg you to help me finally get home, after many years of suffering."

Arete smiled, recognizing the clothes Odysseus wore and guessing where he'd gotten them. She was pleased with the way Nausicaa had handled what must have been a challenging situation and sent her daughter an approving glance. Before she could answer Odysseus, however, one of the noblemen interrupted, urging Alcinous to give the stranger a comfortable chair. Once Odysseus was seated, Alcinous, catching a glance from his wife, said, "Stranger, you're welcome here. Eat; drink! And then be comforted by sleep. Tomorrow, we'll celebrate you properly."

The next day's celebration was grand—twelve sheep, eight boars and two cows were sacrificed to feed the throng. After dinner, the men competed in athletic contests; Odysseus threw the discus much farther than the others and would have taken them on in other sports as well if Alcinous hadn't called upon the bard Demodocus to entertain them. In a clear voice Demodocus sang of how Hephaestus had once laid a trap for his wife, Aphrodite, and her lover, Ares. Above their bed he'd rigged a golden net, as strong as iron but as subtle as a spiderweb, which dropped down upon the lovers as they lay together in lust. Hephaestus caught his prey that day, but it was poor Hephaestus who looked foolish by the end of Demodocus's tale, to his audience's amusement.

Now the celebration was nearly over. The Phaeacians would have set sail immediately to carry the stranger home then, had Odysseus himself not contrived to delay his departure. He cut off a juicy piece of pork and sent it to Demodocus with his compliments. Then he called out, "Sing us another story—sing about how Odysseus conquered Troy by hiding the Greeks inside the wooden horse. If you can sing that, I'll know you're truly inspired by the gods."

So Demodocus sang, and tears rolled down Odysseus's cheeks as he listened. Alcinous, who sat next to him, was alarmed and ordered Demodocus to stop. Then he said to Odysseus, "My friend, a terrible grief must burden your heart! Tell us now: who are you? Where are you from and how did you come to our shores?"

132
A GHASTLY HOST

Odysseus replied:

I am Odysseus of Ithaca, the son of Laertes, well-known for my resourcefulness. After departing from Troy, I visited many strange places and met many strange people; I suffered countless pains at their hands and at the hands of some of the gods, who hate me. All the men who sailed with me are dead now. I am alone.

Soon after we departed from Troy, we stopped on Ismarus, where the Cicones live. We sacked their city and killed their men. My companions were stupid; instead of leaving quickly, many of them were killed before we got away. After nine days of terrible storms at sea, we landed on another island. I sent scouts to find out who lived there, but they didn't return. I eventually found out why: the local people had given them a strange delicacy to eat, a plant called the lotus. It robs you of all desire to do anything other than lie around and eat more lotus. I had to drag my men back onto the ship.

After that, we came to the island of the Cyclopes, who are utterly uncivilized—they don't farm, they don't build ships, they have no laws or councils or any kind of society at all, really; they just assume that the gods will provide for them. Close by there is another island, smaller and thickly forested. I left most of my ships in the bigger island's harbor and sailed over to the small one with twelve of my men, hoping to meet someone more cultivated—someone who would give me gifts, as proper hosts do. I took a few things along, including a skin of remarkable wine that a priest on Ismarus had given me after I spared his life. It was so strong that you had to cut it with twenty parts water before you could drink it. Even then, its smell alone could intoxicate you.

We spotted a cave in the hills and hiked up to it. Inside we found young lambs, baskets of cheese and buckets full of milk. My men said, "Let's grab some and go!" but I wanted to stay and meet the shepherd who lived there, hoping that he'd give us even better things. We ate some cheese and waited. Well—when the shepherd returned that evening, we were shocked. He was enormous! Taller than three men put together, and sturdy. Shaggy and unkempt, too. But strangest of all, he had just one eye, staring out from the middle of his forehead.

After he'd milked his animals and seen to their other needs, he rolled a gigantic boulder across the mouth of the cave—twenty-two carts couldn't have moved it. Then he lit a fire. That's when he saw us huddling in the corner.

"Strangers!" he said. "Who are you and why are you here?"

"We're Greeks, on our way home from Troy. Please, sir; respect the gods and treat us, your guests, hospitably. Give us some gifts and send us on our way."

But he just laughed. "My people care nothing for the gods; we're stronger than they are!" Then suddenly, he lunged forward and grabbed two of my men. He slapped them against the floor of the cave, as one does with unwanted puppies. Their brains ran out onto the ground. He tore their bodies limb from limb and ate up every bit of them: flesh, entrails, marrowbones. He drank a bucket of milk and then fell asleep among his flocks. I went for my sword, intending to stab him—but then I realized that we couldn't move that stone away from the entrance on our own. If I were to save myself and my remaining men, I needed a plan.

The next morning, he ate two more men for breakfast. He left for the day and rolled the stone back into place. I thought even harder about how we might escape and at the same time take our vengeance on the monster. A big log lying in the corner gave me an idea. I sharpened it to a point and then hardened the point in the fire. I hid the whole thing underneath some sheep dung and waited for our host's return.

That evening, he ate two more men. When he was done, I offered him a drink from my skin of wine. He loved it—he couldn't get enough of it, in fact, and drank every drop, just as I'd expected. Soon, he could barely stand up. Then he asked my name and, thinking quickly, I said, "Noman."

"Well, Noman," he chortled slurrily, "you came seeking gifts? My gift is that I'll eat *you* last!" Then he vomited, spewing up chunks of human flesh, and passed out on the floor.

I pulled the stake out of the dung and lay the point in the fire until it was red-hot. My men lifted it while I positioned the point just above the Cyclops's eye. Then we drove it down as hard as we could! The eyeball sizzled, giving off steam that singed the eyebrow and eyelashes. Even the roots of the eye hissed.

The Cyclops screamed and yanked the stake from his eye. He bellowed to the other Cyclopes for help, but when they cried out, "Polyphemus! What's wrong?" he replied, "Noman is hurting me!" So they said, "Well, if no man is hurting you, then you don't need *our* help. Pray to your father, Poseidon." I sure laughed then! But the next morning I realized that I had a new problem. After Polyphemus rolled the stone away from the door, he sat there and touched everything before he'd let it exit. The sheep and goats got out, but we didn't even dare to try.

Some withies that were lying around gave me a new idea. When the flocks returned that evening, I quietly tied three sheep together for each of my men and then tied a man underneath each group. As for me, I grabbed onto the fleece of a great ram's belly and held tight. Sure enough, the next morning we slipped out right under the Cyclops's hand! He never even knew we were there! I let go of the ram and untied my men. We ran for the ship and scrambled aboard, taking a bunch of the sheep with us.

Then I did something that I regret to this day. As we were sailing away, I shouted, "Hey, Polyphemus! It wasn't Noman who blinded you, but me, Odysseus of Ithaca, the son of Laertes!" Polyphemus cried out to Poseidon then, asking him to curse me, by name, so that I'd never reach home—or if I did, I'd lose all my men along the way and find trouble waiting for me once I arrived. And Poseidon listened. Boy, did he listen.

133
CIRCE

Odysseus continued his story:

We reached the floating island where Aeolus lives with his family—six sons and six daughters, each son married to one of his sisters. Around it there are sheer cliffs, topped by a bronze wall. We stayed there a month. Aeolus was a wonderful host and wanted to hear all about the Trojan War.

Zeus had made Aeolus the steward of the winds; he could rouse or quiet each one of them as he pleased. When it was time for us to leave, he gave me a leather bag in which he'd imprisoned all of them except Zephyr, who would blow us straight home. We clipped along nicely for several days and were within sight of Ithaca when, exhausted by all I'd been doing, I lay down on the deck and slept. The men, who didn't know what Aeolus had put in the bag, suspected it was full of silver and gold that I meant to keep all to myself. So—the fools!—they opened it. All the winds whooshed right out and blew us straight back to Aeolus's island. I explained what had happened, but Aeolus told me to leave, immediately.

The gods must really hate me, he said, to let something like that happen. He didn't dare to help me again.

And so on we went, rowing until our arms ached, given that we had no wind. After seven days, we came to Laestrygonia, a land where day changes to night and then back again in the blink of an eye. The people—if you can really call them people, for each was as high as a mountain—turned out to enjoy human flesh as much as Polyphemus did. They scuttled my ships with boulders and then speared my men out of the water like fish. Only the ship that carried me escaped; all the others, and their crews, were lost.

We managed to make it to Aeaea, where Circe has her home. Many mortals had stumbled onto her island over the years and she'd become so adept at conversing with them that she seemed to be mortal herself. In reality, though, she was a powerful goddess, the sister of cruel Aeëtes, whom Jason once confronted, and Pasiphaë, who bore the Minotaur. All three of them were children of Helios—a weird bunch, even among the gods.

But we didn't know all that when we first arrived. We drifted into the harbor and spent two days mourning our lost companions. Then I went hunting, hoping to bring back meat. From atop a crag I noticed smoke rising from a hearth fire deep in the forest, but I stuck to my task. Soon, some god sent an enormous stag across my path and my spear pierced its heart. It shrieked and fell to the dusty ground, its spirit fluttering away. I dragged it back to camp and as we feasted on its meat, I told the men about the smoke I'd seen. Terror seized them—their recent experiences had made them utterly afraid of strangers.

Nonetheless, I sent Eurylochus and some others out to investigate. He returned a few hours later, all alone. He said they'd found a house in a clearing. As they approached it, wolves and lions had loped out to meet them, scaring them half to death. Later, I learned that these were humans whom Circe had transformed with her wicked drugs—the poor souls were just desperate for company of their own kind. Then they heard a woman singing inside the house and glimpsed her through a window as she passed back and forth in front of her loom, weaving an intricate textile. When they called out to her, she opened the doors and invited them in. Most of the men entered—she looked completely harmless, after all—but Eurylochus hung back in the shadows, fearing a trick, and watched everything that happened through the window. The woman made a drink for the men out of barley, cheese, honey and wine, but she must have also mixed baneful drugs into it, for after they drank it, she tapped them on the heads with a wand and snap! They vanished. Eurylochus had run all the way back to the ship, weeping with fright.

I immediately set out to recover my men. As I was walking through the woods, suddenly out of nowhere there appeared a handsome young man carrying a golden wand, who introduced himself as Hermes. He warned me that I didn't know what I was getting into; the woman was Circe, an accomplished magician, and she'd changed my men into swine. Well—they had the *bodies* of swine, anyway, and the grunting *voices* of swine, but inside, their minds were still human, he explained—the horror of how that must feel makes me shudder.

Hermes pointed to the ground nearby, where there was a plant called moly that he said would protect me against Circe's magic. Its flower is white as milk but its root is black as night. Humans aren't strong enough to dig it up themselves, he explained, so he bent over and pulled it out of the soil for me. Everything is easy for the gods, I guess! I tucked it into my tunic and then he told me exactly what to do. When Circe approached me with her wand, I was to pull out my sword and rush at her. Circe would then invite me into her bed, and I should accept, but only after I'd made her swear a great oath not to emasculate me once I was naked. She'd know exactly who I was, Hermes added; he'd warned her over the years that I'd show up at her door, eventually. She'd relish a contest of wits with me and I'd better focus on what I was doing.

I did everything he told me to and it all went according to plan. I kept my head, although frankly, I was dazzled by Circe's beauty. She had hair that shone like polished ebony and eyes that glinted gold. And she moved in a way that was *human*—what I mean is that, although she was divine, she moved as naturally in our world as we do. Not all the gods are like that: even when they disguise themselves as one of us, you can usually tell.

While we enjoyed ourselves in bed, her attendants prepared a feast. I couldn't eat a bite, though, for I was remembering my poor men, who were still swine. Circe led me to the pigsty and let me watch, as she touched each of them with her wand. Their bristly hair vanished and suddenly the men looked just like they had before, only younger and better. They embraced me and I wept. I went back to the ship and got the rest of the men—except for Eurylochus, who utterly refused to return to Circe's house. We stayed with her for a year, feasting every day. Each night, I slept by Circe's side. I might have stayed forever, had my men not reminded me, finally, that we were supposed to be on our way home.

When I asked Circe to help us get back to Ithaca, she said something that broke my heart: the gods had decreed that before going home, I had to visit Hades and speak with the ghost of Tiresias, the Theban seer.

134
VISITING THE DEAD

Odysseus continued his story:

Circe explained how I would accomplish this.

"Raise your sail and let the ship steer itself: Boreas will carry you to the edge of Ocean's stream where the Cimmerians live, a people forever cloaked in mist and fog, forgotten by Helios. Nearby is Persephone's forest, where willows bear fragile fruit and tall poplars sigh. Take courage there and disembark into Hades's kingdom. Dig a pit near a rock next to the infernal river, and all around it pour libations for the dead, promising them that if you reach Ithaca, you'll sacrifice the best of your heifers to them and to Tiresias alone your best black ram. Then cut the throats of a black ewe and a ram, averting your eyes as you do so. Let their blood flow into the pit. Flay the carcasses and burn them for Hades and Persephone. The hordes of dead will clamor forth to drink the blood—but hold them back with your sword until Tiresias arrives. He'll tell you how to get home."

I roused my men from sleep and told them to prepare the ship. One man was past rousing, however: Elpenor, the youngest of all. He drank too much and then he made himself a bed on the roof of Circe's house, where the air was cooler. When he heard me waking the others, he hurried to join us but forgot where he was. He stepped off the roof and broke his neck on the ground below.

When we reached the ship, we found that Circe had already brought aboard the sheep we needed—well, who can see the gods pass by when they don't want us to? So, we set off and did everything she'd told us to. When the first ghosts swarmed forth from the pit, eager for the blood, I saw new brides and young men who had died too soon, old people who had suffered terribly and virgins cut down in their ripeness, slaughtered warriors still wearing bloody armor. The sound of their shrieks was hair-raising; green fear seized me. I kept my nerve, though, and drew my sword to keep them away. Worst of all, at the front of this pack was Elpenor. I asked him how he'd gotten to Hades so much faster than we had.

"It's simple, Odysseus: after I drank too much and broke my neck, my soul flew down here straightaway. But I beg you now, by everyone you hold dear, bury me when you return to Aeaea—if you don't, I'll bring the gods' curse down upon you! Burn my body and raise a mound above it next to the gray sea. Stick my oar into it, so that future people will know I existed."

I promised to do all of this. Then I saw my mother, Anticleia, stumbling vacantly towards the blood and I wept in bitter grief— but even so, I barred her way. Soon, Tiresias approached and I let him drink. When he'd slaked his thirst he said, "Odysseus, you expect your homecoming to be sweet as honey but it will be bitter as gall. Poseidon hates you for blinding his son, and he'll thwart you. You might get home in spite of him, though, if you control your own worst urges and those of your men, as well. Most importantly, leave the cattle of Helios alone! Otherwise, you'll return alone in someone else's ship. At home you'll find suitors in your house, harassing your wife and devouring your wealth. Disguise yourself and use both stealth and strength to kill them. Then, set out once again, walking inland, carrying an oar, until you find people who eat no salt and don't know what the sea is. When someone calls your oar a winnowing fan, you'll know you've gone far enough. Fix it in the earth and make a sacrifice to Poseidon. When you're old and your people are happy, death will come to you from the sea in an easy manner."

I said that I hoped he was right, and then asked why my mother hadn't known who I was.

"A ghost who has fully passed into Hades must drink the blood to be able to recognize you," he answered, and then receded into the throng of dead. So, I let my mother drink. She was certainly surprised to see me! After I explained why I was there, I asked her how she'd died, and what she knew of Ithaca.

"Penelope stays faithful; her will is strong although her heart is breaking," she answered. "Telemachus thrives. But your father, Laertes, is sorrowing at your absence. He neglects his health and will die soon. That's why I died, too, my darling; I missed you so much that I withered away."

I tried to embrace her then, but my arms kept closing on empty air. A sharp pain pierced my heart and I began to cry. "O child!" she said softly. "This is just what happens to mortals. Our bodies die and are burnt, leaving our filmy souls behind. Remember that, and tell it to Penelope." Then the ghost of my mother faded away.

Then Persephone sent forth the ghosts of famous women to tell me their stories: Antiope, whom Zeus loved; Alcmene, on whom Zeus sired Heracles; Megara, the wife of Heracles; Jocasta, the wife of Oedipus, who was also his mother; Leda, the wife of Tyndareus; Eriphyle, who accepted a bribe in exchange for her husband's life; Phaedra, Procris, Ariadne and many others. After them, the ghost of Agamemnon approached. I didn't even know he'd died! After he drank the blood, he began to cry. I asked him what had happened.

"It was that bastard Aegisthus who killed me, Odysseus—with help from my bitch of a wife. Take care, Odysseus; even a good wife like Penelope can't be trusted completely—and after all, she's cousin to both Clytemnestra and Helen. Don't go home openly! Disguise yourself and check things out first." Then he asked about his son, Orestes, but I had no news for him. We were weeping together when Achilles approached.

"Achilles!" I said. "You must be king of the dead! You were always the best among us; we all looked upon you as a god. I'll bet you wield great power here in Hades."

"No, Odysseus," he replied. "It's the same for everyone down here; no pleasure, no joy. I'd rather be a slave to the poorest farmer on earth than a king below. But tell me, how is my son? And my father?"

"I don't know how Peleus is, but Neoptolemus did you proud at Troy—a brave warrior who went home laden with spoils."

Just then I spotted Ajax, the son of Telamon. I tried to speak to him, but he was still angry about that contest over Achilles's armor and stomped away. I saw the ghosts of other famous men, too. Minos sitting in judgment, Orion chasing animals, and others who were being punished horribly for what they'd done: Tityus stretched across the ground, screaming in pain; Tantalus, parched and starving; Sisyphus tormented by his enormous rock.

And I saw Heracles. Well—his phantom, anyway. The real Heracles is a god now. Even his phantom was enough to panic the ghosts, though; they shrieked and fled when he strode through the crowds with an arrow on the string. He knew who *I* was right away and guessed that I was down below because I was facing the same kind of troubles as he'd had when he was alive. I could have seen others—the dead were crowding around me—but I started to worry that Persephone might send Medusa's head up out of the depths. So the men and I got back on our ship and returned to Circe's island.

135
MONSTROUS FEMALES

Odysseus continued his story:

As soon as we landed, we burned Elpenor and raised a mound above his bones. Weeping, we planted his oar on top of it. That night, we dined at Circe's house.

"You're truly exceptional among mortals!" she said to us. "You journeyed to Hades and back; you'll have died twice when others die only once." Then she took my hand and led me away so that we could talk quietly alone. She wanted to tell me about the dangers we'd face on our voyage home and how to survive them. I listened carefully—although I didn't agree with everything she said, stubborn man that I am.

The next morning, Circe dispatched friendly winds to help us on our way and we clipped along nicely. It was then that I told my men about the first danger we'd face: the Sirens. These are birds of prey who have the faces of beautiful women and voices that pierce the strongest heart. They perch in a lush meadow on a small island, singing a song that mesmerizes sailors and draws them near. Scattered in the deep grass all around them are bleached bones, rotting flesh and shriveled skin—the sad remains of those who, spellbound by the Sirens' voices, foundered on the rocks just below the water near their shore.

As I finished describing these monsters, the wind died down and the waves fell still, as if some spirit had cast a spell on them. I could hear the distant hum of the Sirens' melody, thrumming like the string of a lyre when a thumb rubs up and down its length. I took out a wheel of beeswax that Circe had given me and carved off small chunks, two for each man. I kneaded them in my hands until each was soft.

"Listen!" I said. "Put this wax into your ears, all of you, so that you can't hear the Sirens. But as for me: I want to listen to their song. Bind me tightly to the mast and whatever I say or do, don't release me till we're safely past!" They did as I commanded and then laid to their oars, eager to row us out of there.

As we got closer to the island, the sonorous hum resolved itself into words. "Come here, Odysseus! We yearn to meet you—we've heard so much about your glorious exploits at Troy! Truly, you're the very best of the Greeks! We'll tell you things you don't yet know, for we glean all that happens in the world. Come! Listen! Learn!"

How I longed to join them and discover what they knew! I barked at my men to unbind me, but they rowed on. I scowled at them, signaling with my eyes that they should untie the knots, but they only pulled them tighter.

When we'd gone far enough past the Sirens' island that I could no longer hear their song, I came to my wits and signaled that the men could remove the wax from their ears. They did so, and then released me. And just in time, too, for ahead of us I saw billowing smoke and an enormous wave, which Circe had said would signal our next challenge. This time, I didn't share what I knew with my men, lest they lose their nerve and cower beneath the benches, condemning the entire ship to ruin. Indeed, they'd already dropped their oars in fear, allowing the sea to take the ship wherever it wished.

"Row away from the smoke and the wave!" I commanded them. "Behind them is a sheer cliff, and beneath that cliff crouches Charybdis, an enormous maw who thrice a day sucks down the sea's dark waters and then spews them out again. She'll swallow all of us and our ship as well, if we drift near her. Cleave to the cliff on the other side of the strait!"

I didn't tell them what lurked there, though. High on that other cliff was a cave, and in that cave skulked Scylla, a cruel and terrible evil, a bane to sailors. She barks like a puppy, but she's far from cute—even a god would fear her. She has twelve legs that dangle down the face of the cliff and six long necks, atop each of which is a hideous head with a mouth crammed full of teeth, eager to bring grim death. Her bloated body lolls lazily inside the cave, but her heads weave here and there on their necks, constantly scanning the strait for fish or dolphins or any other creature that Amphitrite might send up. When one of the heads spots prey, it darts forth on its neck, striking like a snake to seize its victim.

Circe warned me that there was no way to avoid losing six men as we passed Scylla and cautioned me not to fight her, lest I tarry so long that I lose six more. But I couldn't bear to stand by idle; I dressed in my armor, caught up two spears and climbed to the forecastle to confront the monster.

What a waste of energy that was! As we rowed through the strait, while all the men's attention was focused on avoiding Charybdis and her gurgling gulps, Scylla's heads shot out and snatched six of them. I saw their arms and legs wriggling high above me as they were pulled towards the rocky ledge of Scylla's cave and I heard them shrieking in despair. Even as she began to crush them between her teeth, they screamed and reached out to me. Of all the ghastly things I saw on my voyage, this was the ghastliest of all. "Row!" I screamed. "Row fast!"

136
THE CATTLE OF THE SUN

Odysseus continued his story:

We escaped from Scylla before she could seize six more of us, but all too quickly we approached the next trial, which lay on the island of Thrinacia. There, Phaethousa and Lampetia, two of Helios's shining daughters, pasture the god's cattle and sheep. Both Circe and Tiresias had vehemently warned me against touching these beasts, however cruelly hunger might gnaw us.

Even at sea we could hear them bleating and lowing as we neared the island and I knew that the sound was putting dangerous thoughts of roast beef and mutton into the men's heads. With a heavy heart I said, "Friends, I know we've endured terrible things, but listen to me now: we must stay on this ship and sail onwards, however much we'd like to stop and rest. Both Circe and Tiresias warned me to avoid this island. Landing could be disastrous."

But Eurylochus—the fool!—rebuked me angrily. "You may be made of iron, Odysseus, but the rest of us aren't! We've worked hard and we're exhausted. Where's the harm in going ashore to camp for the night and eating the provisions that Circe packed for us? I don't want to drift around out here in the dark, waiting for a storm."

The other men agreed with him. My heart sank—but what could I do? I made them swear a mighty oath not to touch any cattle or sheep they found on the island and then reluctantly gave the steersman orders to land.

Zeus sent an evil blast of wind against Thrinacia that night; when we awoke, everything was covered by an eerie fog. We were stuck there for the moment. I made another, longer speech to my men, explaining that they mustn't touch the sheep or cattle because they belonged to Helios. They pulled faces but grumpily agreed, eating more of the hardtack and pemmican that Circe had packed. Well, the fog finally cleared but then we had terrible luck with the winds. For an entire month, they blew the wrong way. We were stranded. After the provisions ran out, the men snared what birds and fish they could. Hunger's bony hand held us in its grasp.

I strode off one day to find a quiet place to pray for help. While I was alone, the gods poured sweet sleep upon my eyes—though it proved to be bitter, in the end. For while I slept, Eurylochus spoke to the men.

"We're going to die soon, friends, and I'd rather do so killed by Helios but with a belly full of beef than slowly, by starvation. And anyway, maybe we'll get lucky and be able to sail home soon: if so, we can build a nice temple for Helios on Ithaca, to apologize for what we've done."

They killed some cattle and burned their thigh bones for the gods, hoping to buy their favor. It didn't work: by the time I woke up, Lampetia had told her father everything. Helios strode off to Olympus to demand that Zeus punish us (or so Calypso later told me—she'd heard all of this from Hermes, who was there when Helios stormed in). Helios didn't give Zeus a choice: he threatened to stop shining in the upper world and move his operations to Hades, if Zeus didn't do as he asked.

By the time I got back to camp, it was clear we were in big trouble. The gods were making the hides of the slaughtered cows twitch and crawl along the ground, and chunks of meat were mooing on the spits. It was gross. And yet my men feasted on, enjoying themselves for six full days. On the seventh, Zeus finally sent good winds and we departed. As soon as we were out at sea, however, he hit us with a terrible storm. The mast snapped and hit the steersman, smashing his skull. Then lightning struck the ship and the rest of the men fell overboard and drowned.

I managed to lash the keel and mast together and rode them all the way back to Scylla and Charybdis. You can imagine how terrified I was when I realized where the waves were taking me! But I spotted a gnarled fig tree growing out of a crevice in the cliff above Charybdis and grabbed it just as she was about to swallow me down. I clung there like a bat till she vomited up my makeshift raft and then I used my hands to paddle away as fast as I could. Ten days later, the gods allowed me to reach Calypso's island. You know what happened after that—I had the great good fortune to make it to your marvelous island and be rescued by your splendid princess.

With those words, Odysseus's tale at last was finished. The Phaeacians sat quiet, spellbound by what they'd heard. Finally, Alcinous spoke up, promising again to send Odysseus home, along with all the gifts he'd received while on their island. A final banquet was held, at which Odysseus toasted Arete and Nausicaa, thanking them for their kindness. Arete gave him a fine cloak and tunic that she'd made with her own hands. Then he boarded the Phaeacian ship and departed.

Weariness overcame him and he slept all the way home, forgetting the suffering and pain that he'd endured. When the ship reached Ithaca, the Phaeacians gently carried him ashore and placed him beneath an olive tree, still asleep, with all of his gifts beside him. Then they set sail to return.

Poseidon saw what happened and was aggrieved that Odysseus had reached home in so fine a style—and conveyed by Poseidon's own descendants! He wanted to smash the Phaeacians' ship and drop a mountain on their city. Zeus, however, suggested something even better. As the ship approached the harbor, in full sight of the Phaeacians on shore, Poseidon petrified it and all its sailors, horrifying everyone who watched. Then he raised a ring of mountains around the city, so that no traveler would ever again be able to visit these most hospitable of people.

137
HOME AT LAST

While Odysseus slept beneath the olive tree, Athena cast a mist over Ithaca, obscuring its familiar face. When he awoke, he groaned bitterly at the treachery of the Phaeacian sailors who had dumped him in yet another foreign land. He counted the gifts that lay beside him to make sure that none were missing.

Then Athena, disguised as a young shepherd, approached him. Odysseus spoke. "Tell me, friend, what land is this, and who lives here?"

"Why, you're on Ithaca! I thought everyone knew our famous island," she replied.

Odysseus was jubilant. He bit back his pleasure, however, remembering that Tiresias and Agamemnon had warned him to return home incognito. A long, elaborate lie about who he was and where he'd come from rolled from his tongue like wool from a bobbin.

When he'd finished speaking, the shepherd smiled and turned into a woman, tall and beautiful.

"To outwit you, Odysseus, even a god must be an expert in deceit! I've never met anyone who loved tricks and tales as much as you do. I am Athena, who has watched over you through all your hardships, even when you didn't know I was there. Listen now. We need to hide your treasure in the Cave of the Nereids over there." She waved her hand and the mist disappeared, revealing Ithaca's well-known landscape. Odysseus kissed the ground in joy.

"Next," continued Athena after the treasure had been stored away, "we must make plans. I'll disguise you as a poor wanderer. Go to your loyal swineherd Eumaeus, who for all these years has done what he could for your wife and son and who prays for your return. For the moment, remain there as his guest. I'll go to Sparta to ensure Telemachus's safe return."

"Sparta! Why is my son in Sparta? Is he in danger?"

"Stop worrying. I sent him to the mainland to meet Nestor and Menelaus, so that he might better understand who his father is and begin to win glory for himself. I'm on my way there now to visit him in a dream and warn him about some men who wait to ambush him." She touched Odysseus with her wand. His skin shriveled and his strong body became stooped and arthritic. She dimmed his bright eyes and grayed his hair. The fine clothes that the Phaeacians had given him became dirty, tattered rags. Then Athena vanished, winging her way to Sparta.

Eumaeus had carefully tended the small part of his master's estate that had been entrusted to him. Odysseus found the yard neat and tidy, with new pens for the swine that Eumaeus had built from stones and thorny branches. The watchdogs barked and rushed at Odysseus as he approached. Eumaeus called them off and invited his visitor to share a meal, spreading a goatskin over a stack of wood to make a seat. He killed two piglets, singed off their bristles and roasted their meat on skewers. Eumaeus placed the meal before Odysseus and sat down to share it.

"This is a meager meal, friend, though my master Odysseus's house is a noble one. Arrogant young men have been encamped here day and night for more than three years, gobbling up Odysseus's wealth in his absence, each one hoping to win his wife as a bride. We're forced to slaughter dozens of sheep and swine each day to feed them! How I wish that Odysseus would return! Curse Helen and her blasted beauty!"

Odysseus ate the meat eagerly, washing it down with wine. He listened carefully to everything Eumaeus said, storing it away in his mind. He unspooled another lie about who he was and how he'd come to Ithaca, mentioning that he, himself, had news about Odysseus. He offered to share it with Penelope and Telemachus.

"Don't bother, friend," said Eumaeus. "They no longer believe a word that beggars say. Too many have traded happy news for a meal and then turned out to be liars."

"I swear by Zeus, by your good hospitality and by Odysseus's own hearth that he'll return to rid this house of its unwelcome guests before the new moon rises. The king of Thesprotia recently told me that he'd seen Odysseus at Dodona, inquiring from Zeus's holy oak about how best to come home—openly or in disguise."

"Would that he did!" said Eumaeus. "But don't tell me any more stupid lies. I've heard them all before. They'll earn you nothing from me; I treat you well because Zeus commands us to treat all strangers well."

Soon, the other swineherds returned and drove the pigs into their pens. Eumaeus ordered them to sacrifice a boar and they did so, busily preparing every bit of the delicious flesh, some for the gods, some for the mortals. Night fell just as they finished feasting—moonless, wet and bitterly cold. Eumaeus prepared a bed for his guest and tucked him in with blankets and fleeces before he set out to sleep among his master's pigs just as he did each night, to guard them from marauders.

Meanwhile, Telemachus's ship had arrived on Ithaca, nimbly evading the suitors lying in wait on Cephalonia. When Athena had visited Telemachus in his dream in Sparta, she'd told him to go straight to Eumaeus's hut when he arrived and that was what he did the next morning, glad for a chance to see the old man who had tenderly looked out for him all his life. When he approached, the dogs wagged their tails and licked his hands, and then suddenly, there he was, inside the gate, walking towards the door, closer every moment—Odysseus's own dear son right before his eyes. Eumaeus leapt up to hug Telemachus, but Odysseus willed himself to sit still.

"Eumaeus," said Telemachus, when he'd been made comfortable, "who's our guest here?"

"He's a wanderer who's fallen on bad luck—recently arrived from Thesprotia. He's really *your* guest—you're in charge of this estate—but I've been feeding him till you returned."

"How can I possibly accept a guest in the proper manner with all those loathsome oafs in my house? They might beat him up, just for fun, and I can't defend him alone. Please, keep him here tonight; I'll send some food and clothes for him so you needn't worry about that. And Eumaeus—dash up to the palace and quietly tell my mother I'm safely home."

Athena waited until Eumaeus was gone and then stood in the yard where Odysseus could see her through the window, tall and beautiful. She didn't allow Telemachus to see her, however—the gods need not be visible to everyone, all the time. Odysseus walked out into the yard and Athena touched him again with her wand, making him wondrously young and strong. The lines in his face vanished and his hair and beard grew thick and dark. His clothes were fine and clean. When he strode back into the house, Telemachus leapt up in bewilderment but quickly cast down his eyes, afraid that his visitor was a god.

"Be kind to us, whoever you are!" he said. "I'll burn many thigh pieces to you and dedicate much gold!"

"I am no god, Telemachus; I am your father, Odysseus, returned to you at last. Athena disguised me as a beggar but now she has restored my form."

Then Telemachus threw his arms around his father and the two men wept together. When they'd had their fill of weeping, the two began to discuss how they might rid their house of the suitors. When evening fell, Athena returned and, with another touch of her wand, stripped Odysseus of his youth once more.

138
PENELOPE AND ODYSSEUS

Odysseus and Telemachus had decided that for the moment, stealth was still essential. Early the next morning, Telemachus set out for the palace to greet his mother. Later, Eumaeus led the stranger there so that he might beg the suitors for food from the feast—and also, Odysseus thought to himself, to judge whether any of them should be spared from death.

As Eumaeus and Odysseus approached the palace door, Odysseus spotted an old dog lying on a heap of dung—dirty, mangy, covered with fleas. He recognized this as Argus, who'd been only a puppy when Odysseus departed for Troy. Odysseus furtively wiped the tears from his eyes and said, "This looks like the sad ruin of what was once a very fine dog—why has he fallen into such a dreadful state?"

"Oh," replied Telemachus, "if Odysseus were here to care for him, this dog would still be an impressive sight. He was a wonderful hunter—he could sniff out anything and he always caught his prey! But once he got old, the young men ignored him and the slaves neglected his care."

Argus had pricked up his ears and lifted his weary head at the sound of his master's voice. Now, having looked into Odysseus's eyes once more, he died, content that his master was home.

Odysseus and Eumaeus walked onwards into the great hall. The suitors were just taking their accustomed places after a long morning of sports. Odysseus began to beg from them, stowing the bits of bread and meat they gave him in an old leather bag.

Antinous cried out. "Hey, Eumaeus! Why did you drag this dirty creature in here? There are too many homeless people hanging around already, eating up your master's wealth. Get rid of him!"

Telemachus stood up. "I'm willing to share what *my* house has to offer with anyone who needs it, Antinous. No god will ever see me turn a hungry man away."

"You stupid brat! You've got no idea how to run an estate!" sneered Antinous. Then he picked up the footstool he'd been using and hurled it at Odysseus. It hit Odysseus squarely on the shoulder, but he remained rock-still. The other suitors murmured nervously at that, warning Antinous that the beggar might be a god in disguise, come to judge them.

Penelope heard the commotion from her chamber and summoned Eumaeus to find out what was happening. When he explained, she instructed him to tell the beggar that she'd speak with him that evening, to learn what he knew about Odysseus.

And so the day wore on. The suitors continued to taunt Odysseus—he had to dodge a second footstool—but he endured the abuse silently, knowing that the moment for action had not yet come. Athena watched it all and her gray eyes glinted with a new plan. Hurrying upstairs, she cast into Penelope's mind the idea of appearing among the suitors so that their foolish hearts might swell with fresh desire. Then she poured sweet sleep upon Penelope's eyes and, as she slumbered, anointed her with beauty. When Penelope awoke and descended to the hall, the suitors were dumbfounded; an urgent lust to lie with her arose in each of their hearts.

"The time has finally come for me to marry," said Penelope. "But I've been the wife of a wealthy man and the mistress of a wealthy household; I'm perplexed that my suitors have been so frugal in their wooing. Where are your gifts?"

Odysseus bowed his face to hide his grin of admiration. What a clever woman! he thought; she's charming the wealth right out of their pockets.

Antinous responded. "Wise Penelope! We'll gladly give you gifts, but make no mistake: we're not going home for good until one of us lies in your bed." All the suitors dispatched their slaves to fetch presents, then—elegant robes, amber necklaces, earrings that dripped with jewels. Penelope received the gifts and sent the suitors away for the night. Soon, she was sitting alone with the beggar, next to the fire.

"Tell me, stranger, who are you?" she asked. "Where are you from? Who were your parents?"

"Good lady, the fame of your virtue and charity reaches the skies. You're like a kind and upright king who rules his people well, enabling them to prosper. So don't ask me to share my story; it's full of sorrows."

"Sorrow is my constant companion, friend," Penelope replied. "The gods subdued my strength and beauty on the day that Odysseus sailed to Troy; only when he returns will I flourish again. In the meantime, I'll protect his house as best I can. For three years, I held off my suitors by promising to marry when I finished a shroud for old Laertes. The task seemed endless—because I made it so! Each night, I unraveled what I'd woven that day. But in the fourth year, a slave who'd been seduced by one of the suitors—the slut!—revealed my trick. I was forced to finish the shroud and I can't think how to stall any longer. Those are my sorrows; now tell me your own."

Odysseus spun lies for her that seemed like the truth. He said he was from Crete and had met Odysseus twenty years earlier when he'd stopped there for provisions on the way to Troy. He described in detail the clothing Odysseus had worn—a finely woven tunic that shone like an onion's skin and a purple cloak clasped with a golden brooch, all of which Penelope had given him before he departed. She sobbed as she remembered these things. He said he'd recently heard that Odysseus was at Dodona, visiting the oracle of Zeus, and that he intended to be home soon—before the new moon rose.

"Alas," sighed Penelope, "I wish that your tales were true! But now it's best to turn our minds towards sleep. My slaves will make up a bed for you with warm woolen blankets—first, however, one of them will wash your feet."

"No, lady," replied Odysseus. "I wouldn't want a careless young girl to touch my feet—perhaps there's an old, trusted woman who could do it?"

Penelope summoned Eurycleia and Eurycleia fetched a basin of warm water. She crouched in front of Odysseus and glanced up at him as she prepared for her work. "Ah, stranger," she sighed, "I've never seen anyone who reminded me so much of my old master! He's about your age by now—if he's alive."

She knelt and began to wash Odysseus's feet and legs. As her hands moved upwards, she touched an old scar on his thigh. He'd gotten it on his first boar hunt, while he was visiting his mother's family in Arcadia. Odysseus had killed the beast as it leapt from a thicket, but not before its white tusk gored him. His uncles bound up the wound and sang incantations until at last the gushing blood was staunched, but forever after, a scar had marked the place.

Now, feeling the familiar scar, Eurycleia looked into Odysseus's face and cried out in joy. He quickly clapped his hand over her mouth.

"Quiet, old mother! Do you want to ruin me? Say nothing or I'll have to silence you!"

Eurycleia nodded her agreement. Athena had distracted Penelope while this happened by turning her gaze towards the fire, but now Penelope turned back and addressed Odysseus again.

"Stranger, my nights are filled with sadness—I cry for my husband like the nightingale cries for her child, whom she herself slew. My mind is torn in two—should I keep waiting for Odysseus, or remarry so that Telemachus comes into his property? Last night, I had a dream. I was feeding my pet geese when a huge eagle with a cruel beak swept down from the clouds and killed them all. Then the eagle spoke to me from the roof of this very house, declaring he was my husband. Now tell me, stranger, how should I interpret this?"

"That's easy: Odysseus will return and destroy the suitors."

"Would that dreams were so simple! But I can't tell whether this one flew through the gates of horn, as true dreams do, or slithered through the gates of ivory, as false dreams do. No—I think I'll do this: in the morning, I'll declare a contest. Whoever can string the great bow that Odysseus left behind when he departed for Troy and shoot an arrow through twelve axe-heads, like he used to, will win me as his bride."

139
A CONTEST AND A BATTLE

Odysseus lay awake that night, refining the plan that he'd been crafting ever since he'd awoken on Ithaca. One crucial element was now in place: Telemachus had removed all of the ancestral weapons that usually hung in the hall, explaining that years of grime needed to be cleaned from them. When the battle began, they'd be out of the suitors' reach. And Odysseus realized that

Eurycleia's knowledge of who he really was could be put to use: she could lock away the female slaves when the battle began, preventing them from smuggling weapons to their lovers. Penelope's decision to hold the contest of the bow had given him a good idea, too. Odysseus grinned again, wondering how much his clever wife had figured out. He wouldn't be surprised if she already realized who the beggar really was.

The next day was a feast day for Apollo, the lord of the bow. Telemachus instructed the heralds to drive one hundred cows to the grove where Apollo's temple lay, as a gift for the god. The suitors, meanwhile, sat down to a splendid feast. Telemachus gave the beggar the same amount of meat as each suitor had received and warned them not to abuse his guest as they had the day before. Athena, however, goaded them into bad behavior so as to further embitter Odysseus's heart. Ctesippus, an arrogant, ill-mannered man, shouted out, "Does the beggar want a bit more? Perhaps something he can use to tip the attendant when he visits the baths? Here you go, sir!" He seized a cow's foot from the meat basket and hurled it at Odysseus. Odysseus ducked and the foot hit the wall.

"Good thing you missed, Ctesippus," said Telemachus. "If you'd injured my guest, you'd have felt my sword between your ribs. I'm not a child anymore; I know the difference between good and evil. Stop abusing my guests, seducing my slaves and making free with my possessions—all of you! Go ahead and kill me, if you can—I'd rather die than watch you debase my house."

The suitors sat in stunned silence until Agelaus spoke up. "You're right, Telemachus. But your mother should choose a new husband. After that, the rest of us will leave."

Telemachus took a deep breath. "I'll provide my mother with a generous dowry and encourage her to choose. But I won't force her to leave before she's ready."

Meanwhile, Penelope unlocked the doors of the storeroom where Odysseus had stashed his great bow and deadly arrows before he left for Troy. Iphitus had given them to Odysseus long ago, in the time before Heracles killed him. Now Penelope carried them into the hall herself. Slaves followed behind, carrying twelve double axe-heads. In the center of each, the smith had forged a circular channel, into which a carpenter could fit a handle. Telemachus had heaped up a long, high mound of earth and tamped it firm with his feet. He carefully planted the axe-heads in it so that their hollow channels were aligned.

"Gentlemen," said Penelope, "for years you've courted me. Now I'm setting a contest. Whoever can string Odysseus's bow and shoot an arrow through twelve axe-heads, just as he did, will have me for his wife."

"Try your luck, men!" said Telemachus. "If you doubt it can be done, just watch." And he began to bend the great bow. Three times he made it quiver and on his fourth attempt he would have strung it, had his father not caught his eye and frowned. Telemachus sighed and put down the bow. "Well, I overestimated my strength. Who's next?" Many suitors tried to string the bow then, warming it by the fire and rubbing it with fat, but each of them failed.

Eumaeus and his old friend Philoetius, the cowherd, left the hall to go about their business. Odysseus followed them. "What would you do if Odysseus were to return right now?" he asked them quietly.

"By Zeus, I'd help him clear out these suitors!" exclaimed Philoetius.

"So would I!" said Eumaeus.

"I'm here now, my friends, home at last after twenty years of suffering," said Odysseus. He shifted his tunic aside. "If you doubt me, look at this scar that you know so well. Fight at my side today and if we win, I'll give each of you a wife and wealth and houses next to my own."

They threw their arms around Odysseus and wept until he shushed them.

"Listen. Once I've gotten the bow into my hands, slip out, Eumaeus, and tell Eurycleia to lock up the women. Philoetius, bar the doors so that no one enters or leaves. Then come back and stand ready."

When Odysseus returned to the hall, Eurymachus was peevishly setting aside the bow, having failed to string it.

"Friends," said Antinous, "this is a bad day for playing at archery, anyway; today we should be at Apollo's temple! We'll surely succeed tomorrow."

"Can I try," asked the beggar, "since you're done for the day?"

"*You?*" laughed Antinous. "Do you fancy yourself Penelope's husband?"

"Oh, do let him try!" cried Penelope. "If he succeeds, I'll give him a set of fine clothes and send him on his way."

"The bow is mine to give or withhold, as I please, Mother," said Telemachus. "And it's high time, anyway, for you to leave the men and go back upstairs." Astonished by her son's resolve, Penelope hastened to her chamber, where Athena cast sweet sleep upon her eyes.

Odysseus stroked the great bow with his hands. Then, as easily as a musician twists sheep gut around a peg, he bent the bow and slipped the string into its notch. He plucked it and it sang out clean and clear. Zeus thundered ominously; the suitors grew pale.

Odysseus shot. The arrow whistled through the twelve axe-heads.

"Time to feast, Telemachus!" he cried. Then he threw off his rags and shot Antinous through the throat. Dark death seized Antinous; he flopped forward in his chair and blood gushed from his nose, drenching the bread and meat on his plate. Eurymachus died moments later, when Odysseus's arrow pierced his liver; his fingers pawed at the table, strewing food onto the floor.

Telemachus quickly fetched arms and armor for Odysseus and their friends. At first, the four made good headway against the suitors, who had only their short swords and whatever makeshift shields they could contrive. But soon Melanthius, a cocky goatherd who fawned upon the suitors, managed to sneak arms to them. The tide of battle began to turn. Quickly, Athena swooped down to breathe new courage into Odysseus and then perched in the rafters like a swallow, flicking the suitors' missiles off course and casting terror into their hearts. The suitors ran in all directions then, like maddened cattle, but none escaped. Philoetius sliced through Ctesippus's chest. Telemachus drove his spear through Leocritus's belly. Odysseus decapitated Leodes as he begged for mercy and his head rolled in the dust, still pleading.

After it was all over, Odysseus sent for Eurycleia. When she saw her beloved master standing among the corpses, smeared with blood like a lion home from the hunt, she crowed with delight.

"Old mother," he said, "it's not yet time to exult. Bring me the slave women who dishonored my house by sleeping with the suitors." When they arrived, Odysseus ordered them to clean up the mess. The women dragged the corpses outside, scrubbed the floors and sponged the tables until every trace of blood was gone. Then Odysseus told Telemachus to take the women outside and kill them with his sword. Telemachus, however, begrudged them a clean and easy death. He stretched taut a rope and hanged the women in a row, each neck looped in its own noose. Their feet twitched for a little while, but not for long. Then Odysseus and his friends dealt with Melanthius, cutting off his nose and ears and ripping off his genitals, which they threw to the dogs. They lopped off his hands and feet and left him to die. They washed his blood from their hands.

Finally, Odysseus said, "Eurycleia, bring me fire and sulfur to rid this house of evil." He fumigated the hall to make it pure again. Eurycleia brought forth the faithful slaves and they gathered around their master, weeping and kissing him. And he wept, too, seeing them once more.

140
NEW LIVES

Eurycleia climbed the stairs as fast as her old knees would carry her and burst into Penelope's chamber.

"Wake up, child! Your husband's home and he's killed the suitors!"

Penelope sat up and rubbed her eyes. "Oh, Eurycleia; the gods, in their cruelty, must have addled your mind. Or do you tease me for some purpose of your own?"

Eurycleia tugged at Penelope's hands until she stood up. "No, child, I'm neither crazy nor spiteful. Odysseus is *here*; he was disguised as that beggar! Telemachus and I knew it was him, but we kept his secret while he plotted to win back his house. I've touched that scar on his thigh; it's really him! I wish you'd seen him a little while ago, standing among the suitors' corpses like a lion, covered in gore."

As Penelope descended the stairs, her resolve was torn in two. Should she throw her arms around this man, or keep her distance? When she entered the hall, he was seated with his eyes cast down. As she looked at him, she thought she could glimpse the man she'd loved, but she couldn't will herself to move any closer to him.

"Mother!" cried Telemachus. "Why are you so cold to a man who's suffered for twenty years? Your heart has always been as hard as rock, but this is outrageous!"

"Leave us alone now, Telemachus," said Odysseus. "Your mother will have her own way of deciding what to do. There are plenty of chores for you, in the meantime. We've killed the sons of Ithaca's leading families; they'll want revenge when they find out. For the moment, pretend you're hosting a wedding. Get the musicians to play and the slaves to dance; let the sound of the party drift out into the town. People will assume that your mother's finally chosen a husband. That will buy us some time."

Odysseus left the hall then so that the slaves could wash the blood from his body and bring him proper clothes. Athena made him even stronger and taller than he'd been when he landed on Ithaca four days earlier. She made his hair thicker and darker, too, and cast youthfulness upon his face. When he sat down again across from Penelope, he looked like a god.

"Remarkable woman!" he said softly. "Your heart is obstinate indeed, if it can restrain you from a husband whom you love. But there's no changing you, as well I know."

"I'm not obstinate; I'm careful," replied Penelope. "For twenty years, I've safeguarded what belongs to Odysseus with caution and cunning; I won't act rashly now. Night draws near; we can talk again tomorrow. Eurycleia, move my marriage bed from my chamber into the corridor, so that this man, if he really is my husband, can sleep comfortably in his own bed tonight, even if not by my side."

"Penelope! What have you done?" exclaimed Odysseus, leaping to his feet. "Even a master craftsman wouldn't be able to move that bed! I built it myself around an olive tree that grew up straight and tall where I wanted our bedroom to be, using its trunk as a bedpost."

At those words, Penelope's heart melted, for she knew that only Odysseus shared the secret of how their bed had been built. She hugged him and kissed his face. "Forgive me, Odysseus! The gods are cruel to wives; I was always afraid of being lured into deceitful love, like Helen and Clytemnestra. I've nurtured prudence in my heart because I loved you so well."

They wept together then like travelers who have escaped a storm that killed all their companions, rejoicing to survive but grieving for all that has been lost. When they'd had their fill of weeping, they went to bed and took pleasure in love and in telling one another their stories—stories of all they had endured and of all the clever ways they had survived. Side by side they lay in the olive-tree bed, neither one sleeping until both had finished their tales.

In the morning, Odysseus went to the farm where old Laertes tended his orchards and greeted his father. Athena mediated peace between Odysseus and the families of the suitors. In the days that followed, calm descended upon Ithaca once more. Odysseus sacrificed a black ram to Tiresias and his best heifer to the rest of the dead. He left Telemachus to run the estate and set forth with an oar on his shoulder, looking for people who had never tasted salt. Deep in the wilds of Thesprotia he finally found them. He fixed the oar in the earth there and made a sacrifice to Poseidon. He returned home to prospering crops, abundant herds and a brand new son, Ptoliporthes.

But one day, a storm brought a stranger to Ithaca—a young man with golden eyes that darted here and there, passionate, eager and determined. Failing to realize that Poseidon's power had deviously carried him to the very place he'd sought, he came ashore for provisions and found cattle grazing in a meadow nearby. As he was driving them to his ship, Odysseus arrived. An argument turned into a scuffle; impetuously, the stranger lashed out with his spear. The wound was slight, but moments later, Odysseus lay dead, for the tip of the spear had been carved from a stingray's venomous tail. When the locals came running, the ghastliness of the error that Poseidon's guile had devised became clear: the stranger announced himself as Telegonus, a son whom Circe had borne to Odysseus after he'd left her island. Ignoring his mother's dire premonitions,

Telegonus had set out to find his father but in finding him, had killed him.

Telemachus accepted his brother as a suppliant and purified him of the pollution that clung to him from the unintended parricide. Penelope, who wished to meet the learned goddess who knew how to turn men into swine, asked her stepson to take her back with him to Aeaea. Telemachus, in whom his father's love of adventure had grown stronger as the years passed, put Ptoliporthes in charge of Ithaca and traveled to Aeaea as well.

Athena never leaves untidy ends on her tapestries. She ordered Telegonus to marry Penelope and Telemachus to marry Circe. When old age claimed Circe's husband, son and daughter-in-law, Circe made each of them immortal, and joined them on the Island of the Blessed, where they feasted forevermore in eternal sunlight.

ANCIENT SOURCES FOR THE MYTHS

By the time I was done writing this book, I'd looked at more than a hundred ancient authors and an even larger number of ancient vase paintings and sculptures, comparing the different versions of each myth I wanted to tell. My earliest textual sources date to the late eighth century BCE and the latest to the twelfth century CE. Most of these texts were composed by poets, who were the media stars of the ancient world, but some came from historians, biographers, travel writers or philosophers, some from ancient scholars who industriously collected as many myths as they could, and some from a satirist who poked fun at the traditional myths. Below is further information about each kind of source that's cited in the notes.

POETS

Ancient Greek poems were originally composed to be recited. Then, at some point, perhaps in the late seventh century BCE, poets started writing down their own compositions as well as the older poems that were already in existence. In the fourth century BCE, some poets began composing poems that were intended to be read, rather than recited, from the start. All of these poets frequently used myths as their subject matter.

Epic poets composed lengthy poems about the deeds of the gods and heroes. The best known epic poems are the *Iliad* and the *Odyssey*, which the Greeks attributed to a poet called Homer. We now know that these poems actually evolved slowly over at least a century and were shaped by many different poets. We usually still refer to them as being by Homer, however, as a convenience. They probably reached their current forms in the eighth century BCE.

Another early epic is Hesiod's *Theogony*, which tells about the cosmos's origin, the birth of the gods, and Zeus's ascendancy to the kingship. It also includes the story of Pandora and part of the story of Prometheus's defiance of Zeus. The *Works and Days* is by Hesiod as well. It focuses on practical advice to live by but also includes alternative versions of the stories of Pandora and Prometheus. Hesiod probably composed these in the seventh century BCE.

The ancient Greeks believed that Hesiod had also composed other poems, such as the *Shield*, which tells of Heracles's shield, and the *Catalogue of Women*, about love affairs between gods and mortal women and the heroic children these produced. We now think that a slightly younger poet (or poets) composed these, but we continue to refer to them under Hesiod's name. We also have fragments from other early epics that are slightly younger than Hesiod. The *Thebaid* narrated the story of the first Theban War. The *Cypria* described what led to the Trojan War and the nine years of war that took place before the *Iliad* begins. The *Aethiopis* starts after the action of the *Iliad* ends and finishes with the death of Achilles. The *Little Iliad* tells about what happened at Troy after Achilles's death, the *Sack of Troy* about the fall of the city and *On the Returns of the Greeks* about the journeys home of the Greek chiefs. Other early epics told the stories of Oedipus, Heracles, Theseus, Jason and many others.

Shorter poems were composed in the epic style, too. A collection of these were attributed to Homer and we still call them Homeric now. Each was composed to honor a specific god, and therefore they are called hymns. The longer of them, which were composed between the seventh and fifth centuries BCE, tell about the gods' adventures—Demeter's visit to Eleusis, Hermes's theft of his brother Apollo's cattle, and so on. The shorter ones, which variously date between the sixth century BCE and the second century BCE, focus on praising the gods. In the third century BCE, Callimachus, a scholar, librarian and poet, wrote hymns in honor of the gods, of which six survive. These were meant to be read, rather than performed. A poem that scholars now date to the late third or early second century BCE, the *Alexandra*, has traditionally been attributed to the poet Lycophron, who lived almost a century earlier. Although we are now uncertain about who its author was, we continue to cite it under Lycophron's name. The poem presents the dark and rambling prophecies of the Trojan seer Cassandra, who was also called Alexandra.

Poets continued to write epics for many centuries to come. In the third century BCE, Apollonius of Rhodes composed the *Argonautica*, about Jason's quest for the Golden Fleece. In the early years of the Roman Empire, Virgil wrote the *Aeneid*, about Aeneas's voyage to Italy and how he made his home there. Virgil also wrote other poems from which we derive mythological information. Ovid wrote his *Metamorphoses*, which narrated numerous myths about people being transformed into other things. Although Ovid used Roman names for the gods, almost all of the stories he told had already been told by Greek poets. Ovid also wrote the *Fasti*, which discussed the festivals held on various days of the year and the myths connected with those festivals, and other poems that sometimes took up mythological topics. In the first century CE, Valerius Flaccus wrote his own *Argonautica* and Statius wrote his *Thebaid*, a new epic about the Theban War. Statius began to write another epic about Achilles, called the *Achilleid*, but left it unfinished when he died. In the fourth century CE Quintus Smyrnaeus wrote the *Fall of Troy*, and in the fifth century CE Nonnus wrote his sprawling *Dionysiaca*, about the life of Dionysus and the god's travels to India.

The best translation of the *Odyssey* is by Emily Wilson. For the *Iliad*, I prefer Stanley Lombardo's translation. My favorite translation of Hesiod's poems is by Glenn Most, for the Loeb Classical Library series published by Harvard University Press. My favorite translation of the Homeric *Hymns* is by Martin L. West, also for the Loeb series, as is the best translation of the fragments of other early epics (under the title *Greek Epic Fragments*). For Apollonius's *Argonautica*, I prefer Richard Hunter's translation. For Callimachus's hymns, Susan Stephen's new edition, translation and commentary is excellent. For Lycophron, see Simon Hornblower's recent translation and commentary. For Ovid's *Metamorphoses*, I like Charles Martin's translation and for Ovid's *Fasti* I use the translation by

A. J. Boyle and R. D. Woodard. Charles Stanley Ross's translation of Statius's *Thebaid* is good; for Statius's *Achilleid*, see Stanley Lombardo's translation. Translations of Valerius Flaccus's *Argonautica*, Quintus Smyrnaeus's *Fall of Troy* and Nonnus's *Dionysiaca* are easiest to find in the Loeb series (translated by J. H. Mozley, Arthur S. Way and W.H.D. Rouse, respectively).

Lyric poetry is a collective term for a variety of poems composed between about 600 BCE and 400 BCE. These poems were often, although not always, meant to be performed to the accompaniment of a lyre or other musical instrument. Sometimes, they were sung by choruses that moved back and forth across the performance spaces in stately dances as they sang. At other times, only the poet, or a single singer, performed the poem. Sappho, the most famous of our very few female authors from ancient Greece, was a lyric poet.

The occasions for which lyric poems were composed varied. A poet might be hired by a city or a wealthy family to compose a poem that celebrated a young man's victory at one of the athletic games, or a poem to be performed at a wedding, funeral or festival of the gods.

The lyric poets frequently wove myths into their compositions. Sometimes, the myth illustrated a precept of proper behavior. For example, when Pindar told the story of Tantalus as part of a poem in honor of a victor at the Olympic Games, he used it to exemplify the importance of avoiding arrogance and excess (*Olympian* 1). But whatever other purpose the myths might serve, they were always expressed in exuberant, vivid narratives. Bacchylides's story of Theseus's plunge to the bottom of the sea, composed to be performed at a festival of Apollo, is thrilling (*Ode* 17). Simonides's poem about Danaë singing to the infant Perseus is heartbreaking (fr. 543). Stesichorus makes us feel sorry for Geryon (frs. S 7–S 87).

My favorite translation of Pindar's poems is William Race's, for the Loeb series. The most complete collection of other lyric poets, including Sappho, Stesichorus, Bacchylides, Simonides and others, comprises five volumes in the Loeb series, translated by David Campbell.

Tragedians composed plays that were performed at festivals in honor of Dionysus, the god of theater. The performances were open to any free man who wished to attend; women did not attend the theater. At the festival of Dionysus in Athens, in any given year three tragedians were chosen each to present a trilogy of tragedies whose plots were usually connected or thematically related to one another (for example, Aeschylus's *Oresteia* comprised his *Agamemnon*, *Libation Bearers* and *Eumenides*). The performance of a shorter "satyr" play that was lighter in tone followed each of the three trilogies. A winner was chosen from among the three tragedians by a jury of ten men.

Tragedies almost always drew their plots from myths, and some of our best-known versions of ancient myths come to us through them. In addition to learning about the tribulations of Agamemnon's family from Aeschylus's *Oresteia*, we learn, for instance, about the dreadful experiences of Oedipus and his family from Sophocles's *Oedipus the King*, *Oedipus at Colonus* and *Antigone*, and about Medea's murder of her children and Phaedra's accusation of rape against Hippolytus from Euripides's *Medea* and *Hippolytus*. We have thirty-two complete tragedies and fragments or titles of about two hundred more. Roman authors wrote tragedies as well, often taking as their topics the same myths the Greek tragedians had used. The only author whose work survives, however, is Seneca.

There were also comic plays composed for the stage; the best-known and most successful comic poet was Aristophanes, who lived in the fifth and fourth centuries BCE. I cite his *Lysistrata*, a play about women taking over the state.

There are a number of good translations of Greek tragedies, but my personal favorites are those in a nine-volume series edited by David Grene and Richmond Lattimore for the University of Chicago Press. Occasionally, I cite fragments of otherwise lost works by Aeschylus and Euripides; translations of these fragments were done for the Loeb Library by Alan Sommerstein (Aeschylus) and Christopher Collard and Martin Cropp (Euripides). Emily Wilson's translation of six tragedies by Seneca is excellent. Each generation (or half generation) has its own *Lysistrata*, updated with timely versions of the ancient jokes; right now, the best is Alan Sommerstein's.

PROSE WRITERS

Prose writers contribute greatly to our knowledge of myths. Historians told myths as part of their description of the deep past. The age in which the things described by Greek myths were assumed to have happened was long before the historians lived, but nonetheless was regarded as existing on the same chronological continuum. In the second half of the fifth century BCE, Herodotus wrote his *Histories*, which focused on the war between the Greeks and the Persians but incidentally brought in a great deal of other interesting information, some drawn from myths. We hear about Heracles, Medea and Theseus, for example.

I use several other historians, as well. The most important of these is Diodorus Siculus, who wrote his lengthy *Library of History* in the first century BCE. Diodorus often assumes that the fantastic people and events narrated in myths have some basis in fact, however much exaggerated. Heracles's opponent Geryon, for instance, was not a son of Chrysaor who had three bodies joined together at the waist, but rather *three sons* of Chrysaor who commanded three armies, all of which Heracles conquered (D.S. 4.18.2–3).

My favorite translation of Herodotus is by David Grene. The easiest way to access Diodorus Siculus is through a Loeb translation done by a series of scholars.

We possess the works of many other ancient historians only in fragments—typically, quotations of their works taken from later ancient authors. These are collected in a multivolume publication called *Fragmente der griechischen Historiker (Fragments of the Greek Historians)*, which was first edited by F. Jacoby and which is commonly abbreviated as *FGrH*. Each author is assigned a number and the fragments of his work ("F") are numbered as well. Thus, the notation Pherecyd. *FGrH* 3F71 signifies that a passage is from Pherecydes the Athenian (historian #3) and is fragment #71, which happens to be about the Ceryneian Hind captured by Heracles. There is no single translation of all of these fragments into English, although quite a few of them that concern mythological matters are included in Stephen Trzaskoma and R. Scott Smith's *Anthology of Classical Myth: Primary Sources in Translation*.

One last historical source: the so-called *Parian Marble*, a long list of events inscribed on a marble tablet that had once been set up for display on the island of Paros. The list tells of important things that had happened in the world down to 299 BCE, including events that we would describe as mythic: the great Flood and the rise of the early kings of Athens, for instance. A translation is available in Andrea Rotstein, *Literary History in the Parian Marble*, which is available online through the Center for Hellenic Studies (https://chs.harvard.edu/chapter/1-the-parian-marble/).

Mythographers were ancient writers who collected myths. Some of them, such as the above-mentioned Pherecydes (fifth century BCE), can also be considered historians, insofar as they collected myths in order to write histories of their local cities. Herodorus (fifth through fourth centuries BCE), in contrast, collected myths in order to write a biographies of various heroes, including Heracles. Palaephatus, who probably lived in the fourth century BCE, wrote *On Incredible Things* to rationalize the more fantastic aspects of myths. Bellerophon didn't kill a monster called the Chimera, he proposed, but rather a goat and a lion that lived near a fiery chasm on Mount Chimera. Eratosthenes (third through second century BCE) was a polymath who studied astronomy among other things; he collected myths about the constellations. Parthenius (first century BCE) compiled love stories taken from myths. Conon, a grammarian as well as a mythographer, lived during the first century BCE and first century CE. He summarized fifty myths in prose, as a digest for poets' use.

The two mythographers who wield the greatest influence over modern books of Greek mythology are Hyginus and Apollodorus. Hyginus lived during the first century BCE and first century CE. He may be the same Hyginus as the one whom Augustus made the superintendent of the library he founded on the Palatine, which would have given him ample access to earlier works on myths. He wrote a handbook called *Fabulae* (*Myths*) and another called the *De Astronomica*, which collects myths about people and animals who turned into stars.

Apollodorus is the name that has traditionally been given to the author of a substantial collection of myths called the *Library*, although we now know that the real name of its author is beyond recovery. It was written in the first or second century CE and makes ample use of earlier authors' works. The *Library* was used constantly over the centuries by later mythographers but at some point its last part was lost. In the late nineteenth century, scholars were able to build a basic skeleton of what it contained. This is what we now call the *Epitome* of Apollodorus, abbreviated as *E.* in my notes.

Other late mythographers include Antoninus Liberalis, who lived sometime between the first and the third centuries CE. His *Metamorphoses* includes forty-one short tales about humans who turned into animals, plants and minerals, taken from earlier authors whom he names in each case. From about the same time comes Ptolemy Chennus, a grammarian who collected myths into his *Strange History* in order to entertain the woman he loved. We don't have the *Strange History* anymore, but Photius, a ninth-century patriarch of the Byzantine Church and polymath, gives us a résumé of it in his *Library*. It's from Ptolemy that we hear, for example, that the Nemean Lion managed to bite off the tip of Heracles's finger.

Next comes Proclus, a fifth-century CE scholar best known for his works on philosophy and theology, but also the author of *Useful Knowledge* (*Chrestomatheia*), a digest of early Greek epics, most of which are now lost to us. It is from this digest that we get our best picture of what happened to Odysseus and his family after the action of the *Odyssey* ended, for example. I cite this by the ancient poem on which Proclus is commenting (e.g., *Returns*), and the numbered section within those comments.

Chronologically last among my mythographers is Ioannes Tzetzes, a scholar and poet of the twelfth century CE who wrote a long and learned commentary on Lycophron's *Alexandra*. Tzetzes passes along variants of myths that we wouldn't otherwise have— such as the fascinating tidbit that Bellerophon killed the Chimera by sticking a lump of lead onto his spear and thrusting it into the beast's fiery mouth.

The earliest mythographers are not easy to find in translation, although excerpts from their works appear in Trzaskoma and Smith, cited above. For Eratosthenes, see Theony Condos's *Star Myths of the Greeks and Romans: A Sourcebook*, which also includes translations of Hyginus's *Star Myths* (= *De Astronomica*). Hyginus's *Fabulae* are available in R. Scott Smith and Stephen M. Trzaskoma's *Apollodorus' Library and Hyginus' Fabulae: Two Handbooks of Greek Mythology*. Their translation of Apollodorus is very good as well. For Conon, see Malcolm Kenneth Brown's translation. Antoninus Liberalis is available in Francis Celoria's *The Metamorphoses of Antoninus Liberalis: A Translation with a Commentary*. For Ptolemy Chennus, see entry 190 in the online translation of Photius's *Bibliotheca* edited by Roger Pearse as part of the Tertullian project (https://www.tertullian.org/fathers/photius_copyright/photius_05biblio theca.htm). Passages from Proclus's *Useful Knowledge* are included in West's *Greek Epic Fragments*, cited above. There is no translation of Tzetzes's *Commentary on Lycophron*.

Orators honed the rhetorical skills that all upper-class men were expected to have to an unusually high degree and used these skills to make public speeches advocating political action or to help clients win court cases. They sometimes drew on mythic precedents to shore up their arguments, passing along, in the process, things we wouldn't otherwise know. It's Isocrates who tells us, for example, that the Amazon Hippolyta fell in love with Theseus. Most of the orators are available in translation in the Loeb series.

I cite two biographers in my notes. The first is Plutarch, a late first-century CE philosopher, historian and polymath who wrote biographies of famous men, including Theseus, as well as essays on a huge variety of other topics. We also have some essays that have traditionally been attributed to Plutarch but that scholars now think were written by some other, unknown author(s). We refer to the the author(s) of these essays as Pseudo-Plutarch (Ps.-Plut.). I cite two of them.

The other biographer I cite is Philostratus of Athens, who in the second and third centuries CE wrote a biography of the first-century CE wonder-worker Apollonius of Tyana. I also cite one of his other works, a fantasy called the *Heroicus* in which the ghost of Protesilaus delivers information about the Homeric heroes. Cited as well is the work of a second man named Philostratus, who also lived in the second and third centuries CE. This one, who may have been the nephew of Philostratus from Athens, is usually referred to as "the Elder," to distinguish him from his grandson, who is called Philostratus the Younger. Philostratus the Elder wrote the *Imagines*, descriptions of ancient artworks, most of which illustrated myths. (Philostratus the Younger wrote another, shorter set of *Imagines*, but I do not cite it.)

There are several good translations of Plutarch's *Lives*, but my favorite for *Theseus* is found in Ian Scott-Kilvert's collection *The Rise and Fall of Athens*. For other works by Plutarch or Pseudo-Plutarch, use the translations in the Loeb Library, which were contributed by various scholars. There is a good translation of the *Life of Apollonius* by C. P. Jones and of the *Heroicus* by Jennifer Berenson MacClean and Ellen Bradshaw Aitken (spelled there *Heroikos*). The two sets of *Imagines* are most easily found in the Loeb series, translated by A. Fairbank.

I cite other prose authors who don't fit any of the categories above. One is the Athenian philosopher Plato, who lived during the fifth and fourth centuries BCE. He occasionally referred to or retold traditional myths in the course of making his philosophical points. Cicero was another philosopher, rhetorician and all-around polymath. He was Roman and lived in the first century BCE. Two other prose authors are the travel writers Strabo (first century BCE – first century CE) and Pausanias (second century CE). Strabo, who was born in what we now call Turkey, traveled from Italy to Ethiopia, collecting data about local history, geography and customs. He also studied at the Library in Alexandria. He tucked all sorts of interesting stories and information into his lengthy *Geographica*. Pausanias traveled throughout Greece, collecting information from local peoples about their history, geography, customs and myths and discussed them in his *Description of Greece*.

There is one satirist on my list: the first-century CE Lucian. Religious beliefs and the myths that undergirded them were frequent targets of his wit. Aelian (second and third centuries CE) was a teacher of rhetoric by profession but wrote learnedly on a variety of topics, drawing on his vast collection of anecdotal knowledge. *On the Nature of Animals* is meant to inform readers about what we would now call natural history, but also draws moral lessons from the lives of animals. The *Various History* is a miscellany of curious anecdotes, including some variations of myths and some information on ancient religion.

Finally, there are the scholiasts, who wrote commentaries on earlier works of literature, in the course of which they passed along many myths—often, however, in frustratingly abbreviated forms. The earliest scholiasts date to the fifth century BCE but most of them are much later. Tzetzes, whom I mentioned above in my discussion of mythographers, was a scholiast. Similar to scholiasts are the lexicographers, who composed works akin to our dictionaries and encyclopedias. I cite three of them: Hesychius, from the fifth or sixth century CE; *Suidas*—which is actually the name of the lexicon, rather than that of its unknown author—from the tenth century CE; and the *Etymologicum Magnum*, from the twelfth century (also the name of the lexicon itself).

New translations of the dialogues of both Plato and Cicero frequently appear. Peter Levi's two-volume translation of Pausanias is good. For Strabo, see the Loeb translation by Horace Leonard Jones; for Aelian, the Loeb translations of N. G. Wilson (*Various History*) and A. F. Schofield (*On the Nature of Animals*). There are no translations of the scholiasts or lexicographers.

Some final, technical points on using ancient Greek sources to tell modern stories. There are two ways of transliterating Greek names into our alphabet. In most cases, what is called the Latinate version produces names that are more familiar to us and so I have used that: Cronus (instead of Kronos), Oedipus (instead of Oidipous), and so on. In a few cases, however, the non-Latinate version is more familiar and so I use that: Knossos (instead of Cnossus), Eileithyia (instead of Ilithyia). I have used diacritical marks in cases where it may not otherwise be clear that two vowels in a name are to be pronounced separately. For example, Pasiphaë has four syllables, not three, and Aeëtes has three syllables, not two. With Greek names, a final *e* following a consonant is always pronounced as a separate syllable. Thus, Hecate has three syllables and Aphrodite has four syllables.

Visual representations of myths were everywhere in antiquity and those that weren't firmly anchored in the Greek bedrock are now scattered throughout museums around the world. When I cite these, I indicate where each currently is, where it came from (if we know) and when it was made. Running a Google search with this information usually pulls up at least one photo of the item. The *Lexicon Iconographicum Mythologiae Classicae* ("Iconographical Lexicon of Classical Mythology," usually abbreviated *LIMC*) is also a resource. The libraries of most research universities have hard copies of its many volumes; much of it is now online, as well, at https://www.iconiclimc.ch/limc/tree.php. The Beazley Archive has photos of many of the vases I cite, at https://www.beazley.ox.ac .uk/cva/.

Readers who would like to go further than my bibliographic notes should start with Timothy Gantz's wonderfully thorough *Early Greek Myth: A Guide to Literary and Artistic Sources* (Johns Hopkins University Press 1993). The website theoi.com also gives extensive bibliographies for ancient myths and includes translations of most of the passages cited in each entry, as well as photos of many relevant ancient artworks. Theoi.com does not yet include every myth, however.

Those who are already familiar with Greek myths may be surprised by some of the details they find in my narrations. Rest assured, almost everything I say is anchored by at least one ancient text or artwork. In the handful of cases where I've added something that goes significantly beyond what any ancient source provides, I indicate that in the corresponding note. My additions are no different from what the ancient authors and artists themselves did: in antiquity the myths underwent a constant process of change, small and large, and authors freely reworked what came before them.

The maps included on the endpapers of this book are meant to indicate where some of the major cities, countries and features of the landscape were located—or imagined to be located—in antiquity. The first of them shows Greece and the surrounding countries and waters. The second shows the route of the Argonauts more or less as the ancients imagined it (the ancients didn't agree on all of the details; my map largely follows Apollonius of Rhodes's description of that voyage) and some of the main stops on Odysseus's voyage home. There was a great deal of disagreement in antiquity about the locations of the more fantastical places on

Odysseus's voyage, such as the place where Odysseus dug his pit to pour offerings to the dead. Therefore, I have left these to my readers' imaginations.

The most reliable resource for finding real places that are not on my maps is the *Barrington Atlas of the Greek and Roman World,* ed. Richard J. A. Talbert (Princeton University Press 2000), which is available in most research libraries, or as an iPad app (http://press .princeton.edu/apps/barrington-atlas). I have found that Wikipedia is also a surprisingly reliable geographical resource, when its disambiguation feature is used carefully.

TABLE OF SOURCES

When only one work by an author is cited, the abbreviation includes only the author (for example, "Apollod." means "Apollodorus, *Library*"). When more than one work by an author appears in the notes, citations include abbreviations for those works.

Author/source abbreviation	Author	Work abbreviation	Work	Type of source	Century
Acusil.	Acusilaus			mythographer	6th BCE
Ael.	Aelian			polymath	2nd–3rd CE
		Animals	*On the Nature of Animals*		
		Var. Hist.	*Varia Historia*		
Aes.	Aeschylus			tragedian	5th BCE
		Ag.	*Agamemnon*		
		Eum.	*Eumenides*		
		Lib.	*Libation Bearers*		
		Prom.	*Prometheus Bound*		
		Seven	*Seven Against Thebes*		
		Suppl.	*Suppliant Women*		
		fr.	fragment		
Aethiopis	unknown			early epic poem	7th–6th BCE
Alc.	Alcaeus			lyric poet	7th–6th BCE
Ant. Lib.	Antoninus Liberalis	*Metamorphoses*		mythographer	2nd CE
Apollod.	Apollodorus	*Library*		mythographer	1st–2nd CE
Ap. Rh.	Apollonius of Rhodes	*Argonautica*		epic poet	3rd BCE
Ar.	Aristophanes	*Lysistrata*		comic poet	5th–4th BCE
Asclepiad.	Asclepiades			mythographer	4th BCE

Author/source abbreviation	Author	Work abbreviation	Work	Type of source	Century
Bacch.	Bacchylides			lyric poet	5th BCE
Bion	Bion		*Lament for Adonis*	poet	2nd BCE
Call.	Callimachus			poet	4th–3rd BCE
		H.	*Hymns*		
		fr.	fragment		
Cic.	Cicero		*Concerning Divination*	philosopher, rhetorician	1st BCE
Conon			*Narrations*	mythographer	1st BCE–1st CE
Cypria	unknown			early epic poem	7th–6th BCE
Dion. Hal.	Dionysius of Halicarnassus		*Roman Antiquities*	historian	1st BCE
D.S.	Diodorus Siculus		*Library of History*	historian	1st BCE
Edelstein and Edelstein 1945	E.J. Edelstein and L. Edelstein		*Asclepius: Collection and Interpretation of the Testimonies*	translation and study of texts concerning the cult of Asclepius	
EM			*Etymologicum Magnum*	lexicographic work	12th CE
Eratosth.	Eratosthenes		*Constellations*	polymath	3rd–2nd BCE
Eur.	Euripides			tragedian	5th BCE
		Alc.	*Alcestis*		
		Andr.	*Andromache*		
		Bacch.	*Bacchae*		
		Hec.	*Hecuba*		
		Helen	*Helen*		
		Her.	*Heracles*		
		Hipp.	*Hippolytus*		
		Ion	*Ion*		
		Iph. Aul.	*Iphigenia in Aulis*		
		Iph. Taur.	*Iphigenia in Tauris*		
		Med.	*Medea*		
		Or.	*Orestes*		
		Phoen.	*Phoenician Women*		
		Rh.	*Rhesus*		
		Suppl.	*Suppliant Women*		
		Troj.	*Trojan Women*		
		fr.	fragment		

Author/source abbreviation	Author	Work abbreviation	Work	Type of source	Century
FGrH			Fragmente der griechischen Historiker (Fragments of the Greek Historians)		
Graf and Johnston 2013	F. Graf and S. I. Johnston		Ritual Texts for the Afterlife: Orpheus and the Bacchic Gold Tablets	translation and study of texts attributed to Orpheus	
Hdt.	Herodotus		Histories	historian	5th BCE
Hecat.	Hecateus of Miletus			historian	6th–5th BCE
Hellan.	Hellanicus			historian	5th BCE
Herod.	Herodorus			historian	5th–4th BCE
Hes.	Hesiod			epic poet	7th BCE
		Cat.	Catalogue of Women		
		Shield	Shield		
		Th.	Theogony		
		WD	Works and Days		
		fr.	fragment		
HHAp.	unknown		Homeric Hymn to Apollo	short epic poem in the style of Homer	6th BCE
HHAph.	unknown		Homeric Hymn to Aphrodite	short epic poem in the style of Homer	7th BCE
HHDem.	unknown		Homeric Hymn to Demeter	short epic poem in the style of Homer	6th BCE
HHHerm.	unknown		Homeric Hymn to Hermes	short epic poem in the style of Homer	5th BCE
Hom. Hymn #	unknown		Homeric Hymn [plus number]	short epic poems in the style of Homer	Various dates between 6th and 2nd BCE
Hsch.	Hesychius			lexicographer	5th or 6th CE
Hyg.	Hyginus			mythographer	1st BCE–1st CE
		Astr.	De Astronomica (Star Myths)		
		Fab.	Fabulae (Myths)		
Ibyc.	Ibycus			lyric poet	6th BCE
Il.	attr. to Homer		Iliad	poem	8th BCE

Author/source abbreviation	Author	Work abbreviation	Work	Type of source	Century
Isocr.	Isocrates			orator	5th–4th BCE
		Helen	Helen		
		Panath.	Panathenaicus		
Johnston 1999	S. I. Johnston		Restless Dead: Encounters between the Living and the Dead		
Johnston 2018	S. I. Johnston		The Story of Myth		
Little Iliad	unknown			early epic poem	7th–6th BCE
Livy	Livy		From the Founding of the City	historian	1st BCE–1st CE
Luc.	Lucian			satirist	1st CE
		Dead	Dialogues of the Dead		
		Gods	Dialogues of the Gods		
Lycophr.	Lycophron		Alexandra	poet	3rd–2nd BCE
Naupactica	unknown			early epic poem	7th–6th BCE
Nonn.	Nonnus		Dionysiaca	epic poet	5th CE
OCD			Oxford Classical Dictionary	Reference work	
Od.	attr. to Homer		Odyssey	poem	8th BCE
Ov.	Ovid			poet	1st BCE–1st CE
		F.	Fasti		
		Her.	Heroides		
		M.	Metamorphoses		
		Trist.	Tristia		
Palaeph.	Palaephatus		On Incredible Things	mythographer	4th BCE
Parian Marble	unknown			inscription	4th BCE
Parth.	Parthenius		On the Sorrows of Love	mythographer	1st BCE
Paus.	Pausanias		Description of Greece	travel writer	2nd CE
Pherecyd.	Pherecydes			mythographer	5th BCE
Philostr.	Philostratus of Athens			biographer	2nd–3rd CE
		Her.	Heroicus		
		Life Apollon.	Life of Apollonius		
Philostr. Eld.	Philostratus the Elder		Imagines	philosopher	2nd–3rd CE

Author/source abbreviation	Author	Work abbreviation	Work	Type of source	Century
Pi.	Pindar			lyric poet	6th–5th BCE
		I.	Isthmian Ode		
		N.	Nemean Ode		
		O.	Olympian Ode		
		P.	Pythian Ode		
		fr.	fragment		
Pisand.	Pisander			epic poet	7th–6th BCE
Pl.	Plato			philosopher	5th–4th BCE
		Axioch.	Axiochus		
		Phaedr.	Phaedrus		
		Prot.	Protagoras		
		Rep.	Republic		
		Symp.	Symposium		
Plut.	Plutarch			polymath	1st CE
		Thes.	Life of Theseus		
		Virt. Wom.	On the Virtue of Women		
Procl.	Proclus		Useful Knowledge	polymath	5th CE
Propert.	Propertius		Elegies	poet	1st BCE
Ps.-Plut.	Pseudo-Plutarch (attr. to Plutarch in antiquity)				unknown
			On Rivers		
			Parallel Stories		
Ptol. Chenn.	Ptolemy Chennus		Strange History, as epitomized in entry 190 of Photius's Library	grammarian	1st–2nd CE
Quint. Smyrn.	Quintus Smyrnaeus		Fall of Troy	epic poet	4th CE
Returns	unknown		On the Returns of the Greeks	early epic poem	7th–6th BCE
Sack of Troy	unknown			early epic poem	7th–6th BCE
Sapph.	Sappho			lyric poet	7th–6th BCE
Schol.	Scholiast			commentators	various
Sen.	Seneca			tragedian	1st CE
		Her. Oeta	Hercules on Oeta		
		Med.	Medea		
		Thy.	Thyestes		

Author/source abbreviation	Author	Work abbreviation	Work	Type of source	Century
Simon.	Simonides			lyric poet	6th–5th BCE
Soph.	Sophocles			tragedian	5th BCE
		Aj.	Ajax		
		Ant.	Antigone		
		El.	Electra		
		Oed. Col.	Oedipus at Colonus		
		OT	Oedipus the King		
		Philoct.	Philoctetes		
		Trach.	Women of Trachis		
Stat.	Statius			epic poet	1st CE
		Ach.	Achilleid		
		Theb.	Thebaid		
Stes.	Stesichorus			lyric poet	7th–6th BCE
Strab.	Strabo		Geographia	travel writer	1st BCE–1st CE
Suid.	unknown		Suidas	lexicographic work	10th CE
Telegony	unknown			early epic poem	
Thebaid	unknown			early epic poem	
Theocr.	Theocritus			poet	3rd BCE
		Id.	Idylls		
		fr.	fragment		
Theogn.	Theognis			poet	6th BCE
Tzetzes			Commentary on Lycophron	scholar and poet	12th CE
Val. Flacc.	Valerius Flaccus		Argonautica	epic poet	1st CE
V.	Virgil			poet	1st BCE
		Aen.	Aeneid		
		Ciris	Ciris		
		Ecl.	Eclogues		
		Geo.	Georgics		

NOTES ON SOURCES FOR THE MYTHS

1 **Earth and Her Children:** Ancient Greek poets offered several stories about how the cosmos began, but Hesiod's *Theogony* was the most influential; it was my main inspiration for the first four chapters. For this chapter, see lines 116–206. See also Apollod. 1.1.1–4.

2 **The Titans:** Hes. *Th.* 270–336 and 453–91 and Apollod. 1.1.5–7 were central to this part of my narration. I have also drawn on the east frieze of the temple of Hecate in the ancient city of Lagina, which shows her leaving Rhea's side to carry the stone to Cronus.

3 **The Young Gods Rebel:** This part of the story is drawn mostly from Hes. *Th.* 92–506, 617–733 and 820–68. See also Hyg. *Astr.* 2.28, Apollod. 1.1.5–1.2.1 and 1.6.3, and Nonn. 18.237–67.

4 **Zeus Becomes King:** I drew mostly on *Il.* 15.187–95 and Hes. *Th.* 383–403, 411–52, 517–20, 775–806, 881–921. Cf. Apollod. 1.3.6. A later source, the scholiast on Hes. *Th.* 886, says, "Metis had the power to turn herself into whatever she wanted. Zeus tricked her and, making her small, swallowed her down." I've interpreted this to mean that Zeus tricked *Metis* into making *herself* small, which evokes a folk motif whereby boastful magicians or spirits are tricked into changing themselves into something small that the hero can then imprison (as in The Tale of the Fisherman and the Genie from *The Thousand and One Nights*). The idea that "something small" was a butterfly is my own, added for the sake of the story, but also inspired by the fact that there is a species of butterfly called Metis, genus *Apatura*.

5 **Persephone's Story:** I tell the story here very much as it was told in *HHDem.* 1–90.

6 **Demeter's Wanderings:** *HHDem.* 91–304 is my main source, with details from Ant. Lib. 24 and Paus. 8.25.5–6. For Arion as the steed of heroes, see also chapter 107, below, and Hes. *Shield* 120.

7 **Demeter and Persephone:** I follow *HHDem.* 305–495. See also an Athenian red-figure bell krater from about 440 BCE now in New York (Metropolitan Museum of Art 28.57.23), which shows Persephone rising from the Underworld in the company of Hermes, awaited by Hecate and Demeter.

8 **Athena, Artemis and Apollo Are Born:** These stories were known from early times. As I tell them here, they come mainly from *HHAp.* 25–207 and Hom. *Hymn* 28 (to Athena) with bits and pieces taken from other narrators, of whom the most important are Pi. *O.* 7.34–38 and fr. 33d, Eur. *Ion* 454–55, Hyg. *Fab.* 140 and Apollod. 1.3.6 and 1.4.1.

9 **Apollo Establishes His Oracle:** *HHAp.* 214–546.

10 **Hephaestus's Story:** There were different traditions of Hephaestus's conception and birth. For what I use here, see *Il.* 18.395–405, Hes. *Th.* 924–29 and *HHAp.* 316–21. The story of how Hephaestus becomes accepted among the gods is found in Alc. 349, Pi. fr. 283, *Parian Marble* 10 and Paus. 1.20.3. His arrival on a donkey was a favorite of vase painters, e.g., an Athenian cup from 430–420 BCE now in Toledo, Ohio (Toledo Museum of Art 1982.88), and the

François Vase, an Athenian black-figure column krater from about 570 BCE, now in Florence (Museo Archeologico Etrusco 4209). The encounter that resulted in Erichthonius is narrated by Eratosth. 13, Hyg. *Fab.* 166 and Apollod. 3.14.6. The scene of Earth handing Erichthonius over to Athena was also a favorite of painters, e.g., a red-figure stamnos from Vulci dating to about 460 BCE, now in Munich (Antikensammlungen 2413).

11 **Hermes the Cattle Thief:** *HHHerm.*, plus a bit from Hdt. 1.47.3 and Pi. *P.* 9.44–48.

12 **Dionysus Is Born, and Dies, and Is Born Again:** The stories of Dionysus's birth from Persephone, his kidnapping and his murder by the Titans come down to us only in tantalizing fragments and allusions. These are assembled and discussed in Graf and Johnston 2013: chapter 5. For Semele, Hyg. *Fab.* 167 and Ov. *M.* 3.256–315.

13 **Dionysus and the Pirates:** Hom. *Hymn* 7 and see also D.S. 4.25.3, Ov. *M.* 3.605–91, Hyg. *Fab.* 251 and *Astr.* 2.5. The story is illustrated on an Athenian black-figure cup dated to about 540 BCE, now in Munich (Antikensammlungen 8729).

14 **Aphrodite Experiences Desire:** The tale of Aphrodite and Ares caught in Hephaestus's net comes from *Od.* 8.266–366. The tales of Anchises and Tithonus come from *HHAph.* Other details come from Hellan. *FGrH* 4F140 and *Suid.* s.v. *andra Tithonon.*

15 **Prometheus, Epimetheus and the First Men:** My sources here were Hes. *Th.* 510–14 and 535–64, Aes. *Prom.* 436–506 and Pl. *Prot.* 320c–322a. See also Ov. *M.* 1.76–88, Hyg. *Astr.* 2.15 and *Fab.* 142.

16 **Prometheus Steals Fire:** Hes. *Th.* 521–34, 561–70 and *WD* 47–58 and Aes. *Prom.* were my main sources. The story about the prometheios plant comes from Ap. Rh. 3.844–66 and Val. Flacc. 7.352–70; cf. Ps.-Plut. 5.4.

17 **Pandora's Gifts:** I relied on Hes. *Th.* 512–14 and 570–612, and *WD* 53–105. There wasn't much choice: few ancient authors say anything about Pandora. No one tells us how she came to possess the jar of evils or why she opened it (the idea that she was motivated by curiosity dates to the Renaissance). The type of jar mentioned by Hesiod was used for storing food in ancient Greece; it was the responsibility of women to care for food and ensure that it lasted through the year.

18 **Lycaon Tests Zeus:** We don't have a complete narration of Lycaon's story before Ovid, but we know that early Greek authors told it. Here I relied on Ov. *M.* 1.163–243 but added some details from Hes. *Cat.* fr. 114, Lycophr. 479–81 and the scholiast for line 481. For the cult established following Lycaon's crime: Pl. *Rep.* 565d–e and Paus. 6.8.2 and 8.2.3–6.

19 **The Flood:** Our earliest complete narration of this story comes from Ov. *M.* 1.177–98 and 244–440, but the way in which Greek sources mention it makes clear that the tale was known from earliest times, e.g., Pi. *O.* 9.42–53. See also Apollod. 1.7.2.

20 **Io's Story:** This is another old story, but our first detailed versions come from Aes. *Suppl.* 291–324 and his *Prom.* 561–886. I borrow details from other authors, including Hyg. *Fab.* 145, Ov. *M.* 1.583–750 and Apollod. 2.1.1–4. Argus with his many eyes was a popular figure on vases, e.g., an Athenian red-figure stamnos from 500–450 BCE, now in Vienna (Österreichisches Museum 3729), but a south Italian red-figure wine jug dating between 445 and 430 BCE, now in Boston, showed him with only two eyes—although it gives Io a cow's body with a woman's face (Museum of Fine Arts 00.366).

21 **Phaethon Drives the Chariot of the Sun:** Another old story, although best known from Ov. *M.* 1.751–2.366, who is my main source here. See also D.S. 5.23.2.

22 **Europa and the Bull:** The story was known as early as *Il.* 14.321 and Hes. fr. 89. Here I have drawn mainly on Hyg. *Fab.* 178, Ov. *M.* 2.833–3.5 and Apollod. 2.1.4 and 3.1.1–2.

23 **Callisto's Story:** Yet another old story. Traditions about why and by whom Callisto was turned into a bear vary, although all versions of her story revolve around the fact that she was one of Artemis's followers and that Zeus deceived and raped her. Here I draw mostly on Eratosth. 1

and Hyg. *Astr.* 2.1, but I borrow from Ov. *M.* 2.409–530 and Apollod. 3.8.2, as well. Several authors mention that a few people survived the Flood; I've chosen to add Callisto to their number to solve the mystery of how Lycaon's daughter delivered a son who was regarded as postdiluvian.

24 **Daphne and Apollo:** Our earliest—and almost only—source is Ov. *M.* 1.452–567, although see also Luc. *Gods* 17. The final comment by Artemis is my invention.

25 **Artemis and Actaeon:** The story was popular from early times. My version, which situates Actaeon's fate within the bad luck of his larger family, draws its shape from Call. *H.* 5.107–18 and Ov. *M.* 3.138–252. There are many visual representations of Actaeon turning into a stag, e.g., an Athenian red-figure bell krater dated to the mid-fifth century BCE, now in Boston (Museum of Fine Arts 00.346) and some of Actaeon's ghost still wearing stag's horns in the Underworld, e.g., a South Italian red-figure vase dated to about 330 BCE, now in Toledo, Ohio (Toledo Museum of Art 1994.19). The wedding of Cadmus and Harmonia and Harmonia's necklace: Theogn. 15–18, Pi. *P.* 3.86–96, Stat. *Theb.* 2.265–305 and Apollod. 3.4.2–4.

26 **Niobe and Leto:** We first hear this story when Achilles tells it to the grieving Priam at *Il.* 24.602–17, although it looks as if Achilles extemporaneously changed a detail to suit his purposes. See also Pl. *Rep.* 380a = Aes. fr. 154a, D.S. 4.74.3, Ov. *M.* 6.146–312. I ended with an uncanny shepherds' tale that comes from Quint. Smyrn. 1.290–310.

27 **Arachne and Athena:** Our only narration of this story comes from Ov. *M.* 6.1–151—but see Johnston 2018: 188–91, for another, very different story about Arachne.

28 **Baucis and Philemon:** Our only narration comes from Ov. *M.* 8.616–724.

29 **Hyrieus and His Ox:** We know that Hesiod told this story (fr. 246), but fuller accounts come later: Hyg. *Astr.* 2.34 and *Fab.* 195 and Ov. *F.* 5.493–536.

30 **Orion:** Orion is mentioned by some of our earliest sources, but most of the information is allusive or fragmentary. To make matters even more difficult, there were varied traditions about almost every aspect of his life. The story as I tell it here relies on *Od.* 11.572–75, Hes. fr. 244, Eratosth. 32, Parth. 20, Hyg. *Astr.* 2.26 and 2.34.1–2, Ov. *F.* 5.537–44.

31 **Erigone and Icarius:** This is another story that we have to piece together from brief mentions in many sources. Some of them are Hyg. *Astr.* 2.4 and *Fab.* 130, Apollod. 3.14.7, Ael. *Animals* 7.28. We finally get a fuller treatment from Nonn. 47.132–264. Hsch. and *EM* tell us about the festivals under the entries *aiōra* and *alētis*.

32 **Apollo and Hyacinthus:** The cult of Hyacinthus was established in Sparta in early times and the myth that accompanied it is old as well. Among my sources are Eur. *Helen* 1469–75, Ov. *M.* 10.162–219, Luc. *Gods* 16 and 17, Apollod. 3.10.3 and Philostr. *Eld.* 1.24.

33 **Leda and Her Children:** I have combined several stories in this chapter, relying mostly on *Od.* 11.298–304, *Cypria* frs. 9 and 16, Hom. *Hymn* 33, Pi. *N.* 10.54–91, Eur. *Helen* 16–21, Hyg. *Fab.* 77 and Apollod. 3.10.3–11.2. The topic of Leda and the swan was popular among ancient artists for its erotic possibilities; in 2018, a particularly striking fresco of the subject was uncovered in the bedroom of a wealthy Pompeian villa. Castor and Polydeuces appear as part of the Calydonian Boar hunt on the François Vase, an Athenian black-figure column krater from about 570 BCE, now in Florence (Museo Archeologico Etrusco 4209), and as Argonauts on a metope from the sixth-century BCE Sicyonian Treasury at Delphi; another metope shows Idas, Castor and Polydeuces driving cattle, the portrait of Lynceus apparently having been lost.

34 **Melampus and the Daughters of Proetus:** For the story of the woodworms, Apollod. 1.9.11–12; see also Hes. frs. 199a and b. None of our sources specify what the girls did to offend Hera, although they characterize the girls' behavior as lewd and one mentions a statue of Hera. A painted metope (Athens, Archaeological Museum 13412) and an ivory carving now in New York (Metropolitan Museum of Art 17.190.73), both dating to about 630 BCE, show women who are probably meant to be the daughters of Proetus baring their breasts. Some of the textual

sources I used were Hes. frs. 35, 77, 79–81 and 210, Acusil. *FGrH* 2F28, Pherecyd. *FGrH* 3F114 and 3F115, Bacch. 11.40–112, V. *Ecl.* 6.48–51, Ov. *M.* 15.325–28.

35 **Pan and Syrinx:** Pan's birth is narrated in Hom. *Hymn* 19 and his pursuit of Syrinx in Ov. *M.* 1.689–712.

36 **Echo and Narcissus:** The story of Iynx comes from Call. fr. 685. For the story of Echo and Narcissus, Conon 24 and Ov. *M.* 3.339–510.

37 **The Greed of Midas:** This is one of the best-known Greek myths, but most of us are familiar with a version invented by Nathaniel Hawthorne for his *Wonder-Book for Boys and Girls*, according to which Midas did not repent until he had turned his daughter into gold. In my story, I follow Ov. *M.*, 11.85–193, with some details from other authors, including Hdt. 8.138, Cic. 1.36 and Ael. *Var. Hist.* 12.45.

38 **Tantalus Tests the Gods and Pelops Makes a Bad Decision:** We hear about Tantalus already at *Od.* 11.582–92, but the first in-depth narration of his story is in Pi. *O.*1.35–99, although Pindar avowedly contradicts the mainstream story, which we glimpse at Eur. *Iph. Taur.* 386–88 and get more fully at Hyg. *Fab.* 83 and 84 and Ov. *M.* 4.403–11. See also Lycophr. 52–55. Tantalus, Sisyphus and sometimes women who may be the daughters of Danaus are shown together in the Underworld on vases dating to the second half of the fourth century BCE—e.g., a South Italian volute krater dating to 400–300 BCE now in Munich (Antikensammlungen 3297). For Pelops's part in this dark tale, see also Soph. *El.* 505–15, Apollod. *E.* 2.4–9 and Paus. 5.17.7.

39 **Tityus and Leto:** *Od.* 11.576–81, Ap. Rh. 1.759–62, V. *Aen.* 6.595–600, Apollod. 1.4.1. The story of Tityus's punishment was popular in ancient art, including a metope from the temple of Hera at Foce del Sele.

40 **Ixion, the Cloud and the Centaurs:** My main sources here were *Od.* 21.295–303, Pi. *P.* 2.21–48, D.S. 4.69.3–70.4 and Apollod. *E.* 1.20–21. Several ancient artists showed Ixion on his wheel, but my favorite instead shows a captive Ixion being brought forward to confront Hera while Hermes and Athena wait nearby with the wheel, on an Athenian red-figure kantharos dating to about 460 BCE now in London (British Museum 1865,0103.23).

41 **The Deaths of Sisyphus:** *Od.* 11.593–600, Theogn. 702–12, Pherecyd. *FGrH* 3F119, Aes. fr. 175. See also the metope from the temple of Hera at Foce del Sele, where Sisyphus rolls his stone with a small, winged figure behind him; the scene is also on some black-figure vases, e.g., an Athenian neck amphora from about 550–500 BCE, now in Munich (Antikensammlungen 1494 [J 576]).

42 **The Daughters of Danaus and the Sons of Egypt:** This story stays pretty much the same from our earliest to our latest sources. The story of the daughters' punishment in the afterlife doesn't show up until Plato, however. Hes. *Cat.* frs. 75–76, Pherecyd. *FGrH* 3F21, Aes. *Suppl.* and *Prom.* 855–72, Pl. *Axioch.* 371e, Ov. *Her.* 14, Apollod. 2.1.4–5, Paus. 2.19.6 and 2.21.1.

43 **Asclepius Challenges Death:** In some versions of this story, Apollo learns of Coronis's infidelity when his pet raven tells him and Apollo causes all ravens, which had previously been white, to be black thereafter; here, I have instead followed Pi. *P.* 3.1–60. See also Hes. *Cat.* frs. 55–56, Hyg. *Fab.* 202, Ov. *M.* 2.540–632 and *F.* 6.733–62, Apollod. 3.10.3–4, Philostr. *Life Apollon.* 3.44, Paus. 2.26.3–28.1 and 5.20.2. The final part of my story is taken from documents associated with Asclepius's cult in Epidaurus; see translations in entry #423 of Edelstein and Edelstein.

44 **Minos and Polyidus:** This story barely survives to us before the late mythographers tell it, although we know that it was narrated in several tragedies. I have primarily followed Apollod. 3.3.1–2 with some help from Hyg. *Fab.* 136. See also Palaeph. 26. I invented the idea that Minos tested Glaucus's powers of resurrection after Polyidus had left.

45 **Minos and Scylla:** Virgil's *Ciris* tells us that Minos pursued Polyidus to Megara but does not explain why; at the end of chapter 44, I invented details of what seems like a possible reason,

given what we know of Polyidus's activity on Crete. There are different versions about why Scylla betrays her father (was it for love or money?) and exactly what happens to her afterwards; here I draw on V. *Ciris*, Hyg. *Fab.* 198, Ov. *M.* 8.6–151 and Apollod. 3.15.8.

46 **Pasiphaë and the Bull:** The story of Pasiphaë and the bull is old: Hes. fr. 93, Bacch. 26, Isocr. *Helen* 27, D.S. 4.77.1–4, Hyg. *Fab.* 40 and Apollod. 3.1.3–4. See also a first-century CE fresco from the House of the Vettii in Pompeii that shows Daedalus presenting the wooden cow to Pasiphaë and a fourth-century South Italian red-figure cup, now in Paris (Bibliothèque Nationale de France, Cabinet des Médailles 1066), that shows a disgruntled upper-class woman with a baby Minotaur on her knee—Pasiphaë? Sometimes Poseidon is blamed for Pasiphaë's plight, sometimes Aphrodite; here, I blame both. The story of Pasiphaë's casting a spell on Minos comes from Apollod. 3.15.1 and Ant. Lib. 41.

47 **Daedalus and Icarus:** Ov. *M.* 8.183–259 is the main source for the story of Icarus's tragic death, although we hear about it as early as the fourth century BCE (Palaeph. 12; see also D.S. 4.76.4–77.9, Hyg. *Fab.* 40 and Apollod. E. 1.12–13). I take other parts of my story from Pherecyd. *FGrH* 3F146, D.S. 4.79.1–3, Hyg. *Fab.* 39 and Apollod. 3.15.8 and E. 1.14–15. Sometimes, Daedalus's nephew is called Talus instead of Perdix.

48 **Procne and Philomela:** The story is alluded to at *Od.* 19.518–23 and Hes. *WD* 568–69. I tell it much as Ovid did at *M.* 6.424–676, but behind Ovid's smooth account is a tangle of variants. In some early versions, the two sisters are called Aëdon and Chelidon (literally Nightingale and Swallow). In some, Philomela (Chelidon) is the mother and Procne (Aëdon) the aunt, which makes no sense, ornithologically speaking, given that the nightingale was characterized by the Greeks as singing mournfully and the swallow as scarcely singing at all (as if her tongue had been cut). In other variants, the mother acts alone in killing her child. Further at Johnston 2018: 188–91.

49 **Salmacis and Hermaphroditus:** Although Hermaphroditus is mentioned by a few other authors, the only narration of this story is Ov. *M.* 4.274–388.

50 **Pygmalion and the Statue:** Our only surviving source for the story is Ov. *M.* 10.220–97.

51 **Myrrha and Adonis:** I draw mainly on Ov. *M.* 10.298–739 for these stories. See also Sapph. 140; Bion; Hyg. *Fab.* 58, 248 and 271; Ps.-Plut. *Parallel Stories* 22; Apollod. 3.14.4; Ant. Lib. 34. The name of Myrrha's father is sometimes Theias, and the place they lived is sometimes farther east than Cyprus, such as Lebanon or Assyria. In the idea of Artemis's avenging herself on Aphrodite by killing Adonis, I develop Euripides's version of Hippolytus's story (*Hipp.* 1416–22), as does Apollodorus.

52 **Danaë and the Shower of Gold:** I used Simon. 543, Pherecyd. *FGrH* 3F10, Pi. *P.* 12.17–18, Hyg. *Fab.* 63, Apollod. 2.2.1–2 and 2.4.1. There are several surviving artistic representations of this stage of Perseus's story; see particularly the Athenian red-figure calyx krater dated between 500 and 450 BCE now in St. Petersburg (Hermitage 637), which shows Danaë and the shower of gold on one side and on the other, Danaë and Perseus standing in a chest that a carpenter is finishing while Acrisius looks on; and an Athenian red-figure lekythos from 475–425 BCE, now in Providence (Rhode Island School of Design 25.084), showing mother and child in the chest, on the waves, with birds overhead.

53 **Polydectes and the Gorgon's Head:** We don't get a very good picture from ancient sources about how, exactly, Perseus ended up being sent after the head of Medusa, but it's clear that this had something to do with Perseus not bringing an adequate gift to a party hosted by Polydectes when other young men brought horses. There are also various traditions about how, and from whom, Perseus received the tools he needed. See also Pherecyd. *FGrH* 3F11, Pi. *P.* 12.14–15, Hyg. *Astr.* 2.12, Apollod. 2.4.2.

54 **Some Weird Nymphs:** The traditions about when Perseus met these nymphs, and why, vary. I draw on. Hes. *Th.* 270–73, Pi. *P.* 12.13, Aes. *Prom.* 794–97, Ov. *M.* 4.774–75, Apollod. 2.4.2.

See also the Athenian red-figure pyxis lid from 450–400 BCE that shows Perseus sneakily crawling on hands and knees towards the Graeae (Athens, Archaeological Museum 1291).

55 Beheading Medusa: The story is told or mentioned by many ancient authors. Here I draw mostly on Hes. *Th.* 270–81 and *Shield* 216–37, Pi. *P.* 12.7–20, Ov. *M.* 4.770–803 and Apollod. 2.4.2. The deed was popular on ancient vases, too; often, Athena is shown looking on as if to support Perseus, as in a vase from about 460 BCE now in London (British Museum 1873,0820.352).

56 Andromeda: My main sources are Ov. *M.* 4.663–803 and 5.1–249 and Apollod. 2.4.3–5. See also *Il.* 5.738–42; Pherecyd. *FGrH* 3F11–12; Ap. Rh. 4.1502–36; Hyg. *Fab.* 63, 64, *Astr.* 2.9, 10 and 12; Philostr. Eld. 1.29; Paus. 2.16.2–3 and 4.35.9.

57 Bellerophon and Pegasus: Our earliest traces of Bellerophon's story come from *Il.* 6.152–202. Further on this first stage, see Hes. fr. 69.94–115, Pi. *O.* 13.63–83, Hyg. *Fab.* 57, Apollod. 1.9.3 and 2.3.1.

58 Stheneboea: Eur. frs. 661–62 and the Hypothesis to the lost *Stheneboea*, Hyg. *Fab.* 57, Apollod. 2.3.1.

59 The Chimera: Hes. *Th.* 318–25 and fr. 77, Pi. *O.* 13.84–90, Hyg. *Fab.* 57, Plut. *Virt. Wom.* 9, Apollod. 2.3.1–2. For the trick of melting lead down the Chimera's throat, see Tzetzes's commentary on line 17 of Lycophron; the idea of having Bellerophon see a blacksmith spill lead onto the ground is my own invention. A black-figure vase from about 550 BCE, now in Paris, shows Bellerophon on Pegasus facing the Chimera; the horse rears up slightly, as if in surprise (Louvre A 478). A wonderfully lifelike Etruscan bronze of the Chimera from about 400 BCE was found in Arezzo, Italy, and is now in the Museo Archeologico Nazionale, Florence.

60 The End of Bellerophon: Pi. *O.* 13.91–92 and *I.* 7.43–48, Asclepiad. *FGrH* 12F13, Hyg. *Fab.* 57.

61 Cadmus and the Serpent's Teeth: The story of Cadmus following the cow in order to found Thebes is old, but until the fifth century BCE, we don't get many details. Pherecyd. *FGrH* 3F22 and 88; Eur. *Phoen.* 638–44, 658–75 and 931–44; Ov. *M.* 3.1–137; Apollod. 3.4.1–2.

62 Ino and Athamas: I have twined together several stories for this chapter. Most of them appear in at least fragments of early sources but continuous narratives come only later. Ino's plot and the rescue of Phrixus and Helle: Hyg. *Fab.* 2, Apollod. 1.9.1. The madness of Ino and Athamas: Ov. *M.* 4.416–542. On the wedding of Cadmus and Harmonia and Harmonia's necklace, see chapter 25, above.

63 The Return of Dionysus: I follow Eur. *Bacch.* Fragments of an Athenian red-figure cup dated to about 480 BCE, now in Fort Worth, show the head and torso of Pentheus (his eyes still open!) being grasped by two maenads (Kimbell Art Museum AP2000.02).

64 The Birth of Heracles: Several brief stories about Heracles appear already in the *Iliad* and the *Odyssey*. One of these tells of Hera delaying his birth and hastening that of Eurystheus (*Il.* 19.95–125). I also draw on Hes. *Shield* 1–56; Pi. *N.* 1.33–72 and 10.13–18; Theocr. *Id.* 24; Eratosth. 44; D.S. 4.9.1–10.1; Hyg. *Fab.* 30 and *Astr.* 2.43; Ov. *M.* 9.278–323; Apollod. 2.4.4–8; Ant. Lib. 29; and Paus. 9.11.3. An Athenian red-figure stamnos dating to about 480 BCE, now in Paris, shows Heracles strangling the snakes while Iphicles clings to his mother (Louvre G 192).

65 Heracles Murders His Family: These stories were known by the fifth century: Stes. 230, Herod. *FGrH* 31F20, Pherecyd. *FGrH* 3F14, Eur. *Her.* (my main source here for the murder of Megara and the children) and (for Linus) several red-figure vases, including an Athenian red-figure cup dated to 500–450 BCE, now in Munich (Antikensammlungen 2646). See also D.S. 3.67.2 and 4.29.2–3 and Apollod. 2.4.9–12. The story of the lion comes from Apollod. 2.4.9–10. I take the idea of Megara and her sons having been initiated into the mysteries from a South Italian volute krater dating to 360–340 BCE, now in Naples (Museo Archeologico Nazionale 81666) that shows them relaxing in apparent comfort to the right of Hades's palace (the "good" side).

66 **The Nemean Lion and the Lernaean Hydra:** Two passages in the *Iliad* mention Heracles's performing labors for Eurystheus, including bringing Cerberus back from Hades (8.362–69 and 15.639–40); see also *Il.* 19.95–125. Hesiod mentions labor #1, the lion, and labor #2, the Hydra, along with labor #10, the raiding of Geryon's cattle, at *Th.* 326–32, 313–18, 287–94 and 979–83. Pisand. frs. 3 and 4 add the Ceryneian Hind and the Stymphalian Birds. Vase paintings add the Erymanthian Boar, the Cretan Bull, the Mares of Diomedes, the Amazons, and the Apples of the Hesperides. Only the Stables of Augeas have to wait until the fifth century BCE; the metopes of the temple of Zeus at Olympia showed all twelve. Other sources for the first labor include Bacch. 9.6–9 and 13.46–54, Theocr. *Id.* 25.204–81, D.S. 4.11.3–4, Hyg. *Fab.* 30 and *Astr.* 2.24, Apollod. 2.5.1, Ptol. Chenn. 2. For the second labor: Alc. fr. 443, Eur. *Her.* 419–24 and 1274–75, Eur. *Ion* 191–200, Apollod. 2.5.2, D.S. 4.11.5–6, Hyg. *Fab.* 30 and *Astr.* 2.23. The two first labors were popular among painters—including scenes of the skinning of the lion, e.g., an Athenian black-figure cup from 550–500 BCE, now in Munich (Antikensammlungen 2085).

67 **The Ceryneian Hind and the Erymanthian Boar:** I follow D.S. 4.12.1–13.1 and Apollod. 2.5.3–4 in narrating these. For the hind, see also Pherecyd. *FGrH* 3F71, Pi. *O.* 3.25–30, Eur. *Her.* 375–79, Quint. Smyrn. 6.223–24. For the boar, Hecat. *FGrH* 1F6. Vase painters were fond of the scene in which Eurystheus cowers in the jar while Heracles shows him the boar, e.g., an Athenian black-figure neck amphora dating to 540–530 BCE, now in Paris (Louvre F 59).

68 **The Stables of Augeas and the Stymphalian Birds:** Heracles cleaning the stables is not mentioned until Pi. *O.* 10.26–30; at about the same time it was shown on a metope of the temple of Zeus in Elis. Fuller treatments appear in Theocr. *Id.* 25, D.S. 4.13.3 and Apollod. 2.5.5. (Note: the Peneus River in this story is different from the one who is Daphne's father in chapter 24, above.) There are variations as to how Heracles got rid of the birds—in some versions he killed them—but the use of the castanets is an early detail: Pisand. fr. 4, Pherecyd. *FGrH* 3F72, Hellan. *FGrH* 4F10. See also D.S. 4.13.2 and Apollod. 2.5.6. Heracles's participation in the quest of the Golden Fleece is most fully narrated by Ap. Rh.; see chapters 82–84, below.

69 **The Cretan Bull and the Mares of Diomedes:** The adventure with the Cretan Bull shows up on vases around 525 BCE (e.g., Munich Antikensammlungen 1583) and in literature at about the same time: Acusil. *FGrH* 2F29. See also D.S. 4.13.4, Apollod. 2.5.7 and Paus. 1.27.10. Our first traces of the story of the mares of Diomedes are Pi. fr. 169a, Eur. *Alc.* 481–98 and Eur. *Her.* 380–86. See also D.S. 4.15.3–4, Apollod. 2.5.8, Philostr. Eld. 2.25. Hellanicus tells the story of Abderus (*FGrH* 4F105). See also an Athenian black-figure cup dating to about 525 BCE, now in St. Petersburg, that shows Heracles grasping a horse that has a human head and arm dangling out of its mouth—although there, the horse is clearly a stallion (Hermitage 9270).

70 **Alcestis:** I rely on Eur. *Alc.*, our earliest complete narration, but add some details from Aes. *Eum.* 723–28, Hyg. *Fab.* 50 and 51 and Apollod. 1.9.15. See also an Athenian black-figure lekythos from about 500 BCE, now in New Haven, CT, where Apollo is helping Admetus yoke the animals (Yale University Art Gallery 1913.111).

71 **Hippolyta's Belt and the Cattle of Geryon:** Artistic representations of Heracles's battle with the Amazons are numerous; Ibycus 299 is our earliest literary reference. See also Pi. fr. 172, Eur. *Her.* 408–18, D.S. 4.16.1–4, Apollod. 2.5.9. Geryon is mentioned at Hes. *Th.* 287–94 and 979–83 and his story was told by Stesichorus in a poem called the *Geryoneis*, of which only fragments remain (here I draw on frs. S 10–15 and S 17). See also Pherecyd. *FGrH* 3F18a, D.S. 4.17.1–18.3, Apollod. 2.5.10. The artistic tradition was well developed: e.g., an Athenian red-figure cup, now in Munich, shows Heracles battling Geryon while the dead Orthrus lies between them (Antikensammlungen 2620). Heracles rides in Helios's cup alongside sea creatures on an Athenian red-figure vase from about 480 BCE, now in Rome (Vatican Museum 16563).

72 **Cacus and the Apples of the Hesperides:** The side adventures that Heracles has on his two trips west and home again, such as his confrontations with Cacus, Antaeus and Busiris, are attached to different parts of these journeys by different ancient authors. I have woven them into this and the preceding chapter to make a single continuous story. Sources include Pherecyd. *FGrH* 3F16 and 3F17, D.S. 4.17.4–27.4, V. *Aen.* 8.190–272, Dion. Hal. 1.39–41, Hyg. *Astr.* 2.6.5, Livy 1.7, Strab. 4.1.7, Ov. *F.* 1.543–82, Apollod. 2.5.10–11, Philostr. Eld. 2.21. The apples of the Hesperides and Heracles's search for them are mentioned already at Hes. *Th.* 215–16, 274–75 and 333–35 and Pherecyd. *FGrH* 3F16 and 3F17; see also Apollod. 2.5.11 and the metope from the temple of Zeus at Olympia, which delightfully shows Athena standing behind Heracles, easily doing most of the job of holding up Sky herself, apparently without her younger brother noticing she's there. In some treatments, Heracles goes to the garden himself, slays Ladon and obtains the apples (e.g., Soph. *Trach.* 1090–1100 and Eur. *Her.* 394–407). Several ancient vase painters showed Heracles wrestling with Antaeus or killing Busiris and his men, e.g., an Athenian black-figure amphora from 525–475 BCE now in Tampa (Tampa Art Museum 86.29) and an Athenian red-figure hydria from 500–450 BCE that is now in Munich (Antikensammlungen 2428).

73 **A Journey to the Underworld:** This labor is mentioned at *Il.* 8.367–68 and *Od.* 11.623–26 and frequently thereafter; the action of Eur. *Her.* revolves around Heracles's return from Hades. Vase painters loved the topic; some show Heracles struggling to control the dog, e.g., an Athenian red-figure plate from 520–510 BCE, now in Boston (Museum of Fine Arts 01.8025); in other scenes, Cerberus looks docile or even friendly, e.g., an Attic black-figure amphora from 535–500 BCE now in Moscow (Pushkin State Museum of Fine Arts 70). Hermes is often present and sometimes Athena, as well; I take the idea of Hermes's escorting Heracles back up from *Od.* 11.623–26 and Apulian Underworld vases where Hermes is often next to Heracles and the dog, e.g., a South Italian red-figure volute krater from 360–340 BCE, now in Naples (Museo Archeologico Nazionale 81666). The story of the ghost of Meleager comes from Bacch. 5.56–70. Demeter's special rituals to purify Heracles: see Johnston 1999: 132–36 with sources, including Apollod. 2.5.12, Plut. *Thes.* 30. and D.S. 4.14.3.

74 **Slave to Omphale:** The events in the later part of Heracles's life are arranged in different ways by different ancient authors; sometimes he serves Omphale before his marriage to Deianira and sometimes during his marriage. In this chapter and the next, I have followed the pathway that made the most narrative sense. My sources here include Ov. *Her.* 9.53–118, Ov. *F.* 2.303–58, Sen. *Her. Oeta* 371–77, Stat. *Ach.* 1.260–61 and Luc. *Gods* 15.

75 **A New Wife and New Problems:** My main source is Soph. *Trach.*; see also Bacch. 5.56–70 and 16.13–35, Pi. fr. 249a, Ov. *Her.* 9.111–68 and Apollod. 2.7.6. A charming scene on an Athenian black-figure band cup from 550–500 BCE, now in London, shows Athena eagerly tugging her younger brother towards their father, Zeus, with one hand and with her other hand imploring Zeus to make Heracles a god (British Museum 1867,0508.962).

76 **Atalanta:** Different authors make Atalanta the daughter of Theban Schoeneus or Arcadian Iasion; some call her husband Hippomenes and others call him Melanion. The story of the race is old (Hes. *Cat.* frs. 47–51), but it is most famously narrated at Ov. *M.* 10.560–707. See also Propert. 1.1.1, Hyg. *Fab.* 185 and Ael. *Var. Hist.* 13.1. Atalanta is shown at the Calydonian Boar hunt on the François Vase, an Athenian black-figure column krater from about 570 BCE, now in Florence (Museo Archeologico Etrusco 4209); and wrestling Peleus on a Chalcidian black-figure amphora dating to 550–500 BCE, now in Munich (Antikensammlungen 1541).

77 **A Marvelous Musician:** Simon. fr. 567, Aes. *Ag.* 1629–32, Ap. Rh. 1.23–34 and 1.492–518, D.S. 3.65.4–6 and 5.67.3, Apollod. 1.3.2. On the topics that Orpheus addressed in his songs, see F. Graf, "Orphic Literature," in the *OCD*.

78 **Orpheus the Argonaut:** Pi. *P.* 4.177 and *O.* 4.19–27; Ap. Rh. 1.23–34, 1.492–518, 1.540–41 and 4.895–921; Apollod. 1.9.16 and 25. For the Sirens as daughters of Melpomene and friends of Persephone: Ap. Rh. 4.895–99, Hyg. *Fab.* 141, Ov. *M.* 5.552–63. For texts of the gold tablets, see Graf and Johnston 2013. The idea of Orpheus learning about the Sirens during a conversation with Mnemosyne and the specifics of what the Sirens and Orpheus sang are my own inventions, although I draw on *Od.* 12.205–7 and Apollod. 1.25.

79 **Eurydice:** Eur. *Alc.* 357–62, Pl. *Symp.* 179b–d, V. *Geo.* 4.315–504, Hyg. *Astr.* 2.7, Ov. *M.* 10.1–105, Apollod. 1.3.2–3. The context in which Orpheus first met Eurydice and the topic of Orpheus's song to Charon are my own inventions. Orpheus is frequently shown in Underworld scenes on vases from southern Italy dating to the fourth century BCE, playing his lyre and standing to Hades's and Persephone's right, e.g., an Apulian red-figure volute krater dated to 360–340 BCE now in Naples (Museo Archeologico Nazionale 81666).

80 **The Death of Orpheus:** Eur. *Rh.* 962–73, Eratosth. 24, V. *Geo.* 4.453–527, Hyg. *Astr.* 2.7, Ov. *M.* 11.1–66, Apollod. 1.3.2, Philostr. *Her.* 28.8 and *Life Apollon.* 4.14, Paus. 9.30.4–7. See also the Athenian red-figure hydria from about 440 BCE now in Basel (Antikensmuseum BS 481) that shows Orpheus's prophesying head, surrounded by Muses. For more on Orpheus as an initiator and a poet of the gods' mysteries, see Graf and Johnston 2013: 173–86.

81 **Chiron and Jason:** For the main lineage of centaurs and where they came from, see chapter 40, above. Chiron: Hes. *Th.* 1001–2 and frs. 36–37; Pi. *P.* 4.109–16; Ap. Rh. 2.1231–41.

82 **Losing a Sandal and Reclaiming the Kingdom:** Pelias's request for Jason to bring the fleece back is an early tradition: Hes. *Th.* 992–1002. Here I follow Pi. *P.* 4.70–202, Ap. Rh. 1.1–527 and 3.66–73, Hyg. *Fab.* 12–14, Apollod. 1.9.16. Different ancient authors include different lists of Argonauts, some of which are lengthier than mine.

83 **The Lemnian Women:** I take my story from *Il.* 7.467–69, Ap. Rh. 1. 592–1077, Hyg. *Fab.* 15 and 16 and Apollod. 1.9.17. We hear of athletic games on Lemnos already at Pi. *O.* 4.19–27.

84 **Heracles and Hylas:** The story of Hylas's abduction is old: Hes. fr. 202 and Hdt. 7.193. Here, I also use Theocr. *Id.* 13., Ap. Rh. 1.1078–1343, Apollod. 1.9.18–19.

85 **The Harpies and the Clashing Rocks:** The tale of the Harpies is old, too: Hes. fr. 97. For the stories in this chapter, I primarily follow Ap. Rh. 2.1–910, V. *Aen.* 3.209–18, Hyg. *Fab.* 17–19 and Apollod. 1.9.20–23. For a particularly evocative picture of the Boreads chasing the Harpies away, see an Apulian red-figure volute krater from about 360 BCE, now in Ruvo, Italy (Museo Jatta J1095). There was some disagreement about where the Clashing Rocks were and whether the Argo confronted them on the way to Colchis or on the way back; *Od.* 12.69–72 implies the latter. On the boxing match between Polydeuces and Amycus, see also Theocr. *Id.* 22.1–135.

86 **Colchis:** Aeëtes is mentioned by our earliest sources: *Od.* 10.135–39, 12.69–72; Hes. *Th.* 956–62. We hear of Medea as Jason's wife at Hes. *Th.* 961 and 992–1002. Here I draw mainly on Pi. *P.* 4.213–19, Pherecyd. *FGrH* 3F22, Ap. Rh. 2.1030–3.743, Hyg. *Fab.* 20–22 and Apollod. 1.9.23.

87 **The Tasks:** I draw on Pi. *P.* 4.220–46, Ap. Rh. 817–1407, Hyg. *Fab.* 22, Apollod. 1.9.23. For the prometheios plant, chapter 16, above.

88 **Claiming the Fleece:** I draw on Ap. Rh. 4.1–556, Ov. *Her.* 12.113–16, Ov. *Trist.* 3.9.13–34, Hyg. *Fab.* 23, Apollod. 1.9.23–24. Some ancient treatments had Jason obtain the fleece by killing the dragon himself; I follow Ap. Rh. here. The age of Apsyrtus varies; our earliest source, Pherecyd. *FGrH* 3F32, makes him a child, as do many others. (Ap. Rh. makes him a young man, treacherously ambushed by Jason and Medea, and killed by Jason.)

89 **Circe and the Phaeacians:** *Od.* 7.86–121, Ap. Rh. 4.557–1169, Apollod. 1.9.24–25. On Orpheus and the Sirens, see chapter 78, above. The route taken home by the Argonauts varies from author to author; here I follow Ap. Rh.

90 Home Again: I take my story from Pi. *P.* 4.21–43, Ap. Rh. 4.1228–1781, Hyg. *Fab.* 24, Apollod. 1.9.26–27. A number of vase painters showed Medea's revival of the ram from the cauldron; in some of these pictures, Pelias himself is present instead of or alongside his daughters, e.g., an Athenian red-figure hydria dating to about 475 BCE now in London (British Museum 1843,1103.76).

91 Medea in Corinth: Eur. *Med.* is my main source here. See also Hyg. *Fab.* 25, Sen. *Med.*, Apollod. 1.9.28. There are several stunning artistic representations of Medea killing the children or her flight afterwards; one of the best is a Lucanian bell krater dating to about 400 BCE, now in Cleveland, which shows Medea in her grandfather's dragon chariot high above Jason and the children's corpses (Cleveland Museum of Art 91.1).

92 The Calydonian Boar: There are variations as to exactly how and why Althaea killed her son. Here I follow Bacch. 5.93–154, Ov. *M.* 8.260–546, Apollod. 1.8.2–3 and Paus. 10.31.3–4. The hunt is shown on an Athenian black-figure column krater from about 570 BCE, now in Florence (Museo Archeologico Etrusco 4209, the "François Vase").

93 Athena's City: *Parian Marble* 1, 2, 4, 5, 9, 10 and 18; Eur. *Ion* 9–26, 260–82 and 496; Hyg. *Fab.* 37; Plut. *Thes.* 3; Apollod. 3.14.1–2, 3.14.5–7 and 3.15.5–7. A fuller narration of the conception and birth of Erichthonius is in chapter 10, above.

94 Theseus Travels to Athens: I draw on Bacch. 18, D.S. 4.59.1–6, Apollod. 3.15.7–16.1–2 and *E.* 1–7, Plut. *Thes.* 4–11, Paus. 2.1.3–4. See also various red-figure vase depictions of Theseus's deeds, which often combine them with his defeat of the Minotaur, e.g., an Athenian red-figure kylix from 440–340 BCE, now in London (British Museum 1850,0302.3).

95 A Wicked Stepmother: There are hints of Medea's sojourn in Athens already at Eur. *Med.* 663–758. My main sources for this chapter were Bacch. 18, Apollod. *E.* 1.5–6 and 2.5.7, Plut. *Thes.* 12 and 14, Paus. 1.27.9–10. Persia: Hdt. 7.62 and Strab. 11.13.10.

96 A Voyage to Crete: My main source is Bacch. 17; see also Isocr. *Helen* 28, Plut. *Thes.* 15–17, Paus. 1.27.10 and cf. chapter 46, above. On an Athenian red-figure cup dated 525–480 BCE, now in Paris, Theseus is shown addressing his stepmother Amphitrite while Athena stands between them, as if to facilitate Theseus's request. Theseus's feet rest on the upturned hands of a small creature who seems to be part man and part fish, while dolphins swim behind him (Louvre G 104 plus a fragment in the Museo Archeologico Etrusco in Florence, PD321).

97 The Princess and the Minotaur: Pherecyd. *FGrH* 3F149 and 3F150, Eratosth. 5, D.S. 6.4, Apollod. *E.* 1.8–9, Plut. *Thes.* 19. Artistic representations of Theseus's killing of the Minotaur were popular from an early time; e.g., the Athenian red-figure kylix cited for chapter 94.

98 Theseus Becomes King: I draw mainly on Hes. *Th.* 947–48; Pherecyd. *FGrH* 3F151; D.S. 4.61.6–9; Plut. *Thes.* 21–22, 24–25, 30; Apollod. *E.* 1.10–11. The Amazon who ends up marrying Theseus is variously called Hippolyta, Antiope or Melanippe. In some authors, Theseus goes to Themiscyra to accompany Heracles; in others, he and Pirithous go together. Isocr. *Panath.* 193 is our earliest source for the Amazon queen's falling in love with Theseus, but as our information for this story is sketchy, I have invented some of the details. On Theseus and Pirithous, see also chapter 40, above. The fight against the Amazons was a favorite topic for artists, e.g., the Parthenon metopes and an Athenian red-figure volute krater from 475–425 BCE, now in New York (Metropolitan Museum of Art 07.286.84).

99 A Father's Curse: Hippolyta's death: Isocr. *Panath.* 193, D.S. 4.28.1–4 and Plut. *Thes.* 27. My main source for the rest of this chapter is Eur. *Hipp.* For the resurrection of Hippolytus, *Naupactica* fr. 10 and Ov. *F.* 6.735. Cf. chapter 43, above.

100 New Brides: This was a popular story: *Od.* 11.630–31, Hes. fr. 216, Eur. *Her.* 1169–70, D.S. 4.63.1–3, Plut. *Thes.* 31–34, Apollod. *E.* 1.24. Theseus and Pirithous are shown in Underworld scenes on Apulian vases, e.g., on a volute krater of 365–350 BCE now in Ruvo, Italy (Museo Jatta 1094).

101 The Death of Theseus: Plut. *Thes.* 32–36, Apollod. *E.* 1.23–24 and a detail from *Il.* 2.546–56.

102 The Birth of Oedipus: On the fate of Cadmus and Harmonia: Eur. *Bacch.* 1330–60, Hyg. *Fab.* 6, Ov. *M.* 563–603. On Laius and Chrysippus: Hyg. *Fab.* 85. On the prophecies to Laius: Aes. *Seven* 742–57, Soph. *OT* 711–18, Eur. *Phoen.* 21–27. On the exposure and boyhood of Oedipus: Soph. *OT* 717–19, 774–78 and 1171–76. There is an Athenian red-figure amphora from about 450 BCE, now in Paris, that shows the infant Oedipus being rescued by a shepherd (Bibliothèque Nationale de France, Cabinet des Médailles 372).

103 A Troubling Oracle: Aes. fr. 122a, Soph. *OT* 787–813, Apollod. 3.5.7, Paus. 10.5.3.

104 A Riddle Contest: I draw on Hes. *Th.* 326–27, Aes. *Seven* 776–77, Soph. *OT* 130–31 and 391–94, Eur. *Phoen.* 45–51 and Apollod. 3.5.8. See also the vases on which Oedipus confronts the Sphinx on her column, notably an Athenian red-figure cup now in Vatican City that includes the words "and three" coming from the Sphinx's mouth (Museo Gregoriano Etrusco 16541), and those on which a flying Sphinx clutches a young man in her claws, such as an Athenian red-figure lekythos from 525–475 BCE now in Kiel (Christian Albrechts Universität zu Kiel Antikensammlung B 553). I developed this episode into a longer contest between Oedipus and the Sphinx by drawing on other riddles, and stories of riddle contests, from ancient sources. In ancient sources, the famous riddle of the Sphinx is as I gave it here (e.g., Apollod. 3.5.8). The version we are now familiar with (what goes on four feet *in the morning*, two feet *at noon* and three feet *in the evening*) is a later development.

105 Revelations: My source here is Soph. *OT.*

106 The Theban War: For the final days and death of Oedipus, my main source was Soph. *Oed. Col.*, with additional material from the Greek epic *Thebaid* frs. 2 and 3. For the attack on Thebes, Aes. *Seven* with further material taken from Pi. *N.* 9.9–17, Eur. *Suppl.* 131–61, Apollod. 3.6.1–8 and Statius's enormous *Thebaid*, especially 3.524–46 (for the portent of the swans and eagles).

107 Antigone: My source for the story of Theseus's retrieval of the bodies is Eur. *Suppl.* and for the story of Antigone, Soph. *Ant.* Our knowledge of the second attack on Thebes comes from many passing mentions in ancient authors; Apollod. 3.7.2–4 gives a unified account. In some authors, there is another son of Creon named Menoeceus, who sacrifices himself at the start of the war in accordance with a prophecy that this would guarantee the Thebans' victory (Eur. *Phoen.* 903–1018 and Apollod. 3.6.7). Sophocles seems to conflate Menoeceus and Megareus, for when Eurydice curses Creon, she blames him for the deaths of both Haemon and Megareus (*Ant.* 1301–5)—unless we are meant to assume that Megareus, who defended his gate against Eteoclus, died in a later part of the war.

108 Peleus and Thetis: Our early sources for the lives of Peleus and his ancestors are fragmentary, and some details differ, but Apollod. 3.12.6–13.5 gives the general story. Prometheus: Aes. *Prom.* 755–70. Peleus and Thetis: Procl. *Cypria* 1 and *Cypria* frs. 1–6, Pi. *I.* 8.26–47. Thetis's transformations while trying to elude Peleus were a favorite topic for vase painters, e.g., an Athenian red-figure kylix dated to about 500 BCE, now in Berlin (Schloss Charlottenburg F 2279), which shows Peleus carrying Thetis away while a tiny lion runs down one of her arms and a snake twines around the other, to hint at her transformations. The pictures we obtain from the fragments of an Athenian black-figure vase dating to 600–550 BCE, now reassembled in London (British Museum 13159001), informed my description of the wedding.

109 The Judgment of Paris: Procl. *Cypria* 1–2 and frs. 1, 5–7; Eur. *Andr.* 274–92 and *Troj.* 924–37; Apollod. 3.12.5 and *E.* 3.1–23. The scene of Paris judging the goddesses was a favorite; see, e.g., two Athenian red-figure vases dating to 500–450 BCE, now in London (British Museum 1873,0820.353 and 1849,0518.5).

110 A Promise Comes Due: On Helen's kidnapping by Theseus, see chapter 100, above. For the rest of the chapter: Hes. frs. 154–56 and 247, Procl. *Cypria* 5–7 and frs. 8 and 19, Aes. *Ag.* 403–8, Eur. *Iph. Aul.* 49–79, Apollod. 3.10.8, 3.13.8 and *E.* 3.3–8. It should be noted that ancient sources disagreed on whether Helen had gone willingly or unwillingly to Troy, as well as on what happened during the journey there. Scenes of Helen's departure with Paris are frequent in ancient art and sometimes seem to hint at her reluctance; see, e.g., an Athenian red-figure cup from 490–480 BCE, now in Berlin (Antikensammlung 2291). See also chapter 126, below. On Odysseus and Achilles, see Hyg. *Fab.* 95 and 96 and Ov. *M.* 13.162–70; on the Myrmidons, Hes. fr. 145.

111 **Iphigenia:** I largely follow Eur. *Iph. Aul.* here, with some details from Aes. *Ag.* 104–59. The last part of my story nods to traditions that I take up in chapter 126, below.

112 **Protesilaus and Laodamia:** *Il.* 2.698–702, Procl. *Cypria* 10–12, Hyg. *Fab.* 103–4, Luc. *Dead* 28, Apollod. *E.* 3.29–30. Embassy: *Il.* 3.205–24 and 11.122–42, Bacch. 15, Apollod. *E.* 3.28–29 and 5.21.

113 **Agamemnon and Achilles:** *Il.* 1.1–3.382.

114 **Hera Deceives Zeus:** *Il.* 3.383–461, 4, 5, 6.237–502, 14.153–351. Sharp-eyed readers will spot that here I refer to Europa as the daughter of Phoenix whereas in chapter 22 I called her the daughter of Agenor. The tradition that made her the daughter of Agenor was more common, but when Zeus gives his speech to Hera in the *Iliad*, he says Europa's father was Phoenix, and I did not dare to contradict him.

115 **Achilles and Patroclus:** *Il.* 14.352–522, 15, 16. Embassy to Achilles: *Il.* 9.89–713.

116 **Achilles and Hector:** *Il.* 17, 18, 19, 22.1–404.

117 **Achilles and Priam:** *Il.* 22.405–515, 23, 24.1–697. Several ancient vases poignantly contradict the story as the *Iliad* tells it by showing Hector's body lying under or alongside Achilles's couch while Achilles speaks with Priam, e.g., an Athenian red-figure cup dating to about 490 BCE now in Vienna (Kunsthistorisches Museum 3710).

118 **The Deaths of Achilles and Ajax:** Hector's funeral: *Il.* 24.695–804. Traditions varied as to how, exactly, Achilles met his end, but Paris and Apollo are always involved: *Od.* 24.36–92; Procl. *Aethiopis* 1–4 and fr. 6; Hyg. *Fab.* 107; Stat. *Ach.* 1.133–34, 268–70 and 480–81; Apollod. *E.* 5.1–5. Ajax's suicide: Procl. *Little Iliad* 1 and frs. 2 and 3, Pi. *N.* 8. 23–34 and *I.* 4.35–36, Soph. *Aj.*, Apollod. *E.* 5.6–7. An Etruscan red-figure calyx krater from 350–300 BCE, now in London, offers a horrifying depiction of Ajax falling upon his sword (British Museum 1867,0508.1328).

119 **Neoptolemus and Philoctetes:** Generally: Procl. *Little Iliad* 2 and 3 and Apollod. *E.* 5.8–13. Philoctetes: Soph. *Philoct.*

120 **The Horse:** The Trojan Horse is mentioned already at *Od.* 4.266–89 and 8.487–520. See also Procl. *Little Iliad* 4–5 and *Sack of Troy* 1–2, Ar. 155–56, V. *Aen.* 2.13–267, Apollod. *E.* 5.14–20.

121 **The Trojan Women:** Generally, Procl. *Sack of Troy* 3 and 4, Apollod. *E.* 5.21–23 and Paus. 10.25–27. For Priam: Eur. *Troj.* 481–83. Cassandra: Eur. *Troj.* 65–75, 247–58 and 308–461. Andromache: Eur. *Troj.* 271–74 and 1123–33. Astyanax: Eur. *Troj.* 712–89 and 1133–1234. Polyxena: Eur. *Hec.* 35–608, *Troj.* 622–31 and see the painting on an Athenian black-figure amphora 570–550 BCE, now in London (British Museum 1897,0727.2). Hecabe and Polydorus: Eur. *Hec.* and *Troj.* 275–92, Aeneas: V. *Aen.* See also a remarkable Athenian red-figure hydria from 500–450 BCE, now in Naples, which shows these events encircling the vase (Museo Archeologico Nazionale 81699).

122 **Atreus and Thyestes:** The details of these stories vary quite a bit, and full narrations come only in later sources, but the main lines are clear. Aes. *Ag.* 1191–93, 1215–22 and 1583–1611; Soph. *Aj.* 1291–97; Eur. *Or.* 811–15 and 983–1011; Hyg. *Fab.* 84, 86–88; Sen. *Thy.*; Apollod. *E.* 2.1–16; Paus. 8.14.10–12. Further on the story of Tantalus and Pelops, see chapter 38, above.

123 **Agamemnon's Return:** I follow Aes. *Ag.*, the first play in his great trilogy, the *Oresteia*. See also *Od.* 4.494–512.

124 **Orestes's Return:** I follow Aes. *Lib.*, the second play in the *Oresteia*, with some details from Soph. *El.* See also Apollod. *E.* 6.28.

125 **A Trial in Athens:** Aes. *Eum.*, the third play in the *Oresteia*, is my source. An Apulian red-figure krater dated to 380–370 BCE, now in Paris, shows Apollo dangling a piglet over Orestes's head while Artemis stands at his side; Clytemnestra's ghost rouses the sleeping Erinyes (Louvre 1863 Cp10).

126 **Helen and Menelaus:** There are conflicting traditions about whether Helen ever actually went to Troy and how Menelaus recovered her. I have combined strands taken from several ancient sources, including *Od.* 4.119–32, 219–34 and 348–592; Stesichorus's story of Helen in Egypt (frs. 192 and 193; cf. Pl. *Phaedr.* 243a and Isocr. *Helen* 64) and Hdt. 2.112–17. Eur. *Helen* gives a different picture of Menelaus's recovery of Helen. For Zeus's plan of relieving the weight on Earth: *Cypria* fr. 1 and chapter 109, above. For Iphigenia becoming Hecate: Hes. *Cat.* fr. 19.17–27, 20a and b, Procl. *Cypria* 8, Stes. fr. 215. Another tradition said that at the last moment, Artemis had replaced Iphigenia on the altar with a deer, which was sacrificed instead while the girl was whisked away. An Apulian red-figure krater from 370–350 BCE, now in London, depicts this by superimposing the form of a deer over that of Iphigenia, while Calchas holds a knife above her head (British Museum 1865,0103.21). For the story: Eur. *Iph. Taur.*

127 **Neoptolemus's Return:** Procl. *Returns* 4, Phereycd. *FGrH* 3F64, Pi. *N.* 7.34–47, Apollod. *E.* 6.12–13, Paus. 1.11.1 and 10.24.4 and 6.

128 **Odysseus and Telemachus:** *Od.* 1–2.419. On one side of an Athenian red-figure cup from about 430 BCE, now in Chiusi (Museo Archeologico Nazionale 1831), Penelope sits at her loom while Telemachus speaks to her. Intriguingly, on the other side, Eurycleia washes Odysseus's feet.

129 **Nestor and Menelaus:** *Od.* 2.420–4.847.

130 **Calypso:** *Od.* 5.

131 **The Princess and the Castaway:** *Od.* 6–8. Alert readers may notice that here, the Phaeacians are described as the descendants of Poseidon whereas in chapter 89 they are described as having sprung from drops of blood that clung to the sickle with which Cronus castrated his father. Both traditions existed in antiquity.

132 **A Ghastly Host:** *Od.* 9. Ancient artists enjoyed depicting the blinding of Polyphemus, in spite of—or perhaps because of—the challenges of fitting the large Cyclops within the small confines of a vase's surface. A particularly elegant example is an Athenian black-figure wine jug from 550–500 BCE, now in Paris (Louvre F 342). A lovely small bronze from 540–530 BCE, now in Delphi (Archaeological Museum 2650), shows Odysseus clinging to the ram's belly.

133 **Circe:** *Od.* 10. There are a number of vases showing Odysseus confronting Circe, often with some of Odysseus's transformed men alongside. Interestingly, on an Athenian black-figure cup dating to 575–525 BCE, now in Boston (Museum of Fine Arts 99.518), the painter chooses to show the men with the heads of a lion, a ram and a dog, as well as those of pigs.

134 **Visiting the Dead:** *Od.* 11. An Athenian red-figure vase from about 440 BCE, now in Boston, shows Odysseus at the pit, two dead rams at his feet, and the ghost of Elpenor rising up to speak to him. At Odysseus's back stands Hermes—a logical companion, but not mentioned in the *Odyssey* (Museum of Fine Arts 34.79).

135 **Monstrous Females:** *Od.* 12.1–259. Ancient artists tended to show Scylla as a snake with a woman's torso and head; the dogs grow out from around her waist, e.g., a South Italian red-figure krater from about 340 BCE, now in Malibu (Getty Museum Villa 86.AE.417). Sirens are shown as birds with women's heads and, occasionally, women's breasts, as on a South Italian red-figure bell krater from about 340 BCE, now in Berlin (Antikensammlung V.I.4532).

136 **The Cattle of the Sun:** *Od.* 12.260–13.187.

137 **Home at Last:** *Od.* 13.187–16.481.

138 **Penelope and Odysseus:** *Od.* 17–19. See also the vase cited for chapter 128.

139 **A Contest and a Battle:** *Od.* 20–22.

140 **New Lives:** *Od.* 23 and 24.205–548, Hes. *Th.* 1011–16, Procl. *Telegony*, Hyg. *Fab.* 127, Apollod. *E.* 7.34–37, Paus. 8.12.5.

THE CHARACTERS OF
GREEK MYTHS

In a book that I wrote a few years ago, I explored the ways in which Greek myths helped to create and sustain belief in the gods and heroes who populate them and in the divine world more generally (*The Story of Myth* [Harvard University Press 2018]; see especially chapters 3–5). Here, I summarize some of what I said there, by way of exploring the nature of the characters whom you meet in Greek myths.

One of the things that enabled myths to create and sustain belief in their characters was the fact that the gods and heroes were *plurimedial*. That is, the characters were represented through a variety of different media—epic poems, tragedies, songs sung at weddings, vase paintings, sculptures, and so on. When a character is plurimedial, the people who experience that character draw, usually unconsciously, on all the different representations that they have seen and heard in order to create their own, personal versions of that character. We do this all the time today. Those of us who enjoy Sherlock Holmes, for example, are likely to have unconsciously built our own personal vision of who Holmes is out of bits and pieces of what we particularly like about Benedict Cumberbatch and Robert Downey Jr.'s portrayals, for instance, plus traits that stick in our minds from reading Sir Arthur Conan Doyle's original stories, details from book illustrations that show Holmes in a deerstalker hat, and so on. "My" Sherlock Holmes is unlikely to be exactly the same as "your" personal Sherlock Holmes even if we have seen the same television shows and films and read the same books, because each of us remembers, and values, a different mixture of things from each of those portrayals. The cognitive and emotional energy that goes into this participatory form of character-building forges especially strong bonds between characters and the people who experience them, which in turn makes the characters stick in our minds more tenaciously than characters who are not plurimedial. Because of this, plurimedial characters come to seem more "real" to us and our relationship to them becomes more intimate.

I will use Theseus as an ancient example of what I'm talking about here. An Athenian might have encountered Theseus as a somewhat foolhardy prince jumping into the sea to settle a bet with Minos (chapter 96), as a paradigmatic hero who rid the coastal road of threats and conquered the Minotaur (chapters 94 and 97), as a noble defender of the downtrodden (chapters 98 and 101), as a democratizing king (chapter 98), as a short-tempered father who badly misjudges his son (chapter 99), as a hero who traveled to Hades and back (chapter 100) and so on. An Athenian might have encountered these portraits of Theseus not only in myths presented through words, but also in the artistic representations of Theseus that dotted the Athenian visual landscape and in cults that were dedicated either to Theseus or to gods with whom he was associated. The accretive nature of each person's conceptualization of Theseus made Theseus seem very real, indeed.

Another thing that helped the characters of Greek myths seem real was the fact that their stories were told *episodically*, in the same way that many of our television programs and book series tell stories episodically. If we don't get an entire story at once (if we are compelled to wait a week, a month, or even more between episodes), we tend to think about the characters while we're waiting and to talk to other people about them. This process builds a stronger bond between characters and their audiences not only because the characters are in the audience members' minds for a longer time but also because the characters become a shared experience: if we are all talking about Harry Potter (for example) and speculating on what he will do in the next installment of his story, he comes to seem more real to us than a character whom we don't talk about with other people.

In ancient Greece, many myths were episodic because the poetic narrations through which myths were shared often gave people only part of a story. A person attending a festival might hear part of the story of how Odysseus got home—his encounter with Circe, or his rescue by Nausicaa, for example—and not hear more about Odysseus until another bard or poet decided to recite another part of Odysseus's story. Their knowledge of Odysseus's story would accrue gradually, and in the meantime they would continue to think about him and his adventures.

The plurimediality of mythic characters and the episodic nature of the myths themselves greatly contributed to the feeling that the characters were real. Understanding a third element that contributed requires us to pull our gaze back from any individual character or story and look at the entire body of Greek myths at once. When we do that, we begin to see that the characters of myths were *densely intertwined with one another* in such a way as to create a network. For example, Jason called together the Argonauts . . . who included Heracles . . . who was the great-grandson of Perseus . . . who killed Medusa . . . who gave birth to Pegasus . . . on whom Bellerophon rode to kill the Chimera . . . whose mother (Echidna) was a sister of Medusa. If we add a few more names we get even more connections: Medea has connections to both Jason and Theseus. Deianira has connections to both Heracles and Meleager. Athena, one of the greatest connectors of all, has links to seven of these characters. The diagram on the next page shows what this networking looks like for the characters I've just mentioned; I could keep adding other characters until the crisscrossing lines made parts of the diagram completely black. (Versions of this diagram that incorporate even more names can be found on page 138 of *The Story of Myth*.)

Such networking not only makes any given story more interesting, because it resonates with other stories, but also helps to furnish a mythic story-world in a manner that implicitly lends credibility to each individual myth. If you know that Heracles, who conquered the Hydra and other monsters and who was the great-grandson of Perseus, who beheaded Medusa, had once rescued Theseus from the Underworld, where both Heracles and Theseus spoke to the ghost of Meleager, in whose hunt for a gigantic boar Theseus had once participated—that is, if you know that these heroes had familial or social relationships with one another—then the remarkable things

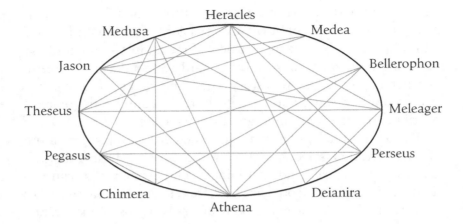

that each of them did help to make the remarkable things that the others did seem more credible. Successfully conquering the Hydra, for instance, doesn't seem quite so impossible when considered against the background of Medusa's beheading, and vice versa, to say nothing of slaying the Minotaur, which any mention of Theseus's name immediately evokes. Something similar to this happens when a character from a successful TV show crosses over into a new show, helping to launch it by giving it instant credibility.

This crisscrossing, self-reinforcing network lies at the very heart of Greek myths. Because of that, I've chosen not to offer the family trees of gods and mortals that are found in many other books of Greek myths. Family trees are linear; they are able to show the lines of descent from one or two particular figures (such as Zeus and Io, from whom many significant characters were descended: see chapter 20), but even the most complex family tree cannot show whom all of those descendants married, or with whom they were friends, or whom they killed, or which monsters they conquered—or any of the other complex relationships they had in the course of their adventures, which are what make the myths so engrossing, so alive. To capture all of that information you have to either read the myths themselves or work your way through a reference book such as Timothy Gantz's *Early Greek Myth: A Guide to Literary and Artistic Sources* (Johns Hopkins University Press 1993), which lays it all out in the course of its 866 pages (eighteen of which are family trees).

In my opinion, going straight to the myths themselves is likelier to guarantee that the relationships will stick in your mind, and it's certainly more entertaining, excellent though Gantz's book is.

By way of making up for this book's lack of family trees, however, I have annotated its index of characters with the names of each character's parents, siblings, spouses, children (except in the cases of most gods, because lists of their children could go on endlessly) and, in many cases, other brief identifiers such as "king of Thebes," or "helped Odysseus." To learn more about how a particular character is intertwined with others, read the chapters of this book to which the index directs you. And if you're still longing for a family tree after that, look at those in Gantz's book, which are very good.

INDEX OF CHARACTERS

Numbers refer to the chapter(s) in which each character is mentioned.

Agenor: Son of Poseidon and Libya; twin
brother of Belus; husband of Telephassa;
father of Europa and Cadmus; king of
Phoenicia: 22, 42

Aglaurus: Daughter of King Cecrops of Athens; sister of Herse and Pandrosus: 93

Air: Primeval substance: 1

Ajax: Greek warrior who fought at Troy;
from Locris: 110, 121, 123

Ajax: Son of King Telamon of Salamis;
fought at Troy; was second only to Achilles in skill: 110, 113, 115, 118, 134

Alcaeus: Son of Perseus and Andromeda;
brother of Electryon, Sthenelus and Gorgophone; father of Amphitryon: 64

Alcestis: Wife of King Admetus of Pherae;
volunteered to die for her husband: 70

Alcimede: Wife of King Aeson of Iolcus;
mother of Jason: 81, 82

Alcinous: Husband of Arete; father of Nausicaa and many sons; king of the Phaeacians: 89, 131, 136

Alcmene: Daughter of Electryon; wife of
Amphitryon; mother of Heracles by Zeus
and of Iphicles by Amphitryon: 64, 66,
114, 134

Althaea: Sister of Plexippus and Toxeus; wife
of King Oeneus of Calydon; mother of
Meleager and Deianira: 73, 92

Amaltheia: Divine goat who nourished the
infant Zeus: 2, 3

Amazons: Tribe of warrior women living
apart from men on the coast of the Black
Sea: 20, 60, 71, 98, 99, 118. See also Hippolyta; Penthesilea

Ameinias: Man who loved Narcissus: 36

Amphiaraus: Descendant of Melampus;
husband of Eriphyle; Argive warrior and
seer; one of the Seven against Thebes;
participant in the hunt for the Calydonian Boar: 92, 106

Amphictyon: Early Athenian king: 93

Amphidamas: Argonaut from Arcadia:
82, 86

Amphion: Son of Zeus and Antiope; husband of Niobe; extraordinary musician;
king of Thebes: 26, 102

Amphitrite: Wife of Poseidon; sea goddess:
45, 90, 96, 108, 115, 135

Amphitryon: Son of Alcaeus; husband of
Alcmene; father of Iphicles; stepfather of
Heracles: 64, 65

Amyclas: Husband of Diomede; father of
Hyacinthus; king of Sparta: 32, 33

Amycus: Barbaric king of the Bebrycians:
78, 85

Ancaeus: Argonaut from Tegea and participant in the hunt for the Calydonian
Boar: 82, 92

Anchises: Father of Aeneas; Trojan prince;
lover of Aphrodite: 14, 121

Androgeus: Son of King Minos and Queen
Pasiphaë of Crete; brother of Glaucus,
Deucalion, Ariadne and Phaedra: 96

Andromache: Wife of Hector; mother of
Astyanax; concubine of Neoptolemus
who bore him three sons; eventually wife
of Helenus: 114, 117, 121, 127

Andromeda: Daughter of King Cepheus
and Queen Cassiopeia of Ethiopia; wife
of Perseus; mother of Gorgophone, Alcaeus, Electryon and Sthenelus: 56, 64

Antaeus: Son of Earth and Poseidon; wrestled travelers to the death: 72

Antenor: Trojan nobleman: 112, 121

Anticleia: Daughter of King Autolycus of Parnassus; wife of Laertes of Ithaca; mother
of Odysseus: 41, 134

Antigone: Daughter of King Oedipus and
Queen Jocasta of Thebes; sister of Ismene, Polynices and Eteocles: 106, 107

Antigone: Daughter of King Eurytion of
Phthia; first wife of Peleus: 108

Antinous: Suitor of Penelope: 128, 129, 138,
139

Antiope: Mother of Amphion and Zethus by
Zeus: 26, 134

Aphrodite: Wife of Hephaestus; goddess
who oversaw sexual passion: 1, 10, 14, 17,
25, 27, 37, 42, 46, 49, 50–52, 62, 69, 76,
83, 85, 86, 91, 96, 99, 108–10, 113, 114, 131

Apollo: Son of Zeus and Leto; twin brother
of Artemis; god of archery, prophecy and
music: 8, 9, 11, 13, 19, 20, 24, 25–27, 31,
32, 35, 37, 39, 43, 44, 52, 56, 61, 62, 65–
67, 70, 73, 74, 79, 80, 82, 85, 93, 95, 98,
102–3, 105–6, 108, 112–19, 121, 123–25,
127, 139

Eileithyia: Daughter of Zeus and Hera; goddess who oversaw childbirth: 8, 10, 19, 64, 91, 108

Elara: Daughter of King Minyas of Orchomenus; mother of Tityus by Zeus: 39

Electra: Daughter of King Agamemnon and Queen Clytemnestra of Mycenae; sister of Orestes and Iphigenia; wife of Pylades: 124

Electryon: Son of Perseus and Andromeda; brother of Alcaeus, Sthenelus and Gorgophone; father of Alcmene: 64

Elpenor: One of Odysseus's men: 134, 135

Empousai: Shape-shifting demons: 126

Endeis: Wife of King Aeacus of Aegina; mother of Peleus and Telamon: 108

Epaphus: Son of Io and Zeus; husband of Memphis; father of Libya; king of Egypt: 20–22, 42

Epimetheus: Son of Themis; brother of Prometheus; husband of Pandora; father of Pyrrha: 15, 17, 19

Epione: Wife of Asclepius; mother of Machaon, Iaso, Podalirius, Hygeia and Panacea: 43

Eriboea: Athenian woman desired by Minos: 96

Erichthonius: Son of Hephaestus and Earth; early Athenian king; part human, part snake: 10, 93

Erginus: Argonaut from Miletus: 78

Erigone: Daughter of Icarius; Athenian maiden: 31

Erinyes: Daughters of Sky and Earth; vengeful defenders of familial rights: 1, 41, 42, 48, 62, 79, 89, 100, 105–7, 116, 125, 128. *See also* Semnai Theai; Tisiphone

Eriphyle: Sister of Adrastus; wife of Amphiaraus: 106, 134

Eris: Goddess of discord: 108, 109

Eros: *See* Lust

Eteocles: Son of King Oedipus and Queen Jocasta of Thebes; brother of Polynices, Antigone and Ismene; defended Thebes against the attack of the Seven: 106, 107

Eteoclus: One of the Seven against Thebes: 106

Eumaeus: Odysseus's faithful swineherd: 137–39

Euneus: Son of Jason and Queen Hypsipyle of Lemnos: 83

Euphemus: Son of Poseidon; Argonaut and participant in the hunt for the Calydonian Boar: 82, 85, 92

Euphorbus: Trojan warrior: 115

Europa: Daughter of King Agenor of Phoenicia (or Phoenix of Phoenicia); sister of Cadmus; wife of Asterius; mother, by Zeus, of Minos, Rhadamanthys and Sarpedon: 20, 22, 23, 25, 27, 42, 44, 46, 52, 61, 114

Eurycleia: Odysseus's faithful old nurse: 128, 138–40

Eurydice: Wife of Orpheus; nymph: 79, 80

Eurydice: Wife of King Creon of Thebes; mother of Haemon, Megara and Megareus: 107

Eurylochus: One of Odysseus's men: 133, 136

Eurymachus: Suitor of Penelope: 139

Eurynome: Sea goddess who nurtured Hephaestus: 10

Eurynome: Daughter of King Nisus of Megara; wife of King Glaucus of Corinth; mother of Bellerophon by Poseidon and Deliades by Glaucus: 57, 58

Eurystheus: Son of King Sthenelus and Queen Nicippe of Mycenae; cousin of Heracles who set labors for the hero: 66–69, 71–73, 84, 122

Eurytion: Centaur who attempted to kidnap Pirithous's wife, Hippodamia: 40

Eurytion: Geryon's herdsman: 71

Eurytion: Father of Antigone and father-in-law of Peleus; king of Phthia; Argonaut and participant in the hunt for the Calydonian Boar: 82, 92, 108

Eurytus: Father of Iole and Iphitus; king of Oechalia: 74, 75

Eurytus: Son of Hermes; twin brother of Echion; Argonaut: 82

Evander: Italian king who welcomed Heracles: 72

Fate/Fates: Three goddesses who determined the length and quality of each mortal's life: 4, 26, 38, 45, 64, 65, 70, 71, 92, 97, 105–9, 111, 115, 116, 118, 126. *See also* Clotho

Force: Primeval entity: 16

Themis: Mother of Prometheus and Epimetheus; goddess who brought order
to the cosmos; counselor of Zeus and
briefly his wife: 2, 4, 15, 19, 108, 109

Thersander: Son of Polynices and Argia;
fought in second attack against Thebes;
king of Thebes; joined Greek expedition
to Troy: 107, 110

Theseus: Son of Aethra and King Aegeus
of Athens (or Poseidon); husband of
Hippolyta and Phaedra; father of Hippolytus, Acamas and Demophon; king
of Athens; killer of the Minotaur and
other dangerous creatures or people; participant in the hunt for the Calydonian
Boar: 33, 40, 69, 92–101, 106, 107, 110

Thespius: King who lived near Heracles; his
50 daughters all conceived sons by Heracles: 65

Thestius: Father of Leda; king of Pleuron: 33

Thetis: Wife of Peleus; mother of Achilles;
Nereid; nurtured Hephaestus as an infant: 10, 82, 89, 108–18, 127

Thon: Husband of Polydamna; warden of the
port of Canopus: 126, 129

Thyestes: Son of King Pelops and Queen
Hippodamia of Elis; brother of Atreus
and Nicippe; half brother of Chrysippus;
father of Aegisthus, Pelopia and other
children: 38, 122

Tiphys: Steersman of the Argo: 84, 85

Tiresias: Blind Theban seer; advised many
people, including, after his death, Odysseus: 63, 64, 105, 107, 133, 134, 136, 137, 140

Tisamenus: Son of Hermione and Orestes: 127

Tisiphone: One of the Erinyes: 25, 62

Tithonus: Son of King Laomedon of Troy;
father of Memnon by Dawn: 14

Tityus: Son of Zeus and Elara; attempted to
rape Leto; tortured in Tartarus for his
crime: 39, 41, 42, 79, 100, 134

Toxeus: Brother of Althaea and Plexippus;
uncle of Meleager; participant in the
hunt for the Calydonian Boar: 92

Triton: Son of Poseidon and Amphitrite; sea
god who helped the Argonauts: 90

Tydeus: Son of King Oeneus of Calydon;
brother of Meleager and Deianira; father
of Diomedes; one of the Seven against
Thebes: 106, 110

Tyndareus: Son of King Oebalus and Queen
Gorgophone of Sparta; husband of Leda;
father of Castor and Clytemnestra; stepfather of Helen and Polydeuces; king of
Sparta: 33, 109, 110, 122, 134

Typhon: Son of Earth and Tartarus; primeval
opponent of Zeus; father of many of the
monsters born to Echidna; 3, 9, 16, 59,
66, 94, 104

Xanthus: One of Achilles's two immortal
horses; spoke to Achilles: 108, 115, 116

Zephyr: God who was the west wind: 32, 89,
129, 133

Zetes: Son of Boreas; twin brother of Calais
and brother of Cleopatra; winged Argonaut who fended off the Harpies: 78, 82,
84, 85

Zeus: Son of Cronus and Rhea; king of the
gods; husband of Metis, Themis and,
finally, Hera: 3–5, 7–30, 33, 36, 38–46,
48, 51–54, 60, 62–68, 70, 72–75, 77, 78,
82–86, 88–90, 93, 96, 100, 102, 105, 106,
108–18, 120, 121, 123, 125, 126, 128, 130,
133, 134, 136–39

ACKNOWLEDGMENTS

I thank Tom Hawkins and Carolina López-Ruiz for convincing me that I finally ought to write this book, and Fritz Graf, Katie Rask, Carman Romano and Karl Stevens for helping me along as I did so.

I am also grateful to the two anonymous reviewers for the press, who made suggestions for improvement; to my editor, Rob Tempio, for his sage advice and unflaggingly good-humored encouragement; to my editorial assistants, Miranda Amey, Sue Hoyt, Ben John, Rachael Knodel and Aristogeneia Toumpas, and my copyeditor, Kim Hastings, for their careful work. I am delighted with the way in which my son, Tristan Johnston, has brought the stories to life visually, and thank him, too.

Before all others, however, I thank my parents, to whose memory this book is dedicated, for supporting and nurturing my love of Greek myths . . . even though I'm pretty sure they wondered, sometimes, why I wasn't spending my time on something more sensible.

ABOUT THE AUTHOR
AND ILLUSTRATOR

SARAH ILES JOHNSTON is the College of Arts and Sciences Distinguished Professor of Religion and Professor of Classics at The Ohio State University, where she teaches courses on Greek myths. Her many books include *The Story of Myth, Ancient Greek Divination,* and *Restless Dead: Encounters between the Living and the Dead in Ancient Greece.*

TRISTAN JOHNSTON is an illustrator and graphic designer whose work includes books for children and adults, as well as storyboards and graphics for apparel. He lives in Los Angeles with his wife and two sons.

THE VOYAGE OF THE ARGO

ITALY

THR

THESSALY

LEMNOS

IOLCUS

SAM

Circe's Island

PHAEACIA

Sirens

ITHACA

ATHENS

Wandering Rocks

Scylla and Charybdis

SICILY

Cyclopes' Island

CRETE

THRINACIA

Land of the Lotus Eaters

Lake Triton

LIBYAN DESERT